THE MARYLEBONE MURDERS

An Inspector Vignoles Mystery

Stephen Done

British Library Cataloguing in Publication Data:
A catalogue record for this book is available from the British Library
ISBN 978-1-904109-21-1

Published 2011

The Hastings Press
01424 442142
hastings.press@gmail.com
hastingspress.co.uk

Set in Garamond
Cover design by Bill Citrine. Photos by Stephen Done.
Printed by MPG Biddles Ltd, Kings Lynn, Norfolk

THE MARYLEBONE MURDERS

An Inspector Vignoles Mystery

~ ACKNOWLEDGEMENTS ~

I would like to thank those who have helped and encouraged me along the way, all my family, close and extended, and especially Irena, for the continuing love and support. Sincere thanks go to Bill for another splendid cover design and to Helena of the Hastings Press for all the support, advice and hard work in preparing the text.

A number of excellent books have been consulted to help provide background to this story, but in particular *Never Again: Britain 1945–51* by Peter Hennessy (Penguin, 2006) and the outstanding *Austerity Britain 1945–51* by David Kynaston (Bloomsbury, 2007). *The Great Central: Then and Now* by Mac Hawkins (David & Charles, 1991) and the glorious photographic books by Colin Walker, of which *Great Central Twilight* (Pendyke Publications, 1986) and *Mainline Lament: The Final Years of the Great Central Route to London* (OPC, 1973) have proved invaluable.

Stephen Done

~ Author's Note ~

The former Great Central Railway ran between London Marylebone, Leicester Central, Nottingham Victoria and onwards to Hull, Manchester and Birkenhead. It was later operated by the London & North Eastern Railway, followed by British Railways. Tragically, Britain's newest main line was gone by 1969, a victim of Dr Beeching in a short-sighted move to save money.

Two lengthy sections of the Great Central have been preserved and may, one day, be reconnected. Readers are encouraged to travel on what is Britain's only preserved mainline double-tracked railway. Its Quainton Road station forms the location for a huge collection of railway stock at Buckinghamshire Railway Centre.

There was never a railway detective department and considerable liberties have been taken with reality to create this work of fiction — and it should be read as such. Fans of Ian Fleming's James Bond will recognise Sir Rodney Vallance as the (fictional) assistant commissioner of Scotland Yard. As Vignoles and Bond were operating at broadly the same time, I felt it appropriate the same man should be in charge. Any similarity to persons living or dead is unintentional.

~ ABOUT THE AUTHOR ~

Stephen Done was born on 3rd August 1960. On his eighth birthday, Stephen declared he wanted to become the driver of a steam engine. On 6th August that same summer, the very last steam locomotives ran in revenue service on British Rail. Unfortunate timing, so he took up writing about them instead.

A museum curator, he has worked at Bristol Industrial Museum, Cyfarthfa Castle Museum in Merthyr Tydfil, and, since 1997, has set up and run the Liverpool Football Club Museum and photographic archive at Anfield. A railway modeller, birdwatcher, avid book reader and collector, Stephen also enjoys a pint of real English ale. Stephen can be contacted via his website www.inspectorvignoles.ukwriters.net

This is the fourth novel in the Inspector Vignoles Mysteries series. For details of the series please see the final pages of this book or visit www.hastingspress.co.uk

~ Contents ~

For Irena

Monday 31ˢᵗ October. The water of the Regent's Canal lay like grey gloss paint poured between its grubby banks. It appeared viscous and unmoving as it clung to the hulls of a row of hardworking narrowboats, the water licking around ropes trailing over their sides and holding fast around two great baulks of timber dumped into the water and now wedged beside a bridge parapet, holding rotting leaves in the triangular pool of stagnant water it embraced. Mist curled from the surface of the canal in a pale layer of bone-chilling damp that mixed with the thick, yellow, poisonous smog choking the very life from the city. It collected beneath bridges and stopped the black holes of the canal tunnels with its evil gas, rendering these dank and claustrophobic places both hostile and virtually unnavigable. It clawed at the little windows and the firmly battened hatches of the boats, seeking out their occupants huddled inside around tiny stoves and causing even the most seasoned river dweller to draw their curtains just that bit tighter together.

'Come along, Scamp. Let's get home. I've had enough of this!' Clive Tustain urged his scraggy mongrel — a loveable, shapeless creature with a shaggy black-and-grey coat and big, flopped-over ears — to cease cocking his leg against a lamp post and hurry along. Tustain coughed following the effort to speak, and after the last painful wrack in his chest pulled a neckerchief back over his mouth and nose. His breathing was laboured and he wanted to get inside the little cabin of the *Primrose,* rub some Vick on his chest and inhale the clean, pungent scent in an attempt to unblock the tar that crawled down his throat and lay heavy in his lungs. Then he would get the stove roaring with the sticks of wood he had collected on their evening walk and settle down with a book and a good shot of whisky.

'It's a filthy one tonight!' He looked down at Scamp, who stopped sniffing some sickly-grey grass at the base of a wide bridge abutment to raise an ear before trotting on, as if agreeing that he'd also had enough of the dank and foetid night for one day. 'It's what Dickens would call "A London particular", and I'm none too particular to it, neither.'

The hairs on the back of Tustain's neck suddenly stood up as a strange, disturbing howl wavered through the thick night. It was a cold, plaintive yell that told of something unknown and unwelcome. Scamp stopped, pricked his ears and made a low growl. Tustain shivered and shook his head. Would he ever get used to those animals in the zoo? He wouldn't mind so much if they didn't sound like a small child in anguish or pain.

'Let's get on home. It's not far now.'

They hurried along the damp towpath and below the massive bridges with their solid supporting pillars that carried the railway into Marylebone station, spanning the canal with a heavy and lowering presence that was exaggerated by the dense smog. Something about the thick, black void beneath, filled with the noxious air, made Tustain involuntarily duck his head, and he was secretly relieved to pass through to the other side, where he could just see a shunting engine huffing and clanging a collection of vans around the parcels and goods sheds on the far side of the canal, its exhaust muffled and reduced to a soft 'whoosh, whoosh'. There was a deep, resonant rumble right above as a rake of brightly-lit carriages was propelled into Marylebone station, to the relief of the waiting passengers no doubt, who would now be able to escape the foul-stinking confines of London.

Tustain stepped aboard the *Primrose* and unfastened the little double doors into the galley. Scamp trotted down the steps without so much as a backward glance. 'Hey, you're eager to be out of it an' all!'

He stopped and coughed again, resting a hand on the cabin roof as he hacked and doubled over, his eyes streaming and face turning red. 'Can't say as I blame you. Oh dear me.' He rested a moment, then stood upright and cast his seasoned eye over his narrowboat, making a final check for the night.

The ropes were secure; his old bicycle was still in its place on the cabin roof; the tarpaulin was secured taut over the hold. The shadowy bulk of more narrowboats and a clutch of permanently-moored houseboats could be discerned immediately behind the *Primrose*, but their shapes were indistinct, swallowed up by a mix of mist, smog and night. A yellow light glowed from a window on the *Brindley & Moorhouse No 2* moored immediately aft. A plume of smoke poured from the stovepipe chimney and Tustain thought he could discern the aroma of bacon above that of burning coal.

He checked the wick of the riding light and hoped it would be bright enough to prevent anyone foolish enough to attempt to navigate the canal during the night from colliding with the *Primrose*. As he did so, a heavy train clanged and trundled out of the station and, unlike the strange sounds from the zoo, its shrill whistle, gruff chuff-chuffing and the rhythmic clickity-clacking of wheels over rail joints were reassuring. This was a familiar sound, and Tustain found it comforting, just as he loved the mournful bellow of the foghorns on the Thames Estuary. The departing train calmed his nerves, frazzled by the disturbing animal cry. Not that a seasoned boatman like Tustain was normally taken with a fit of anxiety, but even so, there was something odd in the air tonight, something other than the stinking smog that was unsettling, and he for one would not delay a moment longer escaping from it.

He stepped down into the galley and lit the oil lamps, filling the small but impeccably tidy space with a soft and welcome light. Scamp was already curled up on his blanket, his scraggy, pale beard below the big, wet, black nose resting on his paws, eyebrows twitching as he watched his master make their narrow little home safe and warm for the night.

'We won't hear any more of those monkeys, Scamp.' The dog flicked an ear, sighed deeply and wriggled into his blanket. Tustain opened the door of his burnished and carefully blacked stove and thrust the sticks of wood inside, followed by a little shovel of coal onto the glowing embers. 'That'll do us.' He watched as the flames eagerly licked around the bits of painted wood. 'Let's turn in for the night and have a bit of a read, eh? But first, I could do with some more of this...' He reached for the jar of Vicks Vapo Rub, but stopped before he had unscrewed the lid.

There was another cry. This was quieter and shorter than before and without that awful wailing and wavering note. But it was still a cry. Master and dog froze and looked at each other, Scamp's ears pricked, and he rolled his eyes expressively towards the double doors.

'Nah. It's nothing, old boy.'

Tustain unscrewed the Vicks jar lid and inhaled the refreshing contents. The scent was clean and intense, filling his nose and lungs and helping to banish the night noises. The railway, raised above on its great bridges, soothed him with its routine rumblings and chattering buffers.

But what was that? It was a sound that Tustain would later describe as a 'sort of a plosh'. It was a deep, solid, well-rounded noise, smoothed and cushioned by the impenetrable smog; the sort of sound that might be made by something heavy entering water.

'Don't tell me — some idiots are throwing stuff about again!'

Tustain heaved a deep sigh, opened the cabin doors and stepped back out onto the stern of his boat, peering fruitlessly into the opaque night. He could see little except the looming shadows of warehouses on either side of the canal, the great black bulk of the railway bridges and the pale, ineffectual glow of lights attempting to pierce the fog from the parcels shed and station behind. He listened intently, head to one side, arm resting upon the tiller. He filtered the various sounds, filing some under 'railway', others as 'road traffic', and then there was the constant low hum and whirring from the electrical generating station that occupied most of his side of the canal. He listened only for those sounds associated with the canal and its slumbering craft, trying to pinpoint the gang of troublemakers he feared was up to no good. But it seemed especially silent tonight. There were none of the hushed voices, feet tramping on the ground and echoing under bridges, the breaking of glass or the aggressive shouts, curses and harsh laughter he knew to expect when trouble was near.

He stared at the water, watching a few ripples disturb the surface. *Primrose* rocked slightly, but already the water was stilling. Something had entered the canal, of that he was quite sure. Tustain shivered, sensing another bout of coughing was about to set in. He turned away, waving a dismissive hand in disgust, and returned below. He could see and hear nothing now; whatever it was could wait until morning.

Seated in his little bunk, snuggled beneath a mound of blankets, the coals in the stove ticking in a series of tiny sounds, he re-read his favourite passages about mud and fog in Dickens's *Bleak House*, until his head drooped and the book tumbled onto the blankets as he succumbed to sleep. But it was not to be a sweet and dreamless sleep; marred as it was by nightmare images of a drowned man and the sound of a crying baby — or was it a monkey? It would not be silenced and it cried and cried whilst a hand scratched at the bottom of the boat, trying to find a way out of the bilge by pushing up the bottom boards that covered the watery sump as Tustain and Scamp desperately fought to keep them in place, the dog snapping and snarling at the hands reaching up; yet his jaws never seemed able to gain a purchase, until the hands became curling skeins of smoke — or was it fog? — pouring between the cracks and chasing them through the narrow cabin, pinning man and dog into the far end of the saloon.

As Tustain tossed and turned in his narrow bunk trying to escape the haunting images, a real hand, its long, pale fingers splayed out as if reaching for safety, touched the narrowboat, fingertips resting gently against the black-tarred hull, a man's face staring with open eyes into the thick soup of the canal. He lay still, the sluggish water holding him in place, gently bumping his hands against the wood as his body slowly stiffened. An eel curled and twisted in smoothly slippery movements around a heavy brogue, then made an exploratory incursion into the dark opening of a sodden trouser leg.

Chapter One

MUCHO DE NADA
Artie Shaw & his Orchestra

The police officers had left their car and Black Maria van parked on Lisson Grove. This was above the short tunnel that took the canal beneath the road, and they had tramped down a set of steep and slippery access steps to the towpath before walking to the mooring of the *Primrose*. They were dressed in dark uniforms or long and equally dark overcoats and so, in the soupy mix of morning mist and smog, they looked appropriately funereal as they stood, smoked, stamped their feet and avoided looking at the corpse they had recently fished out of the filthy water.

The body in question was covered by a heavy tarpaulin that Clive Tustain had fetched from the hold of his narrowboat and it was from beneath this that a dark stain of water slowly oozed and formed into pools on the uneven surface of cinders, mud and clumps of sickly grasses.

A huddle of boatmen and their wives stood nearby, each dressed in donkey jackets, black trousers and peaked caps or in longer, but equally work-stained coats which, on the women, revealed a flash of coloured skirt at the lower edges above wool-lined, gum-booted feet. They spoke in hushed tones, their voices softened in the acrid atmosphere of the filthy November morning, but none passed beyond the tall policeman standing with his arms folded before them; indeed, his presence was hardly needed, as no one showed any inclination to be a step closer to the body now the grisly task of hauling him from the canal was over. Curiosity, however, still drew their attention and they could see their fellow boatman, Trusty Tustain, talking with the Scotland Yard detectives. They were eager to overhear what was being said, hoping to learn more about the man Trusty had found floating against the hull of his boat that morning.

Which was more than could be said for Detective Inspector Tykett of Scotland Yard. This cynical and unsentimental character appeared thoroughly uninterested, and gave the impression of being more inconvenienced than disturbed by the presence of the corpse. He had whinged at his sergeant about parking their car on Lisson Grove instead of North Bank, a road that he insisted was nearer. His sergeant had countered that North Bank served only the electrical generating station and gave no clear way through to the canal side. The debate continued to murmur along throughout their initial investigations. There was a hiatus now, in both the bickering and the act of salvaging the body, and the DI began smoking a cigarette in short, aggressive inhalations, sucking in the smoke with a narrowing of the eyes that made it appear more a necessary chore than a pleasure. An expression of mild irritation mixed with tiredness played across his lined and blotched face. His eyes were red at the corners; his mouth was a thin-lipped line surrounded by the shadow of stubble. He had fallen into a morose silence as he gazed up at the bulk of the railway bridges and their associated abutments.

'You think he could have jumped off there? Or could he have floated downstream?' Tykett spoke at last, addressing the question to both Tustain and his sergeant.

'The canal is flowing sluggish these last days, so he wouldn't have drifted any distance.' Tustain was tired of standing about waiting for a doctor to arrive to inspect the body and confirm what was quite obvious, so he was glad to have something to offer. 'It should be possible to estimate the speed of the flow of the canal and so determine—'

'—Yeah, but it looks like 'e's conveniently got 'imself caught up near the front of yer boat,' the sergeant butted in, stopping Tustain midflow and nodding his head in the direction of the *Primrose*.

The speaker was Sergeant Philip Sidlow, a slight, emaciated man with a grubby Black Watch tartan scarf tied loosely across his mouth. 'We'll 'ave to 'stablish how long 'e was in the water and for 'ow long he'd come to rest near yer barge.'

'The *Primrose* is a narrowboat. Not the same thing as a barge, sergeant. He was at what we call the bow end,' Tustain added quickly.

'Both ends look the same to me. Still, whatever the craft is specifically called, there's still the question of 'ow long the dead man has rested there, and that will, in due course, 'elp us determine at what point 'e entered the water.' The sergeant looked at the DI, feeling pleased with his deductive powers.

'I wonder if it matters what bridge it was.' The DI spoke with a note of resignation in his voice. 'He jumped, and that's about it.' Tykett flicked his cigarette into the grey water. 'Bloody dumb and inconsiderate thing to do.' There was a mocking edge to his voice.

'You're sure it's suicide, sir?'

Tykett made a grimace, took a deep breath and looked at his sergeant, sighing wearily. 'He has an empty bottle of pills in his pocket, he's been face down in the water all night and yet we can still smell the whisky on his breath. Did he bathe in the stuff? Criminal waste of good Scotch.' A shot of black humour from Tykett; his sergeant obliged him by turning up a corner of his mouth in an approximation of a smile.

'Yeah, this looks like a certain way to do yourself in. Either that or he had a bad headache and overdid the pills, went for a right old knees up down the boozer, then fell in the canal on the way home.' Tykett raised an eyebrow. 'I can't say for sure, not until we get the post mortem report, though I'd be amazed if it doesn't confirm my suspicions. All I need is a note saying he wants to end it all to wrap this case up neatly.'

'Yeah. You're probl'y right.' The sergeant glanced back at the mound of damp tarpaulin. 'What makes a man do that, then?' he mused, then shook his head before addressing Tustain. 'You sure you din't see nuffink last night?'

'No gangs of drunks, for a change, and everything was muffled by the smog. You could barely even hear the road traffic.' Tustain did not think these two sour-faced Scotland Yarders were going to have much time for his feeling spooked by the sounds of animals crying in the zoo, although he was starting to wonder if these had not been something else. 'Scamp! Get away!' Tustain rebuked his dog for pushing its nose under one edge of the tarpaulin.

'I thought you said you *did* hear something, and felt the boat move.' Tykett narrowed his eyes and gave Tustain a piercing look.

The boatman visibly curbed his irritation before speaking. They had already interviewed him for some time that morning whilst the sergeant made notes in his slow and pedantic handwriting. 'Like I said earlier, I looked out of the cabin in response to a sound of something entering the water, but visibility was appalling and I could see and hear nothing much, except a quiet sort of a plosh, that is.'

'So, you heard the man falling in?'

'Didn't sound like a man. More like a brick or bottle being chucked.'

'And you say there was nobody about?'

'It was like soup, and it was getting to my chest. I'd just returned from walking Scamp...' His dog looked up and wagged his tail in response to his name, '...and was not in the mood to go back out.'

Tykett pulled a face and looked away, 'I don't suppose I blame you. So if you did hear this individual going in—'

'—I am not saying I did.'

'Accepted. But assuming that *is* what you heard, then it could be he jumped off here.'

They all looked up at the bulk of the railway bridge.

'He could have jumped off any of these bridges,' added Sidlow.

Tustain nodded. 'But he'd make a bigger splash than I heard'.

There was an empty pause before Tustain spoke again, 'I've seen my fair share of these. Bodies, that is.'

'Oh yeah? Why's that?' The sergeant perked up, but the inspector rolled his eyes, knowing that a confession of murder was not about to be forthcoming.

'I worked on the river for years before I switched over to the canal. On the Thames barges — and they really *are* barges,' he glanced at Sergeant Sidlow. 'Anyway, you lot were always fishing them out.'

Tykett managed a sour grin. 'You're not wrong there.' He looked at Tustain. 'This is our fifth stiff in two weeks. Not all from the water, of course,' he shook his head slowly. 'Jesus. We've had all sorts. Look, where's that blasted doctor?' Tykett lifted his left arm with a flourish and glared at his old, heavily-worn watch. A train trundled across the bridge above and his words were almost masked by the noise as a billowing cloud of white steam rolled over the parapet.

'Sergeant, take statements from everyone on these boats,' Tykett made a gesture towards the huddle of onlookers, 'and post two of the lads here until the ambulance takes the body away. Get them to question any passers-by on the off-chance that someone saw him jump.'

The sergeant gave his DI a puzzled look.

'I know, we can hardly see each other in this pea-souper and there's nobody on the towpath, but it only takes one person to have seen something. I'd better go and tell his missus the bad news.' He turned to Tustain, 'We've got your statement, sir, but are you thinking of leaving the confines of the city over the next few days?'

'I'm pottering about today along the Regent's, but it would be very inconveniencing to remain here. I've a living to make, and I can't just go stopping work on a whim.'

Tykett pulled a face, but was sympathetic. 'We might have to ask some more questions, just formalities.' Tykett paused a beat and rubbed his stubbled cheek whilst he considered the situation. 'We should have the post mortem results by the end of the week, so, all being well, the coroner's hearing should be early next week. We'll need you to attend.'

'If I must.'

Chapter Two

YOU COULDN'T BE CUTER
Al Bowlly with Lew Stone & his Orchestra

Listening to the wireless was one of Detective Inspector Charles Vignoles's favourite pastimes. It helped shrug off the stresses and strains that came with his work.

He put in long and irregular hours with the British Railways detective department (Eastern Region, Southern Central Division) and witnessed all manner of unsavoury sights. Railways are dangerous places and people sometimes met with horrific accidents, losing limbs and lives. Vignoles routinely dealt with grisly incidents and occasionally with more sinister and disturbing events. He'd even found his life at risk as a direct consequence of his investigations.

So, all things considered, sitting in his favourite armchair beside the fire at the onset of winter, pipe burning, his wife Anna busy darning or mending whilst they listened to *The Billy Cotton Bandshow*, was a pleasant way to wind down at the end of the day. Bearing this in mind he felt more than a little irritated as he strode out of his office at Leicester Central station and headed purposefully down Great Central Street. The reason was that his beloved Phillips radiogram had blown a valve the previous evening. The timing could hardly have been worse; after enduring the usual litany of woe on the news and a gloomy forecast for more cold and smog to linger for many days in the bigger cities, they were finally rewarded with some cheering tunes and, just as Al Bowlly was getting into his stride, declaring that his girl was *Mighty like a knockout, mighty like a rose*, the song faded away into deathly silence before he could sing of her *cute, fantastic nose*.

This had thrown Vignoles into a fit of frustrated annoyance, much to Anna's amusement. She had merely glanced at the dark, silent cabinet, sniffed at the waft of burnt electrical component and shrugged. 'Oh dear, that's a pity. And one of our favourites, too.'

She returned to her work. The pile of socks still needed darning and her sewing needed finishing, *Bandshow* or no *Bandshow*. However, Anna had been forced to endure her husband's huffing and puffing on his pipe like an old steam engine whilst repeatedly peering into the back of the big, wooden radiogram. It was just a blown valve, and all Vignoles need do was buy a new one and screw it in place. It would be the work of moments, but where could he buy one? Everything was so scarce these days. He just had to hope his local radio supplier would be able to help.

Brook's Radios and Rentals was situated beneath one of the great bridges that carried the former Great Central Railway across Leicester on its super-elevated path. As the city fell away to the southern edge of Leicester Central, the line was supported on a long, brick viaduct, its arches inhabited by a series of cramped motor garages and untidy workshops until the line crossed the Soar Navigation, where the River Soar and the Grand Union Canal blended imperceptibly, firstly on a latticework of steel, then across three deep plate-girder spans. Brook's sat squarely under the shadow of the first of these roaring echo chambers, just one of a thin line of single-storey shops that straggled in a desultory manner towards the rickety warehouses and wharves of the Midland Region's West Bridge branch line. These shops dated from the late 1920s and were an ad hoc mixture of flat roofs and gables. They were rather poor constructions, prone to damp in addition to the continual vibration from the trains thundering overhead and the busy road in front. Storing fragile electrical goods in such a location struck Vignoles as a recipe for trouble.

He crossed the elegant West Bridge, with its ornamented stone towers at each corner, and walked on to St Augustine Street, past Joseph Ellis and Sons, the ironmonger's, that exuded an odour of musty cardboard, mouse droppings and pungent fertilizer, and the little tobacconist and newsagent with its overstuffed window that promised the earth and yet appeared to have little for sale once inside.

Two small, grubby-faced lads in tattered clothes were sitting with their backs against the shop front; a guy, equally ragged, propped up between them. Its misshapen head was a white pillowcase painted with an unmistakable caricature of Adolf Hitler, a badly torn American army cap balanced on top.

'Penny for the guy, mister.'

'Shouldn't you be at school?' Vignoles growled.

The lads scowled up at him, one wiping a runny nose on the back of his hand.

'Come on, mister. Just a ha'penny, then.'

'Hop it, or I'll get the authorities onto you.' Walking on, he wondered if he had been too harsh. He really must soften his mood.

The aquarium next door seemed to be faring the best of all these shops. He read the promises offered on a selection of free-standing boards outside, one of which declared 'Guppies now in!' Although 'We have live maggots!' struck him as nothing to broadcast, and momentarily calmed his desire for lunch.

'We have dead bluebottles!' might have been appropriate for Brook's Radio and Rentals, the window of which was anything but inspiring. What little was on display was faded and everything was lent an unattractive pale grey-beige tone by layers of accumulated dust. An ancient gramophone with a tarnished horn and ripped baize on its turntable sat in the centre of the window, surrounded by two pre-war radios. Little cardboard boxes that once held valves, resistors and other odd bits of electrical equipment were stacked into pyramids, whilst curled cardboard advertisements leant at different angles against the tea-coloured curtains that backed the window display. A handwritten note on a postcard declared, somewhat optimistically, 'You can order television sets here.' A long line of very large and very dead bluebottles completed the look and suggested that it might be a long time before television would reach beneath the railway arches.

As the bell jingled he gave the door a shoulder-shove to close it again and keep the chill air at bay, and wondered why the shop inspired his loyalty. Not only was the window display poor, inside was a dingy, raggle-taggle mess of shelves filled with mouldy boxes, rows of ancient radios, incomplete cameras and all manner of electrical goods of dubious vintage, whilst along one wall were racks of gramophone records in brown card covers and stacks of sheet music.

'Hello, me duck. Not seen you in here a while.'

Quina Brook, known to everyone as 'Queenie', was in her early seventies, but she still possessed a head of rich brown hair that was always tied in a bun and fixed with pins speared into the construction to hold it rigidly in place. Her skin was dry and wrinkled into hundreds of laughter lines, her eyes grey and twinkling; indeed, there was almost an electrical spark of energy to them. She always wore the same shapeless overcoat of an indeterminate dark colour and her hands were ever encased in black, fingerless gloves, irrespective of the ambient temperature. The shop enveloped her in its scent of mothballs and the rubbed-geranium-leaf aroma of hot electrical windings.

Vignoles tipped his hat and smiled, 'Indeed not, Queenie. I hope you are keeping well?'

'As well as can be expected, but it's the damp, you see, ducks. It do get into me joints so. It's terrible this time a-year. And plays havoc with the stock: it gets into the 'lectrics, you see. I have to warn me customers to get everything properly aired and warmed up before use.'

Vignoles smiled. He dipped into his coat pocket and extracted the blown valve. 'I'm looking for one of these.' He handed it over and watched as she ensnared a thin pair of spectacles over her ears with one hand and peered closely at the printing on the side of the valve.

At that moment the shelves started to rattle and there was a jingling sound of glass vibrating against glass as a deafening rumble filled the cramped, gloomy interior of the shop.

'Can't get my hands on anything of this quality. Sold the last of this stock weeks ago. Everything's so short these days. Philips are a pretty good make, but—'

'—you can't get any'.

'Sold the last one only yesterday. Let me take a look...'

She shuffled through an open door into an inner storeroom and commenced opening boxes and moving things around whilst tut-tutting and mumbling. She returned with a cardboard box filled with an uninspiring collection of smaller boxes and loose valves, all of considerable vintage.

'Oh dear, that's an old one.' She shook it near her ear and made a face. 'Broken! The problem is, my most recent order was stolen in transit. Taken out of one of the wagons. Can't you do anything to stop to it, you being on the railways?'

Vignoles pulled a pained expression.

'They nicked fifty valves of just the sort you need. Went missing in London.' Queenie continued, 'I'm a good twenty-five pounds out of pocket. Terrible, it is. I can't go losing that sort of money!' She pushed the box aside and faced Vignoles.

'What rotten luck!' Vignoles continued his futile search. 'But surely you will not have to pay for stock you didn't receive.'

'You'd think not, me duck, but these days, things have changed. Finding a supplier is almost impossible, and when I did get one, they would only let me take five valves at a time for the first few orders. And strictly cash up front. Take it or leave it, they said. Well, what can you do? After a few deliveries I was able to place a far bigger order.' She sighed heavily and her eyes lost some of their vitality. 'But, of course, the big order is that one what's gone missing.'

Vignoles formed a wan smile in response to her sorry tale. 'I'm sure the insurance will pay out.'

'What insurance? I can hardly keep this place going on the few shillings a week I take. I can't afford anything on top of all the rates and the bills. And what with the tax on new radios and gramophones, nobody's buying.' She folded her arms and tipped her head to one side. 'Inspector, can't you find whoever nicked my order? They probably took other people's goods as well. You should put a stop to all this criminality.' Queenie gave Vignoles a stern look.

'We do try.'

'You could telephone them yourself.'

'The thieves?'

'No! The suppliers, silly. Why not speak directly and get them to give you all the details of the shipment, and at the same time you can get a replacement valve. They're only in Loughborough.'

'Yes, I could do that.' Vignoles sounded unenthusiastic, but there was at least some logic in going direct, as she suggested. 'But Queenie, I can't promise I can trace your missing stock—'

'I know.' She sighed heavily. 'Jordan's is their name. Jordan's Import. I must have their address somewhere.' She started to shuffle through an untidy pile of receipts and letters piled up to one side of the till. 'Here you go!' She proffered a small, letter-headed note.

'Thank you.' He folded it and tucked it into his wallet after just a cursory glance. 'I'll stop by if I find anything.' He touched the brim of his hat and, after giving the door a mighty tug that sent the bell ringing wildly, stepped back onto the street.

✻   ✻   ✻   ✻

Ten minutes later, Vignoles was at his desk with an uninspiring sandwich purchased from the mobile Women's Voluntary Service canteen beside a steaming cup of tea that he chose in preference to their tasteless 'coffee substitute'. He placed his feet on the thick hot water pipe that ran under his office window and tipped his chair back a little, all the better to observe the comings and goings on the busy platform.

A beautifully-painted and nicely-cleaned locomotive pulled to a halt at the nearest platform. After adjusting his spectacles Vignoles could read the brass nameplate that identified it as *Kudu*. He nodded approvingly. Suddenly, the big black telephone on his desk rang, the sound startled him and he spilled a few drops of tea on his white shirt.

'Blast it! Oh heck... Inspector Vignoles!'

'Did something just happen?' The voice down the line sounded puzzled.

'Er, sorry. May I help you?' He brushed impatiently at the stain.

'Detective Inspector Tykett, Scotland Yard CID. I am telephoning to ask if you might assist us with a small matter. All pretty routine.'

'I see. Well, we could try our best, though our cooperation would depend on the nature of the work. What had you in mind?'

'The problem is, we're absolutely snowed under down our way. I've got work piled up to my flippin' eyeballs. So we're a bit stretched—' Tykett paused a beat, adding as an obvious sop to Vignoles, '—but I'm sure it's just the same for you.'

Vignoles looked at the pile of paperwork on his desk, all dull and repetitive administration work. He had plenty to do, but nothing that could be considered pressing.

'Indeed. Crime never sleeps.'

'Hit the nail on the head in one, inspector. I've got this case on the go, concerning a chap from up Leicester way. One Jack Pym. Found the blighter floating in a canal yesterday morning, an empty bottle of pills in his pocket — contents presumed swallowed — and it smells like he's drunk a bottle of whisky on top. Suicide. Looks like he jumped off one of your railway bridges on Monday night or early this morning.'

Vignoles smiled at the use of the possessive pronoun.

'His missus has identified the body, and now we're waiting on the PM report. The coroner's set the inquest for early next week on account of the fact we're not getting any particularly bad feelings about this geezer.'

'And where do I fit in?'

'Like I said, he lived up your way. Now, although my gut tells me he topped himself, my innate detective instincts remind me that a little sniff around the family home and his workplace never did any harm.'

'Makes sense.'

'I'm a pro at heart. You'll appreciate my line of thinking,' Tykett paused a beat, 'and we can't find a suicide note — which always disappoints the coroner.'

'Uh-huh. As I understand it, you are in London, and to come here would require you to take out a whole day — time you cannot spare for something apparently routine.' Vignoles had pulled his trusty pipe out of his breast pocket and was sucking on it as he took in the information.

'Got it in one.'

'Could you not send pair of constables?'

'We're stretched to breaking. I can't take men off other cases, not for some pathetic insurance inspector who felt gloomy one night. So, seeing as he jumped off *your* railway — near Marylebone — I got to thinking you might lend a hand. His address is 56 Cherry Blossom Lane, that's in Leicester. His wife is Adeline Pym and they have a young son, Oliver. This Pym worked for the Leicester & Eastern Counties Insurance Company. D'you know them?'

'I've heard the name. I can look up the address in a local directory,' Vignoles found a scrap of paper and started to write.

'He was a loss adjuster. Apparently, that means he investigated major losses on behalf of the insurance company with a view to deciding whether they should pay out or not.'

'Yes, I am aware of the job. Was he in London on business?'

'We believe so — though we couldn't find his briefcase, so have no details, but maybe we'll find that at his hotel, once we've discovered which he was staying at. His wife didn't know, can you credit that?

Anyway, he travelled down on the 31st, ready for an early start the next day.'

'At the risk of sounding callous, I wonder why he didn't save the train fare and do himself in at Leicester.'

'That niggles me, too. Maybe that's why I'm asking you to have a sniff about. His boss told us he was looking into a theft of stock out of Marylebone goods depot.'

Vignoles groaned. No surprise there. The place was like a sieve.

'Have a nose around,' continued Tykett, ask Mrs Pym a few questions about his state of mind, see if there's a note or anything. Similar routine here — we've already spoken with his manager, Mr Taylor, who can think of no reason for Pym to take his life, but there's no harm in asking face to face. But I don't need to teach my granny how to suck eggs, eh?'

'Understood. But you don't expect any surprises.'

'Nah. You'll be working on behalf of the Yard — officially. Take my details and office telephone number.'

Vignoles made more notes.

'Give me call when you're all done.'

'I was not sure that I agreed...' Vignoles began, but found himself speaking to a dead line.

Chapter Three

LET IT BE
Lucky Millinder & his Orchestra

Simon Howerth took a sip of scalding tea from a white enamelled mug with a dark blue rim and waited for his uncle to continue the story. They were seated in the tiny cockpit at the stern of the *Primrose*, and Scamp, his uncle's untidy mongrel, was at Simon's feet, resting his snout on one of his thighs and waggling first one ear then the other in an attempt to induce Simon to continue gently scratching his head.

Colin Tustain had momentarily broken off his tale to concentrate on reassembling a brass and copper lantern he was cleaning. After ten minutes of rubbing and polishing the metal with a tiny piece of Brasso wadding the metal now gleamed, even in the dank and lowering atmosphere of a smog-bound afternoon in London.

'I need this burning brightly or else I'm going to take a hit. Had a couple of near misses these last days and I'm getting the jitters.' Tustain grinned at his nephew, enjoying keeping him in suspense.

'Never mind that. Who did they say he was?'

'Well, they didn't. Of course they searched his pockets and I saw them find a wallet and few sodden bits of paper and no doubt his identity card or ration card. Then they took me down below and gave me quite a grilling.' Tustain shook his head in disbelief. 'I suppose they needed to establish if I was telling the truth.'

'Were you worried they thought you'd killed him?'

'No! I'd never laid eyes on the man before.' Tustain laughed. 'Besides, I'd hardly go leaving the body floating next to my own boat, would I?'

'They've got to check every angle and possibility, I suppose, explore every avenue, no matter how obvious or unreasonable.'

'Well, you'd know: you've had more than your fair share of police involvement, if you ask me.' As Tustain sipped his tea, his twinkling eyes looked through the gentle swirl of steam rising from his mug. 'And I suggest you'd do well to have no more.'

Simon did not respond to the reproach. He continued his questioning.

'Did you manage to find out who he was?'

'Only because old Jackson on the *Lamprey* saw it in the early edition of the *Evening Standard*. That said he was a Jack Pym. A chap from up your way, as it happens.'

'Where?'

'Leicester. The report was only a few lines, said the police are not treating his death as suspicious.'

'After they'd finished questioning you, was it then they decided he had killed himself?' Simon looked across at the towpath where the body had lain earlier that day, vainly hoping it would offer up some explanation or clue to the mystery.

'I think they decided that from the start. My impression was they were not that interested in the dead man. But it did look like suicide.'

'How could you be so sure?'

'What is this? You're asking more questions than that inspector!'

'Oh come on, uncle! How often do you find a dead man right next to the *Primrose*? Simon's eyes were wide.

'And I hope it is the first and last time. I've not felt quite the same about mooring here since. I only stayed till now because we'd arranged to meet. I might go down Little Venice way from now on.' Tustain shook his head regretfully and fell silent. Simon sensed a change in his uncle's mood and refrained from asking another question.

'When you live and work near water in a big place like London, you see all sorts you wish you hadn't. Canals have a habit of passing through the dark and gloomy districts where nasty things happen. They can be rough, dangerous places.'

Simon looked along the curving towpath and watched a figure in black hobbling along with a stick beside the oily water. The scene was framed by oppressively heavy bridges and tall, sooty, industrial buildings with metal windows resembling blank eyes. It was a rather dispiriting sight when cloaked in foul-smelling smog.

'Not to mention the Blitz. Dear me, there were some terrible things during that time.' As he spoke Tustain poured paraffin into the lamp and screwed the reservoir cap closed. After placing the can of flammable liquid on the wooden-planked floor, he struck a match and held it to the lamp wick. A warm, comforting glow reflected from their faces, making their eyes sparkle, pushing the gloom aside and banishing the encroaching winter night.

'Auntie Kathleen was killed in the Blitz, wasn't she?'

'Not in the Blitz, but by a V2 rocket. They came later — worse luck — and even the Hawker Typhoons couldn't chase those from the sky.'

Tustain fell silent for a moment as if considering this fact. 'We had the *Golden Plover* back then; what a lovely craft she was. Kathy went to get some provisions. Standing in a bread queue she was, when the bloody thing landed on a block of flats above the shops. Destroyed the whole place. Turned it all to dust and rubble and left one massive great hole. Killed all in that queue and more besides.'

Simon stared at the floor and, when he finally spoke it was softly and without the eagerness of before. 'Eddie and I used to dream of the war coming closer — coming to us. There we were, in the safety of Woodford Halse, wishing with all our hearts to see the German bombers overhead and then to go collecting shrapnel the next morning after the raids. I wanted to see a dog fight over the fields or to hear a doodlebug engine cut out and wait for the bang! Of course, I realise now how lucky we were to escape it all. I feel rotten even thinking such things, now I know what it was really like.'

'Truth be told, I was captivated by the vapour trails in the sky weaving about high above the Thames, and I admit I found it strangely compelling, almost beautiful. It was hard to understand this was a fight to the death. I don't suppose life will ever have the same thrill and intensity again.' He gave Simon a reassuring smile. 'Anyway, at least it would have been quick for your dear old aunt, God rest her soul. No warning, and no time to feel scared.'

Simon looked across the water at a little J72 locomotive that could just be seen moving wagons around the goods yard, the filthy air rendering it ghostly, all fuzzy and indistinct around the edges. Simon was soon puzzling over the riddle of the dead man again, and returned to the subject.

'Why did that Mr Pym come here from Leicester?'

'Eh? Oh, well, I can't imagine.' Tustain furrowed his brow then stood up and secured the oil lamp onto a bracket on the side of the narrowboat that faced the open water.

'If he jumped from up there, he was trespassing. That's railway property,' observed Simon.

'I should think that would be the least of his worries.'

'What I mean is, he'd have run the risk of being caught before he jumped.'

'The police don't know for not certain where he jumped or fell from. But you'd best leave all this alone. You've got a good life ahead of you, albeit a tough one, on the footplate, so you just keep your head down and get on with the job in hand. You and Edward mustn't keep getting caught up in things that don't concern you.' He held up a hand to silence an interjection from his nephew. 'I accept that you've done some good, shown a bit of nerve, even. But it does not pay to go sticking your neck out. Concentrate on your job and leave police business to the police. I don't want to be reading about you in the back of some villain's van in the middle of a lake again. Tustain smiled, aware that he had been lecturing, 'I'll get off my soapbox now. Let's get below and put the kettle on. I'll brew you some fresh tea and see if we can't make up a couple of sandwiches for your snap tin. What time are you due to clock on?'

'Six-thirty. I'm working a fast goods down to Woodford, but first I need to hitch a ride over to Neasden shed and find my driver and engine. I'd better get my skates on.'

After saying goodbye to his uncle, Simon crossed the slender lattice footbridge that spanned the canal and stepped onto a narrow wharf with a series of rotting steps up to a wooden picket gate, giving access for 'Authorised Personnel Only' into the great expanse of tangled railway lines that lay beyond.

This foggy space was animated by hooting engines, soft coils of smoke and steam and ominous blocks of wagons, some of which would suddenly edge closer in a potentially-deadly, metallic rush and rumble audible only when it was too late to react, then stopped by the teeth-jarring squeals of pinned-down brakes as a shadowy figure of a trotting man dropped the brake levers into place on the free-rolling wagons in a balletic dance of legs, arms and a skilfully-manipulated wooden pole. This indistinct arena was edged with functional offices and mess rooms, coal wharves, swinging mechanical grabs and a long, curving goods warehouse that edged the canal. The open spaces between were studded with tall yard lamps that bore halos of light above road delivery vehicles with yellow headlight beams that cut into the soupy atmosphere as men banged and scraped cargoes between wagon and truck.

However, everything was dominated by the vast, open-sided block of the parcel depot, spilling a soft, diffused yellow light onto the yard and offering a glimpse inside of the many bays filled with parcel vans and platforms crowded with boxes, crates and packages, barrels, tea chests and hundreds of clumps of brown mailbags, all animated by small-wheeled trolleys pushed and pulled by whistling and shouting workers. Beyond this hustle of activity, and imperfectly illuminated by the spluttering gas lamps on the platform ends struggling to burn in the oxygen-starved air, Simon could just make out a hint of the twin gable ends of Marylebone train shed, fading into the impenetrable distance like an incomplete charcoal sketch. The outer reaches of this expanse were rendered invisible on all sides by the smog, and an unfamiliar visitor would find it hard to believe himself surrounded by towering city buildings and that the dull rumble in the background was that of central London traffic.

Simon looked at his watch and decided he was in good time. He identified a locomotive quietly simmering nearby that looked a possible candidate for a footplate ride up to the grand locomotive sheds at Neasden and started to walk towards it. He wanted to arrive at Neasden in good time, so he could acquaint himself with whatever engine he was given, get the fire in good condition and ready himself for the journey ahead. He would be properly prepared for whatever mood his driver might be in and better able to respond if he were a hard-driving man who wasted steam and gave his fireman a tough time of it.

Yes, that was what an aspiring 'passed cleaner' would do. But despite the overwhelming logic of this argument, his mind was still turning over the discovery his uncle had made that morning, and no matter how hard he tried, he could not push it aside.

He changed direction and started to walk towards the main running lines, finding himself drawn — perhaps because the rough footpath veered that way — to the multiple bridges that spanned the canal and came to a stand beside one of the corner pillars. Simon looked at the rusty girders and the narrow path of mud and cinders that ran parallel to the gleaming rails of the main railway tracks, one thought running through his mind: *Mr Pym might have walked along this path.*

He looked back towards the station and saw the blurred shape of a big express locomotive backing onto a line of waiting carriages in preparation for its northward journey. It was a decent walk from these platforms to the bridge and anyone attempting it would need to have their wits about them to avoid being mown down by the frequent train movements. Simon pondered the matter for a few moments. Any local railwayman could do it. Most of the men based here experienced years of total blackout and would be used to the route and unconcerned by the smog, but this Pym fellow was an out-of-towner. He was something to do with insurance, so surely wouldn't know the ways of the railway.

Simon stood about halfway across and peered down into the gloom, trying to discern the shapes of the boats and particularly of the *Primrose*. He could just see the soft glow of their lights. It was not far down to the water; the fall alone would not be enough to kill a man. His uncle had said the man had been drinking. Would that help him drown?

He shivered. These were unpleasant thoughts and he wondered why he was thinking them. What was he doing there? Standing in the horrid, bone-chilling damp that seeped underneath his engineman's reefer jacket and inside his heavy blue overalls and evaded his red-and-white spotted neckerchief. The smog was clawing at his throat, making him want to cough and with each breath he could feel his chest tightening as sulphurous, tarry phlegm collected on the back of his mouth. It would be good to steam away into the countryside and out of this poisonous atmosphere.

He hefted his canvas shoulder bag into a more comfortable position, adjusted his grease-top cap and tilted his head down, the better to find his footing amongst the sleeper ends, signal wires, point rods and cranks and the odd lumps of metal and wood that always littered the edges of railway tracks. The air thickened as the temperature dropped and he was struggling to see very much at all. Taking a few hurried steps forward he was suddenly brought up short as his head thumped into someone.

'Oi! Watch where yer going, yer bloody idiot!'

'Sorry! I didn't see you.'

'Bloody obvious, you din't! You should watch your step, son.'

The speaker was wearing a filthy railwayman's cap and an ancient donkey jacket over faded blue overalls. He had jet black eyes and prominent cheekbones that gave him a hungry, chiselled look which was enhanced by his work-stained skin in which each line and crease was etched by grime and peppered with a day-old growth of beard.

'You en't from around 'ere, are yer?'

'Woodford. I'm working back there this evening.'

'What you doing? Lost?'

'I—I was just looking 'round. Getting to know the place better...' Simon tailed off. It was a limp explanation.

'In this weather? You soft in the 'ead?' The man pulled a contemptuous face, then startled Simon by suddenly forming a wicked grin, followed by a throaty laugh, 'Oh, saints preserve me, it's me what's going soft!' The man's demeanour had suddenly changed and his voice was now chirpy. 'Follow me. You'd never find us first time without someone in the know.' Before Simon could protest the man had ushered him off the bridge with a firm hand pressed against his back.

'You want a smoke? Test the goods? On the house?' He gave a laugh and a wink.

'Sorry?'

'A fag? D'you want one?' A fresh packet appeared in the man's hand, lid open and a cigarette pulled a short way out, inviting Simon to take it. 'Like we said, it's all good stuff. Proper kosher.' He winked, but Simon did not find it an encouraging gesture and was wondering why the man had spoken of 'us' and 'we'. Where were the others? What did he mean by 'kosher'? Where they Jewish cigarettes?

Feeling in a daze at this sudden, unexpected and bewildering encounter, Simon found himself taking the proffered cigarette, anxious to not offend this rough-looking man. He held it in his mouth as his new companion flicked a lighter into flame.

'Thanks. I really need to be going now, must get to Neasden by six.'

'It won't take long. It's through 'ere.'

The man opened an oil-stained door let into the side of an ugly building with 'Thos. Bush Iron Co Ltd' painted in faded letters upon its sooty brick walls, now turning green with mildew in long, wet streaks like drapes of seaweed spilling from broken gutters.

The door lead to a dingy hall illuminated by a fly-spotted bulb that gave a faint, cold, blue light. Simon recognised it as one of the low-wattage type fitted in carriages during the war. He squinted and tried to adjust his eyes to the deathly colour that made everyone look unwell, and was not encouraged by the abandoned appearance of the passageway.

He was ushered into a side room, which did at least have a brighter bulb burning at the end of a grubby brown cord, and the light from this revealed a paint-stained kitchen table in the centre, with four ill-matching chairs scattered about and piles of cardboard boxes and packing cases stacked almost to the ceiling around three of the walls. A window was just visible, but this still had wartime blackout cloth stretched across its frame. The floor was strewn with old newspapers, bits of packing material, dog-ends, an old, greasy jumper and a work boot. It was a cheerless place filled with a haze of smoke lurking in the corners like a disease. A large man was seated at the table. He looked up from his newspaper and scowled at Simon, which did nothing to ally his anxiety.

The man had a round, balloon-like face and tiny, piggish eyes. A shapeless cap of indeterminate colour and at least a size too small rested on the back of his massive head. He appeared to have no neck, his head resting directly on top of a barrel chest that was wide and tightly buttoned inside a dark jacket. His hands were also large, with oddly-proportioned, stubby fingers. He watched with slight unease as Simon entered the room, but relaxed slightly once he set eyes upon the chisel-faced man following close behind.

'Found 'im wandering around.'

'It's a filthy night to be out, that's for sure,' the big man replied. 'So, what were you looking for? Fags or stockings? Or both?' He had a baritone voice coloured by a lifetime of sampling his cigarette supplies.

'Oh, gosh. I'm not sure. What I mean is, I think you may have made a mistake.' Simon's voice was failing him and in danger of becoming an embarrassing squeak. He shut up and gave some attention to his cigarette, his mind racing and heart starting to pound.

'Got a sweetheart?' the big man had apparently taken no notice of Simon's words. 'She'd like the nylons, I reckon.' He squinted at Simon for a moment, and then laughed. 'Nah! So, just the fags then.' Before Simon could reply, a cardboard box had been retrieved from under the table and plonked on top. It sounded heavy and full.

'Good stuff. Park Drive. Oh, and the name's Dennis.' Simon's guide extended a grimy hand as he took a long, heartfelt drag on his cigarette, as if to emphasise the quality of the goods. 'Dennis Parkey.'

'Ahem!' the big man coughed. 'We just stick to first names.' He gave Dennis a sharp look.

'Oh! Er, I'm Simon, just Simon.' He was feeling ever more confused by the situation now unfolding.

'And that's Big Ron. He's the banker, so if you don't pay up, you answer to him. Haha!'

Big Ron nodded almost imperceptibly, probably because he lacked a neck, whilst Simon found his attention transferring to the man's massive hands and the characters tattooed on his knuckles. They were crudely formed and hard to decipher.

'Sealed packs, good as new,' continued Dennis, evidently the chatty one. 'You enjoying that one, en't yer?' He nudged Simon in the ribs in a gesture that should have been playful, but which felt more like the jab of an iron bar. Simon coughed out smoke and wondered what damage the man might inflict if angry.

'Yes. Thanks. Look, I don't think I should—'

'—So, how many is it? Three, four, five? We can do you for more, but I can't see you stretching that far. Not yet, anyway.' Ron's voice cracked into a cough.

'Come on, Ron, give the boy a break; he can't be committing to something without knowing the price!'

'I—I really must be off now.' Simon strained to keep his voice level, hoping he sounded confident and decisive, though inside he was just desperate to flee from these alarming characters. His eyes fixed upon one set of Big Ron's knuckles and discerned the word H.A.T.E. in distorted blue letters.

'No sweat, I'll cut to the chase. Start with five packs, seeing as you are a new customer we can do you a special deal — just eight bob the lot.' Big Ron smiled. It was a frightening sight.

'Can't say fairer,' Dennis chipped in.

'Well below street value,' added Ron.

'Bleedin' daylight robbery, givin' 'im that price.'

The two exchanged looks and laughed. It was obviously a well-rehearsed routine.

Simon's instincts told him to get away, but he was captivated by the sight of five new cartons of cigarettes being extracted from the box packed tightly with yet more. They were in packs of twenty and being offered for a song. Not only that, they were a brand almost impossible to find around Woodford or Leicester, and if available were more often than not sold as singles, split from packs and kept in a shop's cash till, tasting stale and with a slight tang of grubby coins.

Simon heard himself whistle long and low, his apprehension momentarily stilled. There was a strange mix of fear and excitement coursing through him as he realised he was dealing with real black marketeers.

'Um, yes. Yes, please. I have a ten bob note somewhere... I was paid yesterday and still have my wage packet here.'

Simon stopped and swallowed. His stomach dropped. Why had he just told them he had his wages on him? What an absolute chump! They might batter him and take the lot. Feeling sick with fear he stood there with his hand clutching the brown paper envelope whilst he waited for the man with the iron fist to land the first punch.

Evidently reading Simons' face, Big Ron reassured him. 'We en't going to steal your wages! Never bite the hand that feeds, that's the first rule in the book.' Big Ron winked as he took the ten shilling note and quickly stuffed it into a pocket, then just as swiftly brought out two shilling pieces and tipped them into Simon's open palm. 'You're the one gettin' a steal from us.'

Simon stared at the coins. His hand was shaking.

'It's all there. Count it again if you want. Don't forget yer fags.' The packets were being offered by Big Ron.

'Thanks very much!' Simon grinned with relief.

'Good doing business. Maybe you'll want some nylons next time? You can go a long way with a girl when she knows you got some!' Big Ron grinned and winked lasciviously.

Simon stuffed his bounty into his shoulder bag, inwardly glowing with excitement. He was already calculating how much he would make by selling on four of the packs at full price to the lads. Better still, he could split them up and sell them in tens, or even as singles. Crikey, he could turn a tidy profit.

'I'll show you the way out and see you right for a lift to Neasden.' Dennis ushered Simon out of the room. As they stepped into the indigo twilight, Dennis indicated a big black A5 tank engine nearby. 'I'll get you on her. I need to see the driver, anyway.'

Simon noticed a drift of steam just starting to show around the safety valves. They were ready for the off.

'A few ground rules. You don't ask where the stuff comes from, and you don't care. Understood?' Dennis's currant eyes stared hard at Simon, who nodded nervously.

'You don't tell nobody about us. *We* make the contacts. *We* invite people to join the club. We get annoyed when others bring their chums along. Besides, this way you can make a little something on the side — but if everyone's in on it, well, it floods the market, dunnit?'

Simon felt a shiver of fear run down his body. He suspected they had mistaken him for someone else and feared what would happen when they realised. The sooner he got on that engine and fled, the better.

'Of course, we expect a minimum repeat purchase once a month. But you know all that. And you can arrange an increase on what you buy. Everyone does in time. But...' Dennis put a hand on Simon's arm and they stopped a short distance from the hissing tank engine, '...don't ever come here uninvited. Don't forget! You can find one of us most nights, Ron, meself or Vic. Of course, you've met Vic.'

Simon nodded, feeling panic rising. Clearly, he was supposed to know who this 'Vic' was.

Dennis sensed hesitation from Simon, but continued. 'Yeah, most nights one of us is in the Sherbourne Arms. Know it? Out the depot onto Rossmore Road and straight ahead is Harewood Avenue—'

'—I know it. Goes to the station.' Simon felt he needed to say something.

'Correct. You keep going past the rifle range on your left, and immediately after is Sherbourne Place. The boozer is at the end, on the right. The landlord's kosher — he can deliver and take payments, and you can leave him a shopping list and the readies, and he'll sort everything out if none of us are about. Got it?' He clapped Simon on the back and extended a hand. They shook, and Simon knew that, for better or worse, he had signed up to a monthly deal. *Oh Lord, what have I got into?*

Dennis called up to the driver of the A5 in a familiar manner and moments later Simon was invited to climb aboard. As he manoeuvred himself deeper into the warm cab and nodded greetings to the fireman, the driver climbed down to track level. Something changed hands, followed by a cheerful 'ta-ra' and 'be seeing you'. Soon the driver was back aboard, casting an expert eye at his gauges, opening the drain cocks and giving a quick nudge on the regulator handle to start the short train into motion. A brown paper bundle bulged from one of his jacket pockets.

Simon slumped against the cab wall and felt a wave of relief flow over him as the slow, whoosh-hiss-whoosh of the engine gathered pace. Looking over the fireman 's shoulder and through the doorframe, he caught sight of a solitary figure tramping towards the abandoned iron foundry building.

Oh heck, that must be the man they should have been meeting!

Simon winced, but kept his thoughts to himself and sought reassurance in the fact that the black marketeers had not robbed him. In truth, he had made a very good trade. If he was careful, he should be ok, and even a few bob better off.

Chapter Four

A String of Pearls
Glenn Miller & his Orchestra

DI Vignoles firmly believed that when visiting a grieving widow and her young son a woman's touch was appropriate, so he instructed WPC Benson to accompany him.

It was a nondescript, quiet road built to a gentle curve lined by modest, semi-detached houses, each with a postage stamp front garden, a short drive and detached garage, in a housing style known as Tudor or Elizabethan, the rows of semis or executive, detached villas, with their red or green tiled roofs hinting at an over-romanticised ideal of 'Merrie England'. Vignoles chewed on his unlit pipe and wondered at the peculiar nature of the British that compelled them to park a new Morris Minor on the drive of house that pretended to be part of Shakespeare's Stratford-upon-Avon. The lime trees that punctuated the pavements at regular intervals were now virtually leafless and stood like dripping black giants in the morning mist, mingled with chimney smoke that hung low over the estate. The electric street lamps were turned off and hung their heads as if apologetic they could offer no illumination. There was a dank cheerlessness about the road. No cars were parked, no one walked the pavements. There was just a profound emptiness exacerbated only by the occasional yellow light glowing from behind a drawn net curtain.

The Pyms lived at number 56. It was immaculate and the front garden was manicured and swept to perfection. A solitary leaf fell in a series of slow spirals onto the rectangle of lawn that surrounded the stark, twiggy form of a standard rose. The garage doors stood open to reveal the big headlights and bulbous nose of a well-polished car tucked within. This was something grander than a little Morris.

The deep chimes of the doorbell brought to the door a woman in her early thirties, dressed in a suit of fine, very dark tweed, which she matched with a high-collared white blouse with a large bow of black ribbon at the throat. A cameo brooch in black and white was fastened to her jacket lapel and a string of pearls embraced her smooth neck. She was as immaculately coiffured as the front garden, and carried a definite note of perfume above that of furniture polish and pot pourri that greeted them. In the right light she might be thought good looking, but there was something hard to her face and she seemed older than her years.

'Mrs Pym?' Vignoles lifted his hat.

'Yes? If you are trying to sell me something, I—Oh! You must be the detective.' Her eyes rapidly scanned the road that lay beyond them, before returning to Vignoles.

'Detective Inspector Charles Vignoles and WPC Jane Benson'. He flashed his warrant card. 'May we come in?'

'If you really must, though I am not sure what it is you hope to achieve. It is most distressing. I had rather hoped you had finished questioning me and would leave us in peace to mourn our loss. I've held poor Oliver back from school, he's so upset.'

'I quite understand, Mrs Pym. And we offer you our sincere condolences.' As they entered the hall Mrs Pym closed the front door; though, Vignoles noted, not before she had taken another visual sweep of the houses opposite with their net-curtained windows. 'Unfortunately, whenever there is a death under unusual circumstances we must follow due process. It is unavoidable.'

'I see. Actually, I don't. But there again, I almost think that I know and understand nothing lately. Everything has been turned completely topsy-turvy since … since *then*.' She fished a tiny handkerchief from her sleeve and dabbed the corner of an eye. 'Do take a seat. Let's get it over with.'

They entered the lounge, a nicely-proportioned room with a bay window of leaded plain and stained glass. The wallpaper was of a formal design of vertical stripes in shades of brown and pinks; a plate shelf above the picture rail supported many examples of what looked like fine bone china. There were two oil paintings of rural scenes on the walls and Vignoles was struck by the obvious ability of the artist. A sofa of a very traditional design and showing no signs of wear faced a large mantelpiece of polished mahogany surrounding a jet-black grate with a small fire, whilst matching wingback armchairs sat on either side, each decorated with a lace antimacassar. V-shaped magazine racks of brass wire stood to the side of each chair, with women's magazines in one and *Practical Householder* in the other. His and hers.

Vignoles took the armchair alongside the rackful of *Practical Householder*, Benson took the sofa and Mrs Pym sat in her usual armchair. Holding his hat in his hands whilst leaning forwards, Vignoles was about to speak but Mrs Pym beat him to it.

'Have you made a breakthrough? Have you found who did this to poor Jack?'

'No, er, we have not. It looks as though he took his own life.'

'Stuff and nonsense! He would *never* do such a thing. I said exactly the same to that other detective, the uncouth one with the dreadful Cockney accent. He dropped his aitches like a common barrow boy.' Vignoles wondered that Mrs Pym had ever met a barrow boy, but said nothing. 'He was an unpleasant and self-opinionated man. He took no interest in what I thought and has already made up his mind without a proper investigation. I only agreed to this interview today because you were not *him*.' Vignoles wondered if this might be the true reason for Tykett's reluctance to pay a home visit. 'I hope you are both better mannered *and* more able.' She threw a haughty look at Vignoles.

'Anyone who knew Jack would tell you, he would never leave Oliver and I.' She smoothed her skirt and flicked at an imaginary speck of dust. 'He would never be so unthinking and heartless, and besides, he was far too gentle and, well, reserved, to do such a thing.' She now fussed at a thread coming loose on one of the chair arms, brow furrowed as she did so. 'For goodness sake, inspector, one is talking about *suicide*. So humiliating.' Her voice cracked. 'It's simply impossible. He was murdered.'

Vignoles was taken by surprise by Mrs Pym's assertion that this was a case of murder, but he recovered quickly and asked, 'Did he have a falling out with someone recently? Is there anyone you can think of who would want to kill him?' She folded her hands in her lap, twisting the small handkerchief, then looked up and faced him, clearly affronted.

'We are hardly in the habit of associating with known murderers, inspector. And I would hardly think that Jack being in especially ruthless form at our last bridge night and positively fleecing the Philpotts over at number four, would be sufficient motive for their murdering him.' She shot a slightly sarcastic smile towards him.

Vignoles winced. She was correct to stress the folly of the standard police questions.

'So, no, inspector, I cannot imagine who would have done it, but make no mistake, someone killed Jack. I suspect robbery. One often hears of how rough London is getting these days.'

'Was your husband unhappy or depressed in the last few weeks?' asked Benson gently.

'No. We had a happy and loving marriage.' She flashed her eyes. 'I cannot see the reason for these questions. You should be looking for a common thief with a vicious streak.'

'Did he perhaps appear worried about something at work?' Benson continued, undaunted.

Mrs Pym made an effort to control her frustration. 'He was hard working and conscientious and very well respected within the company. He had been elevated to the position of senior loss adjuster only two years ago, and had every expectation of further promotion.' Mrs Pym pulled herself up straight in the chair. She paused, and the mantelshelf clock measured the beats with a solid, rhythmic tick. 'Not that we discussed his work, you understand. That was his domain, and I am — I was — happy to keep it like that.'

'So you have no specific reason to suspect foul play, although you believe that this was the reason for his death?' asked Vignoles.

'You are the detective. I should have thought that was your job. He was probably attacked in the street. Jack often carried more in his wallet than was strictly necessary or sensible and I was always berating him about it.'

'Did he have a briefcase with him?'

'Of course. Have you not recovered it?'

'No. It was not near the... his body. However his wallet was recovered and there was money inside, which rather precludes robbery as motivation and lends weight to the idea that he took his own life.'

'But you are simply repeating what that other policeman said! This just too awful.' Her composure appeared to be slipping. She formed her lips into a thin line. Her face looked gaunt. 'What will the neighbours say? Word has got out already, of course.' Her voice became high-pitched and strained, and she pressed the tiny square of lace to her eyes and sobbed quietly. 'I'm sorry... it's the shock... and the *embarrassment* of it all. The whole road will be gossiping behind my back. Wondering why he chose to kill himself. They won't say anything to me, but I'll know what they're thinking.' Another dab of the tiny handkerchief to her eyes.

Her tears subsided and she breathed more regularly. Her voice regained a lower register. 'No one sends cards of condolence, inspector. Not for such a cowardly way out.'

Vignoles looked up at the cardless mantelpiece. Nor could the vagaries of the Royal Mail be held to blame, since even close neighbours had failed to slip a single card through her letterbox.

Vignoles stood up and carefully picked up a wooden frame with a photograph of a slightly overweight man with neatly trimmed sideburns, a carefully clipped moustache and heavily framed glasses. His hair was immaculately oiled and parted. He was wearing a white shirt with a dark tie and sports jacket. He looked the epitome of solid, reliable middle management.

'Is this your husband?'

'Yes.' She nodded quickly and refolded her handkerchief.

'May I borrow it? I shall take great care of it and return it as swiftly as possible. It helps to have an image. And as you are so sure foul play was involved, I might need it as the case develops.'

'Of course. Very well, if it helps, please take it.'

'Does your husband have an office or a study at home, somewhere he keeps his work things?' asked Vignoles, slipping the little picture frame into his briefcase.

She nodded. 'Upstairs. At the top of the landing.'

'May I take a look?'

'If you must. Let me show you'.

'No need to trouble yourself, Mrs Pym, I can find my own way.'

Benson, taking her cue from the DI, leant forward and touched Mrs Pym gently on the arm, skilfully distracting the distressed widow from her slight feeling of discomfort at having a detective snoop around her home.

'I think what we all need is a nice pot of tea! May I put the kettle on?'

Mrs Pym gave a tearful half smile and gave the response Benson had manipulated. 'Yes, you are right, but you are my guests, so I shall make it.' She stood up and made her way to the kitchen. Benson followed to keep her talking, and away from Vignoles, while waiting for the kettle to boil.

Vignoles quietly walked out of the room and towards the stairs, expertly scanning his surroundings, taking in as much detail as he could. He had no specific idea of what he was looking for, and indeed, there was in all probability nothing to discover, but both he and DI Tykett understood the importance of these opportunities. It was always illuminating, and he was long past being surprised by the secrets people tried to conceal. He also thought he heard feet scampering across the ceiling, but he may have been mistaken.

The house was beautifully maintained and spotlessly clean; the carpet underfoot was deeply piled, even on the stairs. Far better than Anna and he could afford. As he climbed, his feet silent on the cushioned treads, he could now hear a strange whooshing sound that was faintly metallic in timbre, though he could not identify what it could be.

As he reached the landing a series of doors faced him, one of which stood wide open to reveal a good-sized bedroom. On the floor was an extensive train set formed into concentric ovals with a complex interlacing of points and sidings, dotted with a small forest of white-painted signal posts. A big red express engine hurtled around the outer oval, a rake of tinplate carriages in matching maroon rattling behind, whilst a small clockwork shunting engine was travelling in a more sedate manner in the opposite direction on the inner oval, hauling a collection of wagons and tankers.

Vignoles grinned and stepped across to the doorway.

'Hello young man, that's a Princess, isn't it?'

'Yes. *Princess Elizabeth.* A Stanier 4-6-0 Pacific from the

London Midland and Scottish Railway. She's hauling the much-delayed 09:15 from London Euston to Liverpool Lime Street and we have to hope the signalman will not hold her up at any more signals.'

The speaker was a boy of about twelve, dressed in formal school uniform of grey trousers, white shirt, striped tie and blazer. Despite being held back from school, he was still expected to dress as though he were attending. The boy had blond hair cut into a typical pudding-bowl shape, and gave just a cursory glance up at Vignoles before lying prone on the floor, his eyes level with the model trains rushing past just inches from his fringe.

'It's a fine model,' said Vignoles as he watched it circle for a few moments. 'Accurate. That's not a Hornby, is it?'

'Gosh, no! The Princess is a Bassett-Lowke. The very best! The LNER pug is Hornby. It's clockwork. You can see the difference.'

'I can indeed.'

Pym had been a very generous father, thought Vignoles. The train set was extensive and would have cost a pretty penny in its own right, but the Bassett-Lowke engine would have seen little, if any, change from five guineas. It was a quality piece of engineering and Vignoles felt a sudden and unpleasantly inappropriate stab of envy. What would he have given to have such an engine when he had been a boy? He instantly banished such unchristian thoughts in a flood of guilt, remembering that this poor lad no longer had a dad, generous or otherwise, and the gleaming locomotive would now have to serve as some kind of lasting legacy. It did not seem very much.

'Are you a policeman?'

'Yes, I am,' Vignoles smiled.

'Are you here to find out why daddy died?'

'I will try my very best.'

The clockwork engine slowly came to a halt, its spring unwound, but the electric-powered express continued its relentless and unvarying pace around the track, dipping beneath the bed that served as a makeshift tunnel and clattering across the points at the station throat.

'It's Oliver, isn't it?'

The boy nodded his head, 'He promised to get me *Flying Scotsman* for Christmas.'

Vignoles was not sure what to say.

'He told me already, because you must place a special order at the factory. With everyone under austerity, it can take simply *ages* for the factory to make you one.' Oliver looked at Vignoles with a serious expression and spoke slowly, as though weighing up each word, his accent like cut glass.

Vignoles nodded.

'What I don't understand is why daddy would kill himself before he had finished paying for the *Flying Scotsman*? He'd already paid at least twenty shillings of the money.' The boy's eyes widened as he spoke of the vast sum. He looked at Vignoles with a serious and earnest expression. 'I think that rather strange. Don't you?'

'Yes, I suppose I do.' Vignoles swallowed. 'But sometimes people, er, change. Things happen. The plans they make alter because of, er, well, circumstances,' He was floundering.

The boy continued to look at him, holding a stare that Vignoles found uncomfortably long. Abruptly, he turned back to the racing train and very deliberately changed the direction of two of the points. 'Do you mean like this?'

'Careful!'

Princess Elizabeth swung first to one side and then the other as the train altered course at considerable speed, but somehow remained upright on the track long enough to plough at full tilt into the little goods train with a hard metallic crash, scattering wagons across the carpet in an disquietingly satisfying smash, pushing the derailed tank engine backwards, until eventually this twisted sideways and stuck fast and, in turn, toppling the Pacific onto its side.

'Boom! All dead!'

*   *   *   *

Jack Pym's study was small, neat and sparsely furnished, with a portable typewriter on the fold-down front of a heavy oak bureau alongside a photograph of his wife and son sitting on a bench in what looked like Abbey Park. One of Oliver's tinplate railway wagons sat beside the typewriter with a pair of wheels missing. These were lying next to the broken van, together with a screwdriver. Pym had evidently been about to make a repair. If young Oliver was going to stage dramatic rail crashes, then a wagon losing its wheels was to be expected. Vignoles picked the toy up for a moment, and was struck by the awful finality of death, of how these wheels would now never be replaced by the boy's father.

Other than the bureau, there was a swivel chair and a comfy old armchair, a dark oak bookshelf filled with dull tomes on company law and business procedures, an RAC road atlas, a recent Bradshaw's railway timetable, a pile of carefully-folded old newspapers and a selection of *Picture Post* magazines — all of which featured stores about the war — and some tatty American western and lurid crime novels. Vignoles suspected Pym probably indulged himself by reading these paperbacks when he secreted himself away upstairs with the excuse of needing to do some paperwork.

Vignoles turned his attention to the various drawers and compartments in the bureau. There were bundles of receipts and household correspondence with the coal merchant, milkman and mobile fishmonger, bundles of spent ration books and old railway tickets, all held together by elastic bands. Pym was a meticulous man.

One transaction caught his eye, the down payment on a Jowett Javelin car; that would be the elegant beast lurking in the garage. Vignoles knew little about cars, but he did know this was an expensive machine. The initial payment was certainly substantial. There was also a receipt for a string of pearls, possibly those gracing Mrs Pym's neck and, at four guineas, they were top quality. The Pyms had expensive tastes and he wondered how they could afford such luxury.

None of this was particularly illuminating, however, and after a few minutes of fairly thorough searching, Vignoles had not found a suicide note or anything else that held his interest, with the one possible exception of a foolscap workbook containing a list of his insurance investigations over the latter part of 1949. The book had almost certainly been brought home from his office, and Vignoles was sure that the rest of the set, stretching back through the years, would be found there.

Vignoles flipped to the most recent entry.

Pym was looking into the substantial loss of a large consignment of mixed products taken from Marylebone goods warehouse. That explained his trip to London, but did nothing to account for a sudden and fatal dip in mood. However, Vignoles decided to take the book away and study it in more detail, partly because his interest was sparked by one small detail: Jordan's Import and Export Company Ltd of Loughborough had shipped the items that had been lost.

Only yesterday he had heard that name for the first time, when he'd promised Queenie he would investigate the loss of her radio valve order. He still had the letter she had handed him, and he now unfolded it to make sure he had remembered the company name correctly. Vignoles was puzzled that Queenie's order — to be shipped from Loughborough to Leicester — had travelled via London, speeding through Leicester in order to do so. This appeared odd, but he knew the railways were prone to route things strangely, something to do with 'logistics', and certainly could have no bearing on why Pym killed himself.

Aware that someone was watching, he looked up from the workbook. Oliver Pym was standing at the doorway and the boy's oddly unsettling gaze once more fixed upon him.

'Hullo again. I hope there's no lasting damage to the locomotives?'

The boy shook his head.

'I know this is very difficult, but did you notice anything different about your father in the weeks before he died?'

Oliver gazed at the carpet and shook his head, slowly circling one foot through the pile. Vignoles sensed that he should be patient and not hurry the boy.

'Why are you asking *me*? Why not ask Mr Bish!'

'Who is Mr Bish?'

'A horrible nasty man with shifty eyes. I don't like him'

'You met Mr Bish?'

'Yes!'

'I see.' Vignoles weighed this up. It was childish prattle, but there was something compelling about the intense stare Oliver was still giving him.

'Do you think this man might know something about your father's death?'

'Obviously!'

'Why do you say that?'

'He's a spy! You can tell just by looking at him!'

'I see. And this man might know why your father took his life?'

Oliver ran into his bedroom, turned towards Vignoles and said, 'Go and find out for yourself. I hate him — and so did daddy!' With that, he slammed the door shut.

Chapter Five

MONEY IS HONEY
Count Basie & his Orchestra

Mrs Barbara Walsh managed the refreshment room at Woodford Halse station. She held court from behind a high serving counter backed by tall shelves lined with pretty tins of tea and coffee beans, though these were only for show, as rationing forbade such an extravagance, and one of the most ornate examples served to conceal unappealing packets of Rationmix Coffee Substitute.

The room's tall windows held a commanding view across the twin villages of Woodford Halse and Hinton, although the only obvious divide between the two closely intertwined communities was provided by the great embankment and twin bridges carrying the railway slap bang between.

Mrs Walsh loved to watch the regular comings and goings of the railway and village, passing the time of day with anyone with time to listen, sometimes refilling an empty tea can for thirsty footplate men, discussing the late running of a train with a guard or just exchanging a 'hello' or 'lovely day' with a passenger leaning from a carriage window. Although she often expressed the opinion that she held little regard for steam trains, she nonetheless eagerly anticipated the passing of the two flagship named expresses on the line: *The Master Cutler* and *The South Yorkshireman* and, come sunshine or rain, would stand in the doorway or look up from mashing a pot of tea to observe their swift passing, heralded long in advance by distant hoots of the whistle and, if the wind was right, an anticipatory rhythmic beat, like a dance band in full swing.

The stationmaster, buttoned up inside both waistcoat and tails, wearing a glossy, raven-black top hat, made a point of standing and facing each oncoming train, gold fob watch in hand, one eyebrow cocked as he timed its passing. Porters stopped their duties, momentarily resting on wooden handcarts, or pausing between rolling milk churns on their edges. The ticket clerk would turn to catch a glimpse of the roaring green monsters hurtling through the station, rattling the window panes, filling the waiting rooms with coiling steam, blowing loose papers onto the floor and setting the baskets of carrier pigeons awaiting collecting cooing and fluttering.

The locomotives hauling these trains were impressive, and those watching would strain to catch their names cast in brass on their sides. Perhaps today it would be *Sansovino* or *Victor Wild*? Maybe *Solario* or

Grand Parade? The first class coaches looked exotic, their table lamps glowing as chubby businessmen reclined in comfy armchairs with a cigar, reading *The Times* or the *Manchester Guardian*, whilst waiters in white jackets swayed expertly down the aisles, serving breakfast or a hearty evening meal. It was a glimpse into a world where rationing appeared to hold little sway and those able to afford it lounged in comfort in luxurious carriages and had the use of working toilets. It was not for the likes of Barbara Walsh, but she enjoyed trying to catch a fleeting glimpse of this privileged life.

Nor indeed was it for the likes of young railwaymen such as Simon Howerth and his best friend, Edward Earnshaw, who were standing beside the refreshment room door, each cradling a cup of tea and observing, with perhaps a more professional eye, how the top link crew handled their steed.

'*Woolwinder*!'

'That poor wreck. No wonder they've dropped eight minutes.' Simon leant against the doorjamb and took a sip of tea whilst watching the stationmaster give a knowing shake of his head at the hands on his watch.

'It could be a permanent way slack?'

'Could be, but she looks shot to bits, if you ask me.'

'Needs a trip to Donny. They can't just keep thrashing the poor thing month after month.' Eddie pointed with his cup towards the rapidly-approaching locomotive that was clearly trailing steam from the cylinders and below the cab in addition to the great cumulus cloud rising high from the chimney and up and above the train before gently rolling down and over the village rooftops.

The Gresley A3 was indeed in a shocking state; still wearing the pre-nationalised livery somewhere beneath the deep layers of grime and oil, but despite this the elegant shape of the boiler and the curving frames, the 'Doncaster smile' of the smokebox front and the huge, whirling wheels of this 'racehorse of the rails' were still there to admire, and a good crew could always squeeze some running from one of these splendid engines.

'I wish I was crewing her,' Eddie turned his head to watch the fireman bend double over his shovel, then looked for the tell-tale dark grey smoke pouring from the chimney in response as the train disappeared beneath the triple arches of Eydon Road Bridge. 'I've a way to go yet before I make the top link.'

'Are you two going to chunter on out here all morning like a pair of old men, or are you coming inside for your breakfasts?' Mrs Walsh was wiping her hands on her apron. 'You haven't long before you're both down the loco.' She knew the times, the turns, the rhythms of the great locomotive shed almost as well as did the shedmaster himself, accustomed as she was to helping provide railwaymen grab an 'emergency' sandwich and some tea when time was too short to walk to the staff canteen down in the yard. Simon and Eddie were in no hurry, but they preferred the passenger refreshment room to the canteen as its windows commanded a fine view of locomotives as they passed through or stopped at the station. Mrs Walsh was happy to serve them provided they weren't wearing their grubby workclothes.

Both lads grinned at her and walked inside, choosing a table in the corner close to a window. Jenny McIntyre served their two fried-egg rolls.

'Here you go. Now give me those tea cans and I'll fill them whilst you get these down you.'

'Thanks, Jen. Ooh, real eggs!' exclaimed Eddie, as some yolk oozed onto his plate.

'Of course. None of that reconstituted muck here!' Jenny smiled as she took their cream-coloured, enamelled tea cans.

Simon watched her as she crossed the room. 'Nice looker.' he spoke as softly as he could.

Eddie took a big bite of roll and raised an eyebrow, nodding slightly. He swallowed before responding. 'Yes, the A3s are the best looking on the line.'

'Not the engine, you daft bugger! I was talking about...' Simon stopped as saw Eddie's eyes twinkling. 'Thank God, you *are* human after all.' He glanced back across at Jenny. 'I missed my chance there.'

'I never knew you carried a candle for her.'

'Oh, come off it. You've looked enough times.'

Eddie winked. 'Difference is, I realised yonks ago it was just window-shopping with Jenny — same with her lovely friend Kathleen.' He looked rueful. 'Nothing doing there, mate.'

'You're too busy dreaming about that signalwoman, anyway.'

'Keep your voice down!' Eddie looked across the room and met Jenny's gaze. She raised an eyebrow, inviting him to share their whispered conversation. He looked away quickly and felt his cheeks start to burn. 'No one knows anything about Miss Green. Understood?'

'And is there anything *to* know?' Simon leant forward and grinned at his friend. 'I doubt it. Just daydreaming most like; anyway, she's too much older than you.'

'Only four, or maybe five years. It's not *that* much!'

'Are you kidding? Why on earth would she be interested in you?'

'Actually, Laura is always very friendly.'

'Ooh-hoo, it's *Laura* now, eh? Listen, Eddie, she probably talks to everyone and anyone all day long. I hope you've not pinned your hopes on the fact she says, "good morning Master Earnshaw"?'

Eddie remained silent for a moment before replying. 'She sometimes sits next to me in the Mutual Improvement Class.'

Simon rolled his eyes.

'I can't see you doing much courting whilst discussing Rule 55 with a bunch of blokes in a room above the social club.'

'She smiled at me a couple of times and asked to borrow a pencil. She's still got it,' he said, slightly wistfully.

'Oh dear God!' Simon clapped a hand on his forehead with a slapping sound. Eddie switched the topic of conversation.

'Are you going to see those men in London again, the ones with the cigarettes?'

'Don't go changing the subject just as it was getting interesting! What if I am?'

'Er, it's just that, um, do you think they have nylons? You know, stockings?' Eddie flushed.

Simon stared at him, feigning shock. 'You dark horse!' He playfully punched Eddie on the arm, winked cheekily and remarked: 'I'd say you're planning more than just retrieving your pencil!'

Eddie saw Mrs Walsh and Jenny looking towards them with arched eyebrows. 'Keep it down, will you! 'She might go to the NUR fireworks dance, and I thought that, if I dance with her, she might go to the pictures with me and...'

'Go on...' Simon was grinning like the Cheshire cat.

'It could be useful to have a nice present in reserve, in case things take a turn for the best after a few dates. It might impress her.' Eddie was looking flustered. Saying it out loud made the plan sound ridiculous, even embarrassing.

'You might get a slap for your cheek,' Simon grinned, 'anyway, she always wears slacks.' He wrinkled his nose disapprovingly. 'Too many girls wear them. And overalls — yuck! Most disappointing to us lads with an eye for a fine leg.'

'She might wear skirts when off duty. Besides, all women want nylons, and they worked like magic for the Yanks. How much do you think two pairs would cost?'

'Dunno. Give me five shillings and I'll see what I can do?' Eddie fished in his jacket and handed Simon the money.

'You've changed your tune. I thought you didn't approve?'

'I was worried about you getting mixed up with those types.'

'Leave off. You're starting to sound like my mother,' said Simon. 'Sometimes you have to take a little risk; live a little. I'm firing up to Marylebone later. I want more fags, plenty more. I've got a list as long as your arm from lads wanting to buy. I could make a useful bonus from this.' Simon winked.

Eddie caught sight of Simon's wristwatch. 'Crikey, we need to get going, and I want to talk on the way about a really important matter.'

'Girls and cigarettes are not important?'

'I mean, about that dead man you told me about! I've made a list of everything we know so far.' Eddie already had his little train spotter's notebook open, the pages filled with locomotive numbers and jottings, random notes and observations. 'It's not much, though. I wonder if you can find anything about it in the London papers. You might find one in the messroom at Neasden.'

Simon laughed, 'Eddie, you really are the limit! I've decided that I can't go filling my head with that stuff any more. I've turned my back on playing the detective. Finished. The end.'

Eddie looked crestfallen. 'You're not serious.'

'You bet I am.' Simon fought hard to silence his conscience, which was pricking at him by suggesting that he was more interested in selling stolen goods than working on the side of the law. This was an uncomfortable truth that he just didn't want to face.

'Why the sudden change?'

'You should be concentrating on more important things, like the lovely Laura and how to get that well-fitting tunic of hers unbuttoned! You'll not give a second thought to that bloke in the canal once she lets you kiss her.'

Eddie flushed and made a sheepish grin, but his heart leapt just hearing the very idea.

Chapter Six

Strictly Confidential
Bud Powell

Whilst Eddie and Simon were making their way to Woodford locomotive shed, Vignoles and Benson were on their way back into town, heading towards the offices of the Leicester & Eastern Counties Insurance Company.

'So, what did you make of Adeline Pym?'

Benson weighed up her response for a moment. 'She appeared genuinely upset, though I wonder if she is as much distressed by the damage to her social standing as by the loss of her husband.'

'I am inclined to agree,' replied Vignoles, taking a puff on his pipe, 'I'm not accusing her of crocodile tears, but it seems that putting her bridge evenings in jeopardy and the lack of letters of condolence were too high on her list of concerns. But maybe I'm just cynical.'

'A sudden death can make people act oddly. Especially with strangers, and most especially the police. We should not be too hard on her, sir.'

'You may be right. What do you make of her insistence that it wasn't suicide?'

'A natural reluctance to accept her husband committed an ungodly act? It is, after all, a cardinal sin to take one's own life. Pym has left his wife and son high and dry. However, she offered no plausible suggestion for why anyone would want to kill him, other than robbery by a stranger.'

'Which does not appear to fit the facts. Hmm... what about this Bish fellow that Oliver was upset about? He called him nasty, said he hated him and, more significantly, he added, "so did daddy".'

'Would a father take his young son into confidence about whom he hated?'

'Perhaps not,' agreed Vignoles, 'but Oliver may have overheard a conversation, even an argument, between his father and Bish. Mrs Pym did not have much to say about Bish, though I sensed she was also not keen on him. She called him a "work associate". I'm not sure what that implies. Also, she hesitated before claiming not to know where Bish works or lives.'

Benson agreed. 'She was insistent that her husband's work was none of her business. However, Oliver's dislike of Bish suggests they had contact on a number of occasions. Did Bish visit the house?'

'Yes. I'd like to speak with him, if only to discount the accusations of an angry young boy seeking someone to blame.'

'If it *was* murder, does this put Bish in the frame?'

'On what grounds? The dislike of a young lad? Not much to go on.' Vignoles looked at Benson, his pipe jutting from one corner of his mouth.

'I notice the Pyms have expensive tastes, sir: nice car in the garage, house well furnished. She wore fine clothes — no "make do and mend" for her. That cameo brooch was antique Wedgwood, I'd say.'

Vignoles raised an eyebrow. 'How can you tell?'

Benson grinned. 'My mother is passionate about Wedgwood. Not that she could afford pieces like *that* too often. Living with her all these years, I've developed an eye for their work. Do you think Pym's salary alone was sufficient to finance their lifestyle?'

'I doubt it. It might be useful to find out what he was bringing home. Of course, either of the Pyms could have private wealth, or came into an inheritance. We'll make some enquiries, see if there are any skeletons in their cupboards. There might even be something that points to suicide.' Vignoles chewed upon his pipe for a moment. 'And we must find out what life insurance policy there is on Mr Pym.'

'Oh, you suspect his *wife* was involved.' She looked surprised.

'If foul play is suspected, the first principle is: always look into the family circle. Did you not find it odd that she insists it was murder? That she wants it to be so? Now, why would she want such a dreadful thing?'

As the WPC mused on his question, Vignoles brought her up to speed. 'Suicide can, depending on the policy, sometimes disqualify a life insurance payout.'

✻   ✻   ✻   ✻

The pair arrived at Pym's workplace. It was a unique building, located on the side of the New Walk at the end of a short, wedge-shaped terrace. The Leicester & Eastern Counties Insurance Company was located within the thinnest part that terminated in a turret constructed from many tall and elongated glass panes with delicate, stained glass decoration at the top. This tube of glass and wood formed a tower capped by an overhanging and similarly fenestrated first floor with a neat, conical roof of tiles, like Red Riding Hood's cap. A series of shallow bay windows decorated the frontage facing onto King Street that was shared by two other shops with doors set back into shallow porches. The building certainly looked charming and offered plenty of natural light and a pleasing view along

Leicester's favourite perambulation route, but the working spaces inside must be awkward, and Vignoles suspected that the charm wore off with time, an impression confirmed as they stepped inside.

Desks, chairs and filing cabinets were squashed uncomfortably together, leaving little room to move. The office staff sat at awkward angles amidst piles of papers, diligently typing or answering jangling telephones, but the initial impression was not one of order and efficiency, but rather of confusion and muddle and a surprising amount of noise. A middle-aged receptionist wearing rather too much foundation, garish pink lipstick and an invisible cloud of scent greeted them and quickly placed an internal call to the managing director. They were soon shown up a set of acutely steep and narrow stairs, that creaked almost painfully, onto a gloomy landing. More doors and another steep staircase led off this windowless space. Just as Vignoles thought he might expire if he inhaled much more of the receptionist's intensely sweet scent, they were ushered into the office of Ronald Taylor.

The room was in the glass turret and was almost perfectly circular. Taylor sat behind a large mahogany desk with his back to the panoramic view. The room held two chairs for visitors and a bookcase of dull, matching volumes. A large safe squatted like a dark-green toad on one side of the room. His desk was almost clear, save for a wooden plaque with his name in full followed by a trail of letters that proclaimed his professional qualifications. He appeared to be scrutinising a sheaf of papers with great care, an expensive pen poised, ready to pounce upon any mistake.

'Ah, good morning gentlemen — oh, my sincere apologies — *madam*!' Taylor formed an attempt at a smile that fell well short of pleasant and his gaze lingered on Benson. 'Or is it *miss*?' The WPC give an involuntary glance down at her fulsome chest, clearly the object of the managing director's gaze, and replied, rather sternly.

'It's constable, actually, *sir*.'

He peered at the officers through round spectacles with heavy tortoiseshell frames, 'Please, please, do each take a seat. How I may offer assistance?'

Vignoles made the introductions. 'I trust my sergeant telephoned in advance and indicated the reason for our visit? I hope we shall not detain you long.'

'Not at all, not at all!' Taylor said, animatedly. 'Quite an unexpected distraction. Insurance can be a rather dull affair. But I fear we cannot help you, inspector; I feel confident in stating that none of us contributed towards poor Pym's tragic decline in mind, body or spirit.' He was clearly having problems looking Vignoles directly in the eye.

'What can you tell me of Jack Pym?'

'Good man! One of my best. Kept his head down and got on with it.' Taylor picked up his pen and turned it in his hands, shaking his head sadly. 'A tragic loss. We shall all miss him dearly.'

'It came as a shock?' asked Vignoles.

'Absolutely. No warning at all. Can't understand it.'

'Did he seem preoccupied or out of sorts?'

'No, he was same old Jack, nose always in his work. Of course, one feels simply terrible,' he looked at Benson, 'to think that he must have been going through some manner of private crisis and one didn't notice.' He gave a regretful smile and the WPC looked away.

'Did you find anything that could be a suicide note amongst his papers?'

'We have not searched through them. We only picked up the threads of his latest case because one owes it to one's clients, but no more. It has been but three days, inspector. He has not even been laid to rest.' Taylor briefly closed his eyes in what approximated reverence, and placed the pen carefully on the blotter.

'We police officers are trained to ride above sentiment,' Benson replied quickly. 'It would be helpful if we might have a look at his desk and work files.'

'That would be most irregular. There are matters of client confidentiality and privacy to consider, after all, he dealt with sensitive claims and—'

'—and he was found dead in a canal,' Benson reminded him curtly. Taylor looked momentarily floored, and Vignoles silently applauded his WPC's interjection. 'If you could just point us towards his desk? We need not keep you from your work any longer, Mr Taylor.' Jane Benson pushed her advantage home with finesse.

'I shall have to insist that someone accompany you. He shared an office with Miss Buckland.' Taylor dialled a number and a few moments later the landing floor creaked sharply as a young woman entered the room.

'Miss Buckland, these police officers are looking into the sad business of Mr Pym. They need to look amongst his things. Give them full access: we have nothing to hide here,' Taylor looked down his nose at Vignoles.

They filed out after the young woman, leaving Taylor staring wistfully at WPC Benson and tapping his pen on the blotter.

✳   ✳   ✳   ✳

Pym's office, though small, was at least a conventional rectangular shape with a slim bay window and the welcome addition of two potted geranium plants, both still cheerfully in bloom. Two desks faced each other, and the far wall was lined with filing cabinets and a series of shelves holding metal box files, and a set of books matching the one Vignoles had in his briefcase. The room was the very epitome of orderliness. Such was the logic and almost obsessive neatness of everything they looked at, it soon became clear in Vignoles's mind how unlikely it was that they would uncover any surprises within the meticulously maintained case files. Vignoles and Benson selected a number of these at random, with no clear objective in mind, and were struck only by the neatness of his filing system, whilst Miss Buckland hovered around and ensured each was returned to its correct place. Pym was the perfect pen pusher, and his young understudy clearly aspired to the same lofty standards. His desk was, unsurprisingly, immaculately tidy and, if any impression was to be gained, it was of a rather soulless individual.

Vignoles sat back in Pym's desk chair and looked around. 'Where is his diary, Miss Buckland?'

'He usually took it with him, especially if he was going out of town.'

Vignoles nodded. Inspector Tykett had mentioned that Pym's briefcase had not been found. He pulled open the desk drawers and his attention was drawn to a small brown bottle labelled 'aspirin', partially buried beneath some old envelopes and scraps of paper saved for reuse. He picked up the bottle and shook it. Benson and Buckland looked across at the small sound it made.

'Half empty, and the date of issue is... 1944. Gosh! He was hardly a habitual pill taker.'

'Mr Pym has — sorry, had — excellent health. He prided himself on having never missed a single day of work through sickness,' she observed hurriedly. 'I don't think he even had a headache in all the time I knew him.'

Vignoles nodded thoughtfully and stared at the pills a moment longer before replacing the bottle. 'Probably explains the effect on him. No resistance.'

'Did you like working with Mr Pym?' asked Benson.

'I have no complaints. I learnt a lot.' She hesitated, 'I suppose I might even step up to his position. Sorry, that sounds dreadful. I didn't mean—'

'—it wasn't your fault. Dead men's shoes never feel comfortable, but why not seize the opportunity? Advance yourself and get your name on the door,' Benson replied, her mother's suffragette fervour having evidently rubbed off on her.

Miss Buckland stared at the floor.

'Mr Taylor said there was no obvious change in his manner or equilibrium, but you sat opposite him every day and would have a far better appreciation of his moods. Did you notice any change? Any hint of what was to come?'

Miss Buckland considered this for a moment. Vignoles noticed her hesitation and flicked his eyes up from looking at a few papers neatly stacked on the desk to observe her more closely.

'I don't think so... although...'

There was a sudden creak on the desiccated floorboards outside the closed office door. Was this the soft tread of someone trying hard to not betray their presence?

'You appear uncertain,' suggested Benson, softly.

Vignoles was now peering beneath the desk blotter, but his ears were pricked.

'It's my lunch hour shortly.' Miss Buckland looked across at the wall clock. 'I often go to the British Restaurant on Granby Street.' She and Benson exchanged knowing looks.

'I believe we have seen all we need.' Vignoles looked up at the two women. 'I'm quite satisfied there is nothing here that sheds any light on this unfortunate tragedy. We must leave you to your work, Miss Buckland.' He spoke loud and clear, ensuring his voice carried.

'Meet you there, just after one?' Benson whispered to Miss Buckland. Vignoles pocketed something retrieved from beneath the blotter then started buttoning his overcoat in preparation for stepping back into the raw dampness outside. 'We can see ourselves out, and I thank you again for your assistance.'

'My pleasure, inspector. Good day.'

✻   ✻   ✻   ✻

The British Restaurant was little more than a vast canteen filled with serried rows of tables, each with four identical hard wooden chairs, fawn tablecloths and jam jars holding sprigs of greenery. It looked like the pictures in the brochures for the new Butlin's holiday camps, of dining halls filled with happy campers sitting down for their budget meals. The atmosphere inside was a heady mix of steam and the aroma of braised meat, hot gravy browning, boiled cabbage and that peculiar pong of damp Labrador coats. Although the food was simple and would win no awards for imagination or quality, one could eat adequately for two shillings, coupon free, so the restaurant was always full to bursting. However, the bossy but matronly staff ensured that no one lingered long once they had eaten their small bowl of fruit crumble and watery custard for dessert, and so tables swiftly became available.

DI Vignoles, WPC Benson and Miss Buckland were seated at a table in the heart of the room, surrounded on all sides by chatting diners and clattering knives and forks, and this noise served as the perfect cover for the young assistant loss adjuster to speak freely. As each tucked into a plate of braised beef with a solitary, over-boiled cauliflower floret and the regulation serving of two potatoes, Vignoles took time to assess Miss Buckland.

She was of medium height with a fresh-faced, clean-scrubbed prettiness, choosing to wear her brown hair long and straight, almost to the middle of her back in an unfashionable style; he suspected she had worn it like this since she was a young girl, unmoved by changing trends. Her complexion was noticeable for the palest suggestion of lipstick and a touch of colour to her cheeks, though this might equally have been induced by her nervousness. She had strong, dark eyebrows, again unusual in that she appeared happy to leave them unplucked; so very different from the narrow, carefully shaped lines women seemed to prefer these days. Anna would spend ages before the dressing table mirror wincing and pulling faces as she set to work with tweezers, but would never contemplate not performing this agonizing ritual. If looks said anything, Julie Buckland was honest and uncomplicated, if perhaps a little gauche. Despite her clearly having something to gain from Pym's death he could not see her as a valid suspect.

Benson had tried to put the young woman at ease by chatting about the recent availability of tangerines and the ending of clothes rationing, but Buckland just picked at the meat and looked increasingly nervous before finally plunging right in.

'You must think me awfully melodramatic but I had to get away from the office in order to speak freely. The walls are so thin and one never knows who might overhear.' She blushed and looked at her cold meal, the gravy already forming a greasy skin.

Vignoles nodded reassuringly. 'We needed sustenance, and spending our lunchtime with you can hardly be a calamity'. Vignoles smiled. 'You have something to tell us about Mr P? Without using names.'

'I hate to speak ill of the dead, and in a great many ways Mr P. was a good man. Quiet, diligent, efficient, if perhaps a little serious and dry.' She bit her lip at this mild criticism.

She leant forward to speak more quietly, pushing her plate to one side, the food apparently holding no appeal. 'I was given the task by Mr T. of taking on his caseload. It is a huge responsibility and a great honour, so I am uncomfortable saying something that could bring the company into disrepute, having being shown such trust.'

Vignoles remained silent, just raising an eyebrow and nodding as he ate the last of his beef.

'However, I have noticed something a little odd. You might think it awfully unimportant, in fact it may be nothing really, but Mr P. was a meticulous worker, and…' She tailed off.

'You found something that does not fit with his usual way of working?' asked Benson.

'I think so. His current case related to a large quantity of items stolen from Marylebone goods warehouse.'

Vignoles placed his knife and fork on the edge of his plate and deliberately dabbed at his mouth with a napkin whilst looking intently at the young woman.

'Marylebone?'

'Yes. He was travelling to London to make some final enquiries in regard to a particularly large theft, with the intention of awarding full damages. A very substantial sum.'

'But there is a problem?' asked Benson.

'Well, I was surprised not by what I found, but what I did *not* find. It was a very slim dossier, with only the very minimum information. There was nothing wrong with what I read and it was all carefully ordered, as was Mr P's way…'

'You think some papers have been removed?' asked Vignoles.

'No; it was a complete case investigation, but I could find no evidence to suggest Mr P. had sufficiently challenged or questioned the facts surrounding the loss.' She stopped and shook her head, 'I'm sorry, I am not explaining this properly. I need to go back a step.'

'In your own time,' Benson was encouraging.

'I want to make sure that I do a good job so I reminded myself of the first rule I was taught, that of establishing all facts before starting to draw a conclusion.'

'Sound thinking,' Vignoles approved.

'I decided to see if Mr P. had dealt with the same company before. He had. On no less than *seven* occasions over the last twelve months.' She paused and looked first at Vignoles then at Benson with her wide, blue eyes. 'But one must be careful of jumping to conclusions based on that fact alone. However, what intrigued me was that Mr P. had chosen to take on these specific cases. As senior loss adjuster, he would normally pass such trivial cases to me. At first they were a crate of cigarettes or two, a hundred pairs of stockings. Petty crimes.'

'But the losses started to mount up?' Vignoles was filling his pipe as he spoke.

'Significantly so, and I found that odd. I would expect Mr P. to step in only when the losses escalated into hundreds of pounds, so I was a little puzzled that he had been handling the small Jordan Impex claims.'

'Sorry? Is that Jordan's Import and Export, of Loughborough?'

'Oh golly!' She held a hand to her mouth and her cheeks coloured. 'I should never have let slip the name. To betray professional confidentiality is quite unforgivable!'

'Far from it, any information that could have any bearing on a suspicious death, no matter how tenuous, must be shared with us.' Vignoles was trying to keep his voice as low as possible.

'So, what puzzled you was the high incidence of cases and the escalation in goods stolen, all pertaining to the same company and Mr P. dealing with them all from the start. And when you compared the case files with his other work not involving this particular company, it looked too casual?' asked Benson.

'Spot on! He repeatedly agreed full damages without any challenge.'

The three fell silent for a moment, contemplating what this might mean.

'Thank you, this is most useful.' Vignoles smiled. 'I appreciate you taking the time to tell us. I might wish to speak again to you about this,' and handed her his card.

'Do you think this is significant to his suicide?'

'I am keeping an open mind, although it does not immediately strike me that way, so please don't be alarmed.'

'Gosh, that is a relief.' Julie Buckland smiled wanly and looked like a weight had lifted from her shoulders.

Chapter Seven

Mule Train
Frankie Lane

Simon had a final wipe around with an oily cloth over the pipes, gauges and levers on the footplate of the big K3 type engine he had fired from Woodford to Marylebone, a journey that involved stopping at intermediate stations and dropping off or collecting a ragtag selection of mixed goods wagons along the way. It had been an easy run, with the engine steaming well, rattling along with the distinctive beat of the syncopated motion and the exhilarating, unsteady gait that caused the men to dub these engines 'ragtimers' and capturing something of Simon's mood of nervous excitement.

They had dropped off their final load and the engine was to be stabled on one of the lines reserved for coaling and watering engines, rather than being sent back along the line to Neasden shed. Simon had just overseen the topping up of the tender using the small, mechanical loader that tippled coal from even smaller metal trucks that ran on their own short, narrow-gauge line. It was a far cry from the huge, Cenotaph-style concrete coal tower that dominated Woodford loco and which boomed like bombs whenever it emptied its load, but as Marylebone was surrounded on all sides by houses, flats and hotels, Simon presumed that such a noisy monster would hardly be welcome.

His driver had been eager to get off and have a pint and eat whatever his missus had put in his snap tin. To Simon's delight, he left him to drive the ragtimer along one of the crowded stabling lines on his own, stopping just short of a row of engines that included a very woebegone member of the Director class named *Prince of Wales,* now looking anything but regal, and three of the line's ubiquitous B1s.

After winding the brakes on he shut the steam ejector off, checked the damper was closed and had a final glance at the fire. He was satisfied he was leaving his engine in a good state: clean and tidy, topped with water and coal and with a light fire gently glowing in the box. It would not take him long to get her back up to full pressure in three hours' time, when he was expected back. His nerves might be jangling by then, but now he wanted to take a walk, have a pint, and do a little shopping 'on the black.'

Stepping off the footplate, Simon looked around to get his bearings. It was dark, and the now almost permanent London smog was licking around the line of engines, lurking between the locomotive wheels like a sinister gas that coiled and curled around the connecting rods, flared in fiery halos about the gas lamp tops and filled the train shed with a soft blurriness, lending everywhere a strange, unearthly atmosphere. He shuddered and, feeling a sudden kick of nerves, slung his haversack diagonally across his shoulders, took a final deep breath of the poisonous air and ascended a narrow set of stairs cut into a steep embankment leading to the elevated parcels shed.

He didn't want to stumble into Dennis or Big Ron in this place, though there was every possibility of doing so. He was starting to feel anxious and felt his pulse leap as a shadowy figure approached him out of the opaque air, partially silhouetted by the light of a yard lamp. It was an old man, perhaps a beggar, dressed in a ragged coat, a battered hat pulled low over his brow and a scarf tied across his nose and mouth like an Egyptian mummy in a horror film. He was stumping along on a gammy leg with his eyes to the ground, nodding the faintest of greetings as he passed.

Simon breathed again. This was not a good place. There were too many dark corners and constricted corridors between the lines of wagons. If the black marketeers were going to teach him a lesson for taking their cigarettes under false pretences, they could do so here with little chance of being observed or overheard. No, he needed to face them in the pub with the safety of other people nearby. He would explain that it had just been an innocent mistake the first time, but was happy to buy their goods, and regularly. He felt his temples throb. It was not going to be an easy conversation, but reassured himself that his money was as good as anyone's and beating him up was probably more trouble than it was worth, surely?

He walked into the parcels depot, intending to cut through onto Rossmore Road at the far end. It was a scene of great noise and apparent confusion, with great mounds of parcels and mail sacks piled everywhere. Postal workers were driving battery-powered vehicles pulling rattling, wheeled cages that weaved between others standing, talking and smoking on the platforms and the few that were diligently heaving bags into the green British Road Services vans. How did anyone ever find anything here? It looked a terrible muddle. The air smelt of exhaust fumes and locomotive smoke, hessian mailbags, brown wrapping paper and dirty fog. The cavernous space echoed with sharp crashes and bangs, van doors slamming, men shouting and those annoying caged trucks that trembled with a hard metallic sound.

He was glad to walk up the exit ramp and escape to the relative peace of the road. Standing on the corner of the pavement with its black and white painted kerbstones, he had to step back to allow yet another green van to swing into the depot, then watched as a red London bus, followed by a procession of cars and taxi cabs, slowly trundled past, their headlight beams sweeping the ground before them like the searchlights that once probed the sky above.

Simon crossed the road and headed down another that cut between a gloomy black church and a bombsite filled by a tottering pyramid of salvaged wood and rubbish piled into a massive bonfire. That was going to make someone a fine blaze come Saturday night. A cast iron sign salvaged from a wall of the now-destroyed buildings was crudely nailed to a post confirming he was on Harewood Avenue. Simon walked on briskly, the road settling down into lines of three-storey Victorian terraces with occasional gaps, like missing teeth, forming a visual trail of where the German bombs had struck.

On his left the houses gave way to a low, brick shed of some length, with a series of louvred air vents in the wavy roof. It was almost windowless save for a few half-lights below the eaves, some of which were ajar and glowing brightly from lights within. As he walked past, he heard a series of rapid cracks, rather like the familiar snapping of the kindling when starting to raise a fire whilst kneeling on a locomotive footplate in the early hours of the morning. A hand-painted advertisement of faded cream edged with red on the brick wall confirmed what he now suspected: this was Stanley's Miniature Rifle Range. Two men in long overcoats and caps, each holding slim cases that Simon took to contain rifles, stood smoking near the front door on the corner of Sherbourne Place. Simon gave them a wary look as he passed, but they ignored him and continued their conversation about dog racing.

The Sherbourne Arms lay at the end of a short street that stopped abruptly with a brick wall that guarded the steep drop into the throat of Marylebone station. The train shed canopies dominated the scene and a soft cloud of steam from an unseen locomotive formed an almost incandescent pillar from behind the retaining wall until it tumbled down onto the pub sign and twin lanterns illuminating the entrance. The pub and the rifle range were probably the hub of life within this little network of identical terraces built in sickly-yellow London brick, and yet the streets appeared deserted, an impression only enhanced by the smog and a solitary car with a flat tyre. The houses were substantial but down-at-heel, and Simon guessed this was railway workers' territory, populated by men from the goods and parcels depots, by firemen, guards and station porters and the many others subsisting on the slim wage packets of British Railways. The bicycles resting against a wall near the pub backed up this impression, for these were the trusty steeds of almost every railwayman.

As he approached the pub he saw two women leaning against the wall, smoking. One had her leg provocatively lifted to show a considerable expanse of black stocking. As Simon approached they exchanged glances and one threw her cigarette to the ground, leaving it smouldering rather than stubbing it out with one of her brightly-coloured shoes. They both wore a lot of cosmetics, with cherry-red lips and, despite the raw night, their skirts were surprisingly short, barely reaching their knees. Simon kept his head down as he drew level with the pub then vacillated for a moment before opting to enter the lounge rather than the public bar. In that moment of hesitation, the woman who had dropped the cigarette stepped forwards and spoke.

'Good evenin', young man.'

Simon kept his head down.

'Cat got your tongue?'

'He 'ent got no manners, Lind,' the other woman interjected.

'Sorry. Good evening.' Simon looked at the one apparently called Linda. She was leering at him, eyes big and heavily delineated by kohl.

'That's more like it. We ain't going to bite, not at first, haha!' The women burst into gales of raucous laughter, a sound not unlike machine gun fire, and Simon did his utmost not to recoil.

'You got a smoke for a lady?' said Linda, with a playful smile and eyes mischievous.

'Sorry. I'm all out.' Simon mumbled.

'Why you wasting your breff on 'im? He's nuffin' but a kid.' The other woman had stopped laughing and her voice had a sharper edge to it.

'So, you're all out of smokes? Lookin' to get some more from the boys?' Linda nodded her head towards the pub and the hubbub of talking and strains of Frankie Lane singing his recent hit that came from within.

'How about you buy me a drink? A nice port and lemon, I can sit all quiet and *de-mure*,' she divided and exaggerated her final word, then nudged him in the side, winking lasciviously, 'whilst you do a bit of business.'

Simon shook his head and darted through the lounge door. The pub was busy and full of noise, for which Simon was glad as it drowned the sound of the women laughing behind his back, whilst the hot, fuggy atmosphere masked his embarrassment.

It was a typical London pub, all darkly varnished wood, bevelled mirrors and engraved glass; big, brassy lamps and a heavily-ornamented plaster ceiling stained nicotine brown. Groups of men in grubby, railwaymen's overalls stood at the curving bar with their backs to Simon, whilst patrons of both sexes were seated in the alcoves and tables around the room. Three cocky lads in extravagantly-lapelled suits made of shiny black material and sporting garish ties and flamboyant handkerchiefs stuffed carelessly into their breast pockets dominated the room. Pint glasses in hand, fedora hats tipped back in a sophisticated fashion they fancied resembled that of Frank Sinatra, they laughed and joked loudly, surveying the reaction to their noise and bluster with hard, desperate eyes. One of the men spotted Simon, but his look was instantly dismissive, even faintly contemptuous, and he looked away after deciding the young railwayman was no challenge to their swagger. He elbowed one of his mates in the ribs and made a lewd observation about a woman seated opposite.

Simon ordered a light ale, eyeing the landlord as he did so and weighing up whether to mention Dennis or Big Ron. The landlord had a pale scar across one cheek and crew-cut hair, short like the American GIs wore it. Whilst he was civil enough as he pulled the pint, he looked a rough sort and Simon did not feel inspired to speak with him; he just collected his pint and turned his back to the bar. Taking a deep draught and feeling bolstered by the surge of alcohol, he surveyed the room more carefully and was brought up short with a shock of recognition as his gaze met that of Dennis Parkey.

He was seated in an alcove, leaning back against the cushions in a relaxed pose, with another man beside him, a strange half smile playing across Dennis's face as his black, currant eyes stared back at Simon, who took a deep breath and gave a nod of acknowledgment.

Dennis lifted his pint glass and grinned wolfishly, then jerked his head to indicate that Simon should approach.

'Take a pew. This is Vic. Oh, but of course, you two already know each other'.

Simon sat down and met the iron stare of a man in his late fifties with a sharply pointed jaw, pale green eyes and a flat cap pressed onto what was probably a balding head fringed with thin, salt-and-pepper hair. His moustache was narrow and dark grey and did nothing to soften his appearance. He was wearing a donkey jacket over a navy cotton drill blouson with *British Railways* embroidered on the breast pocket, a grubby shirt with the top collar button undone but held closed by a greasy tie.

'Nah. Never set eyes on the scrawny brat,' Victor chewed slowly for a moment before looking at Dennis. 'Who is he? Mate of yours?'

'You didn't introduce him? Here, what's your bleedin' game?' Dennis glared at Simon, who found it an unsettling experience.

'N—no game. You gave me a cigarette and the next thing I knew I was with Big Ron and you in that room and he was offering me some—
'   '—keep your bloody voice down!'

Simon could almost hear his own heart pounding.

'You was looking for us. Wasn't you?' A hint of doubt crept into Dennis's voice.

He glared at Simon and growled, 'If you're up to something, I'll wring your bloody neck.'

'Cor blimey, give it a rest,' Victor implored. He motioned with his hands, his glance flitting between Simon and Dennis. 'Leave it. What's done is done.' He dropped his voice to no more than a whisper. 'You'd do well to smarten up your act, Dennis. You're letting standards slip.' There was something menacing yet understated about the man, and it demanded respect, even when speaking so softly.

'Now, the question is,' Victor turned to face Simon, his green eyes like a panther's, but addressed his next remark to Dennis: 'Since Mr Lucky 'as fallen into our laps, what are we gonna do wiv him?' An uneasy silence hung over the table for a few moments until at last he grinned at Simon. 'So, Lucky, was you 'appy wiv the trade the other day? Satisfied wiv the merchandise?' He spoke in an oddly forced and punctuated manner, stressing many of the words as if used to giving commands and expecting them to be understood.

Simon nodded. The worst seemed to be over now, and the atmosphere less tense. 'Oh yes, very happy. I—I was rather hoping that I might buy some more.'

'Yeah?' Victor looked at Simon in silence for a beat. 'Know what, Den? I fink you might've done all right here. Victor winked at Dennis, who now visibly relaxed, although he still gave Simon a dark look. 'As luck would so 'ave it, we're carrying a little sample of stock wiv us.' Victor flicked his eyes towards the floor and Simon noticed two canvas bags with carrying handles under the pub table. 'See? I told yer you was lucky. Now drink up and we'll step outside and see what we can do you for.'

As they left the pub Simon noticed the two women automatically moved aside in silence. However, he felt their mocking gaze on his back as he walked down the gloomy street and was ushered into an alleyway that stank of tomcat and piss.

A few minutes of brisk trading later, Simon had stuffed ten new packs of Park Lane, a complementary pack of Kensitas ('No one likes Kensitas, so you can 'ave em on the 'ouse to seal the deal') in his haversack together with three slim packets containing nylon stockings. The purchase of these last items had caused Dennis to lighten his mood and quip, 'You hopin' they'll get you a squeeze wiv your gal?'

'Um, yes. No! I mean, they're not actually for me.'

'I should hope not! Haha!' Dennis guffawed and prodded Simon in the ribs. It looked like a playful josh but it hurt like two metal rods being rammed in his side. The exchange had been slick and discreet, however, and Simon was feeling elated, if still a little apprehensive. These men were tough and dangerous and yet, in their own odd way, had treated him decently. He'd got away with accidentally trading without having been formally introduced and made a second lucrative transaction. At the prices he could sell the cigarettes for, he was in for a bumper week.

'Well, I must be off now,' he said brightly.

'We're not done yet.' Victor placed a firm hand on Simon's upper arm as Dennis neatly stepped away from one of the slimy brick walls to block the exit to Sherbourne Road. 'We need to get down to some real business.'

Simon began to feel scared. He could see little of Victor's face in the dim half-light of the narrow alley. His eye sockets were rendered as deep pools of black, his cheeks sunken, and the sickly light made him seem more skull than flesh, with just the thick bush of his moustache adding a welcome touch of life to a hideous death's head nodding on the shoulders of a darkly silhouetted body.

'I've got all I need, thanks very much, v—very much indeed!' Simon grinned affably but felt cold fingers tie a knot in his intestines as Victor's hand tightened like a vice on his arm.

'Correction; *you've* got what *you* want. But there's something *we* want, and no, not the few shillings you just handed over.' Vic's glance flicked across to that of Den, who placed his hands on his hips, legs planted wide in response to an unspoken signal. Simon tried to swallow. His mouth was suddenly very dry.

'Where'd you say you're from?'

'W—Woodford Halse.'

'What's that? 38C?' Victor was referring to the British Railways code used to identify each engine shed on the system.

Simon nodded.

'Good! We might need someone round your manor before long.'

'W—what had you in mind?'

'Checking a few things out, gathering information, or even getting stuck in.'

Simon's eyes were wide as saucers. 'Stuck in?'

'Jesus! Are you always so bleedin' dim?' Dennis looked chagrined. He leant forward so his beery breath blasted onto Simon's face. 'You don't think this stuff grows on trees?'

Simon shook his head. The rest of his body was motionless with apprehension.

'*Someone* has to collect it, and that *someone* now includes you!'

'Oh, no! I couldn't. I mean, I don't want to be involved in—'

'— in what?' Vic's tone was both mocking and threatening. 'Illegal activity?' Simon glanced from one man to the other in panic.

'Too late, son, you're already in it, right up to your eyeballs! One word from us, and you're nicked. You'll be joining the dole queue, or slammed up at His Majesty's pleasure.'

'But—'

'Illegal goods on your person whilst on the *footplate*?' Victor shook his head and tutted, 'and then there's the selling of said stolen items on *railway* property, stuff that was lifted from a *railway* wagon?'

'B—but I never—'

'—they won't believe you. They'll come down on you like a ton of bricks, throw the book at you,' Dennis sneered.

Simon felt sick as he began to realise how cocky and naïve he'd been, thinking he could just buy, sell and make a profit with no reprisals. It had been too easy and he should have realised there would be a catch. It dawned on him that these thugs had him over a barrel. He'd longed to work on the footplate since he was six years old, and now he'd stupidly jeopardised his entire career on the steam engines he loved just to make a few bob on some dodgy fags. Quite apart from losing his job in the most shame-faced way, he would probably end up with a criminal record. What would his dear mother say? Even worse, how could he tell his father? As a signalman with a long service record, this would be just too humiliating for the poor man to bear.

'Listen, don't look so worried; just do like we say and we'll see you're all right.' Victor's voice was calming. He grinned and loosened his vice-like grip on Simon's arm. 'We'll be in touch,' he said chirpily. 'We'll find you, make no mistake. We know who you are and we know where you work, so don't you worry. Just remember, if we ask you to jump, you jump.'

'But—er, what if I can't? I mean, what if I'm busy?'

'Not our problem. Besides, you've got a nice lot of quality goods there. Use 'em to soften up yer shed master. Give 'im some fags, a pair of stockings for 'is missus. He'll be happy to send you wherever we want you to go.'

'Give him those bloody Kensitas!' Dennis laughed. He winked at Simon, who was thoroughly disconcerted by the abrupt changes from physical intimidation to cheery friendliness to veiled threat to laughter, all in the space a few minutes.

Vic slapped Simon on the back. 'Now, get along, Lucky, me lad! And remember to keep yer bleedin' gob shut.'

Chapter Eight

BLUEBERRY HILL
Louis Armstrong

Vignoles was warming his feet on the hot water pipes below his office window, smoking a pipe filled with some decidedly stale tobacco. He'd finished the last of his good stuff the day before and was down to a half-forgotten packet discovered in his desk drawer. He watched the low morning sun dapple the station platform and slice through the steam rising from the hot water boiler on the Women's Voluntary Service mobile canteen, the light staining the white clouds with flashes of lemon yellow. An express fish train thundered through the station hauled by a gleaming V2 locomotive, its whistle shrieking, leaving the pungent scent of the sea in its wake and inducing passengers to sniff the air and wrinkle their noses. This made Vignoles smile.

PC Blencowe and the two WPCs were seated on the other side of his desk beside Sergeant Trinder, who was looking unusually eager to commence taking notes as he was desperate to test his latest purchase: one of the new-fangled Biro pens that had started to appear in the shops.

'It really is a marvel, sir. Apparently, one can write upside down.'

'Do you often have cause to write whilst upside down?' Vignoles swivelled around on his faithful old chair and gave his sergeant a quizzical glance over his spectacles. Benson stifled a giggle.

Trinder looked nonplussed. 'Perhaps at an angle? Leaning against a wall for example?'

Vignoles raised an eyebrow. He was yet to be convinced.

'The chap who invented it was Hungarian,' added Trinder. If this was further evidence of the magnificence of the Biro pen, it failed to impress.

'May I take a look?'

'Be my guest.' Trinder passed the black instrument that looked not unlike any other pen, save for its narrow nib, across the desk. 'It almost never smudges because the special ink dries as it writes, even on wet paper. It has a small rolling ball at the end that collects the ink and transfers it to the paper.'

Vignoles made a few experimental strokes on his desk blotter before writing his name twice and doodling in concentric circles. 'Impressive.' He looked at the many smears and blobs of ink already on the blotter and the annoying stain on the cuff of his shirt that refused to shift no matter how many times Anna scrubbed at it. 'Could you find another? I think it might improve my handwriting no end.'

'I can try, sir.'

He handed the pen back to his sergeant. 'Now, to business. The death of Jack Pym. Following our interview with Mrs Pym and her son Oliver and a visit to his workplace, I'm yet to be satisfied that he committed suicide. Furthermore, there is now a question mark about his honesty at work.' Vignoles explained the concerns raised by Miss Buckland.

'It could be that he was on the fiddle. But that could be irrelevant to his death.' Vignoles took a puff on his pipe. 'If his death is suspicious then we'll concentrate on his wife for now, as murder is usually committed by someone closest to the victim, so let's see what secrets the Pyms are hiding. I want you to consider a few questions. Did he owe money? Has either of the Pyms come into money? Talk to his bank manager. What salary was he on? Has he got another account hidden away somewhere that his wife knows nothing about? Hunt out his life insurance details. At this stage I want you all to go gently and not make too many waves, but I do want to build up a picture of this man — and of his wife.'

'She's the prime suspect? Trinder asked.

'Has to be until we can eliminate her or conclusively prove he took his own life.'

'Do you think we should tail her, sir?' asked Benson. 'It could be illuminating to monitor her movements for a day or so.'

'Ye—es.' Vignoles nodded slowly. 'Tail her. Though, Benson, you'll have to play it extra carefully as she knows your face. You and Lansdowne can work as a team. Blencowe: crack on with the paper trails and work that telephone until its red hot.'

'Righty-o, sir!'

'Sergeant, you and I are heading up to London to meet DI Tykett of the Yard. He's got the PM report and I need to look at the crime scene. You can take notes — better bring your Hungarian upside-down pen.' Vignoles grinned.

The train to London was crowded and discussion about the case had to be put on hold. Since work was off the agenda, Trinder spent his time poring over a sheaf of printed papers, occasionally making an addition to a list he was compiling in the back of his police notebook, or consulting a dog-eared page from a newspaper he had retrieved from his jacket pocket. Vignoles meanwhile, turned to his well-thumbed copy of the *Complete Works of William Clare*, the Northamptonshire nature poet. Looking up from the page and out of the carriage window, he was struck by Clare's perfect description of the view now sliding past, of the gentle rise and fall of hills and hedgerows and winding country roads, and the great stands of trees that appeared to sleep...

...in mist from morn to noon;
And, if the sun looks through, 'tis with a face
Beamless and pale and round, as if the moon.

However, he found his interest in Clare was being overridden by curiosity as to what was so engrossing Trinder.

'John, what on earth are you studying so intently?'

'The latest catalogue of 78 releases. I have a mail order arrangement with a gramophone shop in Liverpool that can get all the newest and hottest cuts from America. They come over on the transatlantic ships and they get them long before the Leicester stores.'

'So your passion for collecting music has not abated?'

'No—o.' Trinder gave a sheepish grin. 'Reined in a little these days. It has to be. Violet has imposed a strict budget on my spending now. We have to save for the future, you know how it is, sir.' He looked a little embarrassed.

'Ah, that's the price of married life, John: compromise! Haha! Found anything of interest?'

'I certainly have, but I can't afford everything so it's a case of making my final choice, and this proved tricky, but I've pretty much settled on Louis Armstrong's latest.'

'He knows a good tune.'

'He does! *Blueberry Hill* is the title. It's getting super reviews in the music press,' Trinder held the newspaper cutting in the air between them. 'I heard it just the once, and was instantly bowled over.'

'I've not yet heard the song — damned radio's broken!'

Trinder's enthusiasm for the subject was clear: 'I predict it will become the hottest thing by Christmas.'

A couple of businessmen turned the pages of their papers rather too noisily, expressing their annoyance about the direction the conversation was taking.

'Is that a review you have there?' asked Vignoles.

'Yes. I tore a page from the *Melody Maker* with reviews of some of the latest releases in the States. I think I must have read them a hundred times!'

A man coughed and sighed heavily. His busy, important life clearly did not allow for such frivolities as reading about Louis Armstrong.

Vignoles took the carefully-folded page and read the report, nodding approvingly before opening out the clipping to its full size, an exercise that involved carefully unfurling many folds and tucks.

'This is almost a work of origami.'

Trinder grinned. 'I should probably have just cut out the relevant part, but I was also interested in an article something on the reverse that has got me thinking — you might find it interesting.'

'Uh-huh.' Vignoles was not really listening, his attention diverted by looking at a photograph showing the cast of a new musical opening on Broadway called *South Pacific*.

'Quite an intriguing story. A big record retailer in the North East was the victim of a nasty fraud and lost heavily. That was early in the year, but the police were successful in tracking down the men behind it and brought them to justice. The case was felt sufficiently interesting to warrant reporting in the music press as a warning of how these gangs are now operating.'

'Really?' Vignoles was intrigued and scanned the page, turning it over in his hands looking for the relevant section.

'Bottom right. The headline reads, "Long arm of the law halts the long fraudsters".'

Vignoles read how a group of men had managed to defraud a music retailer, Hewitt's of Newcastle upon Tyne, out of nearly £400 by setting themselves up as a record wholesaler and subsequently duping Hewitt's into buying from them new 78s at competitive prices. Initially they had supplied small quantities of discs and Jeffery Hewitt, the proprietor, explained how the wholesaler had been 'fastidious in their service, offering an impressive stock list and speedy delivery.'

In reality, the so-called wholesaler was passing on stolen goods, which is how the gang was able to undercut all rivals. The arrangement lasted for about ten weeks, then came the sting. The orders grew in size and value, until Hewitt's decided to stock the shop more substantially, encouraged mainly by the wholesaler's agent, who made a convincing argument about the benefits to their profit margins of abandoning their other suppliers and plumping for their services alone. The only proviso was that Hewitt's had to pay in full and in advance of delivery. Jeffery Hewitt had not hesitated: 'The smooth talking trickster fooled me one hundred percent. He told me that they got the best prices because they had to shell out hard cash in the States. I accepted this, handed over the money and never saw the man or my money again. Needless to say, the discs have never arrived.'

The article explained that the police had eventually tracked down the fraudsters, and caught them red-handed stealing motor-car accessories from a lay-by on the Great North Road as part of their preparation for another of these 'long frauds', as they were describing the villains' *modus operandi*. The system relied upon the gang stealing or otherwise acquiring just enough stock to give the impression of being a major supplier, whilst actually carrying only the bare minimum needed to cover the number of transactions it took to gain the confidence of their victims.

Vignoles was particularly interested in the account given of their method of working. Something about it reminded him of what Queenie had told him about her attempt to purchase new radio valves: she'd paid upfront, too.

'This is intriguing. I've not heard of such a racket before.'

'Jolly interesting, isn't it?' said Trinder.

'I'd like to know more about this "long fraud" swindle.' Vignoles pulled thoughtfully on his pipe for a moment. 'It's a good description and a clever idea. A slowly evolving process, all about winning confidence and making a point of giving people what they want and at a fair price, before making the big hit.'

'Yes, I thought that unusual. An inversion of what one expects, as they reward the victim — at first.'

'And so it is all the more beguiling and tempting,' Trinder nodded.

The view through the window was now one of increasingly murky house backs, punctuated by the noisy passing of dark overbridges and little suburban stations, their lights glowing amidst the enveloping smog, signalling that they were nearing Marylebone.

'We'll talk more about this. Time to make our rendezvous.'

❖   ❖   ❖   ❖

The Kardomah was what DI Tykett had described as a 'greasy spoon of a caff', though he added 'the owner doesn't mind coppers idling their lives away there.'

They had discussed their visit on the telephone the previous evening and, as Vignoles was eager to visit the site where Pym's body was discovered, it made sense to stay in the Marylebone area.

'No sense in you coming down to the Yard, and it's nearer the crime scene, plus we can get a decent cup of char!'

It was a neat arrangement, and now all he and Trinder had to do was follow Tykett's dictated directions whilst negotiating unfamiliar streets swathed in a vile, greenish-yellow smog. They turned up Lisson Grove for a short distance and then made a series of twists and turns down smaller side streets. The pavements were busy with people, nearly all with handkerchiefs and mufflers across their faces. They were shoppers and office workers in the main, but there were a surprising number of sad old men with straggly beards and tatty overcoats, tired-looking women in canvas shoes, and amputee ex-servicemen in threadbare uniforms haunted by and occasionally warding off enemies they imagined were lurking in the fog.

London itself was looking particularly grim that day. Its blackened streets lined with small shops, many still illuminated, even in late morning, in a vain attempt to pierce the shroud of pollution and attract customers into their dingy premises. Other shops were closed or virtually empty of stock, and there appeared to be a profusion of little cafés reeking of chips fried in stale fat, a smell that hung heavy in the air. Vignoles hoped the Kardomah would be less dispiriting.

The character of the area changed as the road narrowed and became noticeably more industrial, with brick warehouses facing onto narrow pavements, some with arched portals leading into yards, whilst more lorries and horse drawn drays passed in regular succession. Both men were surprised, therefore, when the street opened out onto a broad railway yard that sliced across it at right angles. Opposite lay an access route crossing the railway lines on rotting wooden boards, guarded by decrepit gates sagging on their rusty hinges. Tall, grey grasses holding a collection of dented tin cans and soggy cardboard boxes gathered about the gates that, clearly, had not been opened for some time.

The sidings were set within an elongated rectangle of space filled by a filthy mistiness and edged by the pale impressions of warehouses, small factories and tall blocks of dwellings and, to their right, the massive bridge carrying Grove Road. Lost to sight beyond this lay the Regent's Canal and the entrance throat to Marylebone station, where a hooting engine could be heard but not seen.

'I didn't know this was here.' Trinder looked surprised.

'I have a vague recollection of seeing these sidings marked on a map, but I've never had cause to visit.'

'It's almost a hidden world.'

It was indeed. They approached the decrepit gates and looked over into the yard towards a row of box vans and a distant line of open trucks from which coal was being shovelled into bags before being hefted onto the flat beds of a waiting lorry and a horse drawn cart. Small, brick huts and a wooden lean-to shed were the only facilities provided for the men working the yard.

Vignoles looked at the tall street lamps standing like emaciated figures on the pavements. 'Where's this Kardomah got to? Tykett said it was on Carlisle Street.'

A British Road Services van bumped along the road beside them, driven by a large man who apparently had no neck. It swung to the right and turned through the open gates that appeared to be the only functioning access into the railway yard. A black police Rover eased its way along the road the parcel van had just left, a blue glass box with *Police* in white letters was illuminated on the roof above the split windscreen. The Rover pulled over to the side of the road, the motor and lights cut and two men in black coats stepped out and walked directly into a drab little corner café, its windows dripping with condensation and a waft of steam curling from the door as it opened with jingle of a bell.

'Those are our men, and that's the place!' Vignoles quickened his pace and they were also soon inside.

DI Tykett and Sergeant Phillip Sidlow were at the counter exchanging pleasantries with a short and extremely skinny man dressed in a long, white overall coat. He wore spectacles with immensely thick lenses that made his eyes appear huge, like those of a frog. His head was absolutely bald, and a stub of a pencil was tucked behind one ear.

Tykett looked around as he heard the doorbell tinkle. He nodded at Vignoles. A copper could always spot another, plain clothes or not. Introductions were made, hot drinks ordered and they were soon seated by the window at a Formica-topped table. Trinder grinned as a stainless steel receptacle filled with at least six cubes of sugar was placed in front of them.

'Froggy can always get sugar. That's why we keep comin' back.' Sergeant Sidlow had caught Trinder's reaction to the pile of white cubes and deliberately raised his voice to tease the proprietor. 'It ain't cos of the quality of the blinkin' food, that's for sure!'

'Get away wiv' yer!' The proprietor waved his hand dismissively at Sidlow as he returned to his counter.

'A word in your ear, don't touch the coffee. It's just muddy water!'

Vignoles looked worried because, unlike the others, he had ordered coffee.

'Yeah, yeah, yeah.' Froggy was still flapping his hand as if brushing away a fly.

'You're regulars?' Vignoles stated the obvious, but a little friendly chat would ease them into the real work.

'We're often down this way, and it's become a bit of a regular haunt for coppers working this manor,' replied DI Tykett. Vignoles noticed two uniformed bobbies seated towards the rear of the café, their helmets placed on empty chairs, both locked in a private conversation and showing no interest in the new arrivals.

'Righty-o. Shall we start with the PM report? I've already had a read through, but I need to see if anything in it chimes with what you've discovered about our Mr Pym.' Tykett was reaching into his briefcase whilst talking, and Vignoles nodded agreement. 'Not that I'm expecting much.'

The thin report was held together by a green treasury tag threaded through holes punched in the top left-hand corner, and Tykett had already turned a few of the pages over whilst he spoke. 'Most of this is routine, preliminary stuff, we can skip that, unless you really want us to go through it line by line.'

'Cut to the chase and concentrate on the pertinent points. We can always go back if we feel it's necessary,' replied Vignoles.

Tykett looked relieved. 'The obvious question is, how did Pym die? The report is absolutely clear: he drowned, and had a lot of water in his lungs.'

'Which fits with suicide,' observed Trinder, who was looking at the clutch of photographs of the dead man that came with the report.

'It does. Now, if he had not ended up in the canal — and we can come back to *how* he ended up there in a minute — the report says he would have passed out for certain, due to the huge quantity of whisky and a load of pills ingested between thirty minutes to an hour before death. Now, it says he could still have died as a result of the combined effect of this cocktail, even if he had not gone in the canal; he may have vomited and choked, for example. However, the pathologist reckons he was in good physical shape, so he might have survived. He'd be a very sick man, but alive.'

'This is significant. This confirms that his method of suicide — if this is a suicide —was fundamentally flawed. It worked only because he was too incapable of stop himself from falling in the canal and drowning,' observed Vignoles.

Tykett nodded. 'Suicides often don't want to die, just to get attention. It all fits, so I still run with the suicide idea.'

'I'm not so sure.' Vignoles looked like he was thinking about something. 'I would expect a note under such circumstances.'

Tykett shrugged. 'It might still turn up. The stomach contents reveal Pym had eaten a ham sandwich and apple crumble and custard, washed down with tea, about three hours before death. He ingested about four fluid ounces of whisky sometime after his last supper. The painkillers were almost certainly dissolved in the alcohol.'

'That's a lot of hard liquor.' Sidlow commented.

'Easier to swallow the tablets when dissolved.' Trinder was nodding.

'However, this is interesting: an empty pill bottle was found in his coat pocket and from the label and analysis of the dust residue found inside our forensic boys confirmed that he swallowed what was in the bottle. Now, you won't know the make — I'd never heard of them either — because it turns out they're a brand new type still undergoing clinical trials.'

'Should be easy to trace,' Vignoles remarked optimistically.

'They're called "Migranol Solubles", they're especially strong and, being soluble, take effect pretty fast. Made by Hendon Pharmaceuticals.'

Sergeant Sidlow retrieved a small box from his coat pocket. Inside was a brown bottle with a white cap and a blue-and-white printed label pasted to the front. It was dusted with fingerprint powder. 'We got it checked for dabs and found three sets. One was Pym's — the freshest set — overlaying the others.'

'I thought you were too busy to work on this case,' Trinder remarked.

'We are. But this was a piece of cake. The address was on the label!' Sidlow grinned, prompting Tykett to roll his eyes.

Vignoles sat upright in his wooden chair and peered closely at the bottle. 'Pym had a bottle of long-out-of-date aspirin in his desk drawer and when I mentioned this to the woman who shared his office, she was adamant that he was almost never ill. This suggests to me he would be a most unsuitable candidate for a clinical trial of a new painkiller.'

'Maybe his wife was doing the trial and he took the pills off her?' Sergeant Sidlow suggested.

'We need to ask her' replied Vignoles.

'We should be able to get the names of everyone who was supplied these pills for trial. They must have a list of all their guinea pigs.' Trinder made a note. 'I'll get PC Blencowe to make enquiries.'

'They might be unusual pills, but they don't change the fact he topped himself.' Tykett sounded weary as he spoke.

Vignoles was filling his pipe with tobacco. 'Just because we know he took pills dissolved in whisky which rendered him drunk and half unconscious, can we say for certain that he did this himself? So far we have found no compelling reason for Pym to take his own life.'

'We need to find out how and why he ended up in the canal.' Trinder was making more notes as he was speaking.

Tykett sighed wearily. 'There is something else of interest in the PM report.' He turned over a page before continuing. 'The pathologist found traces of bruising, though this was only light, to his upper arms.' Shuffling through the photographs he selected the relevant ones. They depicted pale skin and just a trace of shadow in shades of grey.

'The pathologist suggests the marks could have been the result of Pym being held upright, being supported whilst inebriated, perhaps, and goes on to say there is a possibility he was bound by a cord to a chair.'

'Well, that means foul play!' interjected Trinder.

'Hold your horses, sergeant.' Tykett offered his pack of cigarettes around, then lit one himself. 'Pym was wearing a wool suit and a heavy overcoat. Presumably this cushioned the bruising, so the pathologist will not commit categorically to this explanation. There are bashes to his shins that suggest he collided with something, probably whilst drunk. The pathologist is not able to say that any of these marks were created by a third party.'

'This smells like murder to me. Does no one agree?' Trinder looked around the table at the other three and then at the print showing the marks on Pym's shins.

'This is inconclusive,' replied Tykett, tapping a forefinger on the relevant passage in the report.

Vignoles turned the report so he could read it for himself. 'There is evidence of something other than suicide. We now have a suggestion of forcible restraint and manhandling on a person with no obvious reason to kill himself. It is possible that he was forced to swallow whisky and pills, taken to the canal side and helped, or pushed, into the water.'

Sidlow replied, 'And don't forget, his clothes look like he slid down something rusty and dirty. All down the back of his coat and the heels of his shoes, it was. It don't look like he just jumped off a bridge.' He jabbed a finger at another dark photographic print that struggled to reveal much detail in monochrome tones.

Tykett looked unhappy that his own sergeant was arguing against his theory.

'Now, what would cause marks that? It's almost like he went down a children's slide, you know, like in a park.' Sidlow was looking increasingly engrossed. A murder was much more absorbing than suicide.

'Did the postmortem report say anything about his mouth? Bleeding gums, a split lip, perhaps.' Vignoles was lighting his pipe and scanning the PM report as he asked the question, flicking between the pages.

Tykett sat up in his chair, an unlit cigarette dangling from his lips. Trinder gave a slight nod and a half-smile of recognition, selected two of the photographs and separated them out on the table.

'I'm just running with an idea,' continued Vignoles, 'I'm imagining a man, a little drunk on strong liquor. I don't know where he's drinking, but perhaps it's somewhere private — not in a busy pub.

He's taken unawares by his drinking buddy. No, buddies.' Vignoles was using the stem of his pipe to give emphasis as he looked down at the photographs. 'I think Pym trusts these men, enough to share a bottle of hard liquor. But he's in for a nasty surprise, because just as he's starting to feel a bit squiffy they slip a noose around his body and pull it tight and his arms are pinned to his sides. Why do they do this? Some kind of disagreement, a falling out perhaps?'

Tykett was lighting his cigarette, 'Go on...' He looked grim, but there was a spark of interest burning in his eyes.

'Pym's confused, surprised, he can't understand what's happening, but the next thing he knows he's trussed up like a goose at Christmas and they start to feed him the rest of the bottle, only this time its full of painkillers. These men are rough: forcing his head back, pressing the bottle hard between his teeth because he doesn't want to drink any more. He's trying to struggle, but he can't, not when one of the men is holding his head and his arms are tied to his sides, so he swallows enough of the mix to knock him out. They untie him and they walk, drag, half carry him, towards the canal, banging his legs as they go and... splash!'

'You've got a heck of an imagination, DI Vignoles, I'll give you that,' Tykett exhaled smoke as he spoke. 'But your story has something about it and there is a compelling reference in the report, towards the end.' Tykett flipped the pages. He stopped and whistled long and low as he jabbed a finger at the report. 'It suggests Pym took a nasty tumble, probably at the same time that he bashed his shins, noting that there's evidence of bruising around his mouth and a blister on the inside of his lower lip.'

'A blister? But that means—' Trinder interjected.

'—it was done sometime before he died. Not by falling over moments before drowning! Top marks, Vignoles, I missed a trick there. So did the pathologist. How did he make such an elementary mistake?' He slapped his hand on the table. 'Unforgivable.' Tykett took a thoughtful drag on his cigarette, calming his nerves. 'It could be murder, then.'

'A murder disguised as suicide.' Sidlow grinned. 'I knew there was something fishy about this.'

'Then it was decent of you to let DI Vignoles make the deduction,' said Tykett, sarcastically, as he blew smoke towards Sidlow. 'So, who could have killed Pym—and why?'

'In such a situation one must start with the wife. We've got her tailed today to see if that throws anything up.'

Tykett nodded approvingly.

'We've also got reason to think that Pym was up to something at work,' added Vignoles.

'Maybe he feared the repercussions if he was found out? Maybe he'd just been found out? It got too hot to handle, so he swallowed the pills and whisky.' added Trinder.

'Ten minutes ago, sergeant, I'd have bought that lock stock and barrel, but with this evidence? Forget it. Lean on the wife — my money's on her being behind this.'

Everyone fell silent a moment and concentrated on their drinks, considering the implication of what was unfolding. Trinder had been taking notes, but was now staring between the heads of Tykett and Sidlow and through the rivulets of water dribbling down the window into the limpid liquid light of the pale winter sun, now breaking through the fog being thinned by a wind tossing litter and bits of straw along the street.

He could see the parcel lorry being loaded with boxes from a wagon on one of the overgrown sidings. The two men had worked quickly filling the back of the lorry, and now the rear doors were being locked shut by the large man with no neck, whilst the other was leaning against the wagon lighting a fag. Trinder snapped out of his observations as Vignoles broke the silence.

'Sorry, inspector, but it looks rather like we've just lumbered you with another murder case. I'll get a full report typed up of what we've got so far and have it sent down forthwith. I'll pass on anything I find, of course.' Vignoles leant back in his chair and pulled on his pipe, adding sweetly-scented smoke to the mix of hot fat, damp clothes and acrid smoke that was thickening the air inside the cafe.

'The wife in Leicester and a body in London? This is well off my patch! And besides, it'll require co-operation across a number of forces and it looks like the railway is the thread that binds 'em together.' Tykett grinned. He looked relieved that he'd lightened his workload.

Vignoles nodded. He had become more interested in the case after seeing the pathologist's report and was actually quite pleased it had been handed to him. He could also imagine his boss, Chief Superintendent Badger, puffing out his chest and feeling very self-important as the call came in from CID in Scotland Yard asking him officially to take it on. Yes, the Badger would take the bait.

'Now, you'll probably want to see where we fished him out? We'll take you in the Rover. Tykett stubbed his cigarette out and stood up. 'Ready, gents?'

Chapter Nine

FANCY OUR MEETING?
Al Bowlly

The *Primrose* was no longer moored near the railway bridge and there was nothing to hold their attention on the canal path where Pym's body had been hauled from the water. The four detectives crossed the narrow footbridge, just as Simon had done, and gathered like four black vultures on the edge of the railway yard overlooking the canal, the reflection of the pale disc of the sun slowly swelling and distorting on the gently flowing oily water, stirred into movement by the passing of a chugging boat laden with coal.

'We could do with seeing those interviews with the boatmen,' observed Vignoles.

Tykett nodded. 'I'm not sure there was much in them, but Sidlow will get everything typed up by the end of the day.' He gave his sergeant a look that prompted an immediate, if unenthusiastic, 'Yes, sir.'

'What would this be used for?' Trinder was standing beside a metal disc set into the grey ash of the ground supporting rails, forming a cross shape. 'Is it a turntable of some kind?'

Vignoles looked over to his sergeant and scanned the area, noting how the turntable lay at the end of a long siding with a buffer stop on the far side, teetering on the edge of the steep drop down to the canal. Another line ran at ninety degrees from the turntable parallel to the edge of this drop.

'It is, sergeant. A single wagon could be swung around by hand and pushed along this siding ready to tip its contents into a boat below.' Vignoles started to walk down the centre of the undulating, poorly maintained track to take a closer look.

'So, this is a loading chute.' Trinder was already peering over the side at a rusting metal construction entwined with ivy where it was bolted to the sheer stone retaining wall.

'It looks like it. For ash disposal, I would hazard. They could bring wagons from the stabling point beside the station and tipple or shovel it down this chute to a barge.'

'Narrowboat. You're not supposed to call 'em barges, sir — or so we was told,' observed Sidlow.

'Is that so?' Vignoles nodded. He liked this kind of detail, unlike Tykett, who was glaring at his sergeant. Vignoles had another look around to take in the lay of the land. 'I wouldn't mind betting that they've given up on this method as this looks quite rusted over.'

As if to prove his point, a six-wheeled tank engine was reversing out of the station throat, hauling a string of wooden open wagons, each piled high with clinker and pale grey ash that appeared to smoke as the wind whipped thin clouds of the light dust from the tops.

'It would make one hell of a mess throwing that stuff down there. It would go all over the place.' Tykett was looking down the rusty metal slide at the black water.

Trinder knelt down and peered closely at the contraption; Vignoles stood beside him.

'What do you see, sergeant?'

'Scratch marks. Fresh. A lot of scoring and smudging of the muck and rust on the surface, as if something heavy has slid down here recently.' Trinder turned to look up at Vignoles. 'You could send a man into the water with no problem using this.'

'His momentum would send him right across the canal—'

'—to where the *Primrose* was moored.' Tykett picked up the thread. 'Lying on his back, he'd enter the water with the smallest of noises.' The tough detective gave a rare smile, recalling a fond memory. 'I used to go down a little slide just like that at the lido in Southend when I were a nipper. Me and me brother used to see who could make the smallest splash.' He gave a short laugh at the recollection then took a sharp drag on his fag, as if embarrassed by this revelation.

Vignoles nodded as he looked at the marks Trinder had discovered.

'So he slides into the water, the body gets held against the front, the call-it-what-you-like of the boat and there you go. One dead man in the canal.' Trinder looked triumphant.

'Good work, sergeant. Fits with the marks on Pym's clothes,' said Sidlow

'Yes, you're on form today, Sherlock,' Tykett growled.

'And this,' Vignoles stood with his legs against a metal safety rail placed at right angles to the area where the chute opening lay, 'might be where his shins made contact as he was pulled or dragged here.'

'So, it *is* a railway crime, after all.' Tykett nodded with grim satisfaction.

Vignoles turned away from the disposal chute and watched as a J52 tank engine shuffled some parcels vans about in the entrance to the covered depot.

'Someone working around here must have seen something. Strictly, we should seek authorisation, but do you care to join us in a little nose around?'

Tykett glanced at his wristwatch and shrugged. 'Seeing as we're already doing a bit of inter-service cooperation, I think that would be right and proper. And I can't do with too much standing on ceremony — so let's go!'

The parcel depot was populated by a great number of men, and interviewing every one of them was clearly out of the question. Nevertheless, they split into two pairs and walked the length of the platforms, collaring some of those who stood still long enough, taking names and addresses and inquiring of their whereabouts on the evening of Monday 31st October. They met with suspicious looks and received taciturn answers and few were willing to offer even the pretence of assisting.

'Nothing like being made to feel welcome.' Trinder was fuming. 'To hell with the lot of them!'

'Nobody is ever pleased to see a policeman. We're here unannounced, don't forget'.

'Best time to catch them: when they're unawares.'

'We're just an annoying intrusion to their work'.

'And look what grand work they're doing.' Trinder nodded towards three men who had recently appeared at the depot and were now having a smoking break, all three returning his look with contemptuous expressions through the clouds of cigarette smoke catching the slanting bands of liquid light piercing the covered hall.

As if prompted by Trinder's observation, one of the men pushed himself off the wooden van against which he was leaning, tossed his still-smouldering cigarette onto the track below the wheels and approached the two detectives.

'That's a fire hazard, can't you read?' Trinder nodded towards the 'no smoking' sign suspended on long wires from the roof.

'Since when was that any business of yours?'

Trinder pulled out his warrant card.

'Since now.'

'I see.' The man sniffed and shrugged, his two friends joining him, cupping their cigarettes inside their hands as if unsure whether they should openly flaunt the rules or comply. 'That explains it.'

'Explains what?' Trinder was in no mood for this kind of talk.

'You lot snooping around, stopping my men from fully attending to their rightful and proper work duties and thereby causing an uncalled for and unprompted reduction in productivity.' His voice had suddenly become stilted and overly accentuated. 'I don't recall you seeking permission to enter this place of work, and—'

'—We're investigating an incident on the evening of the 31st. May I ask where you were on that evening, sir?' Trinder flipped a page over on his notebook in a purposeful manner.

'What sort of incident?'

'A suspicious death.'

'You mean the geezer that drowned? He was nothing to do with us.'

'You know about that?' asked Vignoles.

'Of course. It was reported in the papers. Added to which, we saw your lot on the canal bank. He must have floated down the canal, so evidently he was nothing to do with us here.'

'How can you be so sure?' asked Vignoles.

'Stands to reason. He must have gone in upstream, and if prompted to make a suggestion, I would suggest around Camden Lock way.'

Vignoles raised an eyebrow. 'You know an awful lot about the flow of the canal.'

'No, just observation. Now, like I said, I don't recall you obtaining—'

'—Were you working that evening, sir?' Trinder asked again.

The man narrowed his eyes and chewed on the inside of his lip for a moment. 'If you are going to persist with this unnecessary intrusion into the working day, then I shall have to insist this is done following the correct procedures, at a time and place duly agreed and approved. You cannot come here and—'

'—Give it a rest!' interjected Trinder.

The man stared at him. His two colleagues dropped their heads and shuffled a pace backwards, the fat one turning as if he were about to slink off.

'Stay where you are!' Trinder pointed his pencil. 'Were you two at Carlisle Street depot this morning?'

'Say nothing, boys!' The first man waved a cautionary hand. 'What if they were, sergeant what's-your-name. My men will not tolerate being questioned in this intimidatory manner.'

'Cut the hard-done-by worker act,' Vignoles stepped closer to the man, 'or have you a particular reason why you want us to stop asking questions?'

The aggressive man held up a hand in a pacifying gesture and took a breath. 'P'raps we've all got off on the wrong foot in our negotiations.'

'Did you or any of the men hear or see anything odd that evening?' Trinder asked. 'Did you see a drunken man staggering about? Or anything untoward or suspicious in the vicinity of this building?'

'These two have an urgent job to fulfil. Express delivery. I'm sure they can answer your questions later.'

'All right, but I want their names before they go.' Vignoles eyed the two men, who were already walking away, both looking more eager to work than at any point previously.

'On the left is Dennis Parkey and the other is Rodney Mattox. I should advise you that Mr Mattox is a driver with British Road Services and thereby represented by a different union from Mr Parkey and myself.'

'And you are?'

'Victor Millett, local rep. for the National Union of Railwaymen.' He puffed out his broad chest, 'I make it my business to know all that goes on in this place.' Millett narrowed his eyes, a vein pumping on his temple beneath the taut skin as he faced Vignoles. He was a strongly-built man who had no doubt served his time in the army, for his bullish approach and bearing had something of the parade ground about it.

Vignoles was right, though would never have guessed the truth. What Victor Millett did not say, nor would ever admit, was that his position in the NUR, indeed his life in London, was a sham. Nothing but a clever and well-rehearsed smokescreen acted out by a top class mimic, who had used his considerable survival skills to evade the law. Even Dennis Parkey and Big Ron suspected nothing. They just knew Vic as a tough man, an influential motivator and a self-appointed spokesman who'd got himself elected to a position in the NUR. They cared little for his background because, whilst he refused to suffer fools gladly, he lined their pockets with grubby ten shilling or pound notes at regular intervals for doing a few jobs for him on the sly.

'I'd thank you gents if the next time you come calling, you'd see me first, so that way we can get off on a better understanding.' He trotted out the stilted patter of union talk with ease, 'and then I can seek to assist your good selves.'

Vignoles sighed loudly.

'Look, it's just that we run a busy depot and time and tide waits for no man.'

'Or trains,' added Vignoles, dryly.

'Eh? Oh yeah. I get it!' Millett's laugh was forced.

'The evening of the 31st, Mr Millett?' Trinder smiled, his pen poised.

'Off duty. Down the boozer having a few jars and a game of darts, then home to the missus.' He winked.

'Which pub?'

'Why d'you need to know?'

'I like detail. It's an obsession of mine,' Trinder gave an ironic smile. 'The pub?'

'Sherbourne Arms. And yeah, there were plenty of others who will back me up.'

'What time did you leave?'

'Closing time.' Millett hesitated only a moment but Trinder noticed, his steely look encouraging Millett to elaborate. 'Look, it was just close friends. It was just a bit later, nearer midnight, when I left the boozer.'

'An illegal lock-in,' Trinder said, but did not write anything down. 'Don't worry, that's not our concern. Presumably your wife can confirm what time you did, eventually, return home?'

'Of course! Look, his death had nothing to do with me. I don't want you going around causing my missus unnecessary distress and tribulation over some drowned man that I've never set eyes on.'

Chapter Ten

HAIR OF GOLD, EYES OF BLUE
The Harmonikats

Edward Earnshaw was sitting on one of the benches against the wall of the booking office on Woodford Halse station, neckerchief tied tight against the chill air, cap pulled low and hands thrust into his reefer jacket pockets. His legs were stretched out before him, cycle clips still holding his overalls against his thick and heavily darned socks as protection against the dust and dirt of the loco shed. He was contemplating his boots, now grey with grease and ash, and was conscious that his clothes must reek of coal, oil and sweat, though his nose was so full of the strongly pungent smells of the steam locomotive shed that his sense of smell was ruined. His reefer had not had a clean for over a year, but it was better not to wash it as the grime helped hold it together.

He did at least look like a proper railwayman. His face was etched with black in every crease, eyes outlined as if with kohl, the whites starkly accentuated. The light stubble just forming on his chin caught the dirt and gave him a deeper shadow than nature would otherwise have made. Yes, he was one of the boys, and heading towards his exams that would hopefully see him make the grade of passed fireman, exactly what he had wanted when he turned his back on the family bakery business and joined the railway back in the spring of 1946.

Earnshaw's bakery would be wafting delicious aromas along Station Road at that very moment, the shop warm from the bread ovens, his father perhaps wiping his floury hands on his apron whilst his mother would be chatting to customers as she wrapped loaves or placed iced buns filled with their own brand of artificial cream into white cardboard boxes before tying them closed with a strip of ribbon. Or perhaps she was binding little piles of ration coupons with rubber bands whilst discussing the complexities of the points system.

Eddie wrinkled his nose at his stinking clothes and began to recall the familiar scents of flour, sugar, yeast and cinnamon that he'd breathed in daily since babyhood. He felt a sudden pang of wistfulness and wondered if he should have learned the bakery trade so he could take over when his father retired. 'Earnshaw and Son': that would have kept the family name on Station Road. If his little sister Annie took over the shop, when she married she'd doubtless change the name. And if she didn't, then it would be sold and Earnshaw's would be no more.

A baker may get a little dusty, but working with engines his shirts were always black at the collar and cuffs, his overalls endlessly laundered until they were a washed-out pale blue, only to be filthy again within hours of being back at work. It was a depressing cycle of pointless labour that his mother often grumbled about, causing her to dream of obtaining one of those new-fangled washing machines. He could hardly blame her. His hair was always full of bits of char and ash whilst the water in the tin bath was grey within moments of his sitting in it. Oh, for running hot water. And who would want to marry a young man who stank of metal shavings, heavy machine oils and the ever-present coal dust? Yes, it took a certain kind of woman to choose to live with a man working at the dirty end of the railways. Was Laura Green that kind of woman?

He made a face and shifted his position on the bench, inspecting his dark grey fingernails and the palms rubbed pink from being scrubbed with an abrasive mixture of sand, carbolic and hot water. Laura was a railwaywoman, but she worked in a signalbox, and that meant she wore a smart uniform and beautifully-polished shoes. She looked so trim and presentable — just like everything else in her world of work — because in that special, slightly arcane society of signal workers, absolutely everything was fastidiously neat and tidy.

They were notorious for being almost obsessive about cleanliness and order. They washed and polished their linoleum floors until they shone like mirrors, the iron stoves that warmed their boxes were blackbird-black and the envy of many a housewife, whilst the long signal levers gleamed and shone in the sun and were only ever touched through a cloth to protect the metal from greasy finger-marks. Heaven help the luckless fireman who tramped inside with mucky boots; they'd give you a right flea in the ear if you forgot to wipe your feet first. Laura Green was part of the 'clean brigade' that was a world away from the 'black-hand gang'. She was one of an army of 'clean' railway staff — which included managers, office workers and ticket clerks — who did not sully their hands with oil and coal.

A wave of gloom descended over him like the low-lying mist lurking in the dips between the hills, draining both his nerve and confidence just as the chill November air was slowly sucking the warmth from his body. Why would Laura want to go to the NUR fireworks dance with the likes of him? His workmate Simon was right: he'd better leave those newly-acquired stockings at home, hidden beneath his mattress. They didn't look much, anyway. Nylon stockings sounded thrilling as an idea, but the dull, flat packets were uninteresting. No doubt he would feel differently if he was to ever see Laura wearing them, but that seemed increasingly unlikely.

Eddie patted the breast pocket of his grubby overalls, reassuring himself that the two tickets for the dance were safely stowed there. Maybe there was a rival wishing to escort her. How would he know? At least he had managed to discover, by means of some careful questions aimed at Simon's father, the senior signalman at Woodford, that Laura was not working on Saturday, so that was one hurdle cleared. All he had to do was find the courage to ask her.

He was startled out of this gloomy reverie by the sound of footsteps and, looking up, saw the object of his thoughts barely two yards away and approaching him. He sat bolt upright, silently cursing himself for having been caught looking glum.

'Hello! I didn't see you.'

'Well, you've seen me now, Edward.' Laura gave a little smile, though it lacked the usual sunshine.

He stood up, and as this had not been anticipated by the young woman she stopped abruptly and he found himself inappropriately close to her and had to press the backs of his legs against the edge of the bench, wobbling slightly to regain balance and distance. It was a graceless move and Laura also took a step back to improve matters, a look of mild amusement on her face as she did so.

'It's a cold day to be sitting out. Any particular reason?' asked Laura, having allowed Eddie to regain his composure.

'Just passing the time of day.' He dropped his eyes and scuffed a boot on the platform surface, then looked up and smiled at her, instantly regretting doing so, knowing he was appearing foolish. 'Are you going to the Mutual Improvement Class on Monday?' Eddie blurted out.

'No, I won't be able to. Don't you remember, I told the instructor that at the last meeting.'

Eddie had not forgotten; it had made his heart sink at the time, but he'd needed to say something to keep her standing there. *Think of another question, quick!* 'Are you finished for the day?'

Laura gave him a quizzical look. 'Yes, I was on six till two, though I wonder you need to ask, as you seem to know everything about the railway.' She laughed, and Eddie forced a grin, but felt the jibe like a dart. It was nice that she'd noticed him at all, but he wished it had been for something other than being railway-mad.

'I'm walking into the village to try and get some provisions — if there's anything left by the time my turn in the queue comes around.'

'Me, too. What I mean is, that I've also finished work — not that I'm going shopping. Though I could, I suppose.' His nerves were making him sound like a fool.

'I'd take a bath first!' She put a hand over her mouth and giggled. He felt a flush of embarrassment. The two exchanged a glance for a second. 'I'm sorry, that was awfully naughty.'

Her glance drifted to a letter she was holding, and her expression changed, as though she were trying to push something aside that was bothering her.

'Good news?' said Eddie, brightly, nodding his head towards the letter as they started to walk towards the glass-and-wood canopy that sheltered the steps down from the platform.

Laura paused and looked into the distance for a moment, towards the grey, smoking lines of engines stabled outside the loco shed. She sighed. 'No, but I must not be such a goose, and consider it to be good news.'

'Want to tell me all about it over a cup of tea?'

Laura nodded, 'Yes, OK. And you can tell me not to be silly.'

Eddie was too dirty to enter the public refreshment room platform and the staff canteen was a long walk away. There was a scruffy café on the main street used by many of the workingmen of the town and Eddie suggested that was their best option.

'OK, it's on my route to the shops,' Laura concurred.

Seated at the table, Eddie looked at Laura in her smart, tailored black uniform and white shirt, the peaked cap she always wore at a jaunty angle on her wavy hair. The wireless broadcast the Harmonikats' new song 'Hair of Gold, Eyes of Blue'. It described her perfectly, and Eddie yearned again for her to be his 'railway sweetheart'. Filled with a mixture of nervous excitement and intrigue, he watched as Laura stirred her tea absentmindedly while she stared at the letter lying between them on the table. She gave Eddie a wan smile. 'I'm not usually down in the dumps like this.'

'What's up?'

'I'm being transferred,' she touched the official-looking envelope, 'with immediate effect.'

Eddie felt his heart sink like a stone dropped down a very deep and cold well. 'But that's terrible! It must be a mistake.'

Laura gave Eddie a puzzled look, 'How so? You know we get moved around the railway to suit the whims of management. Woodford is my second box already. I want to stay here, of course, it's close to my family and friends, but what can I do? It will be a dreadful wrench to leave.'

Eddie was staring into his tea, feeling almost sick. How could fate be so cruel?

'Where are they sending you?'

'Akeman Street. It's along the Great Central and Great Western joint line, just before Ashendon Junction. I had to look hard to find it on the map.'

'Oh, yes, it's just a tiny halt. Almost nothing stops there now, though maybe they have a siding or two.'

'Then I shall be as quiet as a mouse, with nothing around for miles but trees and fields of cows,' Laura replied. 'Of course I will get a considerable amount of passing rail traffic, but at speed and taking little notice of poor me.'

'Not a very demanding post.'

'I think that's why I'm being shunted off there. Away from the busy Woodford boxes to a place where all I need do is bell trains in and out of my section.'

'Why would they do that?'

'Because I'm a woman.'

Eddie was still wondering why this had any bearing when Laura continued, 'You must know the way railwaywomen have been treated since the war ended? They couldn't recruit us fast enough when the men joined up for the forces, but now we're just an inconvenience. They'd like nothing better than to get shot of us all, and when someone like me refuses to do the "decent thing" and become an underpaid shopgirl or a housewife, we get sent to some God-forsaken place!'

'Can't you speak to the union?'

'Why would they be interested? There's many worse off than me. At least I still have a job, so I have nothing to complain about.'

'But you can't leave Woodford! You just can't!'

'I have no choice! Don't you worry about me. You have your own vocation to look after. Who knows, one day you might be working out of King's Cross, York or some other grand engine shed far away from here, driving a great express engine to Waverley or down to the Cornish Riviera...' Her voice lifted for a moment, but tailed away.

Eddie fell silent. There was so much he wanted to say, but could not find the words. The sudden jump from elation to disappointment had upset what little equilibrium he had when they met. At last he said, 'I'm sure it will be all work out fine once you get settled into the job. At least you will be on the main line and not down some half-forgotten branch.'

'Thanks. That's more the spirit.' She looked out of the window as she continued, her voice now wistful. 'I quite like the idea of having my own little signal box in the middle of nowhere. It will be my own private domain, surrounded only by pretty countryside and the birds singing on the telegraph wires along with the ringing of the instrument bells.' She now managed a smile, at odds with Eddie's mood, which was sinking ever lower by the moment. 'Mind you, I am little apprehensive about the long cycle rides in darkness. I'll have to find a billet in a nearby farm. Father will drive me down tomorrow so I can make enquiries. I have to be ready to start next week.' She glanced at her watch. 'Gosh, is that the time? I really *must* be going if I am to get to the shops. Thank you for the tea and the chat.' Laura scraped her chair backwards and began to stand.

Eddie stood up, annoyed with himself for not handling the conversation better. Leaving the café they paused on the pavement outside and Laura said, 'It's really not so very far from here, I suppose, and I can come visit on my day off.'

'Yes, yes, you can! It's actually jolly close, when you think of it', said Eddie excitedly.

Laura smiled at him. 'Yes, it is. Well, thanks again for the tea, must dash!' With that, she turned and hurried up Station Road.

Oh bother! I forgot to ask her about the dance.

Edward suddenly felt a strong urge to run after her. But what was the point? She was moving away next week and most unlikely to be able to attend the dance. Crestfallen, he stood alone on the pavement, took the two pink cardboard tickets from his breast pocket and gazed at them as symbols of his dashed hopes.

Chapter Eleven

ON GREEN DOLPHIN STREET
Dick Jurgen

Whilst Vignoles and Trinder were in London, WPCs Jane Benson and Lucy Lansdowne were standing on one side of Belvoir Street keeping an eye on the main entrance to the Midland Counties Bank opposite. As this was one of the main shopping streets in the centre of Leicester there was a constant bustle of people and lengthy queues formed outside the butcher, fishmonger, greengrocer and other shops claiming to have stocks of hard-to-find goods, whilst a constant flow of cyclists, delivery boys, buses and motor cars rattled between them and the bank entrance, all of which helped the two women remain unobserved by Mrs Adeline Pym.

They were both in civvies, with Benson choosing to wear a wide-brimmed hat that was perhaps a touch too summery for the day, but by tipping the brim forwards she hoped to reduce the chance of Mrs Pym's recognising her. They were both in fashionably long woollen overcoats in the 'New Look' style, courtesy of the skill and dexterity of Sergeant Trinder's wife, Violet, who was a professional dressmaker. Their hand-knitted scarves and gloves were deployed not only in the cause of fashion but against the raw chill of the day, and each carried shopping bags rather than their usual army-style shoulder bags. These contained flasks of tea, sandwiches, a few biscuits, two bars of Fry's Tiffin and some apples, cobbled together to provide sustenance during their surveillance operation. To a casual observer they looked like two friends out shopping.

Their observations had commenced late morning, and they knew they had a challenge ahead because they could not use the police Rover, whereas Mrs Pym had the option of using her splendid new car. However, as the majority of people took trams, buses, cycles or simply walked around the city, they reasoned that if Adeline Pym was going into town — about two miles away — she was unlikely to squander valuable petrol to do so; added to which, they suspected the car had been her husband's 'baby' and she was possibly unaccustomed to driving it. So the WPCs had decided bicycles offered the most flexible method of transport. They had duly cycled out to Cherry Blossom Lane, where Lansdowne had made an exploratory foray along the road to see if there were any signs of life, whilst Benson remained out of sight.

They were not a moment too soon, because Mrs Pym was just leaving.

Lansdowne had freewheeled along the sleepy curve of suburban houses and caught sight of the front door of number 56 opening as she approached. Realising instantly that this was Adeline Pym in an outdoor coat and hat, Lansdowne pedalled hard to accelerate away, her head down and coat tails flapping (the 'New Look' was not designed for cycling) until she reached the end of the crescent and furiously backtracked down an identical looking street to reach the waiting Benson.

Mrs Pym walked rapidly, her back straight and head held high in a posture suggesting an air of steely defiance or resolution. She wore a long, black coat of fine wool fastened by four large, fabric-covered buttons, tightly nipped in at her narrow waist and cut with a high, fold-over collar that formed a vestigial cape across her shoulders with more buttons down the centreline. This was set off by a small hat of black felt with a dark feather and a wisp of gauze that formed a thin veil across one eye, and black gloves. It was an immaculate, impressively expensive, yet tasteful display of mourning. There was no sign of young Oliver, who presumably had returned to school.

She appeared oblivious to her surroundings, taking no notice of the whistling butchers' boy on his delivery bike, the dustmen humping bins down the path of a neighbour's house or even of the man walking his dog who muttered 'How do?' as he passed. Whilst waiting for the bus she stared into the distance as if in a daze, and by so doing, made the job easier for Benson and Lansdowne.

Tailing the bus was unproblematic as it travelled slowly and stopped frequently, allowing the two policewomen to catch up whilst maintaining a modest pace that was unlikely to attract attention. Once in town, however, Mrs Pym had been a busy woman and Benson's hunch that it might be worth watching her was bearing fruit. She had not come into town to visit the butcher or collect the bread order.

Her first call had been to a small solicitor's office located on the first floor of a building on Bowling Green Street and Benson and Lansdowne could do little else but lean their bikes against the railings outside the imposing curves of the central library and wait, Lansdowne using an adjacent telephone kiosk to call PC Blencowe at the station to supply him with the name of what was, presumably, the family solicitor.

Mrs Pym reappeared after about half an hour, looking rather glum. She trotted off at a furious pace towards Granby Street to pay a visit to an insurance company, though, intriguingly, not the one her late husband had worked for. She was not detained inside for long, and looked yet more dispirited by the time she re-emerged and went into the bank. This was clearly a morning of business affairs, and even without knowing the details, both Benson and Lansdowne felt sure things were not going well for Mrs Pym.

'Here she comes!' Jane Benson alerted Lucy Lansdowne.

'Is she walking towards the bus stops?'

'I wonder if she's returning home. At least we've established her bank, insurance company and solicitor's names, so that's a good start.' The pair pushed their bicycles as they spoke. Lansdowne checked the number of the bus Mrs Pym boarded. 'Yes, she's heading homewards.'

They mounted their bikes and started to weave their way along the street, the wicker baskets slung from the handlebars creaking with each jolt of the cobbles and the weight of their shopping bags. They soon settled into the same relaxed rhythm they had used on the way in, safe in the knowledge that Mrs Pym was unlikely to be straining to turn about in her seat to watch if anyone was following the bus, and so, they spent more time evading the treacherous tram lines and other pitfalls than observing the bus and its passengers, occasionally discussing what their strategy should be once they found themselves back at Cherry Blossom Lane.

It therefore came as a nasty shock to Benson when she realised that Mrs Pym was no longer on the bus that was now noisily grinding its way through the gears and pulling away in a belch of exhaust, but was standing on the kerb barely a yard away as they cycled past, evidently intent upon crossing the road.

Benson ducked her head and kept going.

Lansdowne in that moment of surprise involuntarily looked sideways and her glance met that of Adeline Pym. They freewheeled a few yards further and slowed to a halt. 'Botheration! I think she saw me.' Lansdowne squeezed her eyes closed for a moment in frustration. 'I can't believe we were so lax!'

Making a play of stepping off their cycles and pushing them onto the pavement, they turned about and watched Mrs Pym enter Belgrave Road station. Luckily she appeared to be unaware that she was being shadowed by two velocipedic policewomen.

'Now there's a turn up for the books.' Benson observed. 'Come along, we'd better get these chained up and follow her.'

Leicester Belgrave Road was large and, despite a lifetime of neglect, was still starkly elegant in its almost utilitarian simplicity. It dominated one side of the busy road from which it gained its name and stood in mute testimony to misguided ambitions and hopes unfulfilled by the long-vanished Great Northern Railway Company, now powerless against the combined forces of Leicester Corporation and Eastern Counties buses and coaches noisily gathered on the forecourt ready to convey passengers more quickly and frequently to the same destinations the station claimed to serve. It was the railway equivalent of a white elephant.

The twin train sheds were vast. They vaulted high over the heads of the infrequent passengers, forming two parallel glasshouses in a beautifully narrow lattice-work of iron ribs and spars that managed that extraordinary visual trick of looking both strong and yet insubstantial at the same time. Like two berthed airships stripped of their fabric coverings, these slight metal cages allowed the expanse of empty platform to be flooded with light whilst casting a wonderful net of rectilinear shadows across all they touched. The clarity of this watery sunlight was undiminished by grubby glass because every pane of the many hundreds that once must have cloaked these hothouses of steam had long since been removed in anticipation of German bombs. Carefully stored and marked for replacement once hostilities ceased, the glass now grew green and algae stained in bindweed-strewn stacks at the back of the goods shed, because the will, the manpower and the money had vanished over the intervening years. At least the areas directly above the platforms had wooden planking fixed in place to give some measure of protection from rain, but it was disproportionate to the scale of the vaulting roofs and made little impact on the open and airy appearance.

There were no passengers other than Mrs Pym, who had already purchased a ticket and passed the barrier by the time Benson and Lansdowne walked through the booking hall that smelled of disinfectant and bus exhaust. The roar of the road traffic was so diminished that Mrs Pym's heels tapping on the platform could easily be heard. A train of three grubby coaches and a little tender engine at the front looked almost like a toy within this great cathedral of empty space and was the only sign of activity. Mrs Pym stepped into the second carriage and slammed the door shut, the sound unnaturally loud, prompting a flock of starlings to lift into the air with a squeal of peeping calls before whirling and swooping about the lattice-work like black ink stirred into water.

Lansdowne stepped up briskly to the ticket window, flashed her warrant card and dropped her voice to ask the clerk where the woman in black was travelling. He replied that she'd bought a day return to Melton Mowbray, just as she did every Wednesday. She rejoined Benson and together they crossed the wide, empty concourse to the platform, showing their police issue free travel passes to the ticket collector as they passed the barrier.

'This could be tricky: we might be the only other passengers.' Benson spoke quietly, and with sound carrying with startling clarity, was wise to do so.

'I've only ever been on this line in summer, and then only on a special excursion to Mablethorpe. I don't think many people use it.' Lansdowne replied as they approached the train.

'I can't imagine she'll be going for long; she has to be back at a reasonable hour because of her son.'

They climbed into the nearest carriage as quietly as possible and attempted to shut the door without slamming it. 'Thank goodness we brought our flasks of tea. This might be a long journey and there's not a cat's chance of a restaurant car.' Lansdowne folded her coat and stowed it on one of the brown netting luggage racks, then sank down deep into the faded moquette with a creak, the seat springs long past offering support even for her slight build. A cloud of dust motes thickened the band of sunlight spilling into the compartment and stirred a drowsy bluebottle into action on the windowsill.

Having at least an hour until they reached Melton, the two shared their humble picnic whilst the train ambled through a sylvan countryside of dark copses of leafless trees and fields of cows and sheep that offered glimpses of sleepy distant hamlets swathed in thin layers of low-hanging mist not yet burned away by the pale sun, and encountered stations with names like Thurnby & Scraptoft, Lowesby and John O'Gaunt, each one devoid of passengers either joining or alighting and animated only by the gentle tinkle of the signalbox bell and the guard's strident whistle.

'Do you really think she could be involved in her own husband's death?' asked Lansdowne.

'I think the DI sensed something about her, but I'm uncertain. However, I am becoming increasingly intrigued as the day wears on. But you should know the DI by now, Lucy. He has a knack of seeing things most of us don't. What I've learnt from observing him at work is that he won't just take the easy or most obvious route. And he is always reminding us that things are rarely how they seem at first.'

Lansdowne was nodding, 'Too true. Look at us now.' She peered out of the window at a little winding river with weeping willows drooping over a soggy bank of tall grasses and bull rushes. 'Why the devil is she going all this way out of town, and along the slowest and sleepiest line I've ever ridden on?'

'And dressed to kill!' Benson winced. 'Oh, that was an awful *faux pas*.'

'Did you see her coat? It must have cost a king's ransom. I wish my pay stretched that far.'

'It's strange to think of her sitting alone in the next carriage, her husband so recently dead, and there she is dressed in her expensive clothes as if eager to make some kind of statement to the world.'

'We must not forget she may be completely innocent of any wrongdoing, poor lamb,' added Lansdowne.

'Indeed, and that's why we need to remain discreet. She could just be going to share an hour or two with someone close at her time of grief, a sister, or an aunt, perhaps.'

'Maybe she's only coming to Melton because she likes the pork pies.'

Benson laughed. 'Now, if I am not mistaken, Lucy, we appear to be approaching a town grander than the tiny little places we've passed so far. My guess is, we're here.'

She stood up, dropping the window down with the leather strap and poking her head out. 'We'll let her get out first so she can walk away from the train. It's a reasonable sized station, but there's hardly a crowd on the platform to mingle in with.'

She was correct. The station was virtually deserted, with just the stationmaster meeting the train and an optimistic porter leaning on an empty luggage trolley. A black-and-white cat paused in washing its face with a curled paw, a little pink tongue poking from its mouth as it glanced up, but soon lost interest and continued its toilette.

If Leicester Belgrave Road looked bare without glass, then Melton Mowbray North set a whole new standard. The substantial buildings of smart red brick formed two long blocks facing each other on opposite platforms like a mirror image, each furnished with a splendid set of iron canopies running the length of the buildings in a series of little gables, numbering maybe thirty to each side, and bringing to mind the rows of beach huts crowded cheek by jowl at the seaside. The effect could have been most pleasing and uplifting but this long series of dips and rises in the roofline was rendered infinitely sad by the total lack of any glass. So much ironwork, so many decorative finials and beautifully detailed columns with curved supporting arms but now serving no purpose, save to prop up a solitary bicycle and a man in a long trench coat and dark trilby, finishing his cigarette.

Benson and Lansdowne missed observing the greeting between this waiting man and Mrs Pym, which was perhaps regrettable, however, it was immediately obvious there was a mutual warmth between them, visible in the way they met each other's eye, in the manner they walked together. Adeline Pym was no longer stiff as an ironing board and gone was the defiant jut to her chin as she leaned towards the man and casually linked her arm through his.

'A secret lover?' hissed Benson.

'The minx!'

Benson managed a rueful shake of the head. 'Some people are just not satisfied. She's already got a husband and now a young lover on top, and here's poor me still on the shelf and living with mother.'

'Likewise! But be careful what you wish for — her husband is dead, don't forget.'

Indeed, despite the obvious initial warmth between the two, there was something now playing out that made the two detectives wonder if this was more than just an illicit romantic rendezvous. Adeline Pym was speaking rapidly and quietly, with an obvious attempt at self-restraint, although she appeared upset and animated, whilst the man was at first nodding, then shaking his head with a furrowed brow. They walked as they talked, then stopped abruptly. He was furiously denying something and she appeared to grow angry at his response. They broke apart and she made a gesture expressing frustration. He was still shaking his head, as if resolute on the matter. They came together again, his hand resting on the small of her back, and as he did so he glanced along the platform. The two policewomen immediately concentrated on a timetable pasted to a board on a wall, but the man appeared not to notice them. He gently urged Adeline Pym out of the station.

The couple walked briskly, almost in silence, but it was easy for Benson and Lansdowne to follow, because anyone leaving the station would have to go that way. There was a pretty, double-fronted red brick pub not far from the station with a clutch of cars parked outside; the light spilling out into the mid-afternoon gloom showed that it was still doing a good trade. Adeline Pym and her mysterious man entered the saloon bar and the two WPCs felt they had little choice but to follow, after waiting a couple of minutes for the couple to order drinks and take a seat.

Luck was on their side. The room was quite large with a roaring log fire on one wall and a bar opposite. A huddle of slightly inebriated men and their sober wives stood in the centre of the room, drinking and talking loudly, cradling glasses of brandy, the men dressed in moss green and brown tweeds; their wives in equally robust country clothes. These market-goers were useful in blocking the view of the door from Mrs Pym and her companion. Along the far wall was a series of snug, cushioned benches forming five u-shaped alcoves around copper-topped tables. Short curtains suspended on brass rails ran along the tops of the benches at head height, offering a discreet if insubstantial barrier between each alcove.

Seeing Mrs Pym and her man take their seats in an alcove the WPCs immediately seized their opportunity. After ordering two ports and lemon they quickly seated themselves back-to-back with the couple. Turning to slightly face each other — as two girlfriends quite naturally would while having a cosy chat — they strained to snatch what they could of the couple's conversation over the hubbub in the room.

Eavesdropping proved difficult as the sound ebbed and flowed in the room like the crashing of breakers on a pebbly beach, but it was possible for Benson obtain a very narrow glimpse of the pair through a small gap where two curtains had parted. It was obvious that something was causing an upset between them.

'...and that invalidates the insurance! Can you believe such a ridiculous thing?' Mrs Pym sounded furious. 'They won't pay out if that's the case.'

'That's preposterous. A death is a death. Surely this must be wrong?'

'You doubt my word?'

'No. Of course not, my dearest.'

Benson's eyebrows leapt when she heard this last word. She caught a movement and thought the man had reached across to squeeze his companion's delicate hand.

'I just find it all rather a shock. A darned kick in the teeth, to be frank.' He now looked pale, as though he was scared. He withdrew his hand and commenced fiddling with a silver cigarette case.

'I found out this morning. A sub-clause or some such legal nonsense. It made the policy cheaper, apparently.' Her voice was clipped, and cut through the sound of chatter. 'So typical of that mean, stupid little man to buy a cheapskate policy,' she hissed.

He ran his fingers through his hair and sighed, said something inaudible and looked away, grimacing. 'How on earth did it come to this? I mean *suicide*, for goodness sake. I didn't think he had the gumption!'

'Of course he didn't! We both know it was because your man...' Adeline Pym's voice was drowned as a raucous man guffawed at a joke and his shrill wife and their party joined in with many shouted ripostes and squeals of laughter. Despite straining to hear, neither policewoman caught anything but disjointed phrases for the next minute or so.

'...to look as though he had. I suppose it was clever, in its own way... to be denied at the last moment by such a stupid mistake is beyond the pale...'

Her lover recoiled and shook his head impatiently, dropping his voice whilst speaking urgently. But his words were lost. Whatever was said, Adeline Pym sounded shocked by the time he had finished, her voice now with a sharper edge that helped cut through the noise.

'...I don't understand. I thought you had it all planned... but are you quite sure? It must be a mistake. I mean, if he didn't do it... Jack really took his life.'

'I met him... last night at the club on Green Dolphin Street. It was off. Nothing doing. It was to be for tonight. Why would he lie?' He offered Mrs Pym a cigarette. His hand shook and he dropped a match with his fumbling fingers as he tried to light it. '...death was nothing to do with us. The contract was not...' The rest of the sentence was inaudible.

The apparently hilarious joke had finally run its course and the noise in the pub returned to the hum of two dozen mumbled conversations.

Mrs Pym suddenly gripped one of her lover's forearms. 'Did the fool rumble us? Was this his way of striking back?'

'I don't know. It's hard to fathom it all.'

'Oh God, what are we to do now?'

He muttered something in reply, but it failed to reassure her.

'I'm frightened.' Mrs Pym swiftly pulled a delicate lace square from her sleeve and dabbed gently at her face.

'Stay calm. If he did that — then so be it. At least we're free. And you — *we* — can't be held responsible. We're off scot free!'

'All that money, though. And for nothing!'

'Not for nothing. And I'll see what can be done. I shall meet our man later as agreed.' The man looked as though he scarcely believed this last statement. 'All you need do is keep acting the grieving widow and hold firm.'

The two WPCs shuffled around to the far side of their alcove so they could not be overheard, although they were still careful to speak in hushed tones.

'I can hardly believe it, Jane, but it sounds like they had him killed.' Lansdowne whispered.

'But something seems to have gone wrong. I wish we could have heard more.' She bit her lip in consternation. 'But still, we've enough to call them in.'

'The DI suggested a life insurance claim could lay behind all this and by golly he could be right. But their plan went wrong, by the sound of it.' Benson fell into silent contemplation, re-running in her mind the snippets she had heard.

'It sounded like they were discussing a hired killer.' Lansdowne's eyes were wide with excitement. 'Perhaps the killer tried to make it look like suicide, unaware that's not what his clients wanted, and that ruined the payout. The plot is getting deeper.'

'We'll keep our heads down and just observe them. My bet is they'll stay together until her return train to Leicester. Let's think about how best to play it in regard to her scheming beau. He's the one to watch now.'

* * * *

Mrs Pym left the pub to take the Leicester-bound train, two hours after she had first alighted at Melton Mowbray North station. She had parted after a lingering look and a restrained kiss through the open window of the carriage door, the smoke from the engine caressing the lovers like a scene from a romantic film, the gas lamps creating a pale backlight that enhanced the illusion. It was almost touching, a scene full of pathos and sadness; two lonely people forced to part after their all-too-brief encounter. Neither policewoman saw it that way as they observed from the steps of the footbridge, masked by the pitch darkness that had fallen. To them, the scene was something from a far darker and more deadly tale, and the cold November night that encroached upon the station captured this more unsettling mood perfectly.

Benson and Lansdowne were both now firmly of the opinion these two unlikely figures were nothing less than well-dressed murderers — or at least, would-be murderers. Perhaps they had not succeeded, and perhaps Mrs Pym's husband had either defied them or got himself caught up in a fatal encounter of his own making, but their intent to see Jack Pym dead appeared all too real, and his wife's duplicity undeniable.

As the train slowly eased away to be swallowed up by the impenetrable night, the WPCs' attention turned to the secret lover in this curious tale. The man turned up the collar of his trench coat, adjusted his hat, lit a cigarette and pulled on his leather gloves. Without so much as a glance around the deserted platform, and with head slightly bowed, he strode out of the booking hall, apparently unaware that two women followed close behind. They hung back as far as they dared and the infrequency of the street lamps offered some anonymity as their faces would not be easy to identify at a distance. The little market town was still surprisingly busy as their man made his way along the pretty high street of red-bricked houses and shops. He walked briskly, apparently in a hurry, an impression reinforced by the occasional nervous lift of his arm to peer at his wristwatch. After only five or six minutes of breathless walking, it became clear to the women that he was heading for the busier and more popular Melton Mowbray Town railway station.

'So he takes a different line and a different train and they meet in this sleepy little place away from prying eyes,' Lansdowne observed.

'Yes, and if I am not mistaken this station offers Leicester, Nottingham, Peterborough and, I think, King's Lynn and beyond for its services. We'd better keep our wits about us and be ready to hop on whatever train he takes.'

They had little time to spare. As they crossed the booking hall filled with shoppers and office workers making their way home, their eyes were fixed upon their man's hat bobbing amongst the many. He must have held a return ticket because he went straight past the booking office. They could see a train waiting in the platform beyond and hear the telltale sounds of doors being slammed along its length. The man suddenly accelerated his pace and climbed aboard, a porter closing the door behind him, eager to get the train away on time. Suddenly the guard blew his whistle, prompting Lansdowne and Benson to dart between people reading the evening papers on the platform and sprint through the ticket barrier, waving their warrant cards and travel passes at the startled ticket collector.

Lansdowne, the faster runner, grabbed a door handle, turned it and pulled it open, ignoring the guard's warning cry of 'Stand away, miss!' As the train lurched into motion the pair swiftly leapt aboard whilst the porter rushed towards them, chased the open door a few feet before slamming it shut while muttering a scolding reprimand.

Catching their breath, the WPCs noticed that the carriage vestibule was dimly lit, with at least three others standing within the cramped space. The train was full of commuters and shoppers, and they could hear the sound of feet shuffling along the corridor, of compartment doors sliding open or closed and a rustling of coats mixed with murmurings of people settling themselves down for the journey ahead or enquiring if this or that seat were free.

'Where are we going?' asked Benson, keeping her voice low. 'Did you get a chance to see?'

'Leicester, would you believe?' The quicker and more popular route was along this former Midland line to Leicester's grander London Road station, rendering the slow and meandering line they had traversed earlier that day largely redundant and certainly under-used.

'Unless he gets off along the way, we're going home. That's good news on a number of counts—'

'—Shh!' Lansdowne discreetly touched Benson's arm. A man had just stepped into the vestibule through the rocking and swaying, fabric-covered gangway, pressing close to both women in order to do so. He had one gloved hand raised to hold the brim of his hat as though worried about knocking it off, the other was crossed tightly over his chest with his thin briefcase against his body to make himself narrower as he squeezed through the gap.

Benson's eyes widened as she realised that Mrs Pym's lover and co-conspirator was now standing right beside them, pressed against her shoulder. She looked back at Lansdowne, who was attempting to reach for her magazine, desperate to unfold it and hide her face behind the pages. The train lurched over a set of points in a clatter of wheels and a series of draughty squeaks, compressions and expansions of the connecting gangway, making the man fall heavily against Benson.

'So sorry! Do excuse me.'

The man regained his balance and attempted to create a little space between himself and Benson, offering a friendly smile as he did so. There was a suave and knowing twinkle in his eye.

'Quite all right,' Benson gave him a brief glance, then looked at the floor.

'Always full this train, eh girls? Damned nuisance. I never learn and always leave it too late to grab myself a seat.' He grinned at Lansdowne, who felt she had little choice but to respond and abandon her idea of using the magazine as a shield.

'We had to run to get aboard as well.' Lansdowne realised too late that this implied they had watched him board. 'We spent far too long shopping and gossiping! That last cup of tea nearly did for us.' Lansdowne extemporized and hoped she had rescued the situation. She eased her empty shopping bag on the floor behind her legs.

'Haha!' Clearly, this sort of talk amused him. 'Good idea about the tea: there's no chance of bagging one on board this old train. I don't suppose it's worth trying to fight our way further down. It's dammed rotten luck your having to stand all the way to Leicester.' He suddenly called out in a strong and confident voice above the heads of other passengers and along the side corridor. 'I say — is there space for two young ladies there?'

'Sorry! We're like sardines in a tin already!' came a woman's voice. A few good-natured noises of agreement followed, accompanied by some less cheerful grumblings.

'Please don't worry,' Benson replied quietly. 'We're used to it.' She was concerned they were attracting too much of his attention. She also wondered why he'd assumed they were travelling to Leicester.

'We stand all day in the shops queuing, so what's an hour more on a train?' Lansdowne added.

'Quite so. That's the plucky British spirit, eh?' The man smiled.

His voice was soft with a slight burr that brought to mind the actor James Mason. Lansdowne had the clearest view of the speaker, because her back was pressed against the vestibule wall, leaving her little choice but to face him, and she took the opportunity to observe his manner and his clothes in detail, determined to see what her fledgling detecting skills might reveal.

She noticed that his coat was clean, quite new and certainly of good quality and expensive, prompting Lansdowne to wonder if his profligate lover had influenced this purchase. Adeline Pym was a woman who probably demanded a certain level of style. The WPC noticed, however, that his shirt collar was frayed around the edges. Clothes rationing had only recently ceased and few men had the money in hand to invest in a complete new wardrobe after so many years of going without. His hat looked as though it had been carefully cleaned and a new satin band applied and, whilst presentable, it betrayed signs of overuse. This was typical of so many in Britain, having to make difficult decisions about what to buy with inadequate resources. Unlike Adeline Pym, who appeared to have been able to purchase a completely new outfit in black within days of losing her husband.

The man was looking straight ahead, swaying slightly with the movement of the train and gently humming a popular tune, giving a good impression of a man relaxed and at ease with the world, a man returning home ready for a Friday night on the town. He was of average height, brown-eyed and passably good-looking, though perhaps his mouth was too small and pink. His hair was sandy and there was little sign of five o'clock shadow on his chin, adding to the soft look of his face. His shoes were polished bright with that patina of age that came from having been carefully burnished and mended many times to preserve them beyond their natural life. Again, it was a detail that suggested he lacked the spending power of his lover.

Lansdowne wondered about this. Did he find Mrs Pym's money particularly attractive when mixed with the excitement and danger of an illicit liaison with a married woman? Was he really a cold-hearted plotter of another man's death? Or was he just a foolish idiot, his head turned by a pretty ankle and expensive tastes? Doubtless he would have enjoyed sharing the life insurance payout.

His humming faltered and stopped and he chewed his lower lip. A bead of sweat on his forehead revealed that his relaxed demeanour was merely a front he was losing the struggle to maintain. He looked at the ground, frowned, ran a gloved hand across his face as if wiping away an unpleasant thought or memory. He took a sudden deep breath, then caught Lansdowne's eye.

'I say, are you going to a bonfire party on Saturday? I do so like fireworks!' His voice sounded light, but it was forced.

I bet you do, Lansdowne thought. *Just wait until the rocket goes up when we catch you two.* 'We have nothing planned,' she replied.

'I hear the city is putting on a big, communal fireworks show. I'm not quite sure whereabouts. Might be worth a look, don't you think?'

'You work in Melton?' Lansdowne asked instead.

'No, er, my office is in Leicester, but every Wednesday my work brings me out there. Not a bad run, really, and that's why I should know not to leave it too late to get a seat.' He laughed, though not as heartily as before.

'What brings you there? The market?'

'Gosh, no. I sell kitchen equipment to restaurants and cafés, hotels and such. Good, go-ahead modern stuff — British made, of course. I have a number of valued clients in Melton.' The practised lie was rolled out with the ease of a man who perhaps even believed it to be true. 'And you two pretty ladies?'

Benson looked at Lansdowne, flashing her eyes, desperate they should back away from further conversation.

'Just office girls!' Lansdowne wanted to end the conversation as her hurried explanation did not sound convincing. She lifted her magazine and tried to appear interested in an article. He took the hint and looked away.

Silence fell and someone snored in a nearby compartment as those standing gently rocked and rolled in unison, their bodies occasionally touching, sometimes one of them lost their footing for a moment and lurched into another as the train chuffed with regular beats through the darkness. There was just a blank of black outside the fogging windows, enlivened by the occasional bead of light from a farmhouse window or a string of dim streetlights threading through a small hamlet. The smell of perfume, hair oil, aftershave, sweat and cigarettes mingled with engine smoke was brewed into a pungent mix by a drift of scalding steam escaping from a pipe between the coaches. The tired faces looked wan under the single low-wattage bulb, wishing the train to hurry them home.

Eventually the brakes squealed and jerked as the train slowed, soliciting mumbled apologies and expressions of forgiveness as each fought again to keep his foothold. As the bright lights and noisy bustle of Leicester London Road's great train shed appeared at the window, a friendly porter opened the door, allowing them to almost spill out of the carriage vestibule in a release of cramped limbs, each taking a welcome draught of fresh air.

'Have a nice evening, ladies!' The man tipped his hat then strode purposefully towards the steps leading up to the grand entrance hall on the bridge straddling the tracks.

'You too.' Lansdowne smiled briefly.

Benson tugged at her arm and they slowed their pace to let him ease away in front of them.

'We'll watch where he goes, then dive into a café.'

'Gosh yes, I'm desperate for a cuppa.'

'Not just for tea!' She raised an eyebrow but said nothing else as they ascended the long, wide flight of wooden steps that creaked and clattered with the sound of many feet. They watched as the man passed through the booking hall, crossed the porte cochère outside, now filled with waiting Austin taxis, their engines humming and fumigating the vast covered space, and exited through one of the tall, arched openings onto London Road. He hesitated to allow a clutch of corporation buses to pass before sprinting across the wide road. The two policewomen walked in parallel, but some distance behind and on the opposite side of the road. He hurried uphill before stopping at the double doors of one of the more elegant looking pubs in town, the Marquis Wellington. This splendid creation in pale limestone boasted two tall bay windows in dark oak, heavily ornamented with gilded and painted shields, raised cartouches and fleurs-de-lis, spilling just a little light into the evening from behind heavy curtains partially drawn across the leaded windows. The man appeared to be weighing up the merits of the public bar and the saloon before opting for the former, but not before checking his watch.

'Do we risk following?' Lansdowne asked.

'No. Quickly, up here!' She urged Lansdowne up a footpath lined with iron fencing and tall trees, beneath an elegant filigree archway that declared itself to be Victoria Avenue. 'Make notes, as we don't have much time! He'll discover it's missing any moment and probably rush back to the station.'

'What's missing?'

'His wallet!' Benson pulled out the object in question from one of the large patch pockets on her overcoat and opened it. 'I took the opportunity to lift this whilst we were being thrown together on the train.'

'Golly, Jane, that was dreadfully naughty,' Lansdowne was staring at her colleague in astonishment. 'I just cannot believe you did that. It is against all the rul—'

'—I know,' Benson interjected, 'but we could not risk losing him before finding out who he is. Don't fret, Lucy, I'll hand it into lost property in a few moments. He'll get it back quickly, and no one will be any the wiser. Now listen, I'll read and you write.' She peered at the contents under the blue, fizzing light of a gas lamp. Lansdowne wrote down his name — Terence Peter Wilde — and his address in Leicester. A clutch of business cards revealed he was senior sales manager for Alumex Modern Equipment, a firm of kitchen suppliers.

'At least that's one thing he didn't lie about,' observed Benson.

'He probably invented this regular trip to Melton Mowbray about the time he fell in with Adeline Pym. Or perhaps he met her on one such foray there, and they used this as a smokescreen for their affair.' added Lansdowne. The truth would surely be revealed in the days that followed.

Leaving the banknotes in place, they took a few precious moments to look at a tiny photograph, its edges creased and marked by frequent handling, of a woman whose trim figure was revealed by her short tennis skirt and v-neck top, smiling in broad sunlight, limbs dark with suntan.

'Mrs Pym takes a pretty picture out of her widow's weeds.'

'One can understand his attraction. Though, at the risk of sounding dreadfully bitchy, I suspect this was taken quite a few summers ago and she probably wore less foundation to cover the lines back then.'

'This was taken by her husband, do you think?'

'One imagines so.'

The women exchanged pained expressions, then scurried back to the station, fearful that Wilde would encounter them along the way. Although Benson felt justified in what she'd done, she still felt a pang of conscience that technically she had committed an offence. The lost property office was still open, and whilst Lansdowne kept a lookout Benson ran forwards, pinged the bell on the counter and ostentatiously placed the wallet on the counter, ensuring that the clerk saw her doing so.

'Oi! You need to fill in a form for that! Miss, we need full particulars...'

His voice fell on deaf ears: she had already turned to leave. They could not risk Wilde finding them completing the necessary layers of paperwork that would include declaring their names, addresses and occupations.

'My guess is that Wilde—'

'—Wilde by name, wild by nature.' Lansdowne could not resist the obvious joke.

'Indeed. It is my guess that Wilde is meeting someone in the pub. Once he is reunited with his wallet, I want to see who that person is. We need to uncover as many of this man's secrets as we can before we meet the DI tomorrow.'

'Did you mention a cup of tea?' Lansdowne asked her colleague with an imploring expression as they walked back along London Road.

'Yes, and this café will do nicely. We can watch the pub entrance at the same time.' Benson pushed open a grubby door, setting a little bell tinkling.

It smelled of old fat and damp walls and the tables were crowded into a room far too small. Each had paper covers upon which sat pathetic huddles of sticky bottles of half-used tomato ketchup, Daddie's sauce and malt vinegar. The hard wooden chairs must have been rescued from a church, as the back of each had a wooden trough to hold bibles and prayer books. A woman in a thin, floral-print work coat and a headscarf was standing behind the counter, smoking and chatting to an older woman. A wicker shopping basket filled with produce wrapped in newspaper lay at her feet.

'We're closing in fifteen minutes!'

Her friend glared at the two policewomen as if annoyed that their cosy chat had been interrupted.

'That's OK, just a pot of tea, if we may, please?' asked Benson.

'Suit yourself.' She pushed the cigarette into the corner of her mouth, lifted a monster aluminium teapot and poured out heavily-stewed tea. She tipped some milk into each, but it barely made an impression on the thick and bitter, dark-brown liquid.

Lansdowne still drank it thirstily, although it was long past its best. 'We can wait here a while, but then what?'

'I'm not entirely sure, but we're on to something.'

'There he is!'

Wilde was once again outside the Marquis, now peering into his wallet, no doubt checking that all was in order, with a look of deep relief on his face. He entered the pub as the two women started to play the game of guessing the identity of the person he might be meeting. If their hunch proved correct, it would be the hired killer.

Chapter Twelve

HEED MY WARNING
Louis Jordan & his Tympani Five

The two men were dressed in dark working clothes, like countless millions of others across Britain. They might have been railwaymen, lorry drivers, coalmen, indeed in any of a number of hard and dirty manual jobs in a trade or industry. With dark caps, grubby neckerchiefs, donkey jackets worn on top of blue overalls and heavy work boots, they were virtually anonymous, rendered all the more so by the cold, stinking smog that was yet again forming as the temperature dropped in the capital. The only spark of light and colour about either man were the two orange points of glowing cigarette ends that bobbed in their mouths or described arcs in their hands through the twilight.

They were standing at the top of three curving stone steps before the massive doorway of the Sisters of Mercy Convent School, Marylebone, a gloomy construction of grey stucco and even darker stonework set back a few feet from the pavement behind rusting metal railings that had somehow avoided being commandeered as material for building Spitfires. Dusty bushes of laurel grew each side of the steps and a white-painted statue of Our Lady stood on a plinth overlooking the road, managing to give the appearance of glowing in the dark. Each man was observing the oncoming traffic, squinting to identify the vehicles that at first were just glowing eyes of light, before slowly becoming amorphous dark shapes and finally resolving into vehicles with separate identities. It was perhaps fortunate that the kerbstones were still painted alternately in black and white as a hangover from the blackout.

'It's only proper to warn you that Bash was in town. Came up this evening to have a word.' He used Henry Bish's nickname. It was an appropriate title for a man known to have a cold and steely edge, lacking in emotion when angry and quite prepared to use violence in an effective, almost calculating manner. Vic Millett knew what Bash could do — what they had both done — and the lengths they were prepared to go to keep their past undiscovered.

'You're kiddin' me.'

'Am I laughing?'

'Was it about the police sniffin' about?'

'Yeah, it was, as it happens. We've got a very serious problem developing, and it might get a sight worse yet.' Vic spat onto the steps. 'How in God's name did you two clowns manage to make such a pig's ear of it?' His voice was quiet and controlled, menace lurking in every word he spoke across the foggy space between them.

'Come off it! How was we to know that would 'appen?' Dennis took a deep drag on a cigarette, the following words spoken with the smoke streaming from his mouth and the sound of breath being exhaled from lungs wracked by smoke. 'What were the chances he'd get stuck against a flippin' barge?'

'For Christ's sake.'

'Look, you should've gone somewhere else. It was too close to home. Any dumb fool could work that out. You should have used your brain, if you've got one.'

'Have you ever tried moving a geezer when he's stoned? His flippin' legs din't work properly! We had a right song and dance just getting him across the yard. Anyway, easy for you to say, you just buggered off and left us!'

'I needed to check the briefcase. I had my orders as well.'

'Yeah? And what was so important in there, anyway? I mean, I can see as him demandin' more dosh was a bit out of order, but did we 'ave to top him? What was it you was after?'

'None of your business.' Vic gave Dennis a hard look. 'For your information, there was nothing of value in the case and I slung it in the canal.'

'What? So we could 'ave just put the fright'ners on 'im and left it at that?'

'Always best to be careful.' Vic took a final puff, inspected the smouldering butt held between his finger and thumb, then flicked it across the pavement into the gutter, an odd smile on his lips. 'More than can be said for you pair of goons; you could be for the high jump over this.'

'You're not serious. Aw, come on, Vic, what've you 'eard from Bash?'

'Nothing specific, but he is as mad as hell with you two monkeys.'

'Gimme a break. Apart from the body getting stuck, it was a neat job. Pretty clever how we fixed him up.'

'So why did we have the rozzers crawling all over?'

''Cos they're bound to come visitin', but they'll never rumble us. No chance.'

'You better hope not. Listen, we're making this emergency evacuation because you messed up and the coppers are on the warpath. It's only a matter of time before they find the iron works store and we can't be sure no one saw you drag him from there.'

'No one did!'

'Well, we can't take the risk now, and that's why I wanted him out the way. So you'd better pray this goes well tonight.' Victor glared at Dennis and then nodded his head in the direction of the stone virgin. 'And you'd better pray that Bash is in a forgiving mood. He can get very nasty.'

'Did he say anything about, you know, Top Link?' Dennis dropped his voice to almost a whisper but stopped before he voiced a name. 'What he thinks of it all?'

'Not a dicky bird. He'll bide his time and see how it plays out before he makes any decisions, see what the coppers and the newspapers have to say first. That gives you time to make amends.'

'Yeah, that's right!' Dennis tried a grin for size. 'I'll be all right, won't I?'

A tense silence fell between the two as a woman pushed a large, four-wheeled pram past, the baby so heavily swaddled beneath blankets it was impossible to be sure there was actually a child inside.

'Who d'you reckon he is?' Dennis broke the silence.

'The stiff?'

'No! The geezer, Top Link. I've got my suspicions he's something big down the Yard.'

'What makes you think that?' Vic gave him a careful look.

'He's got the local bobbies more bent than an old nail and it looks as though he can fix anything. He's got influence.'

'I don't know, and it's best to keep it that way. I've heard you don't last long if you ask too many questions. I just hope he can swing something now, cos that stiff on the canal bank looked none too clever.'

'Give it a rest.'

'Of course, he might appreciate that it was just natural forces and not natural stupidity that brought the body against the boat. Haha!' Vic's laugh was heartless and empty.

'Sod off! It ain't funny.'

'No, it ain't.' Victor faced Dennis, the smile instantly wiped away. 'We'll get the stuff cleared out and stashed elsewhere. We just have to hope the coppers have buggered off. From what I understood, Bash has the Loughborough place on standby. Just in case it all goes belly up — so we might have a job for your Mr Lucky. A chance to test him out and see what he's up to — and as he's one of your recommendations, you'd better hope he does well.'

'What? A bit sudden ain't it? We can't be sure he's *sound*.'

Victor pulled a face. 'Nah we can't. But seeing as you brought him, you should think of it as a test of his loyalty — and yours. You have to stand by your recommendations.'

'Come off it, I hardly know the lad!' Dennis looked alarmed.

'Here we go,' Victor stepped out of the porch onto the pavement as a British Road Services van rattled its way over the cobbles towards them. 'I'll tell you more on the way.'

The van pulled up beside them, vibrating hard with the effect of the heavy diesel engine that caused the tailgate to rattle. Big Ron, belly overhanging his leather belt, looked across the cab as the two men slid onto the leather bench seat and slammed the door closed. He let the clutch out with a jerk, and the heavy blanket of smog soon swallowed them up.

Chapter Thirteen

LITTLE WHITE LIES
Dinah Shore

Adeline Pym was seated in the dingy interview room at Leicester Central with her black-gloved hands folded demurely in her lap. She was sitting upright with her chin held at a determined and haughty angle, but her eyes were filled with righteous indignation. Vignoles and Benson were not finding the interview easy.

'I find this quite outrageous, inspector. Why on earth do I have to be subjected to this humiliating experience?' She sniffed theatrically.

'You are not on a charge and may leave at any time. We just wish you to clarify some points...'

'You are attempting — and making a remarkably good job of it, I may say — to insinuate that I killed my husband!'

'It may appear that way, but I see it more that we need an explanation about a few matters. Now, I repeat, do you know a Mr Terence Wilde, a salesman for Alumex Modern Equipment?' Vignoles kept his voice patient and steady.

Adeline Pym said nothing.

'You were seen meeting him yesterday at Melton Mowbray. You had a drink with him in a pub outside the station.'

'He's a friend.'

'Ah. A good friend? You are close?' Vignoles smiled.

'I hope you are not implying what I think you are. That would be quite outrageous and deeply offensive.'

'You did appear to be more than just passing acquaintances,' Benson offered. 'In fact you embraced in a manner that left little to the imagination.'

Mrs Pym fell silent, but she coloured and stared daggers at Benson. Eventually she replied, 'He's an old school friend. We go back many years.'

'Did your husband know about Wilde?' asked Vignoles.

'Of course.'

'Did he know you met every week?'

'No. I—I didn't tell him. You know how it is: people get the wrong idea.'

Benson asked, 'I suggest you are lovers and didn't want your husband to know.'

'Ridiculous!'

'You were seen embracing, kissing warmly and walking arm in arm.' Vignoles gave her a harder look.

'Why trail out to Melton Mowbray when you both live in Leicester?' added Benson. 'You could meet in town, in full view of everyone, if it was that innocent.'

Mrs Pym chewed her lip for a moment. 'Look, it's all rather silly.' She made a weak attempt at a smile. 'We were once sweethearts, I admit that. But it was simply years ago, and it came to nothing, then I married and I love — loved — Jack dearly. It was just a quiet chat about old times, quite innocent.'

'But it might make a husband jealous,' Vignoles replied.

'That was why I never told Jack.' She gave a doe-eyed look of innocence.

'Mrs Pym, you were overheard talking with Wilde and the conversation suggested that your husband was going to get hurt.'

'I have no idea what you are talking about,' hissed Mrs Pym, affronted.

Vignoles exchanged a look with Benson. 'My colleague got the impression that the two of you were angry about something, bemoaning the fact that your husband had committed suicide, which you told me you believed to be out of the question. You were also very uncomplimentary about him.'

Mrs Pym retreated into silence.

'You have lost your dear husband, the father of your son, just days ago, and yet there you were in a public house, discussing the details of his life insurance policy with an old sweetheart!'

Mrs Pym still said nothing.

Benson asked: 'I heard you mention a "mean, stupid little man". To whom were you referring?'

'We were discussing a film,' she blurted out. 'Yes, I remember now, and I was getting into character. Terence and I used to be in an amateur dramatic society together and we do rather get carried away when we discuss films; we both adore thrillers and almost act out the parts as we retell the tale. So it was all a silly misunderstanding.' She gave a bright smile that flashed her perfect teeth.

'I suggest that you and Wilde had planned to kill your husband and claim on the insurance.' Vignoles leant back in his chair.

'This is an absolute outrage!' She banged a fist on the table in an action out of character with her demeanour and which betrayed a harder, angrier side.

'Where were you on the night of 31st?'

She paused, thinking, then relaxed into her chair as a smug smile played across her face. 'With the Philpotts, Oliver was there as well. We played cards — rummy. We stayed awfully late, until eleven or later. With Jack away on business, you see, the house felt empty and we preferred their company, but then I suddenly took a nasty turn during the evening and was ill. Must have been something I ate. Marjorie looked after me. I felt better after I had... after I had been sick, and she made me a peppermint tea. Then we went home to bed. They will confirm everything.'

Vignoles exchanged another glance with Benson. 'I see. We will check this out, of course.'

'Please do. I have nothing to hide. I wish to leave now.'

'There is one more point.' Vignoles opened a small cardboard box and showed the pill bottle to Mrs Pym, although he did not let her touch it. 'Have you seen this before? This particular brand? They're called Migranol Solubles.'

She peered at it. 'No. Never heard of them. Jack was never ill, and if I get a headache I take aspirin. Why?'

'You are not trialling them perhaps?'

'No. I have no idea what you are talking about. Now either charge me with something, or let me go.'

✻　　✻　　✻　　✻

Sergeant Trinder and WPC Lansdowne were faring little better with Terence Wilde. Trinder opened the interview.

'You admit to knowing Adeline Pym.'

'Of course. But there is no crime in knowing a charming woman, married or not.'

'You were having an affair with her, and now her husband is dead.'

'Tragic. Absolutely tragic. I was consoling her, of course. We sat in a pub and had a quiet drink. I'm struggling to see the connection, sergeant.'

'There are two: one is that he discovered your affair and took his own life in despair, the other is that you and Mrs Pym were plotting to kill him and claim on his life insurance.'

'What an extraordinarily offensive — not to mention bizarre — accusation.' Wilde met Trinder's stare with confidence.

'I heard you discuss insurance policies not paying out in cases of suicide. A strange topic to raise,' Lansdowne looked into Wilde's eyes accusingly, 'when consoling a recently-bereaved mother.'

'The pub was noisy. I could hardly hear Mrs Pym speak, so I find it hard to believe you heard anything correctly.'

'I see. What were you discussing, then?' Lansdowne asked, sitting back and folding her arms while still retaining eye contact.

'Oh, some problem at work. Boring, legal stuff. There you go, that *proves* beyond all doubt we are not having an affair.'

'How so?' enquired Trinder.

'Well, sergeant, a man would hardly waste his precious moments with his mistress by talking shop.'

'It certainly did not sound like a work-related conversation,' Lansdowne gave Wilde a sceptical look. He sat impassively, declining to make any further comment.

'Where were on the evening of the 31st?' asked Trinder.

'I was in the pub in Wigston until ten thirty. I have friends who will corroborate that.'

'And after ten thirty?' Trinder was checking his notes against train times to Marylebone.

'I went to a club.'

'On a Monday?' Trinder raised an eyebrow.

'I was not the only one!'

'Did you go with friends?'

'Er, no. Alone. It was the sort of club…' Wilde gave Lansdowne a look then faced Trinder, 'the sort of club a man can visit on his own. For company.'

'I see. And can anyone vouch for you being there?'

'I think her name was Marilyn. And the barman, probably the doorman as well.' Wilde looked a little sheepish.

'I see.' Trinder made notes. 'What time did you leave?'

'I dunno, sometime after two in the morning.'

'Did you meet a man there? The man you met in the Marquis last night.'

Wilde hesitated. 'I don't know who you mean.'

'A stout, thick-set man, with dark sideburns. Wore a flashy suit with very wide trouser legs and a pale hat. I think he would be hard to forget.'

Wilde nodded slowly. 'That would be Dave. He's not really a friend. He… I mean, well, he takes bets on the horses. Gives good odds! Yes, I did see him at the club.'

'And his surname?'

'I don't know it. We're not friends; it was a business arrangement. He's just "Dave".'

'Yes it was a *business arrangement*, Mr Wilde, you were paying him to do a job for you and Mrs Pym. A very sinister job.'

'I cannot imagine what you mean. He took ten shillings for a series of bets, and I met him last night to collect my winnings.'

※　　※　　※　　※

'So, what do you think?' Vignoles asked Trinder, Lansdowne and Benson after hearing how the Wilde interview went.

'They both have alibis, much as we expected. If they are verified then they cannot have travelled to London to kill Pym.' Trinder replied.

Benson added, 'She was definitely lying, though. That ludicrous story about a film, and her amateur dramatics.'

'I agree. And Wilde gave a different explanation: he said it was work-related.' Vignoles was seated behind his desk, an unlit pipe in his hand, rereading the verbatim account of the conversation overheard by the two WPCs. 'We need to prove they paid this "Dave" to kill Pym, but that is going to be hard. We need to get a description of this man to the local constabulary, have them try to find him, bring him in and see if he has an alibi.'

'Right away, sir!' Trinder replied.

'But a great many things are worrying me about all this. You feel certain that Mrs Pym and Wilde are having an affair?'

'Their demeanour was unambiguous, sir,' replied Benson, 'and we overheard evidence that Wilde and Mrs Pym conspired to kill her husband.'

'But you admit that it was hard to hear what they said.'

Both WPCs nodded.

'You may have misheard. That will be their defence. We'd be shot down in flames by their defence counsel. Too many gaps, implications and inferences.'

'Agreed. The director of public prosecutions wouldn't give it the time of day, I'm afraid,' added Trinder with a rueful expression. 'Though it is darned interesting.'

'What are they guilty of? Vignoles chewed on his pipe stem.

Benson looked puzzled. 'Of killing her husband. She as much as said so.'

'The way I see it, the conversation as reported suggests they were not the *actual* murderers, but rather the *plotters* of Pym's demise,' explained Blencowe, 'that would make them guilty of conspiracy to murder.'

'We think that, too,' replied Lansdowne, 'and it sounds as though something went wrong with their plans.'

Vignoles was nodding. 'Exactly! They believed Pym took his own life before their man had a chance to do it for him. Yet we know suicide can be discounted, so where does that leave us?'

'I take your point,' Lansdowne concurred, 'but that means some person, or persons other than his wife and her lover wanted him dead.'

'What a dreadfully unlucky man,' observed Blencowe.

'But can we be clear that these two really *intended* to have Pym killed?' asked Trinder.

'The conversation suggests they hired a killer — a hitman — this chap "Dave", perhaps, to do the dirty deed,' said Vignoles. 'How did the couple behave whilst in the pub?'

'Uncomfortable. Rather preoccupied, I would say,' offered Benson.

'Mrs Pym looked quite unhappy even when they first met,' added Lansdowne, 'though more angry and frustrated than anything else. His reaction appeared to be a mixture of disbelief and confusion—'

'—they acted like two people who have been denied a prize at the last minute,' suggested Benson. 'They parted looking disappointed, but not terribly nervous or scared. I would imagine that if I had just succeeded in having a man killed, I would be having kittens!'

Vignoles gestured with his pipe stem. 'Can we say for certain they were expecting this mercenary to have acted upon their instructions on the day Pym died? This is important.'

'Wilde said that he spoke to "his man",' replied Benson, reading from the transcript. 'Oh, but of course! We heard him say, "*It was off. Nothing happened. It was for tonight*".' Benson looked puzzled.

'So these two planned to have Pym killed but he rumbled their affair and took his own life first. He was unable to live with the shame and humiliation and wanted to end it all. Bingo! We have our answer — it really was suicide.' Blencowe looked around the table.

'Someone tipped drugged whisky down his throat, bashing his gums, bruising him, tied him to a chair, dragged him away and shoved him down a coal chute,' Vignoles reminded Blencowe. 'If he wanted to commit suicide to hurt his wife, none of this makes sense.'

'Of course. So the hitman *did* succeed.' Blencowe observed. 'I think the killer disguised the murder of Pym to make it look like a suicide.'

'A perfect cover — but actually not what Mrs Pym and Wilde wanted,' added Lansdowne.

'Why would this couple pay two killers to finish off poor old Pym? They just needed him to die in an accident that would not attract suspicion. It makes no sense at all.' Blencowe looked crestfallen. 'I think my theory is a dud. He was just a quiet little insurance inspector; he hardly needed a gang of men to bump him off!'

'Dash it, Blencowe, you're right,' Trinder looked equally winded by this argument. 'We're missing something vital here.'

'I think Trinder has hit the nail on the head,' interjected Vignoles. 'A sharp, swift push under a Leicester tram on a foggy night would suffice. Why wait for him to be in London? Why all the complexity with the drugged whisky? Why more than one man to do the dreadful deed? A contract killer costs an awful lot to hire, added to which, the circumstances surrounding his death seen to tell a quite different story to that of marital infidelity.'

Everyone fell silent and Vignoles turned to look out of the window for a moment, deep in thought. 'We can't arrest either of them based on what we have at the moment. We need to trawl through every aspect of Jack Pym's life and find what we are failing to grasp. Blencowe, remind us of what you've discovered to date.'

'The pills were the most obvious place to start. The company who made them, Hendon Pharmaceuticals, was set up in 1946 by Sir Paul Frobisher and Henry Bish.'

'Who was accused by Oliver Pym of being responsible for his daddy's death!' exclaimed Benson.

'Exactly.' He spun around to face them again. 'Bish is the right hand man in a company that makes rare, hard-to-find pills. He also appears to be working for a company in Loughborough. I find that puzzling.'

'Bish is known to have called at the Pym's house. Could he have left a sample behind? Mrs Pym could have passed these on to the hitman.' Trinder was frowning with concentration.

'It's worth bearing in mind, but we still come back to the problem of this plot being far too complicated for their needs. We need to investigate this Bish, as a priority. Now, I am also pretty sure Pym was spending a lot of money lately, possibly far more than his salary could support. Their home life implies this is so. I wonder if he really was taking a backhander at work. We need to push this angle. Maybe his death was related to his illegal activity with Jordan's Import and Export Company. I'm starting to think Mrs Pym and Wilde are just a red herring. A failed pair of amateurs.'

'What's your angle, sir?' asked Trinder, Biro at the ready.

'Pym's son Oliver was most insistent that Henry Bish, warehouse manager of Jordan's, was disliked — "*hated*" to be exact — by Pym. Oliver clearly holds Bish responsible in some manner for his father's death. Miss Buckland, who worked opposite Pym, implied that he might have been up to some kind of fiddle with this company. Taking a payoff?'

'I shall have his bank statements by tomorrow; we can go through them to see if there is anything suspicious,' said Blencowe. I also got wind of a quite separate private savings account with a building society.'

'A secret stash, perhaps? Was this a man desperately spending money on nice things to try and keep his wife sweet?' Trinder suggested.

'It all fits,' Vignoles nodded agreement.

'So he was raking off a percentage to help,' Trinder suggested.

'Yes, and I can't help but think that Bish was in concert with him. Perhaps he placed the rake-off in that savings account.'

'More time with my nose in the paperwork, and I'll nail this!' Blencowe grinned. He was famous in the office for his ability to sift through documents and tease out an answer to such puzzles. 'I've already discovered he paid a large deposit, in cash, on his expensive new car and other significant sums for household goods.'

'Good work. OK, so we have Henry Bish of Jordan's and Jack Pym from the insurance company forming a cosy relationship, with Pym taking a kickback in cash for smoothing things over.' Trinder was thinking aloud. 'But then something went wrong.'

'Pym gets greedy. He needs more money to throw at his failing marriage,' suggested Benson, 'so he seeks a higher recompense.'

'Quite possible,' replied Vignoles. 'So, there is a meeting between Pym and Bish to talk money. It was at the Pyms' home, because Oliver overheard some of it. The meeting goes badly and, as a consequence, Bish arranges for Pym to "take his own life" one night. Except, of course, people don't generally murder someone just because they ask for more money. There must be more to it than that.'

Chapter Fourteen

NICE WORK IF YOU CAN GET IT
Fred Astaire

Julie Buckland looked no less nervous than she had when attempting to eat lunch in the British Restaurant. She was seated in Vignoles's office clutching a large handbag on her knee. Her expression brought to mind a small and slightly alarmed animal. She almost jumped out of her skin when a locomotive suddenly blew off steam with a sharp 'pop'; she then apologised for overreacting.

'They do make an awful racket,' Vignoles smiled. 'You can speak freely, not only because of where you are, but because they make such a deafening noise.'

The sound of the lifted safety valves fizzed around the room, making their ears ring. She smiled wanly in response. 'Yes, I suppose I can. Inspector, there *is* something dreadfully wrong, isn't there?'

He gave a half smile. 'I'm sorry for the short notice, but I have many questions that need answers. I am not being deliberately obtuse, it's just that I prefer to remain discreet whenever possible.'

Julie Buckland nodded. After a moment's pause for reflection, she opened her handbag. 'As you requested, I've brought four reports on losses incurred by Jordan's Import and Export: their very first claim, the most recent, and two in between. I thought this would offer a representative spread.'

'Good thinking. Perhaps you might talk me through each in turn. Indicate the salient details and give me your observations.'

'What are you looking for? Much of this is dull, procedural material.'

'Based upon our previous conversation, I need to understand what you think is missing from the reports.'

She gave a smile that was noticeably more self-assured. 'I took the liberty of also bringing along a file from another of Mr Pym's cases, one quite unrelated to the others, to serve as an example of the level of detail and application he normally showed.'

'Even better thinking!' Vignoles nodded approvingly.

✻   ✻   ✻   ✻

An hour later, after a cup of tea and a few home baked biscuits (provided by Vignoles's secretary) Vignoles sat back in his chair and replaced the cap on his fountain pen, noticing in so doing, that he had ink on his fingers. Wondering idly if Trinder had managed to secure another of those marvellous Hungarian Biros, he looked across his desk, now strewn with case files and his open notebook, and at Julie Buckland, who sat modestly with her arms folded in her lap.

'Very interesting.'

'Do you think I was correct to have suspicions, inspector?'

'Yes I do. There is little doubt in my mind that Jack Pym looked indulgently upon claims made by Jordan's. One could infer a predisposition on his part to agree with everything exactly as reported by Henry Bish. Pym has made little obvious attempt to drive forward the investigations of the transport police who, in turn, appear to have been unenthusiastic and rather too compliant in declaring the thefts as "inevitable", whilst we in the detective branch...' Vignoles winced, '... have not been as thorough as we should. All of which appears to have suited Pym well. The cross-checks you and I have just made with the police case files appear to back this up.'

'I am loath to make excuses, but with so many cases of theft and pilfering piling up on our desks, I can only assume Pym managed to dampen the enthusiasm of my officers sufficiently to allow the investigations to fall fallow. I shall be following this up and we will revive some of the more recent cases. Closing the stable door after the horse has bolted, perhaps, but we should at least make the effort. None of this can be found in any of his files, of course — exactly as you said. None of this would stand up in court either, however, this is still sufficiently odd to raise serious questions in my mind about both Pym and his relationship with Jordan's. You have done well.'

'Thank you.' Miss Buckland leaned forward, 'but what does it all mean? It makes no sense to me.'

'What indeed? You have spoken highly of Pym's professionalism, but I think you have doubts.'

'He is — *was* — a model professional.'

'Perhaps too much so.' Vignoles raised an eyebrow. Miss Buckland looked thoughtful, considering this idea. 'Is it possible that he went out of his way give this impression? Or did he change somewhere along the line? This only makes sense if Pym had a vested interest in Jordan's and was receiving handsome recompense for dealing swiftly and sympathetically with their claims.'

Miss Buckland nodded eagerly. 'I am glad you have said this because I hardly dared think ill of him until now. One must never think ill of the dead.'

'Regrettably, it is my job to do that — and the dead often prove to be both a surprise and disappointment to the living. I would expect Pym to be seeing a decent return for compromising his position so acutely.' Vignoles thought about the new car, about little Oliver's expensive model locomotive on order for Christmas, the oil paintings, the lavish carpets and his wife's fine clothes. An additional income might well explain his lifestyle. 'Perhaps these claims would have gone through unchallenged anyway, but Pym was ensuring their swift conclusion.'

Miss Buckland suggested, 'If he was involved in taking illegal payments, might this be why he took his own life? Through a sense of guilt?'

'This is the first plausible reason we have found for why he might wish to end it all; though in my experience, criminals rarely suffer such depths of remorse.'

Vignoles decided that he would not mention the suspicion of foul play indicated in the PM report. He had no wish to further alarm his already nervous informant. 'Did Pym ever talk of his family? About his wife?'

'Not especially. He mentioned Oliver every so often, but generally he was reserved on the subject. He mentioned his wife only on the occasion of her birthday and their wedding anniversary. Occasionally I heard him talk of a show they had seen.'

'Do you think they were happy?'

'Hard to say, based on such meagre facts,' Miss Buckland fell silent a moment as if trying to remember something. 'Over the last couple of months he asked my opinion about flowers, the purchase of a piece of jewellery and if I could recommend a good dress shop. But I don't suppose that helps very much.'

'Perhaps not.' Though Vignoles privately felt this supported his mounting suspicion that Pym had been driven to crime by the need for extra income to bolster his marriage. 'Did Mr Pym have any other insurance cases in London?'

'Yes, there was one case, a fire. We had insured a small business, and this was badly affected by smoke and water damage when the printing shop next door burnt to the ground. I remember Mr Pym travelled down to deal with it. That was some time ago, at least four months or so, I would say.'

'Can you remember the area?'

'Not far from Marylebone, as it happens. It would be on file.'

Vignoles paused a moment as he weighed this up in his mind, but could find no obvious connection. Information was starting to come in, and discoveries being made, and the layers of wrapping paper were being stripped away in a game of Pass the Parcel. He felt that they were delving deeper into Pym's life, but it was still too early to reveal the truth and hard to know what was important and what was not.

He made a decision, pulled his wallet from out of his jacket pocket and extracted a small slip of paper.

'Do the initials S.P.F. mean anything to you?'

Miss Buckland looked puzzled. 'No, inspector.'

'Does "Top Link" mean anything? It's usually a railway term, but I wonder if you have a business on your files with such a title?'

'No. I can't say it means anything to me. Why do you ask?'

'I found this underneath Pym's desk blotter.' He handed her the slip of paper. 'I am always interested in what a man chooses to conceal — admittedly with little subterfuge in this case — but it was enough to keep it from casual eyes, including yours.'

The paper bore one line in careful handwriting: *S.P.F. = Top Link?*

Julie Buckland glanced up and made a rueful face. 'I have no idea.' She handed back the paper and started to gather up the case files.

'Miss Buckland, I need hardly remind you that everything we discussed here is highly confidential. Furthermore, if you should stumble across anything to suggest unusual or missing payments going Pym's way, do let me know immediately and don't mention it to anyone else in your offices. I suspect any such transactions would have been in cash, and fly well below the radar, but you never know.'

Vignoles remained seated in his office for some time after Miss Buckland had gone, drawing doodles on his own desk blotter, forming arrows and lines making linkages between various names. The Pyms. Bish. A pill company. Marylebone. Top Link. The initials S.P.F. He was seeking connections, but found none. Instead, he peppered everything with question marks.

He rested his chin on one upturned hand and started a new little drawing. It was just a stick man seated on a chair, each element composed of a few simple straight strokes of the pen. He repeated the drawing, refining it, putting it together in stages as he used to do when playing hangman with his younger brother. They'd often idle away the time, all those years ago, in their bedroom in the old vicarage on rainy Sunday afternoons when it was too wet to stand on the fence or footbridge and watch the trains go by. But Jack was long dead — just like the luckless stick man was always doomed to be. He embellished the final version of his drawing with a suggestion of ropes encircling the stickman's chest, then wrote 'long fraud?' beneath the poor creature. He crossed out everything in frustration, crumpled the now-ruined blotting paper into a ball and tossed it into his wastepaper basket.

It was time for action, not idle doodling, and time to seek some answers to the many questions now circling around in his head. He really must bite the bullet and call the Badger. Vignoles had been winging it these last few days, riding on the assurances of a DI he barely knew. He'd been told that Scotland Yard would square it with his commanding officer, Chief Superintendent Badger, but it would be in his best interests to check that this was indeed the case. However, what Vignoles really wanted to do was to visit Loughborough to have a conversation with a certain Mr Bish.

Chapter Fifteen

WATCH OUT
Gene Krupa & His Orchestra

Jordan's Import & Export Co Ltd did little to advertise itself, and despite having its address on the letter-headed note paper Queenie gave him, Vignoles had spent the last ten minutes walking around the various small factories and warehouses that inhabited an area between the Queen's and Empress Roads in Loughborough, trying to find the place. He was now standing in a virtually concealed yard laid out with cobbled setts and weed-strewn railway sidings, bounded at one end by the sluggish water of the Leicester Canal, and the elevated embankment of the railway that strode into the distance towards the bridge straddling the Midland line, before diving behind the great bulk of the Falcon Engineering Works.

The company name was spelled out on a surprisingly small sign on the front of an unremarkable building made of concrete framing and brick infill. It had dirty, brown metal window frames with frosted glass and security bars and a set of big wooden doors opening onto a loading bay. A stovepipe jutted from the curving asbestos roof of the warehouse, leaking filthy smoke, whilst the engine of a flatbed lorry ticked over in the yard, pouring out its own oily contribution from a vibrating exhaust pipe. A six-wheeled tender locomotive busy banging wagons about in Loughborough Central yard was spilling smoke over the concrete fence that lay between and adding to the polluted air. A siding ran along the far side of the warehouse, where presumably there was another loading bay and more doors. Standing on this line were three short flat wagons, each holding a demountable wooden container with lifting eyes at each corner, and branded *British Railways*.

Vignoles was exasperated. He took a deep breath — a bad idea in the acrid surroundings — and rang the doorbell, which sounded faintly inside, and waited. The driver of the idling lorry was busy reading a paper in his cab, taking no interest in either Vignoles or, it would appear, in doing any work.

Time passed.

He rang the bell again. Growing tired of waiting he walked across to the lorry and tapped on the cab door. The driver lowered his copy of the *Daily Herald* and looked at Vignoles, none too pleased to be pulled away from a page of racing fixtures.

'Excuse me, do you know if there's anyone inside?'

The driver pulled a face, but wound down the window. 'What?'
'Are they open?'

'Tea break,' was the curt reply, delivered with a flick of the newspaper that suggested Vignoles took the hint and let him continue studying the racing form.

'They don't answer the door when on their tea break?'

'Dunno.' The driver sighed. 'I just wait to load up. None of my business what they do.' He again flicked his paper impatiently, but then looked at Vignoles. 'You got an appointment?'

'Yes.' A white lie.

'Uh-huh.' The driver turned back to his horses but, perhaps feeling guilty for being so offhand, pointed towards the loading bay door. 'It's not locked, go on in and give 'em a boot up the arse!' He laughed.'

Vignoles tipped his hat to the driver and walked across to the steps leading up onto the bay platform. He gave the wooden door a hefty tug to open it a foot or so and slipped into a modest-sized warehouse containing a great number of neat stacks of cardboard boxes of various sizes and shapes.

A series of trestle tables stood in the centre of the room, upon which were several little piles of paper labels and pots of paste with glue brushes sticking out. There was a stack of sealed boxes at one end of the tables, a second stack at the other, and two boxes placed on the table. Labelling had evidently been abandoned whilst the workers took a tea break.

He walked closer and saw that a label had been freshly pasted on a box, directly on top of one previously affixed. They appeared to be re-branding boxes of nylon stockings for export to Buenos Aires. The British government would be happy, as its export drive was being pushed to almost ridiculous limits in the hunt for much-needed income. Vignoles carefully peeled the still-wet paper label away from the box and looked at another that lay underneath which showed it to have originated from a factory in South Wales. Was that what an import and export company did — just slap a new label on someone else's goods and ship them onwards, no doubt at a marked-up price? It seemed like an easy way to make money.

'Can I help you?' The voice was loud and strong, prompting Vignoles to look up whilst smoothing the wet label back in place. 'This is not a public showroom. We're strictly mail order.'

'I tried ringing the bell.'

'I wondered who was being so persistent.' The man came closer, his shoes tapping clearly on the concrete with the sound of little metal segs nailed in the soles.

'The deliveryman suggested I come in.' He showed his warrant card, 'Detective Inspector Charles Vignoles, railway police, detective department. I wonder if I might speak with Mr Jordan.'

'What's this about?' The man was edging closer as he spoke, his eyes involuntarily flicking down to the fresh label near Vignoles's hand, his brow wrinkling with annoyance.

Vignoles regarded the slim man with his bushy, pale moustache, dressed in grey trousers and a well-tailored sports jacket. His hair was fair and side parted, with the shine of hair oil. He was wearing a collar and tie and his brightly polished shoes looked to be of good quality. Was this how an import and exporter dressed? Vignoles decided the man was very unlikely to be seen humping boxes around.

'Mr Jordan's not here. He travels extensively seeking new export custom. It's the nature of the business.'

'Then perhaps you might be able to help. You are...?'

The man looked as though he were considering how to answer this simple question and took a moment to do so. 'Bish, Henry Bish. Assistant manager.' He did not shake hands but instead folded his arms in a gesture that implied his position carried weight and authority. 'What was it you wanted, inspector? We have an awful lot of work to get on with.'

Vignoles looked around a warehouse devoid of workers. 'So I can see. You're preparing these to ship out?' He touched the box nearest to him.

Bish narrowed his eyes and stepped closer, reaching out and re-smoothing the tampered label, then keeping his hand in place so it covered the shipping address. 'It's a big order going down to the London docks. Nylons. There's a huge demand for the things; in fact, we can't ship enough of them.'

Vignoles smiled, 'I can believe that. My wife and her girlfriends will never believe that I've had my hand on a whole box of them! Though they will be mortified to learn they're to go overseas.' He grinned. 'You send out all manner of items, not just stockings?'

'What if we do?'

'Just interested.' He smiled.

'That's the trade. Buying stuff in and selling it on. We also help others import or export their products: we manage the duties, cut through the miles of red tape, assist with filling in pages of forms and declarations, trade licences and the like. Yes, inspector, we can deal with whatever our customers need us to handle.'

'Dealing with such a great number of companies and the different types of stock, it must be quite a job managing it all.'

'I pride myself on running a tight operation.'

'So you would know if any should go missing?'

Bish chewed the inside of his mouth for a moment. 'That's why you're here? The theft?'

'Thefts in the plural would be more accurate. You've suffered a great many.'

'You don't need to remind me.'

'Does this level of loss not worry you?'

'It's frustrating and the stock can be hard to replace, but we're insured.'

'Ah yes, of course, the insurance. You are fortunate your insurance company has not raised any objections to the frequency of the losses.'

Bish gave Vignoles a long stare, but before he answered there was a sound behind them and he turned towards two men in overalls who had just stepped through a door towards the rear of the warehouse. The men shot suspicious looks at Vignoles and, although neither spoke, their eyes invited a response from Bish.

'It's all right. You carry on with these,' he patted a box. 'I want them all loaded in the next half hour.' Bish turned back to Vignoles, 'would you mind stepping into my office?'

They walked towards an open door in a glass and timber lean-to construction built against one of the walls. The small room held just a desk, two chairs, a telephone and an impressive array of files in neat rows on shelves that ran the whole length of the windowless outside wall. A single bulb dangled from a brown cord, set off by a dusty, enamelled lampshade.

As Vignoles sat down he noticed the lorry driver had joined the other two men near the trestle tables and was now watching him, although as soon as he realised he had been observed, the driver averted his eyes. For some reason the man was now holding a very large spanner in one hand. The lorry had sounded happy enough as it chugged away in the yard, but perhaps it had suddenly developed a fault.

'Is that why you're here?' asked Bish, seating himself behind his desk. 'The theft of our goods?'

'Yes indeed. It struck me that we need to sharpen up our game and do more to stop these dreadful robberies from our railway. It cannot be right that a business such as yours loses so much stock, especially during these austere times, with bare shelves in all the shops and everyone urged to attract foreign money.' Vignoles gave a thin smile.

Bish produced a fresh pack of cigarettes from his jacket and busied himself opening it, placing one in his mouth before offering the pack to Vignoles, who declined. 'Very decent of you, but it's not like the police to go out of their way like this.' He clicked a lighter open and into flame. 'What's prompted the sudden interest?' Bish peered through the cloud of blue smoke.

'Happenstance, if I am completely frank. I need a new valve for my radiogram, but Mrs Brook, my local supplier, was unable to help because all her newly ordered stock...' he adjusted his glasses to emphasise the point, '...formed a rather large and expensive order with yourselves, which subsequently went missing. But the proprietress does not have the protection of insurance. She has been left rather badly out of pocket.'

'Unfortunate. But what can I do? We didn't ask to have the stuff pinched and we always advise our customers to arrange adequate cover.' Bish sat back in his chair, his jaw moving in a nervous, chewing motion.

'I was a little surprised to hear you demanded payment in full in *advance* of delivery. I had not encountered this method of doing business before. This caused the maximum possible financial loss to this customer.'

Bish picked a piece of tobacco from his mouth and inspected it with a look of disgust. 'It's company policy,' he shrugged.

Vignoles sat back in his chair and observed Bish as he spoke. 'I have decided to redouble our efforts on this case and you can rest assured I shall catch the felons responsible.'

Bish concentrated on his cigarette, not looking entirely thrilled by this sudden wave of investigative zeal, and both men fell silent, listening to wagon buffers chattering outside, one after the other, like a row of toppling metal dominoes. 'Have you had a breakthrough?'

'I have a number of lines of enquiry to follow.' It was a hollow statement, but appeared to work on Bish, who returned to inspecting his cigarette, looking unusually preoccupied by it.

'You could help ease the burden of Mrs Brook's loss.' Vignoles took out his pipe and started to fill it. 'After all, you are expecting full recompense. Surely you'd like to do something to help those less fortunate?'

Bish tapped his fingers of one hand on the arm of his chair for a moment. 'What was the name of the company?'

'I have your invoice right here,' Vignoles clamped his pipe between his teeth and extracted the folded letter from his wallet. 'Perhaps you might go the extra mile for her, and in return I'll ensure that we do all we can to stop any more of these despicable thefts.'

'And a new valve for your radio on top, eh?' Bish's eyes were shark-like, and he laughed cynically.

'I wish for no favours.'

'Pull the other one! That's what they all say — at first. You'll soon start to squeeze me for every drop. One good turn deserves another and all that, eh inspector?'

'Certainly not! I would be very happy to pay full retail price for a replacement valve if you could supply one from your stock.'

'So you're not looking for a "mutually reciprocal" deal?' Bish stressed the words. 'A likely story!'

'What do you mean?' Vignoles was deliberately softly spoken.

'Nothing. It's just that I've been in business too long to have not met a bent copper working solo, looking for a quiet little arrangement, something under the counter. And you are here alone, are you not?'

Vignoles gave him a cold stare. He was indeed working alone, Trinder was busy getting the description of the possible contract killer to the Leicester City Police and trying to make contact with Hendon Pharmaceuticals.

Bish suddenly looked away, concentrating on the invoice, brow creased and mouth working overtime. 'All right, this is what I'll do. I'll get the boys to make up a repeat order today and the lorry can run it over later. No charge.'

'That's very decent of you.' Vignoles smiled.

Bish opened a desk drawer and rummaged around for a few moments. 'This was a free sample. Take it.' He pushed a small cardboard box across to Vignoles, a drawing of a radio valve on the side clearly indicating the contents.

'I'd be happy to pay.'

'It cost me nothing.'

'Thank you.' Vignoles peered into the box. It appeared to be the correct size and type, so he pushed it into his coat pocket.

Bish pushed his chair back and started to stand up, then changed his mind and sat down again. 'There's no need to put yourselves out for us.' He made a poor attempt at a smile. 'We're doing all right, despite these thefts. No need for the police to show special concern about us. I'm sure you have more deserving cases for your time and energy.'

'No trouble, and I fully expect a result soon. Things will tighten up around Marylebone from now on.'

Bish took a deep breath. 'I see.'

Vignoles feigned surprise, 'I would have thought you'd be delighted to see an improvement in the protection of your valuable goods.'

'Of course I'm pleased, yes. Thanks.' Bish mumbled the words, his eyes looking distracted. 'Now, if we're all finished?' He forced another smile. He'd probably used up his limited stock of these, and it was a desperately poor attempt.

'Indeed. Oh, but there was just one other thing. Did you often visit Mr Pym at his home?'

'Sorry?' Bish took a long drag on his cigarette.

'You knew Mr Pym, of course? No doubt through his work on your insurance claims.'

'We had reason to correspond, as you would expect.'

'We are talking about *Jack* Pym, of the Leicester & Eastern Counties Insurance Company. I think you did more than correspond with him. His son remembers you,' Vignoles emphasised the point carefully, 'very clearly.'

Bish's face lost a little colour. 'Of course! *Jack*. I meet so many people, so many names.' Bish tried to keep his voice light. Vignoles nodded indulgently, clearly reading the poor attempt at a lie.

'Pym was a hospitable type, preferred to discuss matters in the comfort of his home.'

'I see.' Vignoles was holding his unlit pipe and turning in his hands, 'So you would not know why he would take his own life?'

'No. No idea at all. It was a shock to read about it in the paper.'

'I had not realised it made the national press.'

'Er, no. I was in London, you see. The *Evening Standard* mentioned it.'

'Of course it did. Did you get along well with Mr Pym?'

'Perfectly.'

'No arguments?'

'Never.'

'A professional falling out over the insurance claims? I could well believe that the pressure of such losses and the need to protect the best interests of the company might take its toll on your relations.'

'He was always sympathetic to our losses. What are you suggesting?'

'I wondered if he was upset with you over a long-running dispute, something that might have tipped him over the edge.' Vignoles chose his words deliberately. 'One never knows how nerves can affect a man.'

'I see the point you are trying to make.' Bish stood up. 'But it was nothing to do with me, nor this company.'

'Can you explain why he swallowed pills supplied by your other business interest?'

Bish blanched. 'What other business?'

'Hendon Pharmaceuticals. A successful and profitable concern of which you are a director.'

Bish gave a wan half-smile. 'What I meant was that I—I was not aware of any connection with Jack Pym. He used our pills, did you say?'

'Yes, a new type you are developing: Migranol, currently undergoing trials and impossible to buy.' Vignoles gave a knowing smile. 'How might he have obtained them?'

'I—I have absolutely no idea.' Bish looked genuinely shocked, his face a picture of puzzlement.

'You have not been losing stock from those premises as well, have you?' Vignoles asked.

'No, they are very secure. I am taken aback by your revelation.'

'A puzzle indeed. But one that I shall solve. We have the bottle in question and some fingerprints upon it, and I wonder if you might be good enough to come to Leicester and allow us to take yours? Purely for the purposes of elimination, of course.'

Bish swallowed. 'If I must.' He glanced at his watch. 'Now, I have answered more than enough questions, inspector. I really must get that order made up.'

Vignoles stood and touched the brim of his hat. 'Thank you for your time. When Mr Jordan returns perhaps you might get him to call me before he sails off to another exotic location.' He placed one of his cards on the desk. 'And I'll be expecting your call to say when you can come in and give us your dabs.' He then turned to leave the office, but had to slow his step to avoid the bulk of one of the warehousemen standing immediately outside the door. Vignoles suspected he had been listening because of the way he stepped back as if bitten.

As Vignoles crossed the open space of the warehouse, he felt the gaze of the men follow him. The lorry driver moved away from the partially-opened sliding door to allow him through with a slight nod directed more at Bish than at himself.

He was being allowed to leave.

The large spanner was now propped against the wall, within easy reach of the driver, but at least it looked slightly less threatening out of the man's hand.

Chapter Sixteen

Hellhound on My Tail
Robert Johnson

Simon was in a dark mood. Following the thrill of having been rostered on the regular Neasden and Quainton Road pick-up to and from London that week, he had quickly fallen into the trap of thinking he was something special, that he was suddenly a cut above the other cleaners at Woodford loco. Adding to his newly found sense of self-importance was his newly-found status as the local cigarette tout, a position that had certainly made him popular because he charged good rates and held an impressive stock. As a result, he was now flush with ready pounds, shillings and pence.

He'd come back down to earth with a bump that morning, however, and instead of bowling along the main line to London or even clattering trucks about in the marshalling yards at Woodford, he'd been hastily swapped onto preparing a row of locomotives sitting on one of the three stabling lines at the back of the shed. Shedmaster Saunders had explained that they were short staffed through a bout of influenza; it was all hands to the pumps and Simon had to muck in.

He had not taken the news well and his lack of enthusiasm had not changed when he'd discovered the location of the engines, tucked away from the hustle and bustle of those crowded in front of the shed and from the crews and fitters busying about the main building, offering moments of banter to help make the work go more easily. Apart from a view of the distant turning triangle set in a dank, weedy field with the occasional locomotive negotiating this lonely wilderness, he could see little else but the gloomy rear wall of the shed building.

The morning was to be spent shovelling hot ashes, cascading the fine, lung-choking powder into the pit beneath the engine and getting covered in the process, or tossing out the even finer and darker dust and char that accumulated in the smoke boxes at the front of the boilers, easing the soft black clouds into the waiting wheelbarrow beside the front buffer beam before wheeling this away to an adjacent open wagon, where he had to repeat the process in reverse to empty the barrow. He then had to wash out the boilers with icy water in a task that would smear the ash, coal dust, oil and char into his skin and clothes, caking his boots in mire and freezing his hands. He was not happy.

He whacked a nasty build up of clinker in the far corner of the firebox of an ex-Great Western Railway 2800 class freight engine. The engine had worked up to Woodford from the Western Region via Banbury and had been treated badly by its crew for it was in a shocking state and needed attention before they sent it back on Monday. He cursed loudly, his voice masked by the harsh ringing inside the claustrophobic confines of the still exceedingly hot firebox. He could not reach the clinker mound by leaning in through the fire hole and so had been forced to climb inside, and this was one of the worst jobs imaginable, to be bent double inside a metal oven.

'Come on, you stupid lump!' He started bashing the immovable chunk of clinker in a rapid series of strikes that rattled out an angry tattoo that rang about his ears.

As if this was not enough to put him in a black mood, he'd had a blazing row with Eddie, who'd accused him of not being interested in doing things with him anymore. Simon pushed some lumps of partially-burnt coal through the bars with his boot, stamping on them with annoyance.

Eddie was still obsessed with the drowned man. He'd been going on about him, complaining that Simon had not even picked up any London newspapers or asked around Marylebone about the incident. But it really was none of their business, and besides, who cared about some silly bugger who'd fallen in a canal? It had been intriguing at the time, but Simon's initial thrill of hearing about the dead body outside the *Primrose* had been replaced by the excitement of earning a few bob on the side trading in cigarettes.

Simon whacked the stubborn lump again with his hammer to emphasise his feelings. And that was another thing they'd rowed about: even though he'd offered Eddie some ciggies for free, he'd become all moralistic about Simon's little business. That had really got Simon's goat and they'd exchanged some pretty frank views, and both ended up shouting — until Eddie had stomped off. Simon stopped hammering, letting the awful ringing sound die in his ears, and twisted his convoluted body so he could haul his head and hands out of the narrow fire hole and drink in some precious cool air. Sweat trickled from beneath his cap band despite the chill of the November day.

All Eddie wanted to do was keep on playing detectives. Yeah, it had been fun when they were younger: they'd had some great adventures and got into some terrific scrapes, but his uncle was right. It was time to leave all that to the police.

To top it all, Eddie had made a few pointed comments about black marketeering being illegal, even suggesting the two of them should think about grassing on the London racketeers to the railway police! He coughed up some dusty phlegm. It was stifling in that firebox, beating the bars nine to the bar. As to turning grass on Dennis and Big Ron, fat chance! He'd lose his new income, and besides where was the harm in it? It was just fags and nylons, after all, no one was getting hurt.

Simon turned the little lump hammer over in his hands, then placed it on the cab floor. Shifting his position with much wriggling and pulling, he eased his torso out of the fire hole that only just allowed even a slim man to negotiate, opting to give his boot soles some relief from standing on the hot fire bars. Seated on the battered wooden floor of the cab of the big engine, he took a swig of tea. It was a shame to fall out with his best chum but, all things considered, he was quite pleased with himself. He'd taken heed of good advice from his uncle, and — he patted the left breast pocket of his blue jacket and felt the satisfying bulge of folded ten shilling notes and heavy coins — he was concentrating on advancing his career and income.

OK, if he was completely honest, the real reason he was reluctant to play policeman was because he was enjoying the thrill and rewards of playing racketeer.

He pulled a pained expression. Except he was not playing, and this was no joking matter. He ought to think about that. Vic and Dennis had looked pretty mean in that alley, as though they could hurt someone. Perhaps his pal was right. Was he changing? And what was he changing into? Gamekeeper turned poacher?

He looked out of the cab towards the massive brick wall of the engine shed and the saw-toothed roof of the carriage and wagon repair shops. Between these two great constructions stood the A frame of the sheer legs, from which the front end of a Director class engine was suspended whilst the front bogie truck was extracted. He thought he caught a distant glimpse of Eddie carrying a big paraffin can, but he was lost from sight almost instantly, and he could not be sure, as everyone looked much the same: grubby blue overalls, black caps and dirty faces. Simon felt a stab of remorse. Perhaps he had been unreasonable. He'd stand Eddie a pint or two in the White Hart later and patch things up. He would josh him about his doomed romance with that Laura Green girl — the trousered signalwoman — then talk steam engines and forget their disagreements and about rough, tough Londoners and their dodgy dealings.

Simon was just about to ease himself back into the firebox when he heard a sound, and twisting around to look at the far side of the cab, he saw the face of Dennis pop up over the cab floor.

'All right, son?' The face gave a wolfish grin.

Dennis heaved himself into the cab, towering over Simon, still seated on the floor with his feet in the fire hole and forced to twist his shoulders and neck to look up at his visitor, who flipped down a tiny wooden seat upon which he half sat, half leant, looking relaxed. 'Hard at it?'

'Oh gosh! Dennis. I—I didn't expect to see you here.'

'I told yer I'd come looking when the time was right. So now I 'ave. A bit previous, if you ask me, but then orders is orders and we've got a job on. Smoke?' He already had a cigarette in his mouth, but tossed another down to Simon.

'Thanks. A job, did you say?' Simon swallowed.

'Yeah. But that can wait. So what you up to 'ere then?'

'I've got to get this line of engines cleaned out and prepared for service on Monday morning, so I must get them coaled and watered after I've got the muck out of here.' Simon was glad to talk about something else, as this unexpected visit had come as a nasty shock to his already unsettled equilibrium.

'You're never climbing in there?' Dennis squinted at Simon's legs dangling inside the firebox.

'Unfortunately. It's an awfully tight squeeze. Look, I—I must get back to work — right after I've had this.' Simon indicated his cigarette, hoping that Dennis would take the hint and leave as quickly as he had arrived.

'Jesus!' Dennis whistled, 'Good job Big Ron's a van driver not an engine cleaner. He'd have no chance getting through that rabbit hole!' Dennis laughed, though his eyes remained watchful.

Although Dennis was acting friendly, Simon was starting to wish he were working in a busier part of the shed yard. The only sounds of other human life were a few distant hammer blows and the gruff rumble of the coaling tower. No one had walked past in half an hour.

'Don't let me stop you. We can talk as you work.' Dennis grinned and exhaled smoke from his nostrils like a fiery dragon.

'I had better. The shed master will go spare if I don't get a move on.' Simon decided he was not in the mood for more smoke, his lungs already having their fill, so tossed his cigarette between the fire bars then worked his arms and body back inside the tiny opening. He was bent double once inside and, in a series of careful movements, got his legs and arms into a manageable position whilst facing towards the oval of light and receiving the benefit of a slight draught of fresher air. Behind his head, just an inch of so above his cap, the brick arch radiated heat and he could hear the boiler cooling in little ticking and clicking sounds.

Dennis sat on the cab floor, boots on either side of the opening, and leant forward so Simon could see his face. 'You're in on a job. Vic was eager to give you something to do. I'd say your luck was in.' He sounded enthusiastic.

'Great!' Simon's voice lacked conviction. 'What do you want me to do?' He glanced up at Dennis.

'We're moving some stock, if yer know what I mean.' He winked. 'Ordinarily, we'd send it straight through to London, but we've got some things to arrange down there before we can accept it.'

'Is everything all right?'

'Don't you worry 'bout that. You just listen to what I'm tellin' you and don't screw up. This evening, three containers on flat wagons are coming to Woodford from Loughborough. It'll be late. The consignment notes say they're going on to Marylebone. Rugby Control think that's where they're headed on Monday, and the records will say they did just that.'

'Uh-huh.'

'Now, *your* job is simply to swap the cards on the wagons for these ones.' Dennis pulled three rectangles of buff card from his inside jacket pocket. 'You'll need to do it sharpish, right after the wagons arrive. That way they'll be marshalled correctly to leave on Monday for their new destination, where we'll swap the containers for empties, put the original cards back, an' off they go, a day late. It will look like an unfortunate mix up that will have a few dispatchers apologising down the blower, but no one will be any the wiser. Meanwhile, we'll 'ave got our stuff tucked away and no one'll be any the wiser. Got it?'

'It's not that simple to just swap cards. The yard will be full of people. There's the foreman, two shunters, the wagon examiner, a wheel-tapper and Joey, the 'fat lad' oiling all the wheels — I'd have all these to dodge, not to mention the engine crews. Someone is bound to see me!'

'Then you better take care 'ow you go, and somehow I reckon you know 'ow to skulk around in the dark.' He gave Simon an odd stare and his voice became full of menace. 'You know the place well enough, so just do it.'

'OK.' Simon commenced smashing at some more clinker. As he started to digest his instructions he realised it was not too awful a job. He knew the sidings well, and would indeed operate in darkness. The wagons would probably come into the old 'up' yard, which was smaller and nearer the town than the others. This yard was easier to access and sometimes was used as a cut through by the men going on shed, though this was frowned upon. If anyone did see him there they wouldn't think anything much of it.

'Tonight, did you say?' Simon paused in his hammering, wiping more sweat from his brow. He was overly hot, and that wasn't helped by Dennis almost blocking the only source of air.

'Yeah.'

'But it's the firework party tonight!'

'What of it?'

'Nothing. I could slip away, I suppose. Most people will be attending, that will help. All right, I can do it.' Simon grinned, hoping that that would satisfy the man and he would leave. With the distraction of the fireworks, he might be able to leave and be back before anyone noticed.

'See? It ain't so bad.' Dennis's hard gaze met Simon's. 'Trouble is, though, on my way up here I got to thinking about things.'

Simon looked away as Dennis was speaking and concentrated on trying to see if he had missed any more clinker, peering in the near darkness at the fire bars and the mound of ash in the pan below.

'And I got to wonderin' 'ow it was that you turned up outside our place that afternoon. I mean, that was a stroke of luck. Didn't work out too handy for the other geezer, mind.'

'I was just walking about.'

'Come off it! You could hardly see a thing what with the smog, an' you tell me you was going for a walk?' He thrust his head into the firebox. 'Nah. I don't hold with that, son. Tell me what you were *really* doing.'

Simon started to feel the first gnawing bite of claustrophobia as the light and the cool air were partly cut off, causing an immediate tightening around his chest and an unpleasant tingling in his temples. He had to think of something to say to placate Dennis, if only to make him pull back from blocking the opening. 'I'd heard about a drowned man and I wondered how he'd ended up in the canal. I just wanted to look around.' Simon felt panic rising as the light and air diminished further.

'Why you so interested in the geezer in the canal?'

'My uncle found him, next to his boat. He was questioned by the police and knew I'd be interested because I'd helped the police and—' Simon stopped.

'—Eh? What was that?'

Oh God, what have I said? Simon stared back at the silhouette of Dennis's face, with just the glistening pale whites of his eyes and a flash of teeth enlivening the dark mass blocking the opening.

His voice was low, hard, almost a hiss when he spoke again to Simon. 'You help the police?'

'No, Den, that's not what I meant. It came out all wrong. Look, I need some air...'

Dennis pulled back from the fire hole, 'Stick yer head out then!'

Simon gratefully leant forward, placing one gloved hand on the lip of the fire hole to lever himself forward, but immediately felt Dennis's big hands take hold of his jacket collar and haul him forwards in a swift and aggressive movement, smashing his shoulders against the unforgiving metal and sending darts of pain down his back.

'Aagh! Ow!'

His head was being pushed backwards into an excruciating position by Dennis's hand on his forehead, the other still firmly holding a great handful of jacket collar. 'What's your game? Come on! Speak up or I'll break your flippin' neck, you little bastard!'

'Let go! You're hurting me!'

'Talk!'

'It's not what you think...aagh! ... I just found it interesting, the body, by my uncle's boat...'

'I also heard something very interesting this morning. See, I was keeping me head down, getting the lay of the land around here, and I heard you and another poxy little lad having a right go at each other.' Dennis held his face close to Simon's, his bad breath and rough stubble unpleasantly in evidence. 'You was sayin' as how you was detectives and 'aving work to do in London!'

'Oh! It's nothing — a joke.' Simon was terrified. 'We were joshing each other — ow! Let go... my neck!'

This was awful. They'd made a stupid blunder by broadcasting their argument and now he had to get himself out of this — and fast, but Simon could hardly think straight with his neck almost at breaking point.

Suddenly Dennis released Simon's collar and head, allowing him to collapse with relief, but even as Simon started to breathe more freely and was adjusting his tangled limbs to pull himself out of the firebox, Dennis, with irresistible strength, pushed Simon back inside and slammed the heavy doors closed with a resonant clang. He locked them in place.

Simon toppled backwards, twisting his legs awkwardly beneath him, striking his head on the firebrick arch and landing heavily against the boiler back. It was almost pitch black, although a faint light leaked in around the mound of ash in the pan below making the fire bars look like those of a grimy prison window. For a prison this surely was — and a deadly one. The locked doors could stand a force far beyond that of even the strongest man. Simon could never batter it open, and yet in his desperate and blind panic, he started beating on the metal, begging Dennis to open up. His gloved fists were useless, hardly making a sound, and he could feel the bruises already starting to form and the joints of his fingers becoming raw and swollen as they pounded on the immovable metal.

'Please open up! Please, Dennis — I can explain everything, just let me out!'

He started to cough violently, the poisonous fumes attacking his lungs as his exertions forced more foul air inside. As he coughed he felt his head swim. He was panicking and as fear gripped him ever deeper, he lashed out in impulsive and thoughtless movements, smashing his skull and losing his cap, jarring an elbow and getting his feet painfully tangled between the hot bars. Pain was assaulting him on all sides and he was unable to think beyond alternating between coughing and gulping in more poor air.

'Oh God — I can't breathe! I'm going to *die* in here!'

'Happy, are we, *detective*?' Dennis's voice was calm and gentle, almost soothing as it came from below. He was standing in the pit beneath the engine and the contrast to Simon's obvious distress was all the more shocking.

'Now, you'd better start explaining, because if you don't, I'll just walk away. No one saw me arrive and no one will see me leave. I'll sort the labels out myself if I must, then scarper. It'll be one of those tragic puzzles — how that poor lad got ' imself trapped in the firebox. They'll talk about that for years.'

'I... can't breathe!'

'You'd better not waste your breath, then. Who's this Inspector Vignoles geezer you was arguin' about?'

Oh hell. Did we mention his name? What else had Dennis overheard?

'Listen, you've got to believe me ...' Simon was frantically trying to concoct a story that might satisfy the angry black marketeer. 'It was nothing. We just reported a wagon fire — arson. Some kids messing about one evening.' Simon was bent double, trying to shout down between the fire bars, sweat pouring down his face, his knees unpleasantly hot and the soles on his boots starting to smell. 'We—we live in a small town. N—nothing happens here. Not like in London. So—so it was interesting. Just something to do.' He had to stop as another fit of coughing took him over. 'Meeting the inspector was a big event. But it was ages ago. Please let me out!'

'So what's all this about Marylebone and the stiff in the canal?' Dennis was snarling as he spoke.

'Nothing! It's really nothing. You heard what I said.' Simon's voice was now hoarse, dried out in the dry and dusty firebox. 'I was telling Eddie it was all nonsense and nothing to do with us! You've got to believe me. I'm not a grass!'

Silence fell. Simon closed his eyes, trying to shut out the frightening confines of the dark metal box and concentrate on breathing slowly and trying not to retch.

There was a sound on the footplate and then the metal doors swung open.

'Out!'

Simon lunged towards the opening, thrusting his head out of the oval hole, and then threw up on the cab floor, heaving and coughing, his freckled face, ginger hair and cheeks bright red from the heat, and his exertions combining to make him look like a distressed fox.

Dennis leant forwards, grabbed Simon's collar, hauled him bodily out of the hole and dumped him onto the stinking floor. Simon was unable to do much more than gulp rasping breaths as he lay in a ragged jumble of limbs. Dennis picked up the slack hose and opened the little brass tap, pressing a thumb over the end of the hose to form a jet of cold water. He sprayed Simon in the face and started to sluice him down.

'You should keep yer nose out of things what ain't your business! Got it?' He sprayed a jet of water in Simon's eyes. 'Or you might end up in the canal yerself!'

'Yes, whatever you say.' Simon coughed and sputtered and raised a hand to stop the water.

'Forget the dead man. He topped himself. Case closed, detective.'

Simon nodded gratefully, 'Of course, just as you say.' The icy water was refreshing and he looked up, with water and a trickle of blood from the top of his head running down his face.

'I left the cards in your knapsack.' Dennis dropped the hose onto the floor and let it run. His voice was heavy with menace as he swung himself out of the cab and started to descend the steps. 'Remember — I'll be watching you like a hawk, and if I so much as suspect you've lied to me, or you tell anyone about this conversation, It's canal time.'

Dennis smiled his most chilling smile. 'Toodle pip, Mr Lucky!'

Chapter Seventeen

STAR BURST
Gene Krupa & his Orchestra

The Gorse Hotel was in the hamlet of Hinton, although it was but a short walk beneath the massive twin railway bridges from Woodford Halse, and this convenient location and the surprisingly grand scale of the building made it the perfect location for the railway social club. Whilst the pubs scattered across Woodford and Hinton did a decent trade, it was the 'Gorsey' that was the main focus for railway workers and their families, the first choice for all social events, with its large lounges, where wives and children were permitted, as well as snugger smoking rooms and a public bar where men set the world to rights. Bingo nights, whist drives, parties, weddings and birthdays as well as meetings of two railway unions — it had famously been the home of the 1926 Strike Committee — were all held in this splendid black-and-white, half-timbered building in a distinctive semi-Elizabethan styling.

For these reasons, the National Union of Railwaymen had chosen the Gorsey for the firework dance that Saturday night, and the place was now humming with activity. The bonfire was a vast creation constructed during the preceding week from every scrap of spare wood and combustible material that could be piled high by the many children of the village, ably assisted by the expert abilities of two fire raisers from the loco department. Now reaching nearly twenty-five feet in height, the bonfire was in the centre of the triangular-shaped green in front of the Gorsey, an area bordered by a Methodist chapel and a Catholic church, the congregations of both places of worship also contributing to the construction of the bonfire and the grand spread of food now laid out in one of the hotel's main reception rooms. As the village was almost completely dominated by the railway it made sense that church, chapel and railway union set aside their petty squabbles and the occasional disagreements that beset any community, and combine forces in a spirit of mutual cooperation and celebration.

The guy on the top of this great pyramid of wood and rubbish was also a cut above the average. His body had been skilfully sewn from old mailbags and stuffed with straw, then dressed by the local dressmaker, Violet Trinder, whose husband had yet to return from London that evening, to her increasing chagrin. Violet had put the guy in army trousers and a heavy, grey greatcoat with big, gaudy brass buttons down the front and some oversized medals dodged up from scraps of ribbon and silver foil milk bottle tops. He made a fine sight, securely tied to a pole rammed up his back, saluting the gathering crowd with an inscrutable expression on his painted face — a face that was unmistakably that of Joseph Stalin, complete with a painted-on bushy moustache and beady eyes. Significantly, and much to the mounting excitement of the many children, this Russian bear of a guy was standing beside a large, wooden and cardboard missile that had 'Atom Bomb' painted in garish red on its silver bodywork, the cone of which was formed by a real firework rocket of awe-inspiring size and cost. It was hoped that this would ignite and launch itself into the night sky as the fire took hold and a long fuse had been draped carefully down the side of the bonfire to help it on its way. Stalin had been a popular choice within the village, replacing the perennial favourite of Hitler, who had in turn pushed Guy Fawkes into the shade over recent years. There were some who mourned this rejection of tradition, though others conceded that, as the congregation of the Catholic church were not only present but had also contributed significantly to the evening's events, Stalin was perhaps a more diplomatic target.

The Gorsey had all its lights burning, the curtains left open to cast a welcome yellow glow onto those standing outside. Lanterns hung from the portico and had been placed at intervals around the village green. A string of coloured electric lights draped through the bare branches of a nearby tree and these cast multiple shadows of red, blue, green and yellow onto the gangs of excited children running and scampering about with whoops and shouts of delight. Men were already holding pint glasses and chatting, debating the coming display and the relative merits of different types of fireworks, whilst women brought more bags and baskets of sandwiches, rolls, potatoes for baking on the embers of the fire, homemade cakes and flapjacks, and little cardboard cartons of brightly-coloured jellies from the British Restaurant in Rugby. Inside, the members of the Red and White Concert Party were getting into their stride, playing a medley of popular tunes on their violins, cellos, clarinets, banjos and an upright piano, their efforts amplified through two hefty loudspeakers placed on the roof of the portico by two railway telegraph engineers.

It was a merry scene and a chance for the railwaymen to forget the working week, their slim pay packets, the early morning knock-up calls on their windows and the dirt and hard slog of railway life, and for their womenfolk to dress up in their best and in turn forget about washing, scrubbing and mending, to stop calculating points and coupons, to push aside the weekday queues and the lack of choice in the shops and the struggle against the relentless and colourless drudge of austerity. This was to be a night of noise and colour, of warmth contrasting with the chill bite of the night, to feast on a great bounty of food and drink and to dance into the early hours.

Simon was in the mood to forget everything and get drunk, but no matter how hard he tried, the events of the day weighed heavily upon him. His body ached all over, his knees, elbows and the back of his head were throbbing, whilst his knuckles were red and swollen, and each painful complaint from his bruised and aching body was a reminder of the aggressive thug — and his instructions. Simon feared this unpleasant man was even now lurking in the shadows amongst the lines of stabled wagons in between which he must soon step.

He was wearing fingerless gloves, partly against the cold night, but also to hide the shameful injuries to his hands, and as he handed a foaming pint to Eddie he had to work hard to not let his face betray his extreme discomfort, gently altering his standing position in careful movements that made him look and feel like an old man. He was attempting to ease the pain in his neck where Dennis had so cruelly twisted it.

'Thanks, Si!'

'Welcome.' Silence fell. 'Er...' Simon looked at the damp grass. 'Um... Sorry about all that earlier.'

'It's nothing. All forgotten.'

The two lads looked uncomfortable. Conversations like these were not their forte.

Eddie gave Simon a playful tap on the shoulder with his fist and raised his glass, whilst Simon involuntarily winced and moved back.

'What? I hardly touched you!'

'It's not that. I slipped and gave my shoulder a right bang.' He rubbed it gently with his free hand. 'Quite a tumble, you know what it's like? Hurts like hell.'

'Rotten luck! Is that how you whacked your head? You've got a great ugly red mark above the eyes.'

'Yeah. I tripped up and slammed my head into a regulator handle.' Simon tried a laugh, but it sounded forced. 'It'll be gone soon. I won't even notice it by Monday.'

'Or it'll ache worse, more like! I always reckon it's two days later when you really feel it.'

The pair supped their pints and watched the last minute fussing and fiddling with the bonfire in preparation for being ignited. Simon guzzled down his beer and constantly checked his watch; he was far from his usual, easy-going self. Eddie thought he looked ill at ease, with something on his mind. However, Eddie was also preoccupied, restlessly roving his eyes across the gathering throng, twisting and turning around and unable to settle, his usual stream of eager chatter stilled. However, he finally broke the uneasy silence.

'Take it easy, Si! That pint went down a bit fast.'

'What of it?' Simon looked at his glass with just a few bubbles of froth dribbling down the sides. 'I'm parched. Been climbing in fireboxes all day. The ash makes me thirsty.'

'OK. I'll get you another, but you'll just have to hold on a little longer.'

'Drink up and get to the bar; don't be such a slow coach!'

'Its not that...' Eddie was not even looking at Simon as he was speaking, but closely observing a group of people now stepping out of two cars pulled over on the edge of the green. He was squinting and trying to discern their faces in the gloom. 'I just want to stay here a little longer. They'll light the fire any moment and I don't want to miss it.'

'Ach, we see enough of those every day. It's only nice when it really gets burning.' But Simon's complaint was not heartfelt. He peered at his wristwatch, as he had been doing with increasing frequency, and cocked his head to one side. 'What train do you reckon that is? Is that the Neasden and Cricklewood pick up?'

'Eh?' Eddie was not really listening. He placed his pint glass on the grass, removed his pale grey hat — a recent and extravagant purchase that he was still very self-conscious about wearing — and quickly ran a comb through his heavily Brylcreemed hair. 'It sounds like one of the "runners" to me — it's got a big engine on the front. Si, you've been asking me about the identity of every blooming train this last hour. I thought we were here to watch the fireworks.'

'I'm just interested.' Simon was straining to listen to the train in the distance, wondering if this were the one conveying the container wagons. He would have to slip away soon and find out. 'You're always up for talking trains, so what's the matter? You still under a cloud?'

'Of course not.' Eddie was not looking at Simon, 'Just sometimes I want to think about other things.'

'Look, are you going for another beer?'

'Here's the money, would you get them in? I'd prefer to wait here.'

'You lazy lump. You really want to see the fire lit that much?' Simon frowned. 'Oh, but wait a minute — of course! It's the lovely Laura!'

'Shh! Keep it down!' Eddie looked about him anxiously, hoping no one had heard. 'Have a care and don't be so darned obvious.'

'You don't say she accepted your invitation?' Simon looked to have momentarily shrugged off his preoccupations.

'I'm not sure. I mean, I didn't have time to ask her. Negotiations are at a delicate stage.'

'So *that's* the reason for the spivvy hat and the slicked-down hair!' Simon laughed, finding a release for the tension building inside.

'Leave off! She was out of town today. Maybe she won't even get back in time.' Eddie pulled a face. 'I want to keep an eye out, then, if she should arrive, and did not already have a ticket, I could offer her the one I bought for her.' He stopped and went red, sipping some beer. 'It's pretty lame, I know.'

'I'd better get you another beer. It looks like you'll need some Dutch courage.'

Simon went back into the Gorsey, desperate for another dose of alcohol for his own nerves. He had enjoyed the moment of respite but his own troubles soon crowded back upon him. It was not tracking down wagons and replacing cards that was worrying him, a task that he knew he must put into action sooner rather than later that evening. No, it was the very real concern that Dennis was out there, on his tail. As he leant on the bar waiting to be served, his mind chewed relentlessly over the ominous words of warning fired his way after being almost killed by this dangerous Londoner.

Why must he not speak a word about that drowned man? What a strange thing to say. The trouble was, if he spent much longer with Eddie then this was going to be a hard promise to keep. Luckily Eddie appeared to have other matters on his mind tonight. That was a relief. Simon really did not want to get Eddie deeper into this awful fix. The burning question was why had Dennis been so angry when he'd mentioned Pym?

He closed his eyes for a few moments, his head throbbing with pain. He could understand why Dennis had got twitchy about the police — he was a racketeer, after all — though this fact also pricked Simon's conscience. It was all very well selling on fags to the lads around the shed and making a few extra shillings, but Dennis's anger at the mention of the police served only to remind Simon that he had crossed a line between right and wrong and was being pulled relentlessly into repeatedly breaking the law. How he wished he could just step back from all this. Turn the clock back and not bump into that man that smoggy night. It was too late now, he was in too deep.

But *was* it too late? Should he confess all? He had a friend here he could lean on for courage, and perhaps he should telephone that Inspector Vignoles, just like Eddie suggested, and trust that all could be made well again? The problem with this argument was that Dennis had said he'd throw him in the canal as well if he said a word. If he told the police, how long would he last? Days? Weeks? Or just hours?

'You look half asleep. A long week was it, duck?' The barmaid was speaking to Simon and some of the men propping up the bar laughed as he appeared to jolt awake.

'Not used to Old Hooky, if you ask me. Better watch him, Brenda, or he'll be passed out on your floor!'

'Wakey wakey, Howerth lad! It's good drinking time, this is, you don't want to go wasting that! Plenty of time to sleep it off tomorrow,' another man advised.

'It was a hard day, you're right there.' Simon looked bushed.

He ordered the beers and paid, then walked outside. He wanted to be out of this ugly mess. He'd made a dreadful mistake, but was it really his fault? Had he *chosen* to be in this predicament, or had it just 'happened'? One thing had led to another, almost too quickly for him to know what was going on. He winced as he remembered how he'd actively sought out the men in the pub. That was a foolish error, but perhaps just a momentary lapse of judgement. He had never intended to get involved in some kind of organised crime. But now he was under strict orders and what frightened him most was not just the violence Dennis had been so quick and ready to inflict, but that nagging, cloying, inescapable prickling of fear that the man was responsible for the body in the canal.

Had Dennis *killed* Pym?

Simon took a deep draught of beer and looked for Eddie, who had moved from his spot near the door. He tried to console himself by remembering that the police said it was suicide. But what if the police had made a mistake and he, Simon, the little locomotive cleaner from Woodford Halse, knew different? Had Dennis inadvertently confessed to the killing whilst venting his anger? If that were so, then Dennis was going to realise the mistake he'd made and how dangerous this information was — and he'd come back.

He could feel his hands trembling. He held a deadly secret. A secret he had no wish to have ever heard, nor had he any idea what to do with it.

The bonfire was crackling into life, with thick grey skeins of smoke twisting into the air from the base of the woodpile as bright yellow and orange tongues of flame flicked and licked over packing cases, branches and broken chairs, casting a brilliant warm light upon the people formed in a ring about the base, the fire raisers darting towards the rapidly heating conflagration, jabbing a spar of wood or levering a sleeper end into a better position to catch the eager flames. They stepped back, their work done, and a collective sigh went up as a thin, eager tower of dancing flame forced its way high up near the centre of the fire, showing itself just a yard or so below the feet of the stuffed Stalin.

Simon caught sight of his friend on the far side of the fire, face illuminated by the light, standing near a slim woman wearing a knee-length skirt and an elegant, rust-coloured jacket nipped tightly around a narrow waist to form a flattering shape that enhanced her hips.

'Blimey!' Simon blurted. He whistled softly and thought *That's never Laura Green! In a skirt, and showing some leg as well!* Simon shook his head in disbelief as he walked towards them.

'Hullo! I'm sorry, I would have brought you a drink if I had known.' He handed the pint to his friend. 'I'll go straight back.'

'Oh, thanks!' Eddie looked nervous, and grinned sheepishly. 'Simon, this is, er, Miss Green, I mean Laura.'

'Hello, Simon!' Laura extended a gloved hand. 'Of course we know each other already, I've lived here all my life.' She grinned. 'It's a splendid fire, isn't it? I do so like the guy this year. Mrs Trinder has done a super job.'

Simon just stared. He was surprised at how his friend had managed to be talking to a pretty woman and suddenly he found himself feeling giddy; his world was rocking and spinning. Why was he not entertaining a lovely young woman and enjoying the party, looking forward to a dance with his arm around her waist, instead of being about to skulk around a cold railway yard doing the dirty work for some thoroughly nasty characters? What on earth was he thinking? Was he bonkers?

'I shall fetch you a drink. What would you like?' Eddie asked Laura.

'No, wait here. Let's see Stalin and the rocket go up first — you'll miss it if you leave.' Her gloved fingers touched his sleeve. 'A drink can wait.'

Simon, however, looked grim, scowling into the far distance as he took deep swigs of beer. Eddie watched him down the remainder of his pint in one long draught and thrust the empty glass into Eddie's hand.

'What?' Simon replied to Eddie's curious look. 'You can take this back. I've got to go.'

'No wait! Join us for another. I'll go to the bar right now.'

'I can't. I have to go. I'll explain one day.'

With no further word or a glance back, Simon dashed off, dipping between the gathered crowd and away from the fire in the direction of the dark mass that was the distant railway embankment.

'What on earth has got into him?' asked Laura.

'I'm not sure. He's been in a strange mood all evening.' Eddie was looking puzzled and staring into the night after his friend. 'I can only suppose he's just remembered something urgent by the way he's haring off like that.'

'He was bit melodramatic. Where could he be going?'

'No idea.'

'Look, the fire's catching hold of Joe's feet!'

'Oh yes!' Eddie however looked not at the guy, but at Laura Green in her elegant clothes, her white gloves and little round hat with a dark band placed on the back of her curling hair. Her eyes were alive with the flicker of the fire and she was looking up, her head slightly to one side, a mixture of enjoyment and thoughtfulness on her fresh face. She sensed him looking at her.

'What is it? Do I have ash on my nose? Like the smudge you had on yours when we were taking tea?' She giggled.

'Heavens, no! It's just that you look a bit puzzled by something.'

The crowd made a collective 'ooh!' as the flames started to burn the pillowcase arms, whilst children let out loud gasps of excitement.

'I'm always in two minds about this — it's only rags and straw, of course, but the guy still represents a human being and the idea of burning someone is not very nice, is it?' She pulled a face then smiled. 'It sends a little shiver down the spine, because I admit I also like watching it go up.'

'At least with Joe Stalin we can't feel too sorry to see him go.'

'True, but I still feel safer with Guy Fawkes on the fire. He's ancient history, and so it seems less, well, less real. But this conversation is far too serious — just look how his coat is burning!'

'Watch for the rocket — it's a real whopper and should make a wonderful bang.' Eddie desperately fought off the temptation to take Laura's hand. She was showing no inclination to take his. Together with the crowd they craned their necks, stared at the atom rocket and waited. A cry went up, 'It's alight!'

'The fuse is burning!'

'Any moment…'

Laura stepped slightly closer to Eddie.

'Here she goes! I'm not good with loud bangs,' and she tensed in anticipation, slipping her arm through his. She joyfully creased her face in expectation, steadfastly refusing to look at Eddie, his face glowing with excitement.

With a fizzing whoosh, the great rocket powered into the sky above the Gorsey, a thick trail of yellow and silver fire lifting it high on a wavering, wobbling path as it curved up and over their heads before exploding with an enormous crack that echoed off the buildings below and formed a giant starburst like a silver dandelion clock puffed into disintegration by a strong gust of wind, as countless tiny twinkling stars fell towards the ground like so many seeds.

'Like radiation falling to earth. That's what'll happen if he sends his atom bombs over to us.' A solidly-built man, who had suddenly appeared beside Laura, was speaking. 'That's why we should burn Stalin, Laura my girl! Good riddance to him before he bombs us all.'

'Oh, Daddy! Don't frighten us with that talk.' She slipped her arm out of Eddie's.

'You look a sensible sort of lad, Edward Earnshaw.' He gave him a piercing look, but with a twinkle in his eye. 'You'd agree I was right. The atom bomb will rain its atom dust on to us, just like that rocket above.'

'I suppose so, Mr Green. Though I've not thought very much about it. I'm not really an expert on atom bombs.'

'Daddy! This is no time to put poor Eddie on the spot. Let's just enjoy the firework show and think about nicer things,' Laura laughed, glancing between the two.

'Ay, well. We'll stay for the fireworks, then I'll run you home. We've both had a long enough day and could do with some rest.'

'It has been tiring,' Laura nodded. She turned to Eddie. 'We were looking all day for lodgings for when I transfer on Monday. It was an awful lot of driving and involved talking to farmers' wives and looking at pokey, damp rooms offered at exorbitant rates.'

'I hope you found somewhere nice?' Eddie asked, although his spirits were sinking again.

'I've taken rather a sweet little room overlooking a pretty farmyard. The family seems nice enough and they've agreed I can have exclusive use of the parlour sometimes, to be on my own.'

'You'll get enough of that in the lonely signalbox!' Eddie observed, trying to make light of the situation.

'I think it'll do you grand, Laura. Eh, but some of those grumpy farmers we met! It was a real eye-opener. They'd have fleeced our Laura without a second thought if I'd not been there to put them straight.'

Laura flashed her eyes at Eddie before looking at her father. 'It was not *that* bad, Daddy, and I can stand up perfectly well for myself.'

'Are you not staying for the dance?' Eddie asked tentatively.

'I think not, Edward. Sorry.' Laura hesitated. 'We just came along to see the bonfire. Another time, perhaps.'

'But there won't be another time. With you moving away.'

'True. Well, never mind! Perhaps I am not in a dancing mood, anyway.'

Eddie was again feeling crestfallen. Laura had appeared genuinely pleased to see him, and they had stood chatting together for some time, sharing the atmosphere and the sense of anticipation around the fire. She had shown no inclination to move away and no potential suitor had appeared with a ticket to the dance, so Eddie had naturally begun to assume she would want to dance with him.

'Oh well, lad, I'm quite sure there's plenty of other lovely girls you can ask for a dance instead.' Mr Green winked theatrically at Eddie.

Laura gave her father a stern look. He took the hint and ambled off towards the entrance and the bar.

Eddie was already having to accept the inevitable, that Laura was soon leaving. 'I might go and find Simon. He's acting a bit odd lately.'

'Is he in trouble?' asked Laura. 'You both do have a bit of a reputation for getting mixed up in all manner of escapades.' She gave him a sly look. 'Do please tell me you are on the hunt for a—um, for a *jewel thief,* perhaps! Oooh, I love a good mystery!'

'Jewels? Hardly! Not this time; but something is up with Si. Look, er, why don't you come along, too? It's on your way home.'

Chapter Eighteen

SOME ENCHANTED EVENING
Jo Stafford

Chief Superintendent John Badger patted his new calfskin gloves, instinctively checking that they were safely stowed inside his upturned dress-uniform cap that lay between them on the rear seat, and settled more comfortably. Joyce Badger was dabbing powder on her face using the mirror in the lid of a silver clamshell compact, her scent filling the car in a heady mix with that of the camphor that held the moths at bay from her evening gown, and the rich, earthy smell of the polished leather seats.

A Bentley would have been Badger's marque of preference, but the Armstrong Siddeley Lancaster was still a fine machine and he was delighted the hire company had provided an almost new model, a pretty incredible feat when one considered the almost maniacal zeal of the export drive that saw most of Britain's cars shipped out to Kenya, Ceylon and goodness knows where else. However, he had been at his most persuasive when making the booking and determined to not let them fob him off with some pre-war jalopy.

'We have a personal invitation to a Guy Fawkes night party at the London residence of Sir Paul Frobisher, baronet, and simply *must* have a suitable vehicle.' They had understood, and he was satisfied with the black-and-cream bodywork that gleamed like a mirror and the bright chrome that managed to reflect the lamps outside their house in many twinkling points, despite the muffling presence of the infernal London smog.

The chauffeur was an outrageous extravagance, and on top of the outlay for his splendid new gloves and that shockingly expensive new handbag and shawl for Joyce, the whole shooting match had him delving deep into his wallet. He had the use of his own car for work and the services of a driver, Dick Pedder — but the police Humber was an ancient beast and he felt it would draw unwelcome comment; besides, he didn't want his man smoking and gossiping with the other drivers.

No, the hired car and chauffeur were essential. He pulled a face at his own reflection in the car window and thought of his depleted bank balance. Joyce, however, had insisted they pushed the boat out a bit, and he'd been happy to concur. After all, it was not everyday they were invited to a private drinks party with a baronet. In truth, it was the first such time.

The event, although ostensibly private, had the distinct undertone of Sir Paul wining and dining those in the establishment, specifically, within the world of Law and Order in and about London. Word had it that the baronet was being recommended for acceptance onto the board of the Metropolitan Police and, with voting soon to take place, he was almost certainly canvassing and buttering up anyone he might encounter if he were successful. It was purely Badger's professional position that brought him the invitation. He never threw over a chance to make acquaintance with persons of influence. It was how one got on in life. He had quickly ascertained that they were to be in exalted company, most notably the assistant commissioner of the Metropolitan Police, along with other big guns from Scotland Yard; if that were not enough, there was to be at least one senior member of the British Transport Commission, (the grapevine hinted at Sir Eustace Missenden himself); plus a handful of Conservative MPs (thank God Sir Paul was not one of those modern types who liked to be seen with the Labour shower currently in government!) This was a night to make a darned good impression.

Badger inspected the knife-edge creases in his dress uniform trousers and touched his tie with his fingertips, seeking reassurance the knot was full, tight and perfectly formed, then looked across at his wife. As he expected, she had risen to the occasion. She was no mannequin, but scrubbed up well and when seen in an evening gown (of some vintage, but he had put his foot down on this point) and following a scandalously expensive visit to her hairdresser, she looked the part to a tee. The pearls of her necklace were of fine quality, and that was what mattered; and the big diamond on her engagement ring, nestling beside the wide wedding band of brassy gold, certainly caught the eye. He had been right to splash out — was it really fifteen years ago? — on that impressive rock.

He flipped open his stainless steel cigarette case.

'A smoke?'

'Please, but do be a darling and light it for me.' His wife was dabbing under her chin, 'I may not have a chance for another. One never quite knows the protocol at these dos.' She gave him a swift glance. 'Don't worry, I'll follow the lead set by Lady Frobisher and only smoke if and when she does.'

Badger nodded his approval. Joyce knew how to play things right. He was a lucky man. She instinctively knew how to handle these social occasions. She knew what to wear and what to say, could be relied upon to play a mean hand of bridge, had a decent handicap on the golf course and could serve drinks and put on a cold collation like the best of them.

He flipped his lighter into action and lit a cigarette that was dangling from one corner of his mouth. Once satisfied it was alight, he closed the flame and lit a second cigarette from the one already burning, then pushed this into the end of a long, ivory holder. His wife put away her compact and, with a final touch to her hair, accepted the cigarette holder with a thin-lipped smile. Her lipstick was a deep maroon that looked almost black in the dark interior.

Feeling content, they both looked ready for action and, bolstered by a whisky stiffener before they left home, Badger relaxed back into his seat and looked out into the pale and almost ghostly vision of London beyond the car window. They were close to Marylebone, or at least he believed them to be, as everywhere was curiously transformed by the thick walls of sickly smog filling each side street like cotton wadding and which rendered the car headlights almost physical, like pale cones of solid yellow cutting through the wreath-like barrier, as an icebreaker might through pack ice.

The shops were shuttered, the pavements almost empty, as Londoners huddled inside against the lung-wrenching pollution with damp towels laid across the gaps at the bottoms of doors and loose sash windows. The few people he could see walked with their heads down, scarves around their faces like escapees from a mummy's tomb, others pressed hankies, no doubt infused with vapour oil, to their mouths. It was a bleak and cheerless sight, and Badger was struck by a rare moment of profundity, appreciating that post-war Britain was in so many ways a depressing place. Run down, battered and bombed, it looked worn out, with everything broken or shabby, the people as well as the buildings. Perhaps that damned foolish Labour government would finally come to their senses and realise they should first look after their own instead of sending precious food and clothes to the *Germans* — of all people! Everything bright and new seemed destined for overseas. He watched a lonely bobby walk slowly along the pavement, wrists crossed behind his back.

Oh yes, that reminded him — Vignoles! What was the man up to this time?

The DI had telephoned just as Badger was getting dressed for the evening. If anyone were going to call at a silly time, it would surely be Vignoles! It really had been most inconvenient, standing in the front parlour, receiver in hand, wearing just a shirt with a fly away collar and little else but his sock suspenders. Bloody good job they hadn't invented a telephone with built-in tele-vision!

Vignoles got the job done all right, but he did like to bowl the occasional Yorker and catch him unawares. He'd said he was working with Scotland Yard on some suicide case. No harm in linking up with the London boys, of course, but over a suicide? What could possibly require this level of cooperation? People were always throwing themselves in front of trains, but it rarely needed much more than an unpleasant clean up operation. Vignoles said there was something 'fishy' about the circumstances, though he could find no crime as yet, then started going off on a tangent about thefts from the railway and possible gambling dens.

Badger shook his head in frustration. He had not been in the mood to listen to his DI's ramblings and the moment he had started to mention insurance fraud, Badger had decided that he was not going to stand there trouserless for a moment longer. He'd told Vignoles they would meet on Monday, and if he knew what was good for him, Vignoles would spend Sunday trying to knock some sense into his thoughts.

'Is this Baker Street, John?' His wife was also observing the dank view from the car.

'I can't tell for certain.' Badger shook off his thoughts about Vignoles and peered into the gloom.

'It is, ma'am; the tube station is just ahead,' offered the chauffeur.

'It looks like something from a Sherlock Holmes book, don't you think?'.

'The fog lends everything a melodramatic air,' agreed Badger. 'I say, driver, is it far?'

'Just a few minutes more, sir. I'll be turning up Park Road in a tick, and that'll take us right up to the house.'

Badger looked at his watch. 'About five more minutes, would you say?'

'That's correct, sir. I shall aim to arrive two minutes past the half-hour. One should never be the first to arrive but, of course, one should not be late.' He winked in the rear view mirror.

Badger appeared satisfied with this answer, though unsure whether the driver's winking constituted bad manners.

'Have you been here before, sir?'

'No. It's our first time at Sir Paul's London residence.'

'I've heard it's a fine place. A lovely setting; between the canal and Regent's Park and just a ball's throw from Lord's. I expect you could hear the crack of leather on willow of a sunny afternoon, sir.'

Badger nodded appreciatively.

'Of course, it is also smack bang next to the railway — just missed being swept away when they built the mainline and the tube.'

'Thank heaven for small mercies!' Badger worked for British Railways but he resolutely refused to love trains as a mode of transport.

'That probably accounts for why the place lay empty for a while.

Most of the posh nobs probably didn't want to hear and smell dirty trains at the bottom of their garden.' The chauffeur chuckled.

'I suppose not.' Badger frowned. He was not impressed by that thought, either.

'The story I heard is that the baronet snaffled the place up for a song. Of course, that was still way beyond anything the likes of you or me could afford, but a bargain all the same.'

Badger saw his wife give a toss of her head at the suggestion they were grouped in the same financial class as the driver. He grunted and looked away from the man's eyes in the mirror.

'It was a Red Cross nursing home in the war,' continued the driver, 'and was left in a bit of state, though the gardens were kept nice; no doubt appreciated by the patients to have a walk around in. I understand he's fixed the place up well and proper!'

'These fine houses should always be under the care of the aristocracy. They have the class and the taste others lack,' observed Mrs Badger, to no one in particular.

'Quite. We should count ourselves fortunate to have the likes of Sir Paul. Leave it to the government and they'd have turned it into a children's home or a secondary modern school or something equally ghastly.' Badger stubbed out his cigarette in a little stainless steel receptacle provided for that purpose.

'Here we are, sir!'

The car swung to the right, headlamps glancing off black gates that stood open against stone pillars with small gatehouses to each side. A gravel drive crunched under the tyres as they approached an elegant house in a style that could only be early Regency and managed to shout 'Jane Austen' to even the most architecturally unaware. It was simple, with well-proportioned windows that glowed with a warm, yellow light and offered glimpses of chandeliers, had a stone portico like a small Roman temple, and was topped by a hipped roof with tall brick chimneys. There was a line of cars with chauffeurs opening doors and liveried footmen in attendance as women wearing fur stoles and coats and gentlemen in service uniforms or evening dress with black butterfly ties at their throats stepped out. A white-gloved hand raised a top hat whilst others bowed or saluted.

It was a splendid sight, and Badger inwardly smiled, the thick card invitation already in his hand, clutched with almost boyish anticipation. A footman opened one of the rear doors of their car, and as his wife stepped out, her eyes filled with pride, her face set in an impassive mask as she felt befitted interaction with a servant.

Badger stood on the lower step of the portico, arm crooked ready to take his wife's hand, and he looked back down the sweep of drive at the ghostly shapes and shadows passing on the busy Park Road and where two lorries were noisily labouring in convoy up a steeply graded access road. He could hear the gruff barking exhalations of a heavy steam train pulling away as it started north, its sounds reverberating against the walls of the house, despite the softening strains of a string quartet playing from somewhere within. Both lorries and train were ugly reminders of work, and with relief and a self-satisfied smile he and Joyce walked into the entrance hall, acknowledging the greetings of the footmen whilst looking at the guests already standing with glasses of champagne, and who in turn, were taking the measure of the latest arrivals.

Chapter Nineteen

Do Nothing Till You Hear From Me
Duke Ellington

It was Saturday evening and Vignoles was still thinking about Jack Pym. He was conscious that his artificially imposed Friday deadline for making a decision about whether this was a suicide or a homicide case had long passed, but it was proving an ever more intriguing puzzle, so he could easily justify extending the investigation. However, he was also aware that he had committed his team to a lot of work and not yet given his boss a briefing, trusting DI Tykett's reassurance that Scotland Yard had 'squared' it. He'd been given the case, but was his chief aware of this, and would he approve? Vignoles finally placed a call to Badger, who had been preparing for a dinner engagement. The conversation, however, had been deeply unsatisfactory and Vignoles knew that he had better give a decent and cogent account of himself by Monday or he could expect a thorough dressing down.

The problem was, his officers had gathered all manner of information about the Pyms and were starting to form suspicions about others associated with the dead man, in particular Henry Bish, but he really had nothing substantial to hang on to, and whilst the revelation about Adeline Pym and Wilde was dramatic, Vignoles was increasingly convinced that this was a failed murder plot, which could be placed on the back burner for a day or so. Bish was his current focus of attention, but he felt unable to call the man in for interrogation as he had insufficient information to bring to the table. He was uncertain of his ground and was not sure that he could actually accuse Bish of killing Pym. It was possible, but a long way from proven.

What he needed was to push things along. He'd deliberately stirred Bish up today, of that he was certain and he harboured a suspicion that Bish would not sit back and just hope things blew over. He would react, particularly as he would be aware by now that Trinder had been sniffing around the Hendon operation. Vignoles frowned and shook his head. That was another puzzle, since when did a warehouse manager also co-own a valuable industry such as Hendon Pharmaceuticals? This was verging on implausible. Where did he find the capital? Or, to look at it the other way round, why would a co-owner of a successful business take an assistant manager's job in a warehouse? The man simply was not what he appeared to be.

Vignoles stood up and reached for his greatcoat. He ran the risk of getting into very hot water if discovered doing what he had in mind, but sometimes it paid to take a risk. He would never get a search warrant with nothing more than a faint whiff of suspicion. That the men at Jordan's looked shifty and Bish was not liked by young Oliver Pym was going to convince no one. However, there was something about the place that demanded another look. The best thing to do at such moments was to make a discreet reconnaissance mission to see if anything came to light that might focus his line of enquiry. Ideally he wanted Trinder by his side, but he'd already sent him home to Woodford Halse, and besides, he really should not drag his sergeant into what was, strictly, a rather dubious activity. Not that Vignoles was quite sure what it was he was going to do when he got to the warehouse, nor indeed what he expected to find, but he had put a torch in his pocket together with a set of picklocks he had taken a few years back from a cat burglar he'd caught breaking into the ticket office at Carrington station.

Vignoles stood on the island platform of Loughborough Central in the bitter chill of a November evening, having just stepped off the 5:54pm ex-Leicester Central to Manchester (London Road). It had been a deliberate choice, as this heavy express included the rare and desirable addition of a refreshment car, and so he had been able to eat two peanut butter sandwiches washed down with a bottle of Coca-Cola on the short journey north. Hardly wonderful fare, but at least his stomach had stopped rumbling.

He pulled his coat collar up, tied his scarf tighter around his neck and paused a moment at the bottom of the creaky wooden stairs leading up to the entrance hall. The porter was slamming the carriage door shut whilst the guard stood expectantly, whistle in mouth and paraffin lamp in hand. A capped head could just be seen in the distance looking back from the cab of the engine, now wreathed in slow curls of steam as it waited impatiently to get moving. The big metal barrel of the water tower loomed above the locomotive, its curved arms and water bags like those of a bizarre, twin-trunked elephant. The guard shone his lamp, gave a short blast on the whistle and stepped smartly into his brakevan. The B1 engine launched a volcanic explosion into the night with flashes of red licking the dark grey clouds. It was a real 'snorter,' and the locomotive cab flickered yellow and orange as the fire doors opened and the incandescent light illuminated the rhythmic explosions of filthy smoke that towered high above the station as the wheels slipped on the greasy rails. Vignoles thought the vision had something of the apocalyptic about it, and the occasional rocket fizzing and banging in the night sky added to the impression. As the rhythm increased and the creaking, teak-built coaches gathered speed, the engine smoke rolled downwards and poured around the cast iron supporting columns and open lattice-work of the station canopy as it rushed silently towards him like a great grey tidal wave before ripping apart and disintegrating into tiny insubstantial fragments, harmlessly twisting in the air before vanishing. Where did it all go? How could such an opaque cloud of thick grey just vanish into nothing?

The train chuffed into the distance, leaving Vignoles to look at the inky sky spotted with thousands of stars and the curving trajectories of rockets and colourful gunpowder starbursts. Loughborough was free of the evil smog enveloping London and some of the larger northern cities, and he was happy to take in a lungful of the sharp, chill air. He walked up the stairs to Great Central Road, hands thrust into his coat pockets, clear as to where he was heading, but unclear about what to do when he got there.

He and a few other dark-coated figures hunched against the night walked down the slope of the road bridge towards town, each lost in his own thoughts. If Vignoles had turned about, he would have been surprised to discover that one of these monochromatic men busy staring at the pavement as he walked was Dennis Parkey, who had joined the train at Woodford Halse.

Narrow strips of greenish cloud drifted across the brilliant moon, casting a strong light on the ground, and the air held the scent of burning wood, paper and old leaves from the many bonfires, all tinged with the evocative smell of gunpowder. The streets of two-storey Victorian terraced houses were largely free of traffic except for the occasional car, a freewheeling of numerous cyclists and a snorting, steam-powered dray hauling casks of Sileby Brewery ales. This passed in a whisper of oiled machinery and a rattle of casks caused by the hard tyres on the cobbled street, leaving a faint scent of oily steam in its wake. A couple of hardy lads dressed in tatty jumpers and shorts were kicking a life-expired football against a terrace end, the ball making hollow sounds as it slapped from shoes to brick and back onto cobbles. Through a narrow brick alley between the terraces Vignoles glimpsed a group of people gathered for a bonfire party. A Roman candle was launching red and green balls of light into the air and Vignoles could see shadowy figures in coats and hats, each holding cups and glasses, their faces tinged with the colours of the airborne balls that fizzed and popped.

Vignoles was able to locate the secluded industrial yard more easily the second time and found it illuminated by a solitary gas lamp, bolstered by the moonlight. The ugly premises edging the yard appeared to be shut up tight, much as Vignoles had expected. He still walked carefully however, minimising the sound of his footsteps and trying to stay in the darkest areas whilst keeping a lookout for a night watchman as he skirted the yard and headed straight for the wagon with the demountable container. As he drew closer, he was surprised to see that this had now been joined by two more of these 'conflat' wagons, and all three were coupled together. The shunting engine he had heard at work earlier had obviously paid a visit later that afternoon to bring these new arrivals. Business was booming for Mr Jordan. He must be working wonders on his overseas travels.

Vignoles walked to the far side of the wagons and down the narrow gap between them and the concrete perimeter fence edged with a bank of stinging nettles, and inspected the bill of loading document slipped into a wire frame affixed for that purpose on the side of the container. He risked using his torch, holding it close to the paper to reduce the light it threw. The container was destined for Marylebone goods depot.

This was not surprising, and yet he still felt a tingle down his spine. The only reason Jordan's Import and Export had come to his knowledge was because they shipped their goods to Marylebone, where repeatedly, they had their stock stolen. So why should this feel significant? It proved nothing and gave no clue as to why anyone would wish to fake Pym's suicide, and yet Vignoles knew that somewhere — perhaps inside this container — there could be a clue that might start to help him piece together what was, at the moment, a thoroughly jumbled set of jigsaw pieces. He looked up at the container and the hefty padlocks securing the doors and knew he was not going to look inside without recourse to bolt cutters — or a key. He could not reach up to pick the lock without a ladder and, besides, it felt too risky. This would have to wait, but he felt irked, as it could prove interesting to have a closer look at what Jordan's was really transporting.

Vignoles thought he saw something move on the far side of the yard. He froze. After a few seconds he peered into the dark shadows cast by the moon, but nothing stirred again. He waited almost a minute then decided he had imagined it. He stepped up onto the loading bay platform. The heavy wooden door into the warehouse was pulled closed, but the moonlight revealed an unexpected surprise. The padlock that should have been securing the door was unlocked and dangling from the metal loop screwed to the frame, the hasp pulled open. It had not been forced. Perhaps someone had simply forgotten to lock the place when they clocked off? Vignoles thought this unlikely. If oversight could be discounted, this meant only one thing: someone was inside.

He pressed his ear to the door and tried to listen, but a goods train was passing on the mainline and the sound of this masked everything, not helped by the rocket explosions above. He tried gently rolling the door to his right, hoping to ease it open a fraction, using the slightest of movements and exerting pressure with the tips of his fingers on his left hand and his right splayed flat on the wood. A narrow strip of pale light crossed the loading bay deck and Vignoles peeped through the gap. Finding his spectacles inconvenient he removed them, pressing his eye closer. Although his vision was no longer perfect, it was sufficiently strong to see two men inside — possibly those who had been so welcoming earlier in the day.

However, it was not the presence of these men that caused him to take a sharp intake of breath and question his eyesight. He pulled away from the door and rubbed his eyes before looking again. The warehouse that had been stacked with boxes of every size and shape that morning was now virtually empty. There were but a handful of damaged or empty boxes scattered here and there; the unloved detritus that seemingly was always left behind in a move: the litter of paper, a broom, a forgotten glove and an upturned bucket.

The warehouse contents had disappeared in the space of just a few hours and these men now had stacks of files beside them which they were in the process of methodically destroying. Vignoles suspected these had lined the shelves in the office. The orderly Bish would be horrified to see how these men were unceremoniously ripping out the pages and tearing them into small pieces before dropping into a sooty workman's brazier. Or had Bish ordered their destruction? This was no act of mindless vandalism; they looked intent on burning all the company records, and were being surprisingly careful about how they went about it. They worked fast, exchanging not a word as they bent to the task. Vignoles observed them for a minute longer, until he decided that he had better move. The brazier was now nearly full of torn paper and he guessed what they would do next.

Vignoles dropped down from the platform and melted into a gloomy corner towards the rear of the building, standing against a wall concealed by a dusty laurel bush and a buddleia. He waited a couple of minutes, then heard the door roll open at the same time as the warehouse lights were extinguished — an interesting detail that suggested they were being careful to attract as little attention as possible. Vignoles was convinced this was a carefully orchestrated plan, and suspected Bish of masterminding it.

The two men carried the smoke-blackened brazier between them. They descended the loading platform, swung about and crossed the siding, walked past the container wagons and into the yard. Vignoles followed a distance behind and crouched down behind the wagon closest to the yard.

He had not noticed before, but a small wooden hut about the size of a police box sat close to the entrance into the yard and the men placed the brazier in front of this. One man struck a match and fed the flame through a hole near the base, and soon a bright lick of red fire and a thin plume of blue smoke started to rise, illuminating the night watchman's hut. The brazier looked the part, and as the men tended the fire they would attract little or no attention, especially on a night of bonfires. They were just two cold watchmen trying to keep warm.

One of the men walked back towards the warehouse, forcing Vignoles to hurriedly duck beneath the wagon where he observed the man's legs athletically vaulting onto the platform. Vignoles waited, trying to keep his breathing steady, but he still jumped as a tumble of yet more files clattered to the ground, followed by the man landing heavily beside them. As he stooped to pick them up, Vignoles was able to look at his face, now just a few feet away. It was the lorry driver with the fondness for heavy spanners. So, he was part of this set up.

If the man glanced up now, Vignoles would be discovered. Fortunately he appeared intent on the matter in hand and quickly scooped up the armful of folders and carried them across to the now-roaring fire that was sending little black scraps of charred paper spinning and circling into the night sky like so many starlings above their roost at eventide, urged skywards by the second man prodding at the fire with a stick.

Vignoles quickly darted up the steps and slipped inside the warehouse. He was aware that he ran the risk of either being discovered or getting himself locked in, but he had to take the chance. As the door was open, he could not be accused of breaking and entering, which had been something he had hoped not to have to resort to.

The warehouse had been stripped bare, and Vignoles sensed that, whatever had prompted the exodus, it had been a snap decision rather than the fulfilment of a spectacularly big order and, as with any kind of panic-driven escape, something of interest had surely been overlooked. Bish's office was the most obvious place to start and it also offered a modicum of concealment.

The moonlight cast a pale blue glow through the open door, allowing him to briskly walk over to the office, stooping to scoop up from the dusty floor a bundle of printed labels held together by an elastic band and stuff them in a pocket as he did so. Anything might prove useful.

Another dark shape slipped through the warehouse door and now stood against the wall, melting into the darkness, his breathing slow and almost imperceptible.

The office shelves were empty, and the place looked as though it had been ransacked. Vignoles moved behind the desk and sat in Bish's chair. The drawers had been pulled out and one was upturned on the floor. Broken pencils, paper clips, a scattering of rubber bands, a bottle of ink and other office detritus lay across the desk and floor beside the squat form of a black Bakelite telephone, but there was nothing that held his interest. He cupped a hand over the torch and, using the narrowest beam he could make, started to explore beneath the desk. An address book was too much to hope for, but there had to be something...

He knelt on the floor, placing his face close to the ground, and shone the beam beneath a set of freestanding cupboards. There was a lot of dust clumped into balls, a large spider scurrying away from the light, a golf ball and what looked like an old envelope. That might be worth a closer look. He slid his fingers into the gap and had to strain his fingertips to get any purchase on the paper, grimacing as he pressed his head at an awkward angle against the cupboard. Eventually he felt the envelope move and succeeded in sliding it out and, in so doing, caused the golf ball to roll and come to rest near his body.

Vignoles pulled himself back into a kneeling position, picking up both golf ball and envelope, anxious to prevent the ball from rolling away and perhaps sending him flying if he stood on it. He clicked the torch back on and inspected his haul.

The envelope had been torn apart at the edges and turned inside out to make a useful piece of scrap-paper. Everyone did this since the onset of austerity measures. Vignoles himself had a drawerful of opened-out envelopes ready for rough note-taking.

This particular envelope had been used for financial calculations. A long list of figures, some very substantial, were in a column and letters beside each sum and a small tick suggested the money had been accounted for. There was another list of brands of nylons, with what might be quantities beside each and calculations of value. It struck Vignoles that the sums quoted were wildly in excess of the value of the stockings. He had no idea what this meant, nor indeed if he were interpreting this correctly, but it felt sufficiently intriguing to warrant further inspection at a later date.

He flipped the envelope over and smiled with satisfaction. This felt important, but further consideration of what it might signify could wait until he was safely out of this place.

He clicked the light off and stuffed the letter into a coat pocket. Moving into a crouching position he readjusted his hat whilst he contemplated his next move. It was time to get out. It looked like they had stripped the place bare and he was not hopeful of finding much else. The sudden evacuation of the warehouse might even be enough to warrant a formal visit in the cold light of day. He'd give Tykett a call first thing and see what he made of this intriguing development. He turned the golf ball in his hand for a moment, feeling the dimples in the surface and sizing up the weight in his palm as he wondered at how best to extricate himself from the warehouse without being caught.

Suddenly he froze, the hairs on the nape of his neck standing on end and a clammy coldness instantly forming on his skin. He sensed the presence behind him and only heard the soft intake of breath when it was too late. He thought he smelled coal dust and engine oil and caught the creak of a boot placed carefully on the floor — then came the sharp, dizzying pain as a horribly sickening blow struck his head, prompting silver and red stars to explode in his brain like the fireworks outside, until a scarlet veil of colour moved across his sight like the curtains closing at the end of a cinema screening. He was hardly conscious of the cold linoleum floor rising up and slapping him in the face as his ears rang like a screaming safety valve.

Everything went black.

A gloved hand lifted the receiver and waited for the operator. 'Give me Marylebone 6745. Yes, the Sherbourne Arms.'

He waited until the line connected and sighed with relief when a voice came on the other end. 'Tone, is Vic there? It's urgent.'

The man waited impatiently for a few moments.

'Vic? We're all done here. Cleaned out. There *was* a problem, but I fixed it.' He looked down at the motionless, bleeding figure at his feet. 'An intruder. Snooping around the office, he was, but I put an end to that... OK, keep your hair on! I think he's a rozzer.' Dennis held the receiver away from his ear as he was met with a series of shrieked oaths and curses. 'I couldn't leave 'im watching us, could I?'

Vic's voice continued to bawl down the line. 'Nah, he didn't see me! All right, I'll do nothing until I hear from you. We're out of here now, anyway. Just thought you'd want to let Top Link know.'

Dennis replaced the receiver, ran a hand across his face and silently cursed the unconscious figure of Vignoles sprawled on the floor.

Chapter Twenty
AUTUMN
Antonio Vivaldi

Badger was holding an empty champagne glass, rotating it in his fingers and wondering whether it would be bad form to request a pint of beer from one of the obsequious waiters; however, not even the men from Scotland Yard were holding pints, so he could not risk offending etiquette. Bother! He was no lover of fizzy wine.

His stomach rumbled and he belched, failing to adequately mask the sound and drawing a sharp glance of rebuke from his wife. And that was another thing, these little squares of cold nibbles the waiters brought around on silver trays were all well and good, but he needed some real food to dampen the effect of the bubbly. He was forming the distinctly morose impression that these — what did Joyce call them? Petty Fours? — were all that was on offer. Typical! One gets invited to a house where money and rationing don't matter a jot and they're given the posh equivalent of half-rations — no, quarter-rations.

The Badgers were standing on the wide terrace at the rear of the house, where French windows had been thrown open in anticipation of the imminent firework display (although the appalling visibility was going to render this something of a damp squib), allowing some of the guests to spill outside, despite the chill and the loathsome, smoggy air. Badger did not recognise any of their fellow terrace-strollers, but imagined they were not unlike themselves; numbering amongst the second class on the guest list and eager to seek a few moments respite from standing with fixed expressions on their faces whilst pretending they were 'enjoying themselves tremendously' — but actually bored and irritated by the whole charade.

He and Joyce had walked a little further than most, past stone steps and lengthy balustrading that led down to a pair of long, rectangular ponds of black water partially swallowed by fog. Badger thought the scene resembled something from a Gothic horror story. There was just a suggestion of the brooding, dripping trees amidst the almost impenetrable veil of dank moisture that felt oppressive. The house was not unattractive, and yet there was something unappetising and ugly about the place. It felt more than a little sinister, though he was uncertain why he felt this way. Beyond the oily ponds there was a sickly glow cast by the city lights to their right, the baronet's vast yet unseen gardens and then Regent's Park. But for the traffic sounds, it would be easy to believe they were somewhere deep in the countryside.

Badger ruminated with resentment. He and Joyce were always standing on the margins looking in, permitted to be in the presence of the great and the good, but barely noticed, receiving at best a slight nod of acknowledgment from across the room, but never an invitation to join in.

The evening had started well, however, with Sir Paul and Lady Frobisher smiling and welcoming the Badgers warmly to their 'little place' and hoping they'd have 'a simply marvellous time'; but after this brief, thrilling flurry that lasted little more than fifteen seconds their hosts moved on. Badger noticed that they greeted the other new arrivals by their Christian names and spent longer talking and laughing with them.

Their host was a dapper, self-confident, smooth-talking man in his early fifties, trim and athletic in build and with a suntan not acquired in England's climate. His shirt was obviously hand-tailored and complemented by diamond cufflinks that Badger considered unpleasantly ostentatious. The effect was completed by a silk bow tie. With his Savile Row suit, the raven black perfectly highlighting a brace of medals on his chest, Sir Paul occasionally threw them both a little nod and an empty smile like a movie star acknowledging his fans, but he was always in the midst of sharing a joke with one of his close associates, one hand cupping an elbow, a cigar in the other, listening intently to the thoughts of powerful men. Badger had already recognised the assistant commissioner of the Met, and a man who might be something big in the Ministry of Supply. Both were engaged earnestly in conversation with Sir Paul, who laid on the charm with a trowel.

Joyce sensed her husband sink into a morose silence and, looping her arm through his, steered him along the terrace even further away from the open doors. One wing of the house jutted out ahead, lights glowing from the lower windows. A telephone could be heard ringing with a nagging insistence, growing louder as they walked further from the strains of Vivaldi's 'Four Seasons' drifting from the ballroom. She tried to engage her husband by asking if it was the 'Autumn' or 'Winter' movement, but neither knew for certain. Badger, desperate for something to distract him, began watching a silent charade unfold through one of the lighted windows ahead.

He could not hear what was said, but the telephone's anxious ringing was ended by a blond man in a sports jacket who quickly formed a worried expression, twitching his moustache in consternation and gesticulating with his free hand. Badger was always amused by people expending energy on expressive actions that were invisible to the person on the other end of the line.

The butler entered the room which Badger could now see was an office, perhaps where the house and estate affairs were managed. The blond man cupped a hand over the mouthpiece and barked an order that prompted the butler, looking grave, to nod and immediately leave the room. Moments later, Sir Paul hurried into the room, his usual expression of easy charm replaced by a more dark and uneasy demeanour.

It was many years since Badger had put away his police notebook, and these days he far preferred the swagger stick to a truncheon, but he was still a policeman at heart, and so the mixture of idle curiosity and a detective's innate wish to understand the psychology of men caused him to become increasingly intrigued as to why Sir Paul was speaking in an animated fashion to a man he assumed was Sir Paul's estate manager. Both looked agitated, hurriedly exchanging words, and making every effort to retain self-control. And yet their faces betrayed agitation, even alarm. Angry words were traded, their tone of voice unmistakably heated, but it seemed that a consensus was reached, leading to a message being conveyed down the telephone.

Badger felt his wife pull on his arm and thought she wished them to return to the party, but he stood firm, allowing her to turn so her back was to the window and he could look over her shoulder.

'You wish to stay outside?' asked Mrs Badger, shivering.

'There's no rush to go back to that insufferable dullness,' he replied, without looking at her.

'Is something the matter?' She tried to swivel around.

'Stay as you are please, my dear. I just want to see something...'

'What are you talking about?'

'Don't turn around!' he hissed. 'Just look at me as if we were deep in conversation.'

'What's got into you?'

'Our host is having a most animated discussion, bawling a man out over something, giving him a right dressing down, and the poor man's standing to attention like a squaddie on parade,' Badger whispered.

'You're spying on him?' Joyce sounded outraged, 'How ill-mannered!'

He looked her in the eye and smiled, nodding as if in reply to a witty comment. 'Just keep looking my way, dearest,' he mumbled through gritted teeth.

Badger watched the scene unfold, then felt a chill run down his spine, not induced by the clawing dampness of the air but by something he observed played out behind the window. It was a fleeting gesture: brief but potent. It sent his mind reeling and he physically recoiled, forcing himself with the greatest effort to look at Joyce, smiling as if sharing an intimate moment, hoping that Sir Paul had not met his gaze as the baronet glanced nervously into the darkness through the glass before yanking the pull cord that brought a roller blind down across the window.

Badger ran a hand over his face. 'This champagne is really not agreeing with me.' He looked pale, as if in shock. 'What say we rejoin the body of the kirk and warm ourselves?'

Mrs Badger gave her husband a quizzical look but was happy to acquiesce. Her new shawl was warm, but the night air was leeching the heat away and she felt another shiver pass through her body, not helped by her husband's perplexing behaviour and the gloomy surroundings.

'You look like you've seen a ghost.'

'I'm fine. A funny turn, that's all.' Badger was keeping his face impassive, running the scene over in his mind, trying to find an interpretation that made sense. He forced a half laugh. 'I do think our host is having a few problems with his affairs, but as you quite rightly said, it is none of our business.'

They strolled back towards the sweet strains of Vivaldi, but as they did so Badger felt his wife's hand tense on his.

'If I am not mistaken, Sir Paul is heading our way in a most determined manner. If he saw you spying on him, it will be simply too embarrassing for words!'

Seconds later the baronet, the assistant commissioner of the Met — and his rather fierce-looking wife — stepped through the French windows. Sir Paul appeared to be searching for someone. He caught Badger's eye and made a beeline, accompanied by his two companions. The AC's wife surprised the Badgers further by breaking into a smile so wide it was reminiscent of a shark, whilst exclaiming with exaggerated enthusiasm how delighted she was to meet Mrs Badger 'at last'. Before Badger had time to do more than shake hands, his wife had been whisked off 'to see the fabulous porcelain collection'.

'It's John, isn't it? And do call me Paul; no need for titles between friends, eh?' Sir Paul's face beamed, though Badger noticed that his eyes lacked sparkle and there was a hint of colour around his neck that was perhaps the lingering trace of the recent contretemps. His brow also betrayed emotion, covered as it was with a faint sheen of moisture. The baronet extended a hand, showing a flash of the expensive shirt and a diamond glinting with a cold light.

Badger tried to suppress a feeling of immense pride suddenly swelling inside as a result of being addressed by his forename and regarded as a friend. His sense of shock and unease was pushed aside as he became the centre of their attention.

'You know Ronald, of course.'

Badger had never met the assistant commissioner in person, however, Sir Ronald Vallance expertly sidestepped this potential embarrassment by extending his hand.

'Good evening, chief superintendent.' He offered a practised smile, though he looked ill at ease and his face quickly became impassive.

The butler appeared at their side and three large balloon glasses filled with cognac were offered from a heavy silver tray.

'It's darned fine stuff, John. A 1928 Hine Grande Champagne Cognac,' Sir Paul explained, expertly spinning the liquid around his glass and wafting a rich aroma that cut through the stink of house-coal smoke that lay like a thick carpet all about. 'Bloody expensive and well-nigh impossible to find. I struck lucky with some chums in France who secured me a few cases. They were sequestered by a Nazi general for his private enjoyment after the fall of France, but he had to leave them behind after we kicked 'em out. At least the beastly man had taste!' Sir Paul gave John Badger a conspiratorial wink. Badger felt another shiver down his spine but blanked the memory.

'Bottoms up!' They raised their glasses as the butler drifted silently back towards the house.

'Thank you!' Badger sniffed the heady liquor. It was deliciously warm and rich, and even just a lungful of the aroma was warming. The first sip was smoother than the softest silk and caressed his throat as it slipped down. Sir Paul's story was reassuring and Badger mentally upbraided himself, forcing his silly doubts into a deeper recess of his mind.

'I say John, old chap, I wonder if I might have a word,' the baronet placed a strong hand upon Badger's upper arm and steered him towards one of the sets of stone steps leading down to the twin ponds of black water. 'As you're probably aware, I've been proposed for election to the board of the Met, and with a fair wind in one's sails, I'm pretty confident of securing sufficient votes.' He glanced across at Sir Ronald. 'Indications suggest everything's heading in the right direction.' He smiled smugly.

Badger took another deep sip of the astoundingly fine cognac. The evening was taking a most extraordinary turn. He felt another tremor of doubt pass through his mind, but his concerns were being rapidly drowned by flattery and fine liquor and he fought to keep his face impassive whilst offering an understated nod of agreement.

'If one is successful, it could open up all manner of opportunities to work the corridors of power.' The baronet sipped his drink and fixed his eyes on Badger. He grinned, showing immaculate teeth. 'But, look, and this is most important, John — I've heard such good things about this detective department of yours. Jolly innovative idea for a railway.'

'Indeed. We plough a lone, but a successful furrow.' Badger felt his chest almost explode with pride. He lifted his chin as he continued, 'it was quite daring and the old London and North Eastern went out on a limb when they started it up.' He rose up on his toes then lowered himself again as he spoke, aware that he was shorter than either the baronet or the AC. 'A dedicated detective service is almost unique and, dare I say, I have personally overseen some notable successes.' He risked a glance at Sir Ronald, who gave the faintest of smiles.

'Splendid! And the quality of your work precedes you, John.' Sir Paul threw an obvious look towards the AC. 'And, as luck would have it, Ronald and I were just discussing a few ideas this very evening that will interest you, hence the private chinwag.'

They were standing beside one of the rectangles of water, mist creeping low over the dark shapes of lilies on the surface and enveloping with a thin veil the pale marble figure of an almost naked girl on a plinth who appeared to be running towards them whilst drawing an imaginary string on a stone bow, ready to release an arrow directly at them. Her sculpted hair was streaming behind and her limbs were lithe and perfectly formed, one leg thrown forward to land on her toes, the other kicked back by her leaping run. Badger found himself staring at her pale breasts and the gently curve of her belly as he listened to Sir Paul, trying to keep his expression impassive.

Fresh glasses of cognac arrived and Badger was urged to finish his first and start another. As he swallowed the fiery liquid the unwavering gaze of the huntress fixed upon him, her unmoving lips formed into an unreadable expression. His head started to swim and he suddenly became aware that Sir Paul was speaking.

'...that I might be able to put in a good word and look to expand this idea across the board. A British Railways detective department covering all regions. Sounds like a winner, don't you think?' The baronet was in full flow, his rich, mellifluous voice was so easy on the ear that Badger was finding it hard to keep a hold on reality. 'Let's be frank, there could be enticing prospects for the right man. I know you share my thoughts on this matter, Ronald.'

'Indeed.' Sir Ronald made a point of brushing a sleeve of his immaculate uniform, tailored from cloth of superior quality, the gold and brass of his buttons, the heavy braiding and the medal ribbon on his chest glinting in the faint glow from the house. 'I am inclined to agree that a case could perhaps be made to expand your remit. It would be quite a little empire.' He risked raising an eyebrow to emphasise the point.

'The man in charge would be a heavy hitter in the policing world.' He raised his glass and gave Badger a steely look that was hard to fathom.

Badger gulped, seeking air like the koi carp that moved below the inky water. He swallowed more cognac. 'That would be bloody marvellous!' Realising that the alcohol had allowed the emergence of an expletive, Badger pulled himself back under control. 'That is, I would certainly be interested and would be grateful for such an opportunity.' He averted his eyes, feeling a flush of excitement and meeting the reflection of the stone Diana in the still pond water.

Through the corner of his eye Badger caught an unspoken exchange between his two companions and a slight nod from the baronet appeared to prompt the AC to continue.

'One of the benefits is that one could ensure a proper level of inter-service cooperation between the railways and Scotland Yard on the trickier matters. The transport police do a splendid job, of course, on the daily grind of keeping law and order, but we both know there is a world of a difference between the decent copper pounding the beat and the acute antennae of a detective and the particular abilities of Special Branch.'

Badger nodded sagely.

'With the railway infiltrating London from all directions, it cuts deep into our territory and is a perfect conduit for the hardened criminal. The level of serious crime involving use of the railways is on the increase and we must ensure that Scotland Yard and the British Transport Commission work in harmony to combat this crime wave.'

'Quite so, Sir Ronald.' Badger rose onto his toes again, but swayed sideways as if aboard a ship. He dropped back on his heels rather too quickly, made his back ramrod straight and took a deep breath, adopting his practised stance of the parade ground sergeant major. The brandy and the giddying attention being paid him were taking effect.

Sir Ronald gave an indulgent half smile. 'However, as in all things, striking the correct balance is so important and it can be a ticklish job to achieve a happy medium. It's all too easy to let one's enthusiasm run away with one.'

Badger looked into Sir Ronald's grey eyes, sensing a sudden shift in mood, but the assistant commissioner's were giving nothing away. He had absolutely no idea what the man was angling at.

'You have a chap in your department by the name of Grenobles, er, Vignobles?' asked Sir Paul.

'DI Charles Vignoles?' Badger felt as though he had been pushed face first into one of the icy ponds.

'Odd name. French Huguenot, I suppose.' Sir Ronald considered the matter a moment as if he were interested. 'He's a decent detective?'

'Excellent.' Badger marshalled all his reserves of self control and met the AC's gaze.

'Splendid. An effective detective is so hard to find, one should ensure his time is used profitably. You should keep him away from all those distractions and low-level affairs a junior officer could handle.'

'Those dead end cases going nowhere, eh?' Sir Paul drained his glass and laughed. He glanced at his watch, a flicker of impatience crossing his brow.

'I appreciate that liaising with Scotland Yard will have a certain appeal for a provincial. The glamour of the Big Smoke and working with men at the top of their game is undeniable. However —'

What has that bloody fool Vignoles done now? This must have something to do with whatever it was he telephoned about. Blast! I should have listened more carefully! Badger desperately tried to recall the hurried conversation.

'—One must remain focussed at all times,' Badger blurted out, 'I drum this into my men constantly.'

Sir Ronald inclined his head indulgently. 'I don't doubt it. However, as I was about to explain before you interrupted,' the rebuke stung Badger as if the arrow from the sculpted Diana had now been loosed and let fly into his chest, 'I fear he may have become a little overzealous in his desire to assist one of our chaps.' The assistant commissioner made an indulgent gesture with a hand. 'From information I saw today, it would appear they have got themselves into a bit of flap over nothing. In the heat of the moment one of my men transferred the whole case over to yours. One can appreciate the frisson of collaboration is a pleasant diversion for your Inspector Grenobles, but you and I have a duty to take a more dispassionate view, ensuring our men concentrate on cases equal to their rank, not dabbling in trifling matters.'

'Quite so, Sir Ronald.' Badger emptied his glass whilst inwardly screaming blue murder at Vignoles. He remembered what it was now; some foolish story about a suicide. Had he not told Vignoles it sounded like a complete waste of time? Now he had the embarrassment of the AC upbraiding him in a most humiliating manner.

Still, there had been a lot of encouraging talk before this hammer blow, and he would take heed. These men had obviously not stage-managed this 'unexpected' conversation in the garden for nothing, and Badger knew if he tightened up his act and pulled Vignoles into line he could recover the situation.

'So, are we agreed, gentlemen? Excellent!' Sir Paul beamed.

'I shall have my secretary call you; we can continue this conversation over lunch at my club tomorrow.' Sir Ronald looked at Badger, who was lost for words.

Sir Paul then spoke. 'This really was most useful, glad I had the chance to get the two of you talking — but, gosh, I'd better scoot. The firework display is set to start, and one must be there to kick off the proceedings.'

The conversation drifted into a gentle winding down whilst the baronet gently but firmly guided them up the dank steps and towards the chatter of the ballroom.

Badger found time to wonder at Sir Paul's sudden mood swings and his decision to seek him out just minutes after receiving what appeared to be worrying news in the estate office. The two events appeared connected — certainly by proximity of time. However, such thoughts were quickly overtaken by the thought of lunch with Sir Ronald at his club. Gosh, he'd struck gold tonight.

He spotted Joyce walking slowly towards him, her expression one of quiet pride and the manner in which she touched her hair and gave little glances around the room communicated without words how much she had enjoyed her time with the assistant commissioner's wife.

Badger swiped a glass of red wine from a passing tray in a waiter's hand and drank it down heartily. Why worry? He had probably got the wrong end of the stick. If he played his cards right, he might be hobnobbing with the likes of ACs and baronets on a daily basis.

Chapter Twenty-one

NOTHING BUT TROUBLE
Bob Wills and his Texas Playboys

Whilst Vignoles lay unconscious, Badger was drinking himself towards a hangover and Eddie was romancing Laura, Simon walked with his head hunched low towards the railway embankment that lay across the road in a massive rampart of earth and grass like an ancient Neolithic earthwork and not a Victorian construction of a little over fifty years in age. The impenetrable black of this great slab of earth made the night sky appear pale in contrast, lightened by a moon veiled with a thin gauze of bonfire smoke. Where sky and embankment met, life appeared in a twinkling necklace of red and green signal lights and the cheery glow from the signal cabin and station buildings perched above the road.

He needed to get on top of the embankment, head away from the station and cross the tracks into the 'old down yard' that lay just beyond. The signalbox posed a problem, however, as this guarded the yard entrance and the signalman (assuming he was doing his job properly) would be keeping an eye on the approach lines, alert to the movements of the pilot engine that was still chuffing about the yard. Simon knew he could not risk crossing the running lines close to the box, as he would surely be noticed. Walking around the yard, whilst perhaps provoking a raised an eyebrow if he encountered one of the men working there, would not cause too much surprise and he could easily invent some daft excuse that would suffice, but crossing the busy main line at an unapproved point would be impossible to justify and only serve to attract attention, as well as a severe reprimand.

He walked beneath the twin railway bridges, past the passenger entrance set between the arches with its steep steps leading to the island platform above and onto Station Road. The White Hart Hotel lay to the right, beside the sweeping incline of the station access road and the rows of allotment gardens with their ramshackle collection of sheds and the silhouettes of beanpole wigwams. On the opposite side was a small, single-storey garage with the shapes of two pre-war vintage cars parked outside with 'for sale' cards in their windows and a long row of shops climbing uphill, though now all were in darkness, their canvas awnings pleated back against the walls.

Simon knew there was a narrow road to the rear of the garage that gave access to the lengthy gardens behind the row of shops. He and Eddie had once had a memorable experience hiding some forged banknotes in an air raid shelter down there, and he was familiar with the layout. He needed to be, for there were no street lamps and the infrequently-used road was heavily overgrown with weeds, nettles and stiff brambles with spiny fingers encroaching on either side.

He remembered that at the end of the road he would come to a concrete gulley that allowed the narrow River Cherwell to flow beneath the embankment, and at this point there was the barest trace of a route, not much more than a sheep track, up the steep, grassy slope to the yard. The path was not worn by the passage of cloven hoofs, however, but by maintenance gangs on their inspections to ensure the river was flowing freely. Eddie and he had followed the path on numerous occasions when they were young lads as a means of observing the train movements within the yard.

Simon moved quickly, safe in the knowledge that almost the whole village was presently transfixed by the shower of rockets and whizz-bangs exploding in the sky behind him. Even the men working the yard would be distracted by this noisy diversion.

Clawing his way up the bank of bleached autumn grass, he could soon see the outline of the lines of wagons in the yard. It looked full, and he could hear, though not see, the yard shunting engine clattering wagons and the occasional whistle or call by one of the men working alongside. Other than this, everywhere was very still. He bent low and tried to peer beneath the wagons, but the inky darkness was impenetrable.

He hunkered down on his haunches and lit a cigarette.

What am I doing creeping about like a cat burglar? He took a deep lungful of smoke. He was part of this railway, part of this village. All his friends, family and workmates were near to hand, and yet here he was, sneaking around prepared to commit an act of... of *what*, exactly? Tampering with railway property? Conspiracy to steal? Sabotage?

Closing his eyes, he tried to calm the headache building in his temples. The sounds and smells of the railway were comforting. He could sit on a station platform or on a bench by the side of the engine shed and happily soak up the atmosphere at any time of day or night. An hour or two beside the racks, peering through a fence or sunning himself on Charwelton station whilst nothing much happened was luxury for him. It cost nothing, and needed no annoying points or coupons either. The government couldn't ration the all-pervading stink of oil, the reek of creosote on hot sleepers, the taste of coal smoke or the squeal and clatter of shunted trucks and the bells from the signalbox followed by the whirr and twang of the signal wires or the toot of a whistle.

He wished Eddie was here, and that they could stop their squabbling and just take down some locomotive numbers and play silly betting games for sticks of precious chewing gum on what type of locomotive was approaching, judged only by its sound alone; talking about girls and swigging beer and having a smoke. Times past, they would be sitting here, high above the village, discussing their latest mystery and plotting and planning how they could find out more.

Simon groaned out aloud and opened his eyes.

The drowned man!

Like a bucket of ice-water tipped over his head, he was rudely pulled back from his reverie into the harsh reality of the here and now. He felt an icy chill run through his body and a sickening feeling of apprehension as he thought of Dennis. The way he had become so angry and worked up about the police and the dead man had been terrifying. It had played on Simon's mind ever since he had been released from the confines of the firebox and the fearfulness made him feel far worse than the many physical aches and pains wracking his body.

There were so many dark and concealed areas all about and the few yard lamps offered only a poor light. Dennis could be watching and waiting. Ready to reach out and grab him by the throat or maybe smash an iron bar onto his skull at any moment.

No matter how hard he tried, Simon could not shake off the stomach-churning suspicion that Dennis had killed the man in the Regent's Canal. If that was the case, he'd had an actual murderer's hands around his neck. Simon felt his palms become clammy. His very life may now depend on his doing whatever these men demanded — what if he failed? Perhaps that was why Pym was dead.

The lyrics of a popular song that was being played regularly on the wireless came into his head. 'Nothing but trouble...' Dennis and his chums had been 'nothing but trouble' ever since he'd fallen in with them. The song refrain refused to go away and was like a warning siren.

He pulled the replacement bill of loading cards from his pocket and turned them over in his hands, his brow furrowed in thought. He placed them on the ground and smoked silently for a few moments, still hunkered down, trying to steady his nerves. He really should walk the lines and find the container wagons, make the switch then get away from here as fast as he could. Yes, he would do what the London gang asked, do it well, and win their approval. He would prove he was reliable, loyal and trustworthy and that Dennis had nothing to fear. And no one in Woodford would ever suspect him. He'd be back at the bonfire party in under half an hour, drink another beer or two, find Eddie, and life would go back to normal.

Nothing but trouble...

Except it wouldn't.

What was 'normal' about being forever on tenterhooks, looking over his shoulder, half-expecting to be challenged or bludgeoned at any moment as he walked down a dark alley or ducked into a firebox hole? This feeling of apprehension was going to hang around, grow stronger and dog his every step. It was inescapable. It was not just the threat of the thug Dennis that lay heavy on him. He'll have actively taken part in something illegal, and once he switched these cards he was part of it and could not plead ignorance nor put it down to a moment of poor judgement. He would be guilty.

Simon picked up the cards and started to walk, his boots crunching and trouser bottoms swishing through the weeds and grasses of the embankment top. His limbs felt heavy and his energy seemed to be draining away through his boot soles. He stopped. There had been another sound, of footsteps walking almost in time with his. He listened, but the fizzes, bangs and whooshes of rockets were all he could identify. Whoever was following him had stopped at precisely the same moment. Or had he just imagined it?

There was a gap in the line of wagons where one group was separated from another, so Simon stepped between them and crouched down low in the inky shadows cast by the moon, careful to keep his head clear of the buffer beam. If the yard locomotive suddenly shunted these wagons he wouldn't stand a chance.

He listened and waited. There was a call, a whistle and a deep, resonant clunk, followed by a chatter of buffer touching buffer and a long line of wagons that lay opposite shifted and rattled as the yard pilot engine coupled up. A lamp beam flashed on the ground some distance away. Another shout sounded from deep in the yard with an answering toot on the locomotive whistle, then the wagons across the way slowly groaned into motion. This was a dangerous place to be at night, especially as the men working the yard were unaware of his presence, but Simon stayed where he was, confident it would be some minutes yet before the engine could turn its attention to the line of vans concealing him.

Hearing one of the shunters approach, he stood up. His mouth was dry and clammy. Stepping away from the vans he walked, peering at each wagon as he did so and keeping pace with the rolling train of wagons on his left and listening to the track creak and groan beneath the weight of each wheel as it passed over the track joints and an axle box squealing for lack of oil. He varied his pace before suddenly stopping and spinning around, hoping to catch his shadow by surprise.

What was that? His imagination playing tricks again? No, something had moved! The darkness seemed to form shapes that moved before his eyes. He took a few deep breaths to try and calm his nerves and stared. A head with a long snout and pricked-up ears peeked out from below a wagon and stared back at him for a moment, and then a large fox trotted across the yard and was gone. Simon almost laughed out loud with sheer relief.

As the line of wagons pulled away, the moon was also unmasked and another row of wagons was revealed, perfectly illuminated. Amongst this motley mix of wooden box-vans and tarpaulin-covered open trucks were his targets: three bauxite-coloured wooden containers on their little four-wheeled flat wagons.

Simon felt a jolt of excitement. There was something thrilling about seeing them sitting there, as promised. This was not some wild goose chase after all, but part of a complex operation and he was to play his part in it. They were just three containers, and quite unremarkable, and yet they had the power to compel him to cross the tracks in a run. His fear had evaporated. This was *it*!

Nothing but trouble... Would the words of that damned song ever stop flashing into his mind? It was driving him mad!

The moon passed behind a thick bank of cloud again and darkness rapidly washed over everything, reminding Simon how rash he had been in crossing the tracks in such a brazen manner. He looked around but all he could see was a lamp beam swinging in the far distance near a pale, incandescent puff of steam from the engine.

He pulled the nearest bill of loading card from the spring-loaded metal frame and peered at it, biting his lower lip. His brief rush of excitement was extinguished when it came to actually doing the deed and his hand shook.

Something was wrong. This was a set up, and he had been stupid enough to fall for it. Dennis could easily have switched the cards himself! He'd travelled all the way from London, so why get Simon to do this job and risk trusting someone he hardly knew? No, Dennis had lured him there, and he, like a dumb fool, had walked right into the trap. He was never going to be rewarded for this — since when did gangsters throw their money around? They never did in the Cagney films he watched at the Savoy cinema. It was ludicrous to believe these tough Londoners were going to be pally with him, and he, like a proper chump, had lapped it up. A mixture of greed and bullying had brought him here. He was expendable. He was nothing to them. *Well, I'm in a fine old mess. Stay here and get killed, or do something to try to save myself? Nothing to lose now!*

The shunting engine halted and the clinking of coupling chains followed. The men were getting on with their work. It was just another mundane evening for them and they were probably wishing they could knock off, have a pint and watch the fireworks. Simple pleasures, but to Simon they were now something to be craved. He might never get a chance to sup a pint with Eddie again. *Damn and blast those men! Why, oh why, did I get in with them?*

Acting on impulse, he suddenly ripped the cards from the holders on the other two wagons and swapped them for three cards on adjacent wagons. He was not sure why he did this, but he knew it would mess things up for a day or so. He then sprinted back between the wagons on the outside edge of the yard. Breathing heavily, he tore the cards given him by Dennis into quarters and tossed the pieces under the nearest wagon. *Go to hell!*

It was too late to change his mind and Simon was determined not to be dragged any further into this life of crime. If Dennis were really after him, then he'd go down fighting and attempt to salvage some pride in so doing. But he was living on a knife-edge now, and time was short.

Where could he go? Not home; Dennis would easily find him there, and besides, Simon could not drag his poor parents into this vile, stinking mess. No, he was going to have to live on his wits until he could find some hard proof that might convince the police of what Dennis had confessed. If he helped them nab a murderer, they might forgive his sins — if he lived long enough.

Simon peered at his wristwatch and screwed his face up in concentration. The late train to London was due in twenty minutes. It was risky to head deep into 'enemy' territory, but they would not expect him to do that, and besides, if he was going to find something to nail on Dennis, it was going to be in London.

He jogged towards the place where the little trampled pathway dropped down to the Cherwell, and half threw himself down it, eager to get away as fast has he could. He slid over the grass, found his footing again and ran full tilt along the tarmac surface of the road, paying no heed of the encroaching vegetation — and smacked hard into someone blocking in his path.

He heard a sharp exhalation of air.

'Ouch! Watch it!'

'Eddie! What are you doing here?' Simon felt a wave of anger rise inside. Eddie shouldn't be mixed up in this.

'Is something wrong, Si?'

'No! Just get out of my way!' Simon lunged at Eddie, pushing him into a tall tangle of briars and causing his friend's new hat to fly off backwards and catch on a tall frond, where it bounced on the end in a faintly ludicrous manner.

'You stupid oaf, I'm stuck on the thorns…'

'Just leave me alone!' Simon shouted at his friend, but as he turned to run, he was pulled up short yet again.

'Not so fast, Simon Howerth!' Laura Green, arms akimbo, stood blocking his way. 'Is that how you thank your friends for showing concern?' She glared at him, furious and not in the least intimidated.

Simon looked thoroughly confused. 'I didn't ask for your help.'

'Maybe not, but you look as though you need it.'

'I can't explain right now. Just don't get involved, that's all!' Simon looked at Laura then at Eddie, who had extricated himself from the briar and had a very black look on his face. 'Forget you saw me here — it's important. I have to go—go away for a day. Eddie, tell my mum and dad not to worry!' Simon eased Laura aside with a strong hand on her shoulder and barged past, sprinting into the dark. 'I hope I can explain one day…'

'That's not the Simon I know.' Eddie said to Laura, staring down the overgrown road. They looked up at the dark mass of the embankment and the blocks of wagons, just discernable against the night sky filled with bonfire smoke.

'Leave him to sort out his own business.' Laura, affronted at Simon's rudely thrusting her aside, folded her arms and looked down the dark lane towards Station Road. Edward was desperately trying to retrieve his hat. This was inadvertently a blessing, as Laura started to laugh at the comic scene of Eddie repeatedly leaping up to reach for it, only for his hat to evade his grasp and bob up and away on the thick and elastic wand of thorny briar.

Her mood softened. 'Of course, we were following Simon and not everyone appreciates being followed. I know I wouldn't.' She glanced around at the dark bulk of the embankment and the silent house backs.

'Got it! No damage done.' Edward was peering at his hat.

'What do you think happened up there?'

Eddie looked up at the towering embankment. 'Something scared him. And I think we alarmed him even more and he just lashed out, in surprise, not really in anger.'

They exchanged looks.

'I really should walk you home now. There's no point in standing here.'

'Yes. Please do.' Laura Laura shivered as though suddenly feeling cold.

Everything was black and he felt as though he were on board a small boat that was rocking gently; a sensation that might have induced a deep sleep — something he dearly craved — but unfortunately someone would insist upon repeatedly thumping the back of his head, and that was decidedly unpleasant. His nose was flattened against a smooth and cold floor and, whilst uncomfortable, the coolness was at least soothing and offered a little succour to his pounding skull.

After a few moments more of head beating and boat rocking, he made a small, exploratory lift of his head, only to immediately relax again, this time with one cheek flat to the linoleum, taking the pressure off his nose. Stars burst in his eyes and a wave of nausea overtook him as the boat appeared to be hit by a series of far bigger waves, the floor rolling horribly. He lay still and breathed deeply for a long time until the seasickness passed. He could smell and taste blood.

Vignoles kept his head completely still and turned his attention to wiggling the fingers on each hand and, when satisfied that all appeared in order, turned his attention to flexing his toes. This was promising. Cautiously he tried easing his arms and torso into a different position. Everything seemed to work, and this realisation made the pain in his head a touch less alarming. At least he was in one piece and definitely alive. There were no ropes restraining him and as far as he could tell he was still in the office inside the empty warehouse.

He would have to risk sitting upright. It was a horrible experience and the sloe-black darkness served to emphasise the swimming colours behind his eyes, but at last he was able to lean against a wall and start to get the circulation back into his cold limbs, breathing in short gasps through his mouth because his nose was aching and blocked by dried blood. His palms were sweating, despite the acute cold. After a few minutes he was ready for the next stage, and leaning forwards until his groping hands found the edge of the desk he hauled himself upright, then rested on it heavily, leaning over with his head drooping low. After a few breaths he felt for the desk lamp and turned it on.

He paused. Tense and fearful, his breath forming pale clouds from his mouth, knowing the light would surely alert his attacker. But nothing happened. Perhaps his assailant had thought he was dead — an impression no doubt aided by the dramatic pool of blood on the floor that had flowed copiously from his bashed nose. He looked at his watch. Nearly ten o'clock. He had been unconscious for a few hours.

Feeling annoyed with himself for allowing someone to get close enough to assault him, Vignoles looked at his shirt and tie, now stained a deep brownish-red. They were a write-off, but perhaps his trusty old greatcoat could be saved, although he was not sure, and gloomily brushed at the damp stains down the front in a futile gesture.

He had made a basic error in assuming there was not a third man lurking inside. Clearly these men had a big secret and were prepared to take violent action to protect it.

Vignoles had a desultory scout about the muddled and disordered office for a few moments in the vain hope of finding something of interest, but the pain in his head and nose made bending down a nauseating experience.

What was that?

He stood stock still and listened.

Voices...

He turned off the lamp. As his fear-induced adrenaline kicked in and took the edge off his pain he moved swiftly to the office door and slipped into the echoing expanse of warehouse. He had no wish to be cornered a second time. There were a number of people outside, all talking at the same time — and none too quietly. Clearly stealth was not on their agenda. He stayed tight to the walls, edging towards the sliding door that was pulled closed and muffling the sound, though the voices were getting louder.

'This is it!'

Was that Trinder's voice? Vignoles pulled up short.

'Give me a hand with this door!'

Good Lord, it really is Trinder! Vignoles gave a slight shake of his head in disbelief and immediately regretted doing so.

'Perhaps there's someone inside. We should be careful!'

Hell's bells, surely that was not Anna?

'They'll jolly well answer to me if they are! It's unlocked...'

Vignoles stepped into the expanding pool of moonlight that flooded across the dusty concrete floor as the door rolled back and the elongated shadows of his sergeant and two other figures animated the cool blue rectangle like a shadow puppet show.

'Anna! Good grief! What on earth brings *you* here?'

'Charles!' She ran forwards and, to his immense surprise, threw her arms around his neck as she kissed him in a immoderate and unrestrained manner. 'Oh, my darling! Are you hurt? What happened? So much blood! Oh, you poor thing! You were gone so long, we were so worried. What happened?'

'Ouch! Stop!' Vignoles gently eased Anna's arms away from the back of his head, her enthusiastic embrace unfortunately restarting the sickening pounding on his skull. 'I took a blow to the head. Quite a smash.' He looked pale.

'Oh, my poor love… sit down.' She steered him towards an empty packing case. 'You need a doctor. Could someone *please* call for urgent help?'

'Anna, please! No need for all the fuss. An aspirin will do the trick. The blood is from banging my nose on the floor, it looks worse than it is.'

'Did you see who did this to you, sir?' Trinder was inspecting a board of Bakelite switches on the wall. He selected one and flooded the room with light.

Vignoles winced in reaction, and promptly sat down on the packing case.

'You look terribly pale!' Anna was fussing around, 'and your poor head needs attention. A cold compress, iodine and a bandage and plenty of rest is what you need, at the very least.'

'Don't touch!' Vignoles winced, 'It's a bit sore…'

'I always carry a few painkillers in my handbag and we have some hot, sweet tea in the flask.' Violet Trinder was rootling within a small and elegant handbag as she spoke.

Anna was soon offering two small, white pills. Vignoles took them from her whilst she unscrewed the metal cap on a thermos flask into which she poured some tea. He swallowed the pills and, whilst he was not normally a tea drinker, the hot, sweet liquid was exactly what he needed. He drank it thirstily.

'We need to get you to hospital,' Anna stated firmly.

'I hardly think that necessary. Now, in answer to your question, John, I didn't see who did it, but I did get a good view of two men busy burning what I presume are records in a brazier.'

'I saw that. It was still smouldering.'

'It could have been either of those or a third waiting inside. Either way, they surprised me.' Vignoles made a face as he confessed his mistake. 'Dammed foolish on my part.'

Anna glared at him.

Vignoles peered at his wristwatch. 'I may have been out cold for some time.'

'You might have concussion.' Violet said, looking worried. 'Is your nose broken?'

'Can you see straight?' Anna was giving her husband a searching look, bending at the waist and trying to peer into his eyes.

'Enough questions! I'm quite all right.' He looked white as a sheet. 'But what on earth brings you all here?'

'Good timing and a jolly big dose of luck!' Violet grinned.

Anna disagreed. '*Bad* timing would be more accurate.'

'We left it late to come to your rescue, but we were in a quandary about what was best,' explained Trinder.

'It's a hard place to find,' observed Violet.

'Quite possibly deliberately so.'

Trinder was using the points of his shiny shoes to probe scraps of paper and other abandoned detritus on the warehouse floor as he explained, 'Violet and myself were planning to head into Leicester. We have tickets for a show tonight, and—'

'—and then I spoiled your evening.' Vignoles now noticed that Trinder and his wife were dressed in evening clothes beneath their warm topcoats, Violet wearing expensive-looking shoes with a hint of maroon dress visible beneath her flared coat hem, and Trinder looking very dapper with a black dickie-bow at his collar and highly-polished patent leather shoes that he seemed determined to cover in concrete dust.

'Think nothing of it, sir. On the way I just put my head around the office door to see if there was anything Blencowe needed, and was surprised to find Mrs Vignoles in the office enquiring after your whereabouts.'

'And no one had seen or heard from you for hours,' Anna added, with a steely edge to her voice.

'Blencowe said you'd gone to Loughborough, and I got a feeling something was wrong, so I decided to come and find you. I told both ladies to go home, but they would have none of it, and, well, truth is, I was outnumbered.' Trinder threw a brief, accusatory glance at each woman.

'What possessed you to go on a foolish jaunt like this on your own? It was quite irresponsible!' Anna had evidently decided her husband had recovered sufficiently to receive a scolding.

'I planned to just have a quiet look around. It was never my intention to encounter anyone.'

'We're a jolly funny rescue party, equipped with a flask of sweet tea, a couple of torches, an evening gown and a pair of tickets for *High Time*!' added Violet, though with a playful smile, apparently in high spirits and not in the least put out by their change of plan.

'Even if you won't see a doctor I must get you home and make you rest.' Anna stood upright, looking determined and in no mood for dissent.

Vignoles got to his feet and walked towards the open door, then stopped abruptly. 'Well, I never! They've gone. The siding is empty!'

Trinder stood beside Vignoles. 'What's gone?'

Vignoles explained about the three container wagons. 'That could explain why they whacked me on the head. They needed to lay me out whilst they hauled the containers away.' He looked thoughtful. 'Now, where's my pipe? I need to think about this.' He patted his coat pocket then grinned as he brought it out, safe and unmarked. 'I wonder what happed to my hat? I was in the little office back there...'

'I'll go and look,' answered Violet.

'Do you think the contents of the warehouse were placed inside the containers?' asked Trinder.

'Seems likely. When I visited the first time, the place was full of boxes and they must have stowed them somewhere. Jordan's appear to operate by re-labelling all manner of stock for re-sale and not very much else, from what I could see. The container wagons were to be conveyed to Marylebone goods depot.' Vignoles was filling his pipe, enjoying the sweet smell of the tobacco cutting through the sickly iron tang of old blood.

'I've found your hat!' Violet called cheerfully from across the open floor of the warehouse, waving it above her head. 'It's a little dusty.'

'Thanks.' Vignoles nodded gratefully, then immediately looked back at his sergeant. 'How did you get on at Hendon?'

'A blank,' Trinder replied. 'Bish and Frobisher were not there. However, we may have found the drinking den at Marylebone in an abandoned iron founders adjacent to the yard. It was locked shut, but the constables found one plucky chap prepared to admit that some of the men are invited there of an evening. He thinks black marketeering takes place in there. It could also be a possible location for the attack on Pym as it is not far from that chute leading into the canal. We could get a warrant to force an entry. But sir, do you remember that article I showed you, about the long fraud?'

'I do indeed.'

'It's got me thinking about all this. I'm just wondering if Jordan's are part of something similar.'

Vignoles nodded and grinned. 'Great minds think alike. I've been trying to puzzle out how such an idea might fit what we know about this case, and—'

'—all that can wait!' interrupted Anna, placing her hand on her husband's arm. 'We should get out of this horrid place, it's giving me the jitters. And do stop talking, Charles. You really need to rest.' She ushered both her husband and Trinder along the loading bay platform towards the steps, whilst Violet switched off the lights. Trinder heaved the door into motion on its oiled runners so that it closed with a boom.

'I want you to take it easy until tomorrow, at the very least' insisted Anna.

'I can't; this is too urgent.' But Vignoles yawned as he replied, suddenly feeling tiredness roll over him like a wave. 'We must... we must talk.... Important...' His voice was losing some of its usual energy.

'Shh! I'm putting my foot down.' Anna shot Trinder a stern look that stopped him short just as he was about to speak. He closed his mouth and remained silent.

The air was pungent with the smell of bonfires and spent fireworks and opaque with the soft haziness of smoke as they walked in silence towards the station. Vignoles, blood-stained, tieless and dishevelled, was puffing reflectively upon his pipe, hat balanced upon his throbbing head.

Ten minutes later they were warming themselves at the pretty cast iron fire place in the general waiting room at Loughborough Central, each holding a cup of Vimalto, generously supplied by the friendly porter, whilst they awaited the arrival of the York to Swindon express that would take the Vignoleses to Leicester and the Trinders to Woodford Halse. Vignoles regained some of his colour as a plate of Rich Tea biscuits did another round, but, as he held a second biscuit in his hand, his eyes suddenly felt very heavy and his head slumped forward, hat tipping low over his brow. Anna gently rescued his drink before it spilled. He was asleep.

'Knowing Charles, he will absolutely insist upon meeting tomorrow. There's really no point in my trying to stop him, but can we at least agree that you two, Jane and Lucy will come to our house for a late lunch? That will be far less tiring for him than going to the station.'

'We'd be delighted.' Trinder had experienced Anna's hospitality before and knew better than to refuse. Her parents owned Carelli's Italian Ice Cream Parlour in Leicester and always seemed to be able to obtain wonderful food that everyone else could only dream of finding.

'I have a freshly baked fruit cake and a couple of jars of bottled damsons I can bring,' added Violet, her cheeks flushed with a rosy glow from the evening's excitement.

Chapter Twenty-Two

APPETITE BLUES
The Big Three Trio

It was raining hard in Leicestershire. Pale curtains of water crossed the zinc-grey sky and battered the windowpanes with a sound like tossed rice grains, lending a cosy feel to those squeezed companionably around the dining table in the Vignoles's modest semi that lay but a short walk from Belgrave and Birstall station.

The invitation to lunch had been gratefully received by the two WPCs and extended to include the apparently tireless PC Blencowe, who had gamely manned the office until the early hours of the morning, awaiting the safe return of the rescue party.

The consensus was that hunger, combined with the fine spread of food that Anna had somehow managed to rustle up despite the endless privation of rationing, demanded their full concentration, allowing room only for light-hearted chit-chat about the weather ('the rain will at least clear the awful smog in London'); the recent changes to the points system; the latest dress patterns ('I've just got hold of a simply *divine* design, exactly like Princess Margaret was wearing'); and thoughts about yesterday's football results, ('that Stan Cullis is a terrific player for Wolves'). The conversation veered briefly into darker territory when Vignoles, seated at the far end of the table, shoe-horned into a narrow space between the window and a bookcase, and wearing around his head a theatrically bold white bandage holding a compress, mentioned the deteriorating relations between East and West over the 'Berlin question', but, fortunately, fears of an impending Third World War were instantly repelled by the timely appearance of Mrs Trinder's promised damsons presented in a variety of small glass dishes with great scoops of Bepe Carelli's vanilla ice cream topped with multi-coloured hundreds and thousands. The vanilla was, they unanimously agreed, 'back to its best.'

With a pot of coffee oozing a delicious aroma and the prized wireless, now restored to working order, gently playing the Light Programme in the background, the conversation finally turned to serious matters.

'Where shall we start?' asked Vignoles, rhetorically. The informal atmosphere prompted him to use his staff's forenames: 'Thanks to Lucy and Jane, we strongly suspect that Adeline Pym and Terence Wilde conspired to have Pym killed. However, their conversation in the pub implied that their hired hitman did not do the deed. We asked the city police to find their would-be assassin, and once questioned I will not be surprised to discover that he, like the two lovers, has a strong alibi for the night in question. Pym died because of the actions of at least two other people and for reasons unrelated to his wife's affair.'

Everyone looked grim, but there were no dissenting voices.

Vignoles reached into the bookcase and extracted two small pieces of paper he had placed on top of a row of books. 'I found this under Pym's desk blotter in his office off the New Walk.' He showed everyone gathered around the table the scrap of paper. 'I do have a suspicion of who this S.P.F. might be, but I shall come to that in a moment. The implication of this note would appear to be that S.P.F. also goes under the name of Top Link.'

'A nickname?' asked Anna.

'Yes, or a code name. The top link are actually the crews of crack expresses, but I cannot imagine for one moment Pym's note is referring to Kings Cross engine drivers.'

'However, such a word used in a railway context would attract little attention if overheard, so it could be a useful cover,' observed Anna.

Vignoles agreed. 'This note was tucked out of sight and reads to me like a man making a connection in his mind.'

'Putting two and two together—' Blencowe was writing as he spoke.

'—and reaching a deadly deduction.' Vignoles raised an eyebrow to emphasise the point. 'Last night at Jordan's, shortly before being knocked silly, I pocketed this.' Vignoles placed the opened-out envelope on the table. 'We all reuse envelopes for making rough notes without sparing a thought for the address on the other side, and that's exactly what Bish has done here. I think this is might be one of those details that helps turn a case.' Vignoles puffed on his pipe as they paused to digest this statement. 'Bish was listing sums of substantial amounts of money and products, probably tallying up the takings of their illegal trade.' He pointed with the stem of his pipe. 'But perhaps more significant is that Bish has pencilled a note for "T.L. to agree". Quite what he is to agree, I don't know, but that's not out primary interest at this juncture.'

'And "T.L." is Top link?' Trinder grinned.

'I think so. We now have references to Top Link written by both Pym and Bish, which establishes a strong connection *and* is a step away from their professional relationship.' Vignoles turned the envelope over to reveal a name and address that astonished the others.

'Sir Paul Frobisher, baronet.' Benson read aloud.

'A London address, near Lord's... and close to Marylebone,' added Lansdowne.

'S.P.F!' Violet chimed in.

'The man who, with Henry Bish, set up Hendon Pharmaceuticals, the source of the pills that helped to kill Pym,' Blencowe underlined his notes to that effect with a flourish. 'He is the link. The top of the tree?'

'Agreed. Perhaps he is also the so-far-invisible Mr Jordan of the Loughborough operation. I think he is the man masterminding the whole operation.'

'An underworld gangster! But just like Al Capone he's a prominent and powerful businessman.' Trinder's voice was excited.

'I'm thinking this way. Our task now is to prove it. We need to uncover exactly what he and Bish are up to, and find a way to get to them.' Vignoles sat back in his chair and looked around the table.

'Who is Sir Paul Frobisher?'

'I checked *Debrett's Peerage & Baronetage* this morning and the darned fellow is not even listed,' answered Vignoles. 'It is the 1939 edition, but even so, not a squeak. Nouveau riche, I would guess. A wealthy social climber who has bought himself a title, perhaps. We've seen a lot of people muscling in like this since the war, opportunists to a man and just the type who might run a complex racket that turns a tidy, and very illegal, profit.'

'We need to run more checks on this fellow, sir,' observed Blencowe. 'Perhaps we can rope in some of the civvies to lend a hand on the paperwork.'

'Agreed. Chase up every angle.'

'This sounds like we're really on to something.' Lansdowne was impressed.

'It's no more than a start. We are a long way from proving that Bish and the baronet killed Pym.'

'What do you think these two men are up to?' asked Anna.

Trinder picked up the thread. 'Sir Paul is the head of a gang and Bish was overseeing the Jordan warehouse, which is now empty, abandoned at short notice following your visit which, I presume, must have spooked them.' Vignoles nodded agreement. 'Perhaps this was only a temporary set up. Perhaps Bish ran a few other such operations located elsewhere.'

'And don't forget the iron founders in Marylebone.' Blencowe looked up from his notes. 'From what the constables reported, that sounds like it could have been filled with knocked off stuff.'

'You're right! So we have warehouses at both ends of the line, stuffed full of stolen goods. They're constantly buying in and sending out... and re-labelling and re-packaging, you said.' Trinder was counting off the elements on each finger as he spoke.

'Go on, sergeant...' Vignoles urged Trinder on. 'I sensed last night you were on to this.'

'They shipped out stock from Loughborough to London and carefully contrived to have this robbed at Marylebone by their own men!' Trinder grinned. 'Remember that obnoxious union rep. down there? I just knew he and his pair of gorillas were up to something. By heck, it's starting to add up. Pym is in their pocket, taking a percentage, to ensure that nobody asks awkward questions about the frequency of the thefts. I think we've found ourselves a long fraud!'

'I don't understand.' Lansdowne said, looking puzzled.

Trinder unfurled the dog-eared article from the *Melody Maker* and briefly summed up the case of the music retailer.

Vignoles took up the story. 'When I needed a new valve for my radiogram, my supplier told me a sorry tale of how she had been trading with Jordan's, only to see her most recent — and largest — order go missing. I think Bish and his team obtained a stock of radio valves, almost certainly by stealing them. Using this batch of valves, they set up what looks like a legitimate company offering highly competitive prices and an excellent service, the only caveat is they take payment up front and in full. Once their initial stock runs low, they move in for the sting. They urge the customer to place a huge order and pay up front, this order is then "stolen" en route. They claim the insurance on the "lost" items, with Pym's assistance, and melt away into thin air, never to be seen again. They can make money three times over, by selling stolen goods to legitimate traders, by claiming insurance on the same, and once they have "stolen" back their stock, they sell the twice-knocked-off items for cash in pubs or at the back of factories and warehouses, probably around Marylebone, using the iron founders as their store and shop. And so the story is repeated over and over again with cigarettes, nylons, chocolate, you name it, whatever they can lay their hands on, using a host of different company names.'

'They make three sets of income on one set of stolen goods. The ultimate example of capitalist exploitation.' Violet shook her head in disbelief.

'Gosh it's clever, though!' Blencowe whistled. 'And that explains why they burnt all the Jordan's records. To conceal the false company names and destroy the paper trail.'

'Needs a brilliant mind and a lot of men to make it work,' observed Anna.

'I agree. We are not looking at amateurs. This is highly organised crime with the potential to earn vast sums of money. Someone very intelligent is masterminding this operation. Frobisher could be that man.'

'Do you think Pym rumbled the connection? Worked out who was behind this and perhaps confronted Bish, foolishly thinking he could use the information to increase his earnings?' asked Trinder.

Vignoles nodded. 'That might account for the fractious, ugly encounter that Oliver overheard between them. We'll let Adeline Pym and Wilde stew a day or two longer, as we have more urgent work to do, looking into the activities of Frobisher, Bish and their gang. We urgently need to find where Mr Bish and the three container wagons are. The containers must be tracked and placed under surveillance. Anna, you may be able to help us here.'

'I'd love to. Just give me any information you have on their intended journey and I can look through the records, find who placed the order, the delivery point and contact names and addresses when I get to the goods office tomorrow. Don't worry, I won't let the other clerks know what I'm up to!'

'Excellent. They surely won't be stupid enough to stage another robbery after fleeing Loughborough, but we do need to see where they store the containers and their contents.

'John, get down to Marylebone with some uniformed officers and search that iron founder's building, and go through the parcels and goods depots like a dose of liver salts! Presumably there must be more than a few men up to no good and working for Top Link and Bish, and I would suggest that bolshie union rep. is one of the worst offenders.'

'Victor Millett.' Trinder made a face. 'Yes, he was certainly full of his own self-importance, wasn't he? Do you think he knows something about Pym's death?'

'Certainly his unwillingness to cooperate could be based on fear that we'll rumble him and his racketeering, if nothing else. Give him the works and don't be too nice about it.'

Trinder nodded, relishing the opportunity.

'We need to follow the paper trails between any businesses suffering sting operations in the manner that the radio shop experienced. There must be others out there and looking afresh at them might throw something up. And I want Jack Pym's briefcase. It still bothers me that we didn't find it.'

Vignoles and his team spent another hour making lists of things to do and angles to explore, and as they did so Violet's delicious cake was eagerly consumed. Afterwards, they allowed a sense of satisfaction to engulf the room, comfortable in the knowledge that, whilst the case was far from cracked, it was starting to show fissures and they were sure that after a week or so of hard work, they would split it wide open.

But even the best made plans have a habit of falling apart, and come Monday morning, everything was to take a very different and unexpected direction.

Chapter Twenty-three

OVERTIME
The Metronome All Stars

Things started to go wrong the moment Vignoles stepped into the police offices at Leicester Central. The telephones were jangling with that insistent tone that somehow suggested they tolled only bad news and already everyone wore harassed expressions, despite only having recently arrived at work.

Mrs Green was pulling a face that suggested she was sucking an especially sour lemon. She was gesturing from behind her typewriter with a frantically flapping hand that flashed red nails like a warning sign, demanding that Vignoles wait whilst she spoke in a conciliatory tone down the telephone. She handed him a collection of notes and glared as he made another attempt to walk away.

'...of course sir, I shall tell him right away, sir... the very moment he steps through the door, sir.... of course, sir.' She replaced the handset. 'You'd better rush down to London on the very next train: the Badger wants to see you. He was expecting you first thing.' She gave him a reproving look.

'Oh botheration! I had quite forgotten.' Vignoles pulled a face, his head still throbbing from the assault. 'He'll just have to wait. I can be there by lunchtime — at a push.'

'I'm sorry sir, but you'll want to be on the very next train. You'll understand the urgency when you read that first message.' She pointed to the pieces of paper in his hand.

Vignoles had still not looked at the notes. He'd come to work with a to-do list as long as his arm and was eager to crack on. Merely being reminded that he had to go to Marylebone had already dented his equilibrium. 'Where's Trinder?'

'He also telephoned. He has a missing person reported in Woodford Halse and will be here once he's looked into it.'

'A missing person in a tiny place like Woodford? That takes a bit of doing!' Vignoles shook his head and finally looked at the first note on the pile. 'A fatal accident in London? Oh, for crying out loud. That'll take hours. What a dratted inconvenient day to get killed.' He bit his lip as he met Mrs Green's admonishing look. 'Sorry. Poor chap. I'll go right away. Is Lansdowne here?'

'Sir?' The WPC was just passing, clutching a file to her chest.

'Did you type that report on Mrs P. and Wilde? I could do with something — *anything* — to placate an angry Badger.'

'Got it right here,' she smiled proudly.

'Splendid. They're not the main thrust of our investigation right now, but it'll serve to keep him quiet.'

'Sorry to have to report this, sir, but there's a problem with some missing goods wagons. Benson's gone to investigate. It might be relevant.'

'Are we *ever* going to get *anything* done?' Vignoles threw his hands in the air and the papers fluttered out of the slim folder Lansdowne had handed him. It was going to be one of those days.

❊   ❊   ❊   ❊

It was easy for Vignoles to find the scene of the incident. A small group of onlookers stood around smoking, chatting and staring, looking as though they wanted to help but were unsure how to. A locomotive sat on one of the loading dock lines, its crew leaning on the cab rails, also watching. If pairs of eyes merely looking got things done, the mess would be sorted in moments.

A petrol-blue ambulance was parked a discreet distance away, close to the big station turntable. The crew were seated on the tailgate with a canvas stretcher deployed beside them, awaiting the call to remove the body. A deep-maroon saloon car was parked alongside bearing a small, illuminated sign reading *Doctor*. A police patrol car was untidily slewed across the top of the steeply-inclined road that straddled the Bakerloo Line, blocking the road to all traffic, with a uniformed bobby standing sentry. There was another constable close to the crash site, who saluted and waved Vignoles through the imaginary cordon holding the curious onlookers back.

The bonnet and cab of a massive British Road Services milk tanker was crumpled and distorted into an ugly shape, wrapped as it was around the base of tall yard lamp with pale shards of glass littering the ground and glinting from the surface of an expanding pool of sump oil. Someone had thrown a dirty tarpaulin over the misshapen cab to shield the body trapped inside from inquisitive eyes.

The immediate impression was that the tanker had careered down the steep access road into the yard and failed to take the sharp turn at the bottom of the ramp, smashing into the lamp post and the back wall of the Express Dairies building that edged the railway lines at Marylebone station throat.

Had the driver lost control, or was it brake failure? Vignoles ran his hand across his face, took a deep breath and prayed that it would not take too long to wrap up this case.

A chubby man with sandy hair and a handlebar moustache was hovering about near the cab. Dressed in a Harris tweed three-piece suit, he held a doctor's case made of leather, and was talking with a man in oily overalls who was looking pale and depressed.

'Ah, you must be the inspector chappie.' The fair man stretched out his hand to meet that of Vignoles. They introduced themselves, and the doctor advised him that he'd pronounced the driver dead at 7:30. He then peered at the inspector's battered face. 'I say, you need that nose seeing to, it's dreadfully swollen, possibly broken. Quite a shiner you've got, too,' he pointed to Vignoles's black eye.

After dismissing the doctor's comments, Vignoles ascertained that the worried man in overalls was from the British Road Service maintenance garage and responsible for the safe operation of the fleet. He was concerned that he might somehow be blamed for the accident. Vignoles reassured him the police didn't jump to hasty conclusions, then turned back to the doctor.

'Shall we take a look?'

Vignoles and the BRS mechanic, assisted by the constable, pulled the tarpaulin back far enough the reveal the man beneath.

'Ugh! Poor chap,' exclaimed Vignoles.

'Rather a lot of blood, I'm afraid, which is significant.' The doctor took care to hold his suit away from the vehicle. 'Split his clean head open on the windscreen upright and the many lacerations to the face and neck are from the glass.'

The smell of blood, oil, sweaty clothes, old cigarette smoke and mildew was overpowering. The glossy, pillar-box red paint of the mangled cab seemed to emphasize the bloody horror of the scene. The deceased was slumped over the distorted steering wheel, his big head a horrible mess of browning blood. Vignoles recognised the broad, stubby hand with crudely formed letters on the knuckles that spelled out H.A.T.E. The dead man stared at him with an unblinking eye. All life in this strong body had long drained away, vanished, like the coils of smoke and steam that faded into nothing on a station platform, and yet, there remained a trace in this one eye of the contempt and defiance that Vignoles had detected when they had met in the parcels depot.

'He's local?'

'S'right, guv. Works 'round Marylebone,' the BRS mechanic answered, 'name of Rodney Mattox. Everyone knew 'im as Big Ron. Good darts player, was in the pub team what topped the league last year.'

'He was equally skilled as a driver?'

'Of course. He was in the army transport corps, joined us in '48. He could handle a tanker, no problem.'

'But not this time. I wonder why.' Vignoles stared at the body of Big Ron and immediately sensed this was going to take longer than an hour or two. Was it just a tragic accident? He suspected not. Vignoles asked the young constable his opinion.

'Well, sir, apparently he turned down the road at about seven and just went smack bang into the lamp post. The tank's full to bursting, so the weight would take it downhill at a fair lick.'

'Witnesses?'

'Visibility was far worse than it is now, sir. And it was dark, so no eye witnesses as such.'

'Who reported it?'

'A man working in the milk depot, sir. He heard the crash, came straight out to see what was up and then called us. I have his name and address.' The constable was young and eager to help. He was also having trouble looking away from the unsettling eyeball fixing them with its unwavering gaze.

Vignoles nodded. It would have made quite a noise, even with the many train movements close by. At that moment there was a loud whine that grew to a crescendo followed by a rattle and a flash, as a tube train whizzed past just a few yards away on a brief escape from its narrow rabbit hole.

He took a moment to run his gaze over the onlookers, nearly all of whom were dressed in work clothes, although he noticed an elderly man leaning heavily on a walking stick some way at the back and two women with big prams, shopping bags dangling from the upswept handles. It struck Vignoles as odd that the annoying union rep. was absent. He turned to the medic and asked, 'What can you tell me, doctor?'

'As I am *quite* sure you are tired of hearing from member of my profession, we'd rather get him on a slab before we make *too* many pronouncements, but the position of the body in the cab also gives much information. Death at about seven o'clock is consistent with the state of rigor. My initial belief was that the cause was the impact with the windscreen pillar: severe head trauma combined with severe blood loss. Certainly it looks that way, and I think that is how we are supposed to interpret the situation. However, I wish to introduce a note of caution. Notice the way his arms are beneath his body. Now, if you lost control and knew you were about to hit a solid brick wall moments later, you would attempt to turn the wheels, or open the door and bale out, or at the very least shield your face. And yet it appears he clutched himself around the chest or midriff. Now, you're the detective, why might he do that?'

'Heart attack?'

'Good, good.' The doctor nodded approvingly. 'But it could be something swifter and more disturbing.' The doctor gave Vignoles an arch look. 'Could you lend a hand again, constable? Pull the chap upright.' They heaved the stout corpse backwards then stepped sharply away as Big Ron's head rolled to one side and stared at them, his face a ghastly mess of gore.

'Ugh, I'm gonna throw up!' The mechanic, who had watched with grim fascination, turned away, bent forward and retched.

The doctor, unflinching, moved to one side and urged Vignoles closer. 'Look, something interesting just... *here.*' Reaching across, he used a pencil to prod the far side of the man's chest. 'There is an incision right through his clothes, quite a deep one, from what I can tell from this awkward angle. The pathologist will be able to corroborate my suspicions, but my guess is that someone in the passenger seat stabbed him in the heart with a knife or something equally sharp and narrow. The heart pumped for a short while, hence the blood.'

'Good Lord,' blurted Vignoles, surprised at the doctor's suggestion.

'That mechanic chap, who is now being sick in a most spectacular fashion, observed that the vehicle was in neutral when it struck the lamp post.'

'So the driver drew to a halt at the crest of the hill, placed the gear in neutral and pulled on the handbrake. Why? Perhaps he was going to let someone out of the cab. His passenger then stabs him in the heart. He clasps his chest, the handbrake is released by the killer, who promptly jumps out, and the heavy tanker rolls down the hill and slams into the post.'

'Jolly good, inspector!' said the doctor. Vignoles thought his lighthearted cheeriness rather inappropriate, given the circumstances. 'Now, are you quite sure I can't take a look at that nose?'

Chapter Twenty-four

Deep Water

Bob Wills & his Texas Playboys

Sir Paul Frobisher was smoking a particularly fine Cuban cigar whilst seated in a leather armchair behind a highly-polished cherry-wood desk in his private study, a chunky ashtray of Bogotá silver near his right hand. In his left he held a lighter which he was idly flipping open and closed, enjoying the solid, well-machined *clunk* as it did so. He couldn't fault German engineering.

A roaring fire burned in a cast iron fireplace edged with blue and white tiles, and the heavy mirror above the mantle shelf reflected candles in tall, silver sconces together with light thrown by the electric chandelier in the centre of the ceiling. The room was encased on three sides by floor-to-ceiling bookcases lined with volumes bought as job lots in auctions. He'd never opened them, but they gave the right impression — and helped soundproof the room. He was most circumspect about eavesdroppers, hence his annoyance at that idiotic slip up the other night. A flicker of doubt passed over his face. That was a rare moment of weakness, a symptom of them all becoming too blasé. He stared reflectively down at the large, antique Turkish carpet of superior quality that overlaid the polished floorboards.

This carpet was his pride and joy. A precious gift from SS Obersturmbannführer Otto Skorzeny, though his old commander was no longer known by that name or title. It had been delivered to Sir Paul's door one day in August 1948, a thank-you present for his vital work in 1944, and for making over the funds and men to stage Skorzeny's daring escape from Darmstadt internment camp. Sir Paul was doing a valuable job fundraising to help maintain the 'ratlines' and it was appreciated. Of course, everyone thought the rug had been sent by a professor of antiquities at one of the larger museums in Egypt, and the note accompanying it was suitably short and sparse. But he knew from whom it had originated, and why.

He looked at the intricate pattern of woven silk on the floor, regretfully pushed aside fond memories of his daring escapades in the forests of Belgium and considered his present situation. Things were suddenly taking an awkward turn and perhaps it was time to shed the image of the landed English country gent, like a snake sheds its skin. They'd had a good run of it and banked considerable funds over the past four years, but lately too many elements were causing trouble or not running smoothly. In this game one had to know when it was time to cut one's losses and run. It was a delicate balancing act juggling the many strands of his various concerns, whilst ensuring their secrets remained undiscovered.

He took a long drag on his cigar and decided the carpet and the silver lighter with the engraving of the death's head were two extravagances he would allow himself to take to Argentina. He'd travel light, of course, but he could have the carpet shipped out. Everything else would be put up for sale. He'd get a good price for the house, but then he'd spent heavily on it and the organisation would be expecting a decent return. Lady Frobisher was a problem, and he suddenly betrayed a rare flash of remorse. She was supposed to be a trophy to help give the right impression in society, yet he'd grown genuinely fond of her. He sighed and flicked some ash from the cigar. At least there was a contingency in his escape plan. He was to meet with a 'fatal accident' once in Buenos Aires and Lady Frobisher would be called to identify the body and make the necessary arrangements. Once there, she would have the choice of accepting him as being very much still alive, and for what he really was. She would have to swear loyalty to the cause or face the consequences. But how would she play the do-or-die card? There could be no way back for her once the truth was out. Poison was the most humane way if she refused…

He spun the flint on the lighter with his thumb to make a flame and his face glowed yellow, but his eyes were as blue and cold as the Hebridean sea. The lighter was too obvious in London society but would be well received in Buenos Aires. He smiled as he imagined the exchange of knowing looks as he leant forward to light another man's cigar, carefully observing his companion reading the motto of the SS engraved on the side, now smoothed and polished by regular use. He might casually explain it was no more than a ghoulish souvenir, whilst the other might smile knowingly, understanding the pretence. As they sounded each other out with little signals and clues, they would start to exchange stories, testing each other's allegiance as they recalled the glory years.

His was a good story, if not in quite the same league as the more battle-experienced, but it was still one of daring and courage, of how Sir Paul Frobisher, baronet, dressed as a Belgian peasant, had lifted the lighter from the frozen hand of a tank commander from Hasso von Manteuffel's 5th Panzer Division as the brave man lay dead in the snow near Bastogne. Yes, he had been in the terrible, frozen forests of the Belgian bulge, battling against hunger and perishing cold whilst knee-deep in snow. He'd observed close up those heroic men trying to warm barrels of frozen diesel and the tragic sight of the mighty King Tiger tanks — impregnable and without equal as a fighting weapon — stilled only by a lack of fuel or the vice-like grip of ice, their crews captured or killed as they worked to dig snow from the tracks and between the wheels.

Sir Paul drew on his cigar and drifted back into memories. They had been crazy, adrenaline-fuelled days and he pined to be back, living on the edge, hour by hour as he expertly finessed a masterful double bluff on his fellow countrymen. He had been deeply undercover with Churchill's personal favourites, the Special Operations Executive, infiltrating the ranks of one of the most feared fighting forces in the world, feeding the grateful Allies with scraps of tactical information that plunged the Wehrmacht into ever deeper trouble and ultimate defeat. His affiliation to the SS, however, had never once been suspected, even now, and operating so deep inside the organisation, he had been expected to appear outwardly sympathetic. Yes, he'd run the perfect 'double cross' system; undermining the ordinary German foot soldier in the Ardennes whilst working tirelessly to buy the SS valuable time, if not victory. What did he care for the common soldier? The SS were a class apart, and anyone lucky enough to bear the twin silver lightning flashes on their collar knew their own survival was paramount. So a few thousand ordinary foot soldiers were sacrificed to pay for their survival? It caused him not one moment of regret.

He was most proud of his part in Operation Greif, serving under Skorzeny and his battalion of carefully-schooled, English-speaking German soldiers dressed in British and American uniforms. He'd helped train each on the finer points of the English language and its idioms, the plots of popular films and the lyrics of the best-loved songs, barrack room jokes and the correct way to swear and curse. Some of the men were so good it was uncanny. They were word perfect and the very best had even survived capture.

Ultimately, von Manteuffel had not managed to break through and secure the vital oil reserves in Holland, despite their work in disguise, blowing communication lines and ammunition dumps and spreading incorrect information, but Frobisher had supplied a number of senior SS officers with new identities, supplying the documents they required and details of safe escape routes, the collection points for train and boat tickets and the myriad other details that successfully allowed so many to escape as the dream of the Thousand Year Reich collapsed. The joke was, he had many of the false papers made by the SOE's own small army of backroom forgers and, under the mantle of his 'deep cover', had smuggled them easily to the enemy. Skorzeny had been appreciative of that most rare and peculiar commodity — a real Englishman eager to serve the 'enemy', even bending a few rules to have Frobisher officially recognised as a member of the elite, despite having never undertaken the compulsory training. Perhaps having a German mother had helped seal the deal? The little card with his name and SS number made him proud.

The problem was, he could not find that membership card no matter how hard he looked. It had just vanished. He must have put it somewhere in a moment of crass stupidity and forgotten where. It was no longer in the safe and, as no one but he knew the combination, he could blame only himself. He was acutely worried.

There was a knock and Henry Bish entered upon his command, closing the door with its heavy, leather-studded covering behind him. Frobisher asked him to turn the key and take a seat on the other side of the desk, offering a cigar and closely observing his trusted second-in-command for a few moments in silence, noticing how he handled the cigar with less composure than usual. Bish's hands trembled ever so slightly as he cut the end with the special silver scissors. It was not like 'Bash' to show nerves. He was a cold-blooded killer, notoriously ruthless and efficient in his day. He'd been one of his best pupils, one of Skorzeny's finest. His German identity long abandoned, Bish did an impressive job acting the English middle manager; indeed, he was a natural mimic. Sir Paul realised that the situation must be bad if his number two was starting to betray nerves. This did little to ease his private worries.

'I trust it went smoothly this morning.' Sir Paul almost chewed on the pungent smoke in his mouth as he asked the question. He might have been enquiring if his estate gamekeeper had bagged a few brace of pheasant.

'As well as can be expected, sir. He didn't suspect a thing.' Bish fiddled with his cigar. 'Though a half-decent policeman will soon rumble what was a hasty job. I'd say we have but a few hours' grace until it becomes a murder hunt.' Bish may have been nervous but he never let his immaculate command of King's English slip. A professional through and through.

'I see.' Sir Paul nodded as he took this in. 'Then you'll need to find a way of deflecting their attention away from us, as I fear they do indeed have a half-decent detective on the job.'

'I'm working on it, sir.'

'The weaker elements need weeding out, even if it creates a few more problems to solve. He and his idiot friend drew too much attention with that laughable execution, and I won't stand for it. I've had to sail pretty darn close to the wind, pulling strings at Scotland Yard to try and get that blasted DI Vignoles off our tail. He's no plodding local policeman — unfortunately.' He puffed on his cigar, his face masked by a cloud of blue smoke, 'I'm not happy about this, as it might raise the odd eyebrow in the wrong places, but it might buy us a little time. I need three, maybe four days to make arrangements. It's time to think about baling out.'

'I see. May one ask why?' Bish kept his face impassive, but a little ash from his cigar dropped onto his leg, shaken off by a slight twitch in his hand.

'I'm not sure we're out of the woods.' Sir Paul pulled a face. 'The Jordan operation is ruined and now I understand a policeman has been making enquiries about this Pym fellow at Hendon Pharmaceuticals. Asking if Pym was trialling one of our new painkillers. Now, why would he be doing that?'

'No idea, sir.' Bish swallowed. 'I cannot see how there can be a connection with Pym.' Bish, however, felt a tingle of doubt crawl over his skin, forming a clammy sweat, but he worked hard to suppress showing it. *Those two idiots used whisky laced with painkillers... don't say they opened one of the boxes of medical stock stored near the contraband?* Bish kept this opinion to himself, but was concerned. *If they had, they were compromised.*

'Hmm. It may be nothing. I'm unhappy the pharmaceutical branch of the business has attracted attention. It would be unfortunate if we had to abandon that lucrative wing of the operation. Find out what prompted their enquiry.' He narrowed his eyes and looked at Bish. 'I trust the relocation of the Marylebone stock went without a hitch?'

'All stowed and correct, sir. The big man was a hard worker, if not the brightest spark. In some ways it would be a pity to kill him, as he got the job done all right.'

'Humph! And the delivery from Loughborough arrived as expected?'

'I'm sorry to report it has not.' His Adam's apple bobbed.

'Why not?'

'There has been a small hitch: the containers were inadvertently sent elsewhere.'

'What?' Sir Paul rose to his feet and stared at Bish, a vein pumping in his forehead. 'Are you telling me you've lost the containers! Have you forgotten what is *in* that consignment?'

'No, sir! Of course not, sir!'

'Each packet contains five pounds sterling! Ten thousand pounds in cash and all genuine notes, you dumb idiot! They had better get to London docks and be sailing for Egypt in two days' time or you will live to regret it. I will not accept this failure.' His eyes were unwavering as he stared across the desk.

'It is just a temporary problem, of that I am quite sure. I shall have the matter resolved as soon as arrangements can be made. On that you have my word of honour.'

'Is everything so ill-starred at the moment? You used to run it like clockwork.' Sir Paul stood up and strode away from his desk, pacing the room and collecting his thoughts. His voice was quieter when he next spoke, though still laced with anger. 'Explain how such a simple error could happen.'

'I understand there was a mix up with the cards that determine where they should be delivered. We entrusted the task to a young man — along the lines you demand we follow. We chose someone ignorant of the operation and quite unable to provide incriminating information if challenged. But it appears he was not up to the task.'

'Go on...'

'We now have three wagons laden with fertilizer and farm machinery parts, whilst a farmer in Buckinghamshire has our three securely-locked containers sitting in a siding in the middle of nowhere. We have been able to establish where the containers were delivered by looking at the delivery notes on the farmer's consignment.'

'How will you recover them?'

'I'll take Millett and two drivers with flat bed trucks. We'll hire a mobile crane from a local supplier to unload the containers then drive them directly to the ship, as I think taking them forward by road would be wiser. They have attracted enough attention. We should be able to have this matter put to rights by... er, tomorrow evening, I hope.'

Sir Paul nodded. There was no doubting his man was an able operator and could be relied upon to find swift solutions to almost any problem. His felt his anger simmer down. This was a time to remain calm and make balanced judgements and he should not have lost control as he had earlier. His nerves were frayed, for some reason. 'Make sure it goes smoothly and cover your tracks.' He gave a tight-lipped smile that was supposed to reassure. Silence fell and was held for some time. Sir Paul was standing beside a small table, drumming his fingers lightly, and after a few moments he pulled the stopper from a cut-glass decanter and poured two generous slugs of brandy into glasses. He handed one to Bish and, swirling the amber liquid in his glass, looked down at him.

'*Hau weg das Zeug!*' He winked as he gave the toast.

Bish lifted his glass in reply.

'I've made a decision. We shall put the escape plan into action with immediate effect. Secure this important delivery then make your way abroad in the manner we have previously discussed.'

'So suddenly?'

'Things are on the verge of becoming unsustainable. We must stay a few steps ahead and cannot risk another close shave as we had with the Water Street operation in '46.' They both exchanged knowing looks as they recalled it.

He placed his glass on the desk then walked across to a set of bookshelves beside the fireplace. With two deft movements that involved pushing a set of books until a small rectangular section swung open he revealed a secret wall safe. Bish could see the gunmetal colour of the heavy door behind, but not the white numbers of the black dial that was expertly spun one way, then the other. With a slight click the lock was released.

Sir Paul took out a small rectangular metal box and carefully laid this on the desk between them. Sitting down, he unlocked the box using a key on a chain attached to his gold fob watch and lifted the lid. Bish stared at the box like a hound might observe his master opening a tin of dog food as a series of documents was carefully lifted and laid out like cards in a game of patience.

'Our tickets to a new life.' He raised an eyebrow, then took up an Argentinean passport, flipped it open and scanned the pages. The face of Señor Juan Santos Rodriguez, senior sales director of a canned meat company, stared back at him. 'I shall make an appointment with my barber. A rinse of dark hair dye might be advisable, d'you think? All these documents look excellent.'

Bish sighed audibly. 'He was the best.'

'So I understand.' He replaced the passport at the top of a column of documents associated with his new personality and moved across to the next set. Sir Paul critically compared the photograph with the man seated opposite. 'You could put on some pounds and grow out the moustache, but the photograph was supposed to have been taken a few years ago. Hmm? You'll pass muster, if you take care.' He tapped an official-looking envelope in the same column of documents. 'You know your contact in Cairo. The letters of invitation are in here.'

Bish nodded. He was fighting the urge to snatch up the documents and be sure of securing his escape. To be denied at the last hurdle would be unbearable. His commanding officer was displeased and might withdraw the offer of an escape route.

Sir Paul scooped up the Egyptian passport and associated items and held them in a bundle in his hand above the desk, tantalizingly close.

'It was indeed most unfortunate that our master forger met with such a sudden end. He had proved himself invaluable.'

'He had an old shop and all those solvents he used, like the printing inks and varnishes, are terribly flammable. He should have taken more care.'

'Quite.' He smiled at Bish. 'Still, every cloud... he took his secrets with him, eh? That could prove a lifesaver for us.' He handed the documents to a grateful Bish, immediately followed by another set. 'Millett has also proved his worth. These should get him to Egypt as well. He might be useful out there.' He dipped into the box, extracted a hefty bundle of Egyptian banknotes and slid them across the table. 'That should tide you over for a month or two.'

'Thank you, sir!' Bish felt a wave of relief as he pocketed the precious sets of irreplaceable forgeries. His commander locked the metal box and returned it to the safe.

Bish hoped that Sir Paul had not noticed that his SS membership card was missing. Hopefully, he'd be by the Nile before the baronet realised it was gone. It was Sir Paul's fault, anyway. Allowing it to slide inside one of the stolen passports used to make the forgeries was stupid. The problem was, that snivelling little creep of a forger had taunted him about the card when he'd gone to collect the finished documents. He had said that it was tucked away 'somewhere safe' as a 'guarantee of a long and profitable life'. Well, he'd put paid to that nonsense. The failed blackmailer was incinerated.

'Another? Yes, let's enjoy our last drink together for the foreseeable future.' Sir Paul walked across to the decanter as he spoke. 'Start shutting everything down immediately. No contact unless absolutely essential. Oh, and could you arrange for this rug to be forwarded?

Chapter Twenty-five

'Baby, It's Cold Outside'
Dinah Shore & Buddy Clark

Simon sat on one of the narrow bunks, knees pulled up under his chin, peering anxiously through a small gap between the faded brown curtains and the steel window frame, looking quite the picture of dejection. His uncle was clattering about in the tiny galley muttering and grumbling, half to Simon and half to himself. Scamp sat on the wooden floor, one shaggy paw on the bunk beside Simon, his gaze continually roving from the galley and back again, eyebrows and ears in a constant state of flux as he responded to Tustain's grousing and the banging of the kettle and cups, then to Simon's frequent sighs and nervous twitches.

The *Primrose* was an unhappy and unsettled boat.

'You want me to *lie* to my own *sister*?' asked Tustain, his tone making it clear that was out of the question.

'It's not exactly lying, just say you've not seen me. I need a couple of days to sort out this mess I'm in.'

'She's probably going half spare with worry and here I am, able to put her out of her misery and you want me to let her suffer. I can't do it.' He poured boiling water into a battered old teapot.

'But if they know where I am, they'll be in danger, too! These men are thugs! If mum and dad don't know my whereabouts then they can't force it out of them.'

'If they're as bad as you say, then it might be better if your parents *can* speak up.' His uncle looked concerned. 'Look, I'm not scared of them; I've met enough rum fellows in my time on the river, some were right nasty sorts. Trusty Tustain can handle a marlin spike all right!' His voice was defiant, but his hand shook slightly as he held the pot. To mask his nerves he swirled it around, ostensibly to speed the mashing of the brew.

Simon pleaded, 'Just give me until midnight, then you can tell them I'm here.'

'Midnight? How can I telephone at that hour? I'd have to wake the Windybanks at number 12 and get them to run around in their dressing gowns. I'll give you until ten. And not a minute more.'

Simon fell silent and stared at the grey water lapping against the wooden piles of the wharf wall, reflecting the grubby warehouse on the far side of the canal. He could see a tall chimney belching yellow smoke that stretched and contracted as the canal water slopped between the sides. It was bitterly cold outside and the view did nothing to warm Simon's spirits. 'We need to get going.'

'We'll cast off after we've drunk our tea. I can have us there in under an hour. The question is, what are we looking for?'

'I wish I knew. And how do I find whatever it is?' Simon accepted the cup of tea gratefully and gave a weak attempt at a smile. 'I spent all yesterday trying to find something useful in the newspapers and hunting up and down the canal bank looking for clues, but there was nothing. I've got to find something. Anything. I think my life depends on it.'

Tustain sat on the bunk opposite, sipped his tea and tried to calm his nephew's panic. 'Let's not get melodramatic. We need a plan of action, not bull-in-a-china-shop stuff. This Dennis and his gang know the area a darn sight better than you, and they will have plenty of friends to lend a hand. I still think you should walk into the nearest police station and tell them all you know. Let the law take its course.'

'But I've nothing to tell them — no real evidence. Not only will I lose my job for handling stolen goods, I'll still have these brutes on my back.'

Tustain nodded silently. Simon swung his feet off the bunk and sat upright. 'What am I missing? If Dennis killed Pym then he also threw him in the canal, a little way upstream of where the *Primrose* was moored. Does that sound right to you?'

'Well, the police were very uncertain on that point.'

'That doesn't help, then. But we know he sells stolen goods from an old building near Marylebone yard and drinks in a local pub, so he probably met the man and killed him near there.'

'I suppose so,' agreed Tustain, although he could see many holes in this argument.

'I need to find somebody who saw Dennis with Pym that same evening. Someone who will admit seeing them together. That might just convince the police that he's worth questioning!'

'It would be a start. But how will you find such a person and convince him to speak up? You can hardly ask his friends or associates. The moment you do that...'

He met Simon's gaze and left the sentence unfinished.

'Golly, things do look bad. But what can I do?'

'Listen, we'll make our way back to where I was moored that morning and I'll start putting the word out amongst the boatmen, but discreetly. They'd never talk to the police, as nobody likes them nosing into their business, but they might talk to me. This Dennis might be known to a few of them, as I wouldn't be surprised if the less honest didn't trade with his gang, what with them operating so close to the canal. Perhaps I'll strike lucky.'

'I'll sniff around Marylebone yard and see what I can find. Then there's the pub. It's awfully risky, but worth a try.' Simon blanched at the thought, his copper hair and freckles standing out against his pale skin. 'I've rather put this off all yesterday, but I need one person with some information. Just *one*.'

'I'll head down to Little Venice and ask along the way. I'll still be pretty close, so just follow the towpath west if needs be. Tonight I'll head towards Camden Lock, aiming to pass Marylebone at nine-thirty. You be ready to jump aboard!'

✻ ✻ ✻ ✻

On Monday morning Sergeant Trinder was just finishing his solitary boiled breakfast egg when there came a knock on the back door. It was not the confident strike of a tradesman wanting payment or the cheerful rap of the postman, but a more hesitant sound, as though it did not really want to be heard. However, as he and Violet were seated at their kitchen table just a few feet away, it was clear enough. With bright red braces crossing his white shirt, a tie draped around his shoulders and top collar button undone, he glanced up at his wife and raised an eyebrow before opening the door to see who wanted them so early.

Mrs Howerth, the signalman's wife, was standing in their yard wringing her hands and wearing a look that mixed anxiety and apology in about equal measure. Trinder quickly disguised his disappointment the knock had not heralded the postie bringing his much-anticipated 78 of 'Blueberry Hill', and asked how he could help her.

She launched immediately into a rapid-fire explanation of her presence that gave little time to draw breath, lurching from her concern about Simon's disappearance to agreement with her husband that she was just jumping the gun and there was probably no need to get worried, not yet anyways, as lads will be lads. But then, well, you know how it is, what with him not showing for work this morning? He'll be docked pay! Which has never happened before and that is unsettling and quite out of the ordinary seeing as how Simon was always a good lad, and gave us no worries; well, of course, apart from that time with those men when he was in the van on the ice, but then of course officer Trinder, sir, you would know all about that. He had been at the dance and quite a few had too many and he had been looking a bit worse for wear earlier. Maybe he could be somewhere nursing a sore head after drinking a bit too much, sleeping it off in a ditch somewhere? Oh, my goodness, what if he's had an accident? It's been two nights! He's old enough, I know, and at first I just tried to think nothing of it. But a second night? He could be injured…

Trinder finally teased out the facts, aided by Violet ushering the poor woman into the warm kitchen and offering her a cup of tea. Mrs Howerth eventually calmed down and went home, whilst Trinder telephoned the office to explain his delayed arrival.

As it stood, young Howerth's disappearance was not causing Trinder any particular concern. The lad was a sensible sort and old enough to look after himself. No, his worry was the thought of having to tell the inspector that the somewhat notorious Simon Howerth, half of a double act with his chum Edward Earnshaw, the baker's son, was yet again a thorn in their side, delaying knuckling down to the long list of things needed to further the investigation.

He was inclined to think Simon had drunk too much at the fireworks dance and was nursing a hangover somewhere, or even slinking out the back door of a young woman's house. No doubt he'd turned up at the engine shed today. But since Trinder knew the Howerth family and Violet was insistent that he made *some* attempt to look into the matter, he accepted the inevitable and acquiesced. As Violet put it, 'the lad is both a railwayman and from this community, so that makes him practically part of the family. The very least you can do is make some initial enquiries then get the local constable to follow up if needed.'

Somewhat reluctantly, Trinder went to Woodford engine shed to look for Simon's chum, Eddie, whom he found preparing an engine for the day's work ahead. That the postman had propped his red and black bicycle outside Violet's shop and entered the front door, holding a slim but perfectly square package as Trinder breasted the Church Street hill on his way to the engine shed, only added to his sense of frustration. He'd have to wait till the evening now to hear his new Louis Armstrong record.

Soon he and Eddie were seated on a paint-stained wooden bench set against the inside wall of the shed, facing the pretty green locomotive named *Jutland* that Edward was making ready. A sickly-yellow wad of smoke curled from the chimney as damp coal, aided by oily rags, caught flame whilst the engine ticked and sighed as the metal warmed, warm water dribbling from a copper pipe beneath the cab creating a little steaming pool on the concrete floor.

A woman in blue overalls cinched at the waist by a thick, leather belt, her hair held up in a brightly-coloured headscarf that matched her glossy lipstick, was perched high up the side of the boiler, rubbing the smooth barrel with a lightly-oiled cloth to create a rich lustre to the Brunswick-green paint. Trinder was trying not to notice how the overalls highlighted her nicely-proportioned hips that waggled provocatively each time she polished the boiler with circling arm movements.

'So, the last time you saw Simon was on Saturday night. Was that at the fireworks dance?'

'No, I saw him after, down the back of the railway embankment. He was quite out of sorts. I've known him since I was little, so I can read him like a book.'

'Any idea why, or what he was doing there?'

Eddie hesitated. He had a few ideas, but was wary of confessing them to a policeman. He suspected it concerned the black marketeers, so played safe by replying, 'No, sergeant.'

Trinder made an effort to appear professional, with notebook open on his knee and Biro poised, although as yet he had written nothing other than the date and Edward's name. He found his gaze drawn again to the cleaner, who was stretching to reach across to the steam dome, overalls pulled taut across her curves. Reluctantly, he looked away and down at his notebook.

'We were by the bonfire, chatting, when Si suddenly rushed off, then myself and, um, well, a lady friend, bumped into him later, down that little back access road off the bottom of Station Road.'

'The one that runs behind MacIntyre's?' His wife's shop still carried her maiden name. Edward nodded. 'But it leads nowhere.' Trinder gave him a penetrating look. 'I hope you were not up to any monkey business.'

'Of course not! We followed him because we were worried. Station Road was deserted, then I remembered the little road behind the shops. We made our way along it and suddenly he came crashing right down the embankment, bang into me! Sent me into the brambles.'

The view of the cleaner was distracting, and the revelation that Edward Earnshaw had taken a girl down a back lane in the dark was also mildly diverting. 'Who was with you?'

Eddie gave a sheepish grin. 'You don't need to write all this down, do you?'

'That depends.'

'Miss Green. Laura.'

'Oh, the signalwoman.' Trinder grinned. 'Quite a catch. But isn't she a bit older—'

'—only by a few years!' Eddie blushed, but was enjoying the sensation of mentioning Laura.

'So, Master Earnshaw, what was the *real* reason you went down the lane?'

'No, honestly, we weren't, um, we really were following Simon.'

'Sounds like you got your priorities wrong!' Trinder laughed heartily as he folded his notebook away. He wanted to return to Leicester and get on with some proper work, but not before he'd given Edward the benefit of his worldly experience.

'Listen, young Earnshaw, let me give you some advice. When a smart and pretty girl like Miss Green chooses to accompany you to a secluded place, practically in the middle of the night, she would not be too surprised to have to fend off an amorous advance. Now, don't go getting silly ideas and do anything rash — she throws signal levers all day, so is more than able to give you a slap you won't forget if you overstep the mark, but I think an arm around her waist might have been worth the risk.' Trinder winked.

'She was pretty good about it all.' He gave a cheeky grin and enjoyed the memory as he played it out in his mind. 'I'd been telling her how Simon and I were investigating the mystery of the dead man in the canal, and she was really interested. Quite excited, I think. I'm sure she likes the thrill of the chase quite as much as we do! What a terrific girl she is...'

Trinder stopped midway through putting away his notebook and listened more intently as Edward gabbled on.

'... and she told me about the time the inspector kept watch from her signalbox a few years back and we suddenly realised we had loads to talk about. Then Simon ran off. I told Laura I was fed up because he was no longer bothered about solving the mystery and that I was worried he was getting in with bad company. Then I suggested we follow him. I suppose it was an excuse for an adventure and, um, well, to walk her home,' he said, sheepishly.

'Can we just go back a step? What's this about a dead man in a canal?'

'Oh, Simon's uncle found the body at Marylebone, where he has a narrowboat. We were intrigued; well, you know how we like all this Dick Barton detective stuff?' His eyes grew wide with excitement then paled again as he added, 'But Simon lost interest soon afterwards, probably because he got in with a gang who were selling...' Edward stopped himself in mid flow, realising he'd said far too much already.

Trinder spoke under his breath. 'Tell me everything you know about the man in the canal.' He took out his notebook out again and was looking stern.

'Hardly anything, just what we heard from Si's uncle.'

'What about this gang? Do you think your friend is mixed up with them? This is no time for silly-boy games, Edward. Simon is missing. He could be in danger.'

Edward closed his eyes for a moment. He knew he'd let the cat out of the bag and there was no way back. He told Trinder everything he could remember Simon had told him about the men at Marylebone, and the cigarettes and nylon stockings under his bed.

'This is very serious. Your pal is in trouble and I don't just mean about selling stolen goods.' Trinder felt a strange prickle of fear run through his body and, despite the cold and dank weather, his palms felt sweaty. Violet had been right: he *did* feel familial affection for young Simon. His main concern right now was to find him.

'Tell me everything Simon told you about these people. Every last detail. And then I need all the packets of cigarettes and stockings you have. Even empty ones. They're evidence and could provide information. If you do a thorough job, and do it quickly, I'll try to forget you told me you knew the stuff was stolen when you bought it. Understood?' Edward assented, looking guilty.

They talked a while longer, attracting the attention from Mr Saunders, the shedmaster, who came to enquire what was keeping Edward from his work. Trinder sent the lad back onto the engine before talking for a few moments with Saunders, skilfully deflecting questions about his presence there. Saunders was easily pacified, being in a chatty mood and eager to discuss the weekend's football as the two men watched a heavy goods engine roll forwards out of the shed into the iron grey light outside, closely followed by another on the same track. Trinder thought they looked like racehorses being readied for the gallops; the men leaning out of the cab windows with an arm stretched across to the regulator handle and firemen hanging off the lower steps, ready to drop down and throw a point lever, were like grooms holding their bridles, their steel chargers panting and snorting as they met the bracing air.

There was work to be done, however, and Saunders said as much, but a moment after parting company he called Trinder back.

'Sergeant! I almost forgot, the shunter up at the Old Yard, handed these in.' He pulled out the neatly torn pieces of the three bill of loading cards discarded by Simon. 'Found them in one of the yards on the track this morning.'

Trinder looked unimpressed.

'The odd thing is, none of the wagons anywhere in the vicinity were missing cards. You might want to check with Central Control. I reckon someone might be missing three wagons!'

Trinder humoured him by scrutinising the cards, turning them in his hands, and extracted some enjoyment from showing off his deductive skills. 'They look brand new. Not damp, at least no more than you'd expect after maybe a night on the ground. I don't reckon they've been used. If you put the pieces together you'll see there's no creasing where the wire frame would have held them in place. Those springs can snap back and trap your fingers something rotten and they bend the corners.'

'I know your DI Vignoles loves puzzles, he'd like to see those.'

I doubt it, thought Trinder, but he thanked the shedmaster nonetheless and pocketed the pieces before heading off towards the station, his mind engaged in thinking about the men Edward had mentioned — Dennis, Big Ron and Vic. Trinder knew who these characters were and was looking forward to another encounter. However, he was unaware that, in the case of Big Ron, it was already too late.

Chapter Twenty-six

PREACH MY WORD
The Five Trumpets

Vignoles had been kept busy all morning organising a photographer to record the scene, fending off a brace of newspaper men sniffing after a story, telephoning the office to have Mrs Green explain the situation to the Badger and calling Scotland Yard. He could not yet establish a direct link, but he sensed this murder was tied in to that of Jack Pym. When he arrived and appraised the situation, DI Tykett was inclined to agree. Vignoles was pleased to have a second opinion.

They now stood some way from the smashed milk tanker, smoking and watching the ambulance solemnly remove the remains of Big Ron to the mortuary as the firemen who had cut the body free started to hose down the oil-stained road and sprinkle sand about the area. A huge, six-wheeled rescue vehicle rumbled into view, a vicious-looking hook dangling from its sturdy jib. The smog was thinner than in previous days and allowed a pale light to filter through from the sun, but the air still smelled vile and rested heavily upon their chests. Everything had a ghostly quality.

Vignoles told Tykett and Sergeant Sidlow that he believed Mrs Pym and Wilde were not responsible for the murder, then outlined his belief that Jordan's Import and Export was just one arm of a complex 'long fraud' operation controlled from the St John's Wood area by Henry Bish and, quite probably, Sir Paul Frobisher. They were in agreement that Bish was a senior partner in this crime operation, and he was to be a priority target. The Scotland Yard men were intrigued by the way the case was developing, and even the cynical Tykett appeared impressed. He promised to make some enquiries of his own and see if they could get wind of an operation of the size Vignoles was talking about.

Vignoles could now leave the crime scene. He accepted a lift in the Met police car for the short run to 222 Marylebone Road. They parted with a promise from Tykett to get in touch 'as soon as he had anything'. As their car melted into the mass of traffic on Edgware Road, Vignoles adjusted his tie and hat, checked he had not forgotten to put the all-important report typed by Lansdowne in his briefcase, and entered the premises of the British Transport Commission immediately in front of Marylebone station.

The beautifully-grandiose construction had once been the Great Central Hotel, but was unceremoniously sequestered by the powerful

BTC upon the nationalisation of virtually all transport services in January 1948. It was a fabulous building of pink midland brick and yellow terracotta that had escaped damage in the war, still boasting a tall clock tower that would not look out of place on a Flemish town hall, a light and airy porch of curved glass and steel that supported great gas lanterns, and a florid entrance archway guarded by two sturdy stone maidens wearing breastplates, robes and faintly bemused expressions.

Chief Superintendent Badger's office had once been a large and lovely bedroom decorated in high Victorian style with rich, overblown Morris wallpaper, heavy encrustations of moulded plaster on the ceiling and ornate coloured glass in the upper sections of the windows. Although mutilated, it was still one of the more fortunate survivors following the conversion to BTC HQ, in that the walls had been left unspoilt — probably because suitable paint to cover the entwining briar rose design was in such short supply. Venetian blinds now hung unsatisfactorily in place of the missing heavy drapes and a new ceiling had been crudely inserted at picture rail level, from which were suspended on chains long tubes of the new fluorescent lights in ugly metal shades, the whole ensemble resulting in that curiously unhappy and unapologetic amalgam of old and new that only modernising socialists could achieve with such ease. The fine Wilton carpets had been replaced by something fawn and hard wearing, whilst dark green filing cabinets and a set of simple shelves lined one wall where a tall wardrobe once stood. Someone had screwed a cheap row of hooks for hats and coats to this same wall. However, two large photographic portraits in gilded frames, one of the king, the other of Winston Churchill, looked at home against the Morris wallpaper and lent the office a warmer aspect and a whiff of old Empire. Vignoles suspected the commission's mandarins would have preferred Badger to have chosen a monochrome image of the new locomotive testing plant in Rugby or one of those ungainly DC electric locomotives working the Woodhead route, presented in pale, grey-and-white utilitarian frames.

Vignoles found Badger sitting behind his brand new, utility-style desk, a bottle-green Anglepoise lamp illuminating a sheaf of papers before him. He looked up as Vignoles entered, nodded a greeting and gestured to indicate he should sit in one of the new and uncomfortable office chairs made of bent steel tubing and moulded plywood. The light of the lamp flashed from the nib of his pen, an effect exaggerated by the failing light of a day already losing the battle in the face of thickening airborne pollution. He fastidiously replaced the cap on his expensive fountain pen and laid it carefully on its black lacquered pen holder, adjusted a few papers and other items that were already perfectly happy in the position they occupied, and settled back in his chair.

'Hell's bells, Vignoles! What the devil's happened to your face?'

Vignoles brought his boss up to speed, but thought it wise to imply that he had been outside the warehouse at the time of the attack rather than admit having entered the premises illegally.

'You probably disturbed a burglar.' Vignoles declined to set him right. 'Have you found the man who did it? No?' Badger made an irritated expression. 'Well, what have you got on your current caseload? And don't give me a long-winded, tedious account of complicated insurance frauds. Keep it snappy.'

Vignoles had anticipated this and on the journey had considered how best to distil the many complex aspects of what was shaping up to be a major investigation into something more digestible. It was not easy, and now the murder of Ron Mattox had to be added to the mix. He decided to offer the Badger two small 'snacks': the tanker smash and the revelation that Mrs Pym and her lover had been plotting to hire someone to kill Jack Pym. He laid the WPC's neatly-typed report on the desk, knowing it would make a favourable impression.

He waited whilst Badger read the resumé on the top page. He did not delve deeper, choosing instead to question Vignoles. They talked for a few minutes, during which the DI was at pains to stress that the couple's hired killer did not kill Pym. When asked to explain why he had made this deduction, it was with some trepidation that he tackled the idea of the long fraud and the sudden abandonment of the Jordan's warehouse.

'Ah, now, you see, Vignoles, this is all very interesting, but it touches upon one of the reasons I particularly wanted to see you today.' Badger spoke slowly and with his most clipped and carefully enunciated voice, a clear signal he wished to communicate something he considered important. 'I can't help feeling one is straying further and further away from our core business — policing our railways. Now, I can quite understand the attraction of linking up with those splendid chaps over at Scotland Yard. It must be quite an adventure—'

'—excuse me for interrupting, sir, but may I point out that it was *they* who made contact with *us*. In fact, they practically threw the case at me.'

'That's as maybe, but I took luncheon with Sir Ronald Vallance, assistant commissioner of the Met, in his club yesterday...' Badger enjoyed name-dropping and relished giving Vignoles the impression that he frequently hobnobbed with such luminaries, '...and spoke with him again this morning, whilst you were wasting your time with that tanker accident—'

'—that was no accident,' Vignoles attempted to interject, but Badger brushed his comment aside and continued, '—the AC and I are both firmly of the opinion we must not overreach ourselves. For example, the sudden demise of a milk tanker driver, despite the proximity to both main and underground lines, is not exactly a railway matter, eh?'

'I feel sure there is a connection with the death of Jack Pym. I just need a little time to establish how and why.'

'Ah yes, now we come to the man in the canal. This is British *Water*ways territory, and you are most definitely a British *Rail*ways detective.' Badger gave a self-satisfied smile, aware that he'd scored a point.

Vignoles remained silent; he was still considering something Badger had said. He knew the drill: let the chief have his rant, agree to anything he asked, then carry on though the conversation had never happened. But Vignoles was startled by the revelation that Badger had been talking to the AC.

His chief was still droning on, '...were both in agreement to keep focussed and knuckle down to what's strictly relevant, and this particular case, the body in the canal, cropped up as an example.'

'It did?' Vignoles was not aware Badger knew of it.

'He was concerned that some of his officers were palming off low-level cases to ourselves—'

'—I'd not call this low-level—' Vignoles's attempt to interrupt was ignored.

'—which are strictly outside our remit. There could be an opportunity for us to greatly expand our little empire, and he's tipping us the wink to ensure we stick to what we know best.' Badger paused for effect then continued, with an annoyingly self-satisfied tone to his voice, 'Of course you were aware that I knew Sir Ronald?' Badger knew perfectly well that Vignoles was not aware of this fact, but was enjoying dropping the name and indeed had been doing so to everyone the whole morning.

'I was not.' Vignoles was puzzled by the turn the conversation was taking.

'Thoroughly decent sort, as you'd expect from someone in *his* exalted position.' He gave a little smile. 'Yes, we had quite a tête-à-tête, touching on some pretty interesting matters.' He polished his nails on a trouser leg. 'It might pay you to sit up and take notice.'

'Of course, sir. I'm all ears.'

Badger was in no hurry; he was savouring the opportunity to mention Sir Ronald whilst repeating parrot fashion the lines the AC had trotted out in his exclusive club. Badger picked up a card with gold and navy blue lettering upon it, slowly turning it in his hands as he continued. 'I also met Sir Ronald at a rather enjoyable soirée.' He pronounced the word without a trace of a French accent and gave a rare smile. 'Darned well-connected crowd.' Vignoles realised his boss was conspicuously showing off the invitation, allowing the desk lamp to catch the golden lettering. He obliged by trying to read what was printed on it.

'Have you heard of Sir Paul Frobisher, baronet?' Badger preened his immaculate uniform and adjusted a cuff on his brilliant white shirt so it protruded a regulation half inch from beneath his jacket sleeve. Vignoles suddenly became alert.

'Yes. I heard his name for the first time just the other day.' He felt his pulse quicken.

'Splendid fellow. We hit it off so well he insisted we be on first-name terms.' Vignoles raised his eyebrows, smiled and nodded to convey that he was suitably impressed. 'His London residence is not a stone's thrown from here, as a matter of fact. It turns out he's a bit of a mover and shaker within the policing world. Between you and me, I think he could prove darned useful to our department.' Badger winked extravagantly.

'Is that so?' Vignoles's mind was turning cartwheels. Like the rockets exploding on bonfire night, thoughts, ideas and disjointed images flashed in his head in a riot of snapping synapses. He felt himself mentally reeling as his sore head and nose started to pound, making him feel faint and slightly nauseous.

'You seemed surprised when I mentioned Sir Paul's name.'

Vignoles took a moment to answer. 'His name came up during our investigations into Pym's death.'

'What? How on earth could that be possible?' Badger glared at Vignoles.

'I found a short note. Just a scrap of paper really. I have it here...' Vignoles extracted it from his wallet, having not had time earlier that morning to add it to the murder case file on his desk.

'What is Top Link?'

'We think it could be someone's nickname. I believe S.P.F. is Sir Paul Frobisher. He might also be Top Link.'

Badger stared at the note again. 'Even if the baronet has a silly nickname, that's hardly a crime!' He glared across the table, seemingly personally offended.

'Think of it more as a code name. He appears to be linked to a number of strands of our investigation...'

'You'd better have some damned hard evidence for such a preposterous accusation,' exclaimed Badger, folding his arms defensively.

'The Top Link reference cropped up on another document, one written by Henry Bish, from whom Jack Pym is believed to have taken back-handers for insurance fiddles. Bish trades on the black market, works some very clever frauds, and Sir Paul Frobisher is the owner of one of the firms involved. He also appears to have a similar role in another company. There is a clear link between all three men. I think Pym discovered something and was killed to shut him up. The pills found in his body were made by a company owned by Sir Paul.'

'Are you suggesting that Pym was killed because he knew something about Sir Paul?' Badger sent the invitation card spinning across his desk, coming to rest facing Vignoles. 'You are suggesting that a fine, upstanding member of society, a *baronet*, no less, would consort with criminal types?'

'We are drawing closer to the answer every day. I think Pym died because of something he knew and not because his wife wanted the life insurance payout. What draws everyone together, the central lynch-pin, is Henry Bish. And he works with Sir Paul.'

'And that's all you've got? Far too tenuous. This note could suggest absolutely anything to someone with sufficient imagination, of which you appear to have ample. We cannot say for certain these initials are those of Sir Paul Frobisher. And even if they are that piece of scrap paper means nothing. You've really overstepped the mark on this one. I sincerely hope you have not broadcast this hare-brained opinion.'

'Just to my officers.'

'Thank God! No great harm done.' Badger stood up and paced the room, then swung around to face Vignoles. 'Sir Paul moves amongst the most elevated circles, has the ear of politicians and is a personal friend of the assistant commissioner! Good Lord, you would have made this department — *and me* — look foolish if you had publicised your ridiculous theory. It was most fortunate that Sir Ronald and I spoke earlier: he warned me of potential trouble with this case.'

'He did? I find that most surprising.'

'You do? Well, you had better learn that men like Sir Ronald Vallance make it their job to know *exactly* what's going on. No one pulls the wool over their eyes.' Badger gave a grin as he scored a point. 'Vignoles, that scrap of paper of yours is quite meaningless.'

'But it *is* a coincidence, is it not?'

'And you are always telling me you don't believe in coincidences.'

'Perhaps that is my point, sir.'

'DI Vignoles, you're just the sort of man who would read that blasted Orwell chap and believe every word he writes. I suggest you leave the scaremongering in *Nineteen Eighty Four* and join us in the real world. Top Link could be the name of a company or a new product. SP.F. could be a Super Polishing Fluid or Sally Penelope Fisher!'

'May I ask, what you actually know about Sir Paul Frobisher? He has a title; he wines and dines influential people, but does that mean it's impossible that he could ever break the law?'

'You should be very circumspect about making such allegations,' Badger's voice was chilly and low. 'He's about to be elected to the board of the Metropolitan Police, which proves he is above suspicion.'

Vignoles spotted the circular argument, but humoured his chief. 'Maybe he is not involved, but one of his close associates almost certainly is. He may well be an innocent party, but it needs looking into.'

They both fell silent, Badger breathing heavily after his outburst and holding Vignoles's gaze for a few moments longer. Eventually he looked away, clasping his hands behind his back and looking out of the window at the darkening bulk of Marylebone station.

'You will cease this line of investigation as of this moment. Do you understand?'

'But sir—'

'—that is an order! Do not make the mistake of disobeying me on this.'

'No, sir.'

'Very well, then.' He swivelled around and gave his usual, perfunctory twitch of the corners of his mouth that stood in for a smile. His voice was more relaxed when he next spoke. 'Our ladies did a darned good job on Mrs Pym, I must say. A quite *excellent* example of detective work. Your belief in undercover surveillance actually paid off this time. Do please communicate my appreciation.'

'Of course.'

'We could get a most satisfactory result here,' he tapped the slim report. 'Sadly, it's not quite in our area, a little off the beaten railway track, so to speak. The ladies will just have to settle for an honourable mention in dispatches. Scotland Yard will take the case back, as Sir Ronald and I agreed. It never should have landed on your desk in the first place, of course, but I suppose it was a stroke of luck really, as our ladies caught them red-handed. The London boys will call those two scheming devils in for questioning again and my hunch is they'll crack in no time and have 'em bang to rights, along with their paid assassin. A most pleasing conclusion.'

'But they didn't have him killed—'

'—oh, you do *so* like to complicate matters. Just you wait and see.' Badger smiled. 'The solution is staring us right in the face and all you want to do is go off on a tangent! Now, you have your orders. Dismissed.'

After Vignoles had left the office Badger sat behind his desk quietly. Small feelings of doubt began to creep in. He had been decisive in dealing with Vignoles, just as he had promised Sir Ronald; and yet, now that he was alone, no longer having to be seen to win the argument, to pull rank, or to exercise power and control over Vignoles, he could hear a little voice in his head nagging away. He felt less self-assured and this led him to re-evaluate the situation. Lunching with the persuasive Sir Ronald had massaged his ego and he had lapped up everything like a cat who'd got the cream. But now he felt uncomfortably as though he had been fed a story. What did it all mean? He rearranged the items on his deal desk and fussed with his uniform jacket for a moment whilst he regained his equilibrium. No, Scotland Yard was right, the Pym case was just a deadly domestic drama, and he should concur.

But no matter how hard he tried, he could not ignore the questions Vignoles had posed about the baronet. Pride had prevented him from admitting to his DI that he might be right to have suspicions about Sir Paul. But he was damned if he'd give Vignoles the satisfaction of making him look a fool after he'd bragged about his burgeoning friendship with the baronet. He stared at the invitation card. What did he know about this man? Virtually nothing, if truth be told. Everyone respected and trusted the baronet as bona fide because everyone else did. The phrase 'the blind leading the blind' came to mind and his mouth formed a tight-lipped line as he pressed a switch on his desk telephone. When the voice of his secretary crackled through the squawkbox he spoke in a hard, perfunctory voice.

'Please get Digby Wyatt of the *Daily Telegraph* on the line. Tell him it is a most urgent police matter.'

*   *   *   *

Vignoles needed a beer. Correction, he needed two beers. The London Pride served in the station refreshment rooms was quaffable and as he supped his second pint in a more measured manner, having downed the first almost in one, he stared thoughtfully into the amber liquid, watching a little stream of pale white froth slide down the outside of the glass. His head ached and he needed an aspirin, in fact he could do with one of those extra strong soluble things poor Pym had been forced to swallow.

He really had better snap out of his mood and get back to work. He reached into his jacket and extracted two telegrams that had been wired down to him whilst he had been busy that morning. He'd not been in the right frame of mind to bother giving them even a glance. In fact, he had been seething with frustration and annoyance. But the first pint had mellowed these feelings to a more manageable level and he decided he'd better see what they said. The first was from Sergeant Trinder:

```
SIMON HOWERTH STOP REPORTED MISSING STOP PRESUMED IN LONDON
STOP BELIEVE KNOWS UNION RAT AND GANG STOP IN DANGER STOP
```

Vignoles stared at the telegram for a few moments, trying to assimilate what it meant. Damn, this was all he needed! He'd just been ordered off the case and now he had this devastating piece of information to take in. Whatever Badger might think, this was serious and Trinder was correct to be worried. Hours had passed since the telegram had been sent and Vignoles just had to trust that his able sergeant had taken the initiative and alerted the transport police and Scotland Yard. There was no time to waste, however, and he scribbled a reply to that effect and one saying much the same to Tykett, then, leaving his pint unattended, hurried to the police offices to have them sent. Feeling yet more frazzled he returned to his beer and sank down in the leather chair to study the intriguing contents of the second telegram. It was from PC Blencowe:

```
HENDON PILL COMPANY INVESTS HEAVILY IN ARGENTINA STOP JORDANS
IN EGYPT STOP BIG FUNDS OUT OF GB STOP INTERESTING STOP
```

What was he to make of this? They invested heavily and were shipping their profits abroad. Was there any significance in the particular countries, neither of which immediately struck Vignoles as likely choices? Squirreling their funds away from the taxman and the clutches of the law, most probably. Blencowe had clearly been working hard and delving deep, though Vignoles could not yet decide if this was interesting or not. He knew too little about imports and exports, overseas investments and the trade in headache pills to be able to make any clear deductions from these bare facts. What he did know was that for some reason the boys at Scotland Yard were playing games with him and had reeled Badger in hook, line and sinker.

He shook his head in disbelief, but then managed a wry smile. *I must admit, I gave Badger exactly what he needed, delivered on a plate in the form of a perfectly-presented report that appeared to confirm the misguided thinking of the assistant commissioner. He could hardly complain.* Upon mature reflection, Vignoles decided that it could play out rather well. Scotland Yard could deal with Adeline Pym, Wilde and the rogue hitman, sweeping up those loose ends, whilst leaving him to duck under the radar and if he moved swiftly and carefully, he just might crack the case. But he had little time and had better not get caught doing so.

He spent nearly an hour supping his second pint and smoking his pipe in a thoughtful manner, occasionally writing in his police notebook and barely glancing at the city gents coming and going at the bar, nor at the two young men playing billiards on the table through the archway to his right. Nor did he notice Dennis Parkey hunched over the bar in the corner behind him, drinking pints in quick succession after his recent arrival back in the Big Smoke from up north. The man was apparently oblivious to the world, and his dark mood would not have been improved if he had recognised the man he'd left for dead in the warehouse sitting so close by. Dennis left the bar after about ten minutes.

Vignoles was trying to recall everything he'd learnt about this bewildering case, attempting to piece together little oddments of information in the hope they might add up to something substantial. He was also trawling his memory to try and retrieve a little nugget hidden deep inside. If he could just snatch hold of it, he felt sure it could be a missing but vital piece of the jigsaw.

'Got it!' He sat up straight and slapped the tabletop, causing the barman to look across. He shook a pile of coins out of his pockets, selected those he needed, hurried onto the station concourse and into one of the telephone cubicles set into a wall, closing the wooden door and illuminating the light as he did so. He had a number of calls to make.

Chapter Twenty-seven

In the Blue of the Evening
Tommy Dorsey

Simon was scared and with tiredness and hunger added into the mix was also feeling thoroughly sorry for himself. But no matter how much he wanted to stop tramping the railway yards and backstreets of Marylebone, he was driven onwards by the fear of what might befall him if he failed in his task or just gave up. He felt desperate to find something that would convince the police that Dennis Parkey killed Pym. He wanted to find someone who saw Parkey with his victim on the night he died. Yet he had no real idea where to go, or where to start. He was driven more by fear than logic. The moment he lowered his acute level of vigilance, that would be when the arm would snake around his throat and the knife blade slide into his side. He would bleed to death in a London gutter, unseen by those passing in the filthy, opaque night, his blood pooling around the cobblestones because, the way Simon saw it, Parkey was after him and with murderous intent.

He'd spent much of the afternoon around Marylebone yard. He could blend in with the railwaymen and was thankful he'd worn his fireman's reefer jacket and work boots for skulking about Woodford yard, but knowing who to avoid was the most stressful part. If he confronted one of Parkey's mates, he was done for. However, he discovered that fate had played him a curious stroke of luck, although luck was perhaps not the appropriate word. Just about everyone was talking about the sudden death of Big Ron Mattox, who appeared to have crashed his vehicle because he'd been drunk at the wheel. Everyone had a point of view on the matter, and given the slightest of prompting would offer it. As Ron's untimely demise had followed only a week after the drowning in the canal Simon would raise few eyebrows if he introduced the subject of Jack Pym. However, despite much discussion over mugs of tea and cigarettes, as early evening deepened and the day shift straddled their many hundreds of bicycles, and thousands of clogs and heavy work boots clattered over the cobbled streets, Simon had made little significant progress. He had nothing that would interest the police, just idle speculation, and he was feeling desperate.

If that were not bad enough, the sheer size of the city was overwhelming him. He was just a little fly scrabbling about on this great smoky, filthy, bomb-blasted metropolis that felt too big for him to comprehend. The buildings were taller than he was used to, hemming him in on every side, the bridges big and ugly and then the constant hum of traffic speaking to the hinterland of smoke-blackened buildings that stretched away for miles in each direction. The narrow side streets were little better, seedy and populated by strange men with haunted faces, tough-looking workers with tattoos, and drunks staggering out of doorways, lunging towards him with wild eyes begging for 'thruppence to buy a cuppa, mate'.

Worst of all, he was starting to get a horrible, nagging sensation of being followed. Not by Dennis Parkey, but by a strange little crippled man dressed in a dark coat. Simon could outrun the man any day, even in his heavy boots, but wherever he went and no matter what tiny, gaslit alley he ducked down or what lengths he made to double-back upon himself, and even despite the appalling visibility, this stalking presence always seemed to reappear after a few minutes of respite.

How Simon longed for the cramped warmth and security of the *Primrose* and the unquestioning companionship of little Scamp. He leant against a doorway and drew breath for a few minutes. There was now nothing for it but to step like Daniel into the lion's den and tackle the Sherbourne Arms. It was to be his last roll of the dice.

As he approached the pub, everything looked much as it had the first time, the streets still lifeless and the windows of the houses like dark eyes peering through the veil of fog. The footsteps of the infrequent passers-by were muffled and came from strange directions, putting him even more on edge. He stopped and listened to what might have been the limping, stuttering walk of that dratted old man, but if it was then the sound was lost beneath the mournful hoot of a large engine in the station. It sounded sad, like a great night bird on a mist-shrouded cliff top.

He took a deep breath and walked up to the woman he remembered was called Linda. She looked, in her own way, like some kind of exotic bird and was standing in what must be her habitual pick-up spot outside the pub. She was alone, and he was pleased. Two against one was too intimidating. Simon was so tired and dogged by nervous exhaustion he wished he could just invite her inside, warm himself whilst seated on a softly cushioned bench and drink the evening away, forgetting about everything in a haze of alcohol and gazing at the great lengths of pale leg and the tantalizing curves of her all-too-visible and impressive cleavage.

He was prepared this time, proffering a cigarette with a smile, ready to strike a match and light it whilst trying not to let his hand shake as he held the tiny flame to the white stick balanced on her red lips, the light highlighting the excessively-applied foundation that tried to mask her drawn features.

'Bit friendlier tonight, en't yer? Liked what you saw and thought you'd 'ave a closer look?' She gently jiggled her ample chest and smiled at Simon.

'Not exactly. I mean yes!' He tried not to stare at her chest but it moved with a soft fluid motion he found captivating. 'I—I need to ask you something.'

'Oh, for Gawd's sake! I can't stand 'ere all flippin' night talkin'! You want some comp'ny or not?' She fluttered eyelashes coated in lumpy black mascara and gave a provocative smile. 'Don't be shy, now.'

'No, please, I need some help. It's about, about Den. You know who I mean?'

'Yeah, course. What you want to go discussing 'im for?' She gave Simon a sly look. 'It don't do asking questions about the likes of 'im. Nor his mates.' She pulled away from Simon and looked wary, glancing along the street.

'I know, but, well, I thought that as you are here quite a lot, you probably see things.'

'You wouldn't believe half of what I've seen, I can tell you.' She took a long and deep drag on her cigarette and winked lasciviously. 'I seen it all, luv.' Linda narrowed her eyes and put her weight on one leg, thrusting a hip to one side. 'Now, forget about that shower and decide if you want to see some more for yerself?'

She stared into his eyes, holding the look for a few seconds, but then suddenly became serious, her face changing in an instant. She pulled herself up straight, blew smoke from the corner of her mouth as if clearing it away in preparation for what came next and stepped close, the scent of sweet perfume was intense. When she spoke it was in a voice that had shed its brash edge.

'You're really scared, en't ya? You in trouble?'

There was a clatter of buffers from the railway behind the retaining wall.

'I might be. I don't know who to trust—maybe I can trust you?'

She looked taken aback. 'Luv a duck! I'm flattered. Not many as bother to talk to me, let alone trust me.' She made a pained expression. 'Come on then, out with it.'

He almost whispered. 'It's about Dennis. I need to know if he was seen with someone on the evening of 31st October. The man from out of town who ended up in the canal.'

'You a bloody rozzer?' She stepped backwards as if scalded. The sound of chatter and the soaring tenor of Mario Lanza from within the pub mixed with that of the locomotive moving in the station below.

'No, of course not. It's just that— that— Den might be in trouble. Was he with the man or not?' It sounded lame and his voice betrayed his lack of conviction. The words of the song being played at full volume leaking from the pub seemed to echo his desperation.

'Listen, you don't want to go gettin' nosey, and the way you're talking is like you want someone to grass on 'em. Everyone knows Den and that gang what he hangs about wiv. I never liked 'im, nor his mates, but I don't go shootin' me mouth off.' She tossed her cigarette butt on the ground, crossed her arms in a comforting motion and, rubbing her bare upper arm, inadvertently revealed a dark bruise beneath the short sleeve.

Simon saw this and she noticed, pulling her hand away quickly and adjusting the sleeve. 'As I said, it don't pay to get on the wrong side of them sorts.' She spat the words out. 'Get out of it,' she dropped her voice, 'or you'll end up like that fat, vicious, good-for-nothing Ron.'

Simon looked surprised. 'You heard?'

'Course I 'ave. It's the talk of the bleedin' town.' She narrowed her eyes. 'D'you know how he ended up dead?'

'No.'

'Only the word around here is, they knocked him off.'

'Who would do that?' Simon thought he might faint.

Her voice was now barely a whisper, but it was softer in tone. 'You know who. Nasty pieces of work to a man and happy to do over one of their own, so you take my advice and hop it back to where you came from. That's the best help I can give you.'

Simon nodded then sprinted away, darting down the side alley, his feet echoing on the stone flags and off the damp walls on either side. He'd had enough. He just wanted to run and run and be away from all this, but the end of the alley was lost in smog and he felt like he was running through a cocoon of dank cotton wool, his vision limited to bricks, tatty wooden doors leading into back yards and stinking rubbish littering the ground that he stumbled and clattered into. He slowed to a walking pace, then nearly jumped out of his skin as one of the wooden doors suddenly reverberated beside his ear with a sharp sound like a something heavy had been flung at it, followed by a crazy series of barks from a dog.

He shouted 'Shut up!' and the dog's voice diminished to a low and menacing growl. He was giving in to panic and that was when mistakes were made, and he was already telegraphing his presence by making such a noise.

A husky voice floated out from a dark doorway, disembodied and yet distinct. It was a voice that seemed to tell of a lifetime of cigarettes and alcohol, cracked and on the edge of breaking into a heavy cough.

'Where are you going in such a hurry, young man?'

Simon stopped dead.

'Here! Over here!'

The voice broke off into a series of deep, wracking coughs that betrayed the man's ruined lungs. Simon should have fled, but he was not sure if the man was alone, nor whether he was in front blocking his way or standing behind. He was gripped by indecision.

'Found what you're looking for? No? Hehehe, I thought not.' The laugh was soft and low and sounded slightly demented.

A dark figure draped in a filthy overcoat, a crumpled hat of indeterminate shape pressed low over straggling strands of lank, greasy hair and leaning upon a wooden walking stick stepped out of the dark towards him. A thin arm with twisted, tangled fingers like the twigs on a winter tree reached towards him, twitching at his sleeve. Simon recoiled, partly from the touch and partly from the appalling stench of unwashed body and rotting flesh that coagulated around the two of them in the oppressive atmosphere.

'I know what you're looking for, and I've got it.' He twitched at the sleeve again with surprising force, then his cough took over and Simon stared in horror at the twisted creature wreathed in mist, oddly compelled by the old man's claim and yet repulsed by his appearance.

The man looked up at Simon, stepping even closer, the smell increasing to an almost physical level. His face was a bright pink and livid red with ugly blotches, the skin stretched taut until shiny on one side, whilst fantastically creased on the other like scrunched paper, one eye socket distorted so it was pulled permanently wide, the other almost closed. His mouth seemed to have no lips, just a narrow slit surrounded by thin straggles of moth-eaten beard. 'I've got it. I've got the insurance... You need insurance in this bad world and I was too clever. Hehehe. I hid it, see?' He gave an oddly conspiratorial look.

'Hid what?' There was a knot of disgust in Simon's voice.

'I saw them, on the street with the milk bottle filled with petrol. They mixed a Molotov cocktail just for me.'

'Who? I don't understand.'

'I was watching for them. I was clever. Unlike that big man with hate on his hands and now he's paying the price. Hehehe!' The old man gripped Simon's sleeve and despite the horribly mangled fingers with the skin melted and reshaped around the bones it felt like metal forceps pinching his flesh. 'You want what I've got! But it will cost you.' He yanked at the sleeve in an angry motion.

'Leave me alone! What do you know about anything? Here, take this, have a cup of tea and leave off.' Simon thrust a shilling towards the man.

'I want more than a cup of tea!' He batted Simon's hand from below so the coin went spinning into the air before landing with a little tinkling sound. 'Listen boy, I dragged it from the canal. I was watching them.' The staring eye rolled conspiratorially. 'But there's something missing.' He shook his head unhappily like a caged circus lion. 'Very important things missing.'

Simon was about to push the stinking old tramp away, but stopped. 'What's that about the canal? Is this about the drowned man?'

'Shh! Quiet! You are not so much in a hurry now, are you, eh? You have time for a crazy old man now. Oh yes!' He clawed again at Simon's sleeve before breaking off into another bout of terrible coughing. Once it was over, he continued in a low voice that forced Simon to bend closer and inhale the terrible stench of rot. 'A man going in the water. Splosh! Plop! In he went, so smoothly, so quiet, oh, it was ver-ry quiet. Clever.' He stopped and stared at Simon. 'They burnt me, but I can still see and I can still hear and I can still think.' He tapped his head with a forefinger and turned away, his words drifting over his shoulder as he stumped off. 'I can't stand fire though... I like to be near water. And so I saw them carry him.'

'Please stop talking in riddles.' Simon was following, stumbling along in his noxious wake. 'Who did you see? Tell me!'

'The man you are asking about, stupid. I saw him and his fat friend together with the nasty one. I've watched you all day. I'm good, eh?' He momentarily checked his stride to cast a strange, wild look at Simon. 'I can get along fast with my stick and I know every corner, street and alley.' He smacked the stick on the ground as if to make the point, but then broke down into ever-worsening coughs, eventually spitting what looked like blood on to the ground, making Simon recoil.

'You're none too clever.' He leered into Simon's face. 'But I need you. So we work together. I lost something. You find it and we get a great reward. Follow...' He stumped away at some speed.

'Need me for what? Where are you going?'

'Not safe here.' He looked over his shoulder up at Simon, his distorted face ghoulish. 'Keep quiet and follow.'

Simon did follow, unsure why he was doing so and fearing this was nothing more than a lonely, crackpot man playing a stupid game just for the company, and yet he was intrigued. Could this really be the piece of luck he was seeking? He had no idea what he was letting himself in for, but with only about an hour before the *Primrose* passed Marylebone, he felt he had no options left.

They moved rapidly through the fog, dipping down back alleys and stairways, swiftly cutting across the bigger streets filled with traffic, the hobbling man preferring to take quieter roads and cross desolate bombsites. Simon was having a problem keeping his bearings, desperately trying to read and remember street names if he caught a glimpse of them as the pair wove a complex path through the grubby underbelly of London. He sensed they had made almost a complete circle and were probably not so very far from where they started, but on the opposite side of the Regent's Canal and within the electrical generating station yard.

'I've had enough of this. You're just taking me in circles!'

'A long way around, but it pays to be careful. I was careful. That's why they didn't burn me to death.' The man started coughing again.

Simon felt alarmed, what was all this? It was disturbing hearing this talk of being burnt and the man's melted skin brought vivid memories flooding back of being trapped inside the hot firebox, feeling the oppression of the over-heated darkness pressing in on him, his throat dry like ashes, and lungs burning and he suddenly felt a disturbing connection to these crazed ramblings about fire.

The old man was now stomping his way across a tangle of overgrown railway sidings, finding his way with the sureness of a mountain goat, picking a way across the rails, rotting sleepers, point rods and signal wires, apparently able to see through the combined effect of night and the wall of smog. Simon stumbled and lurched along behind, aware of the looming shapes of solitary wagons and the clankity-clank and hiss of a moving engine. They arrived at a small, ramshackle hut constructed of tarred sleepers, now far from the perpendicular, with a rusty, corrugated iron roof draped in thick festoons of Russian vine that almost enveloped the building. There was a rotten door out of kilter with the drunken slant of the opening. The old man unpegged the latch and swung the door open on one hinge. He stepped inside, beckoning for Simon to follow. It took all his courage to do so, but he decided it was too late to turn back now.

The elder man lit a pair of sooty railway lamps and pulled the door closed, dropping a curtain of potato sacking across to block the light. The hut was small and housed a dirty mattress and dark blankets on the ash floor, a wonky table and a short wooden bench. There was the lower part of an old kitchen dresser supporting a few books, a tin mug, a military canteen set broken apart into a frying pan, metal plate and short flat utensils. Old newspapers were strewn on the floor, presumably as insulation. A window was boarded up with layers of water-stained cardboard. A rusting, pot-bellied stove stood cold in the corner and the air hung heavy with damp and mould. The man placed a lamp on the table close to their faces, the light of which immediately pushed the dank air back into the gloomy corners.

'Sit!'

Simon cautiously lowered himself onto the bench. His railwayman's cap had been scraping the metal roof so he was glad to be seated. The old man rootled about in the dresser, mumbling the whole time in an odd monologue, then stood up, clutching a brown leather briefcase to his chest and grinned. It was a terrible sight.

'Look. He dropped it in the water.' He laid the still-damp briefcase on the table. 'You will help me, young man. It's agreed?'

'I—I don't know. I don't know what this is about and how I can help. Please explain.'

'Look! Look inside. See for yourself.'

Simon opened the case. It smelled of damp paper and wet leather, though this was far better than the appalling odour emanating from his companion. There were bundles of waterlogged typewritten papers welded into sodden clumps. He removed one and attempted to turn the pages but only succeeded in tearing a great chunk from one corner.

'It's ruined.'

He tried to read the top page in the poor light and saw it concerned a claim for stolen goods. The other bundle was much the same, though this peeled apart more readily, but again was just business stuff about insurance. He pulled a face.

'Go on!'

Out came a soggy railway timetable, a train ticket, and what felt like a piece of thin metal wrapped in brown paper. The covering was torn and stained and had clearly been badly rewrapped around whatever it concealed. The paper came away easily to reveal a copper plate, etched with fine line, its polished surface now stained green and black in blotches that echoed the man's poor face. Simon squinted at it and then grinned. 'Five pounds... Golly gosh! Is this for making money?'

'For printing counterfeit bank notes of the most perfect quality.' The crazy old guy made a horrible sucking noise with his non-existent lips and a strange gesture with one twiggy hand. Simon realised it was an attempt at a theatrical kiss. 'The most exquisite printing plate, though I say it myself. I was the best in the business.'

'This would print five pound notes?'

'In the right hands.' The man was nodding. 'Of course, it is not easy, even with this, but in the hands of a skilled printer... Hehehe!' His laugh broke down into a cough that lasted for a long time. 'It made a lot of money at one time.'

'The man in the canal had this plate? Why? I mean, was this why they killed him?'

'Dennis and his big friend killed Pym. I can tell you where, when, even the exact time. But there was someone else there, a nasty piece of work. He's worried, though. There are certain things he wants so much that he'd kill for them. And he thinks I had them in my possession. He thinks I'm dust now... hehehe... a pile of ash along with my papers.' The old man stopped suddenly and changed the tone of his voice. 'Pym played his cards all wrong.' He tapped the copper plate, 'this is not what that nasty piece of work wanted, so it went into the water with the case. I watched as it floated for a minute or two then sank. A few hours with a hook and a stick for a fishing rod... I needed to be sure, to understand.'

'So do I. I'm lost.' But Simon felt his heart leap. He'd got a witness who, despite appearing a little bonkers, was starting to sound convincing. He could prove that Dennis Parkey and Big Ron had been up to no good. The old man was right — he'd given him something to take to the police, but he just could not understand the story.

'Listen: Mr Pym did not understand, and made a mistake. Or he got greedy! He played with fire, and I know you don't play with that. Not without getting burned.'

They both shivered in the dank hut.

'After my shop burnt Pym was there, looking at it. He wanted to help. Seemed a good man at heart. Deep down.' The old man was nodding slowly and looked tired, the exertions of the day seemed to have suddenly caught up with him and he was visibly flagging. 'I'm finished. I'm gone. I know that. But I want to take those bastards down with me!' He slammed a fist on the table. 'He promised to help...' He broke down into a long and painful cough and Simon could only watch helplessly.

'He took some things from me a few weeks ago. Special papers I'd hidden away from my shop. I gave them to him for safe keeping — my insurance policy, if you like.' The man nodded very earnestly. 'He was going to use these to get revenge.' He spat on the floor. 'Phah! I don't understand. Did he think this plate was the most valuable, the most *dangerous* thing I gave him? Stupid man!' The man pulled a contorted expression that approximated surprise. Simon looked confused and just stared. 'I think he betrayed me. He was just the same as the others, trying to get something for himself.'

Simon's eyes were like saucers. Heaven knows what this all meant, but he'd stumbled on just what he needed. He had a witness and he had evidence.

'But we still have luck on our side. They imagine this piece of useless metal was all he found in the ruins of my shop. They imagine Pym played his ace and were pleased it proved useless. He's dead, the plate in the canal. Problem solved. But Pym must have hidden the really important things somewhere. Small paper documents. Small yet deadly...'

*　　*　　*　　*

Five minutes later, Simon was running, the damp briefcase tucked under his arm, cap rammed hard on his head, heart thumping in his chest, stumbling and tumbling over rail and sleeper, dodging tall pylons as they appeared to step out of the gloom and bar his way, but his mind was focused on escape and he somehow ducked and dived and kept his footing. He was completely alert now, the adrenaline coursing through his veins as he hurtled as fast as he could between the great, humming buildings of the electrical generating station, a greenish light emanating from tall, arched windows along the side of the massive turbine halls illuminating the strange tangles of wires and insulators above his head in a confusing cat's cradle of fizzing power lines.

Was he too late? It was too dark to read his watch and struggling to do so would just waste valuable time. He had to get down to the canal, but was foiled by towering metal fencing he could never scale. There was a narrow way through at one point leading onto steps down to the towpath, but in his panic and the poor visibility, he just could not locate it. He stopped, chest heaving and tried to get his bearings. Was that the low dum-dum-dum of the *Primrose*'s engine? Or was it the regular beat of a man running? The old man said Simon was in grave danger. He had made his presence too obvious all afternoon.

He looked about in desperation, forcing himself to take a moment to properly identify the massive buildings around him.

I've done it, just mustn't blow it now...

Ahead lay the main railway line on its elevated course across the massive bridges, so to his right was the canal... and yes! Between those two buildings must be the steps onto the towpath. He ran forward and his heart leapt as he recognised the place. The sound of his boots clattered off the walls as he flung himself headlong towards the gate as all attempt at concealment was forgotten. The gate was bolted but not padlocked and he flung the bolt to one side with a clang.

There was the *Primrose*, chugging sedately past as a drift of smoke from the stovepipe crossed the narrow divide between boat and bank.

'Ahoy! Ahoy!' He waved madly.

Tustain sprang alert and instantly steered closer, the engine note changing to neutral, then hard reverse, kicking up a splash of water around the stern and creating a wash of little waves and a cloud of diesel exhaust. Tustain said nothing, concentrating only on collecting Simon, who was fortunately accustomed not only to boarding a rocking boat but also to the crazy movements of a locomotive footplate, and so leaped confidently aboard the still-moving craft.

It was not a moment too soon. Tustain knew there would be time enough to ask questions and was feeling nervous to breaking point, so immediately pushed the engine into forward gear, willing his craft to accelerate as it inched away from the bank and slowly gathered speed with frustrating sluggishness. A man was running along the towpath. He was strong and solidly built, obviously fit and running easily and gaining on them steadily, his jaw set in a mask of grim determination and there could be no doubt whom he was after.

'Cripes, it's Den Parkey!' Simon hissed. 'Hurry!'

'Seen him. Get below and keep your head down. He can't jump us now and no man can keep pace once we get up to speed. We can keep this going all night if needs be.' Tustain peered into the dark at the figure loping along in long steady strides. 'Though there is a problem looming ahead.'

Parkey continued his run. He knew the canal like the back of his hand and could afford to let them ease ahead. He'd catch up once they reached Camden Lock. That would delay them a good fifteen minutes. OK, there were two of them aboard and that could prove tricky, but he'd think about how best to handle it. This time he was going to finish the lad off.

But he was in for a shock.

Chapter Twenty-eight

There's No Tomorrow
Tony Martin

As the narrowboat turned a corner and was masked by the thick abutments of a bridge, Dennis Parkey was brought to a sudden and shuddering halt as Victor Millett's carefully placed foot sent him sprawling along the cinder path, his palms scoured by the fine ash as he tried to soften his fall. Millett placed a boot on his neck as he lay panting and momentarily stunned with shock and surprise.

'Don't get up until I say, and no funny stuff that might make me angrier than I am already.'

'We just want a little word, that's all. There's been another problem with the arrangements.' Henry Bish lit a cigarette, the flame flaring in his dark and soulless eyes as he stood, almost invisible, under the bridge. 'We'd like your opinion on how this happened.'

He gestured to Parkey to stand, and the three walked along the towpath, the tension between them almost palpable. Millett hung a step back, Bish walked beside Parkey, the raw graze marks on his palms stinging viciously and doing nothing to help improve his foul mood. He was sweating after his exertions and feeling the effect of the two pints he'd swiftly downed in the station bar before someone had tipped him the wink that the dumb kid was in town asking awkward questions about him.

'Mr Bish, I was on to him.' Dennis growled. 'I'd have collared the little bugger and beaten seven bells out of him.'

'I'm not interested in the brat! He's nothing but a waste of breath,' spat Bish. 'The problem is, we've got a warehouse full of very valuable stuff gone missing, no thanks to you.'

'How's it missing?'

'That's exactly what we'd like to know. The wagons never arrived. *mucho de nada*, as our guv'nor would say.'

'Did you get the lad to switch the cards?' Millett's voice came from behind.

'Yeah. You told me to, remember?'

Millett made a noise that was ambiguous.

'Come off it! It was your bloody idea in the first place. It should have been a piece of cake for the little bastard,' said Parkey.

'Trouble is, Den, we've heard that you had a spot of bother with the lad in between times. Is that so?'

'How d'you know about that?'

'We've got eyes and ears all over. You best remember that.' His voice was menacing.

'It must have been serious,' remarked Bish, 'or why bother?'

'It was nothing, just a misunderstanding.' But Dennis did not sound convincing.

'Putting the frighteners on the lad is all very well, but it looks like he bottled out of the job as a result. Worse still, he's been looking for you all day. Asking some very odd questions, he was. Now what would all that be about?'

'I dunno.'

'You don't seem to be very well informed these days. That's a pity.' Bish smiled at Dennis in a manner that sent a chill through him. An ominous silence fell for a moment. 'But right now, the missing wagons are giving us more serious concern.'

'They can't just vanish!'

Bish shrugged. 'It would appear they have, Mr Parkey.' His exaggerated politeness did nothing to lessen the menace. 'Turned into three box wagons of fertiliser, if you really want to know. You'd better hope ours turn up soon.' He was not ready to let Dennis know they had already been located. It was time to make the man squirm.

The men started climbing a slippery flight of steps that brought them to the edge of a busy roundabout. The noise of grinding motors, the searching beams cast by fog lamps and the burning braziers placed on the roundabout to warn motorists of its presence were a strange, other-worldly contrast to the sluggish calm and quiet of the canal side. They picked their way between the slow-moving traffic towards a darkened building with wooden boarding over the windows and rusty chains padlocked around ornate iron gates closing a series of entrances beneath a long wooden canopy. At each end of the frontage were poor little shops and a tiny petrol station, although they were dark and closed for the night.

'Where are we going?'

'To show you the new depot. We should have thought of this ages ago.' Millett swiftly unlocked the padlock and slid the chain away. 'There are more discreet ways into the place, but in this filthy night no one's going to see us nip through here.'

They stepped through the gate and Bish flicked on a torch as he pushed open one of a pair of wooden doors. They entered an abandoned railway booking hall. It had an unsettling stillness to it, with odd shadows flickering in the corners from the torch beam. Everything smelled of rat droppings. A cold draught blew from the far side, bringing an even stronger whiff of damp concrete and sewage.

'Follow me.' Bish strode across the litter-strewn tiled floor, past the rows of empty ticket windows towards an archway opening onto a sharply-dipping tiled corridor lined with dirty white and maroon glazed tiles that bore the station name 'Lord's'. A pair of escalators lay idle, gathering rubbish. Old posters stared from the walls as the men clattered down the staircase, trying to avoid the piles of abandoned clothes, odd shoes, a tin helmet, empty beer bottles and great drifts of paper that had gathered like autumn leaves. Posters of Churchill, the Land Army and handsome RAF fighter pilots giving a thumbs-up sign silently watched their progress from the curving walls.

Parkey did not like the London Underground. He had never eradicated his lifelong, irrational fear of the narrow tunnels and steep steps leading into the unpleasant bowels of the city. He always found the Tube either far too hot and stuffy or icily cold, never a comfortable temperature. As the torch beam swung about, Parkey's eyes took in a bright red poster with white lettering urging him to 'Keep Calm and Carry On'. He set his jaw in grim determination to try and do just that, and fell into step.

'We've moved the iron works stock down here. Bit of a hike, but secret and well out of sight,' it was Millett who broke the silence, sounding calmer and more relaxed than earlier. 'We can bring up what's needed for one night's trading, and keep the rest out of harm's way.'

Dennis tried to mask his growing sense of dread. 'Did Big Ron and you lot shift it whilst I was up north?'

'Correct. Worked all night, we did.'

'Where is the big guy? Not seen him since I got back into town.' He tried to sound relaxed.

'Rodney? He's gone away. We moved him on,' Bish chimed in. 'We thought it best to relocate him.'

'Gone? Where?'

'Oh, you'll soon find out. You'll be joining him, as it happens. With you being mates, we thought that would work out fine.'

Dennis concluded that things were not as bad as he'd feared. He'd be working with Big Ron again, probably in some rotten, dingy part of the city, but it could be worse.

When they arrived at platform level Bish stepped up to an electrical cabinet on the wall and fiddled about until the station became illuminated by a string of low wattage lights. Although not bright, they appeared so after the thick blanket of darkness. A rat scuttled across the tracks and there was the sound of trickling water. Parkey looked around, trying to assess the situation, his fists balled tensely at his side.

'That's better. They need these for the maintenance gangs and fluffer girls cleaning the tracks. The station closed down before the war, though it was used as an air raid shelter. That's why there's so much ruddy junk down here.' Bish nodded at a stack of rusting bed frames stacked against a wall. 'Now it's just full of ghosts!' He grinned. 'Follow my footsteps, as it gets narrow and hazardous. Remember to keep well clear of that electric rail.'

'Where we going?'

'For a little walk.' Bish nodded towards the narrow train tunnel entrance. 'There's a whole maze of tunnels and hidden rooms through there. It's a secret world.'

Dennis felt his skin become damp. The gloomy station and the black hole of the single track tunnel were getting to him. 'What's going on? First you jump me and nearly knock my blummin' teeth out, then you tell me Big Ron's been moved on somewhere and you're filling me with stuff about how I've lost the flippin' wagons and how I'm in trouble. Now you want me to go down some soddin' rat hole! Let's talk here. Come on, out wiv it! I've done yer dirty work, just like you asked. I done the shop fire and I finished that Pym geezer off! What more d'you want?'

Bish walked briskly towards him, beady eyes flashing, moustache twitching, making Parkey take an involuntary step backwards closer to the platform edge. 'I suggest you simmer down. All right, here's as good as anywhere to talk. So you did what we asked? Yeah, and we paid you handsomely too. Trouble is, we expected a good service, and we're not pleased with the results.'

'I've had enough of this. All I get is an ear bashing. Do your own dirty stuff from now on!'

Bish stepped right up to Parkey, his mouth close to other man's unshaven face. 'The body in the canal was a complete balls up. The police are close to seeing right through that. Top Link himself had to patch things up. We've had to ditch Loughborough as a write off, no thanks to you getting heavy with a bloody cosh!'

'I didn't know he was a copper!'

'No, you didn't. But the stuff was already stashed and the records burnt, so why the violence? All you've done is stirred everything up—'

'—I risked my neck doing that—'

'Bish continued without pause, '—and now you've gone and lost the bloody stock! Everything started with you and big fat Rodney not doing a neat enough job in the first place. We've straightened things out with Ron. Now it's time to do the same with you.'

'What d'you mean?'

Dennis felt a push of chilled air escape from the narrow bore hole ahead and heard the distant clack and metallic rumble of a train. He glanced nervously down towards the tracks. He hated that electric rail, there was something about it that gave him the jitters and made his knees feel like jelly when he stood too close to the edge. It seemed to lie there like a malevolent snake, silent, and yet in his mind he was sure it fizzed and hissed in a low sound on the edge of hearing. He looked back at Bish and to his surprise could detect fear in the man's eyes. For all his shout and bluster, for all his anger and aggression, Bish was scared too.

'Gawd, the air down here dries my throat.' Millett was unscrewing the cap from a bottle he'd pulled from his shoulder bag. 'You need to drink plenty of water.' He took a swig. 'Want some, Den?' He offered the bottle.

His tongue was almost stuck to the roof of his mouth. 'Thanks.'

Bish stepped a pace back whilst Parkey took a swig, then accepted the bottle in turn. He appeared to relax, the dressing down over for now. As he held the bottle he looked at Parkey. 'Things don't always turn out as planned. Disappointing, but no hard feelings.'

Suddenly he shoved Dennis hard with one hand, his foot expertly curled around the calf of the now-unbalanced man, sending him toppling helplessly over the side of the platform to straddle the running lines and the live rail in a swift movement that lasted barely a second. The glass bottle was tossed after the falling Parkey with expert accuracy onto the live rail, where it shattered in a flash of blue sparkling splinters that reflected the light like a silver shower from a rocket, as arcs of water conducted the lethal electricity into his outstretched arms and onto his face. The fizz, bang and crackle was stomach-churning as his body flexed, tautened and bucked with just one short, horribly loud scream.

'Amateur!' growled Bish, contemptuously.

They instantly turned away, Bish dousing the emergency lights, leaving just a trace of ominous blue flickering from below the platform edge. As the sound of an approaching train grew louder, the two men stepped back into the shadows of the entrance arch. They stood and watched without emotion as a Bakerloo Line train sped through the station, its cold steel wheels instantly butchering the parts of Dennis Parkey's body that lay across the rails.

'It's so hard to find men of the calibre we're accustomed to,' observed Millett, his green eyes keen as those of a big cat out hunting. 'He was just a roughneck foot soldier.'

Bish nodded, his jaw set firm. 'There can be no room for weakness. Absolute discipline at all times.'

With just the faintest trace of light spilling from the speeding train, and unseen except by Bish, Millett stood rigidly to attention, his work-booted heels clicking softly as he offered his assent, though the words were barely audible: 'Zu Befehl, Herr Hauptsturmführer!'

'Your loyalty does you credit, but don't speak it aloud.' Bish scratched an itch below his left armpit where the tattoo bearing his SS number had been inexpertly removed.

'Jahwol!' The reply was barely a whisper.

'We're getting out, with immediate effect. It will take time of course; a few weeks to sell the stock, longer to find a buyer for Hendon Pharmaceuticals, but I have the necessary documents and money to make a safe escape. Keep them ready to use at short notice and prepare your disguise. Use all the skills at your disposal to avoid discovery.'

The man known around Marylebone as Victor Millett, but who had been christened Jürgen Sonnenfeldt, and subsequently known by two other identities since he abandoned his uniform in 1945, drew himself up tall and nodded, already thinking about the preparations he must now make to turn himself into a vehicle spare parts dealer working in Cairo.

'We need to collect those containers and get them shipped out. We have our orders, and we, of all people, cannot fail. We are better than these...' Bish indicated where the mangled and burnt body lay between the rails.

If the driver had seen anything between the tracks, it had been too brief a glance to cause him to slow, and so the series of thumps along the bottom of the train were unexpected, however, they didn't seem to impair its progress and the driver decided it could wait until he stopped at St John's Wood. Only when he stepped out of his cab to take a look did he notice a piece of something bloody, and disturbingly unpleasant, lodged in the front bogie. Flecks of crimson spattered the dusty frames and wheels and the terrible reality dawned on him that his train had struck someone. The line closed for service ten minutes later and the shaken driver offered his report to the station supervisor. Half an hour after that, the power was switched off and a further twenty minutes later, six maintenance men with heavy hearts, wearing long, thick rubber gloves and carrying waterproof bags would start to walk the line, followed at some distance by a stubby London Underground pannier tank engine in deep maroon and golden-yellow lettering hauling an open truck.

By the time the severed limbs and torso of Dennis Parkey were discovered, the two men who knew how he came to be lying there were long gone.

Chapter Twenty-nine

Don't Get Around Much Anymore
Duke Ellington Orchestra

It was after midnight and Vignoles was on the train back to Leicester after a busy but fruitful evening.

He'd placed a telephone call from Marylebone to the governor of His Majesty's Prison, Wormwood Scrubs. They knew each other, having studied in Leicester at the same time, too many years ago. They rarely spoke more than once or twice a year on the telephone, but liked to exchange news and a few words about their home life, chew over the fortunes of Leicester City football club and, once in a blue moon, have a pint or two in Leicester or at one of the grand Victorian London pubs Vignoles was so fond of. However, requests relating directly to work were a novelty.

The unexpected nature and urgency of Vignoles's call had puzzled the governor, who almost certainly would have rebuffed this type of request at such short notice, but was prepared to make an exception because it was Vignoles.

'Visiting ends at six. You still have time if you take a cab. In the meantime, we shall speak with the prisoner and see if he will agree, but I must warn you he does not welcome visitors. He may very well refuse and you will have a wasted journey on a grim night.'

'Do what you can. I just need ten minutes alone with him. Please do try to get him to acquiesce. It might even improve things for him when he's released into the big wide world.'

'May I enquire what this is about?'

'I'd rather not say at this juncture, but it could be significant to a case I am working on.'

'I see. Well, I fear I shall have to be satisfied with that, eh, Charles? Very well, I'll try to bring some influence to bear on the prisoner.'

It took Vignoles some ten minutes to pass through the security checks at the prison, leaving a few moments in which to chat with the governor in person.

'I'm sorry to be so darned cloak-and-dagger, but sometimes it pays to play one's cards a bit close. If my hunch pays off, I promise to give you the full run-down. If not, then I'd ask you forget all about my visit.'

'How very intriguing.' He raised an eyebrow. 'The prisoner has agreed to give you exactly ten minutes. Perhaps I was too literal in conveying your request.' They both laughed. 'He's deemed low risk: he's kept here rather than an open prison purely for his own safety. Criminal gangs have long memories and considerable influence, even within prison walls.' He gave Vignoles an arch look, 'I suppose that's why you're being so circumspect.'

Vignoles gave an ambiguous shrug in response.

'Ready? We've given you a private interview room with a guard outside.'

When the prisoner was brought in, Vignoles was struck by how much he had aged since 1946. His remaining hair was snow white and thinning; the crown of his head quite bald, although his moustache remained bushy. He wore new National Health prescription glasses with thin wire frames and walked with a pronounced stoop. When he sat down, he did so carefully, as if easing his knee and hip joints into place. He looked like an old man. If prison had done anything to punish him then it was by robbing him of any last vestiges of youth. He gave Vignoles a brief glance then stared at his lined and creased hands resting on the table, making it clear he considered the visit an intrusion.

'Mr Price, are you keeping well?'

'The Scrubs is no rest cure, so can we dispense with the pleasantries and get on with it?'

'It was good of you to see me at such short notice.'

The prisoner said nothing.

'You may wonder why I am here.'

Silence.

'I need to ask you something about the events in 1946. There's been a development and I think you can help.'

'I am serving my time, inspector. I admitted my culpability and accepted my punishment without complaint. I have nothing further to say.' He stared at the table.

'Something has come to my attention that appears to link with the Water Street case.'

Ken Price gave Vignoles a sharp look. There was a twitch in one eye and a tensing in his shoulders. 'Listen, I have a simple and quiet life. I look after the library, I get along with the screws well enough and the food is almost edible. I've three more years to serve, maybe less, if I'm lucky. The cons leave me alone because I'm of no interest to them now, and I like it that way. I never discuss what happened.'

'I appreciate what you are saying, but I need to ask you about the man who masterminded the whole money counterfeiting and laundering operation that you were part of. The man at the very top of the ladder in the Water Street gang.'

'I never knew who that was! Why would I?' Price snapped.

'Come off it, you or one of your co-conspirators at some point must have referred to the man behind it all. The boss?'

'Leave it out!'

'You were paid by him and he must have a name. A nickname?'

'Bugger off.'

'Do yourself a favour, Price. Help me nail him and you'll lose this poisonous thorn from your side forever.'

'I can't do that! I don't know who he was, and besides, I'd soon be dead if I went blabbing my mouth off.' His hands trembled slightly. 'They use razor blades. In the showers. Horrible.' He dropped his voice to barely a whisper. 'They've got ears and eyes everywhere.' He flicked his eyes towards the door.

'Don't panic: officially, I am a relation.' Vignoles leaned forward and spoke softly. 'This is strictly between you and me. Now, I'm going to write something down and I just want you to nod or shake your head if this is the name you heard.

Price glowered.

'I feel sure the governor could look favourably upon your parole date at the next review if you are helpful now.'

He was tempted. No prisoner shirked from the suggestion of an earlier release date. He stared as Vignoles slid a page from his notebook across the table. 'Did you ever hear this name spoken?'

After looking at the note for a few moments, his eyes widened and his hands tensed, then almost imperceptibly he nodded his head.

'Are you sure you knew this as someone's name? It could be easily confused with a word used for train crew.'

'I was a driver, remember.' He looked at Vignoles with a bitter expression. 'Look, I knew this was nothing to do with the Leicester boys. That was obvious at the time.' He spat the words out with contempt.

'How did you know?'

'The way it was said.'

Vignoles was now sure that Sir Paul Frobisher had masterminded the Water Street money counterfeiting operation they had smashed in '46 and was the man behind the long frauds and associated robberies for which Jack Pym had helped smoothed the way. His long ruminations over a pint in Marylebone had paid off, leading him to suspect there was a connection. But he needed more,

Vignoles screwed the note into a ball and stuffed it into his jacket pocket. 'Any idea about the identity of the man concerned?'

'No.'

The two men studied each other across the plain wooden table.

'No one will know it came from you. I give you my word of honour.'

'I've said too much as it is. I want this interview to end now.'

'Why are you so scared? You're serving your time and will walk free before very long. You can retire to the country and grow dahlias in your old age and put all this behind you.'

'Give it a rest.' Price was angry but there was something in his eyes, a hunted look.

'Trouble is, there you are, in your little garden, pottering around in the shed when suddenly there's someone at the gate. Unexpected. Unwelcome.'

Price swallowed.

'Or there's a ring on the doorbell in the night. Of course, they *may* never come, but you won't ever rest easy.'

'They wouldn't bother. I'm nothing now.'

Vignoles shrugged. 'Some people have long memories,' he paused a beat, 'and they don't like a grass.'

'You set me up! You dirty rotten—'

'—Calm down! I've done nothing of the sort, I'm being level with you. You're not free now and won't ever be, not until I feel the collars of those at the top of this gang. But when we do, they'll be out of your way — permanently!'

'Why should I believe you?'

'Because from where I'm sitting you don't have many options.'

Price chewed at the inside of his lower lip then dropped his voice to a bare whisper. 'I heard a rumour he was supposed to be a bit high-hat. Well off. A big shot in the city or something, with cash to throw around. Micky Rollo let that slip out once and got a right dressing down for it.'

'Who put him straight?'

Price stared at Vignoles for a long time. 'He had a nasty sort working for him. A deputy, you might say. I never met him, but young Jimmy was there when he tore a strip off Rollo. He told me about it.'

Vignoles nodded, he recalled that Jimmy Creswell had met a particularly nasty end all those years ago.

Price was almost whispering. 'They called him Bash. I've never said a squeak of this to no one, and I won't ever repeat it again, not in court, nowhere.' Price leant back in his chair. 'Hardly worth you coming out for, was it?'

'Far from it. Your assistance is much appreciated.'

'I would like to go now. Guard!' He raised his voice and the door opened immediately. 'My uncle is leaving.'

Vignoles sat in the corner of an empty compartment of the last through train from Marylebone to Leicester, smoking a pipe and feeling content. This had been an oddly satisfying day, despite following a course quite different from the one planned. His boss had given him strict orders to drop the enquiry, but he knew it was too late to stop now. He would just have to tread carefully because he could ill afford to be caught blatantly defying Badger, not until he had the case wrapped up.

He was after two men. One known as Top Link, aka Sir Paul Frobisher, aka Mr Jordan; the other his ever-present deputy, Henry Bish. He knew they were masterminding complex and lucrative swindles similar to that reported in the *Melody Maker* article, but were they involved in the deaths of Jack Pym and Rodney Mattox? The post mortem report and fingerprints from the smashed lorry might reveal something, but so far he had nothing to link them directly to either man's death.

As the train chugged northwards the wheels clickity-clacked in a regular rhythm over the rail joints and the coach rocked gently to the beat of the three-cylinder engine. Vignoles's battered body demanded rest, and he succumbed to a deep and dreamless sleep, his hat tipped low over his face and gently resting on his bruised nose, a hand in his lap cradling his unlit pipe.

He would have been surprised to learn that, in a genteel semi-detached villa in south London, Chief Superintendent Badger was lying awake in his bed, tossing and turning and disturbing his wife, who had resorted to pulling more of the of the heavily-embroidered satin counterpane across to her side of the bed to form a small bulwark between herself and her ever-fidgeting husband. Badger was bothered. An unpleasant sense of unease had steadily crept over him all that evening like a bad attack of stomach ache. A couple of stiff whiskies as they listened to the wireless had done nothing to settle him. It was most irregular, especially as he had been so confident and decisive with Vignoles that afternoon and he was not predisposed to ever question his own orders once given. Self-doubt was something he rarely suffered, but he was struggling tonight.

Was it self doubt? Or an attempt to fend off a gnawing sense that something was wrong? Not for the first time in the last few days, he had cause to revive the dormant detective inside him as he chewed matters over like a dog worrying at a bone. It was time to shrug off the mantle of management and new policy implementation, time to forget staffing quotas, crime reports and the obsequious bowing and scraping to his paymasters and return to the eager sleuth he had once been: a copper who by pure instinct could sniff out something fishy from twenty yards.

He'd telephoned Sir Ronald Vallance the moment Vignoles left the office and suggested Scotland Yard arrest Adeline Pym, Peter Wilde and their hired killer immediately. He explained this was a strong tip off based on sound detective work and would secure a surefire result. Sir Ronald had been most appreciative, indeed almost fulsome in his thanks, indicating that Special Branch would have the matter cleared up in no time and advising Badger to stand his men down from any further involvement.

The strange thing was, Sir Ronald had relaxed from his ultra-reserved self, almost as if this news was a weight off his mind. They had discussed a few minor points, almost as close colleagues might, the assistant commissioner complimenting Badger on the work of his WPCs. However, as Badger replayed the conversation in his head he remembered something odd. Sir Ronald had used the past tense when conveying Sir Paul Frobisher's appreciation of Badger's help in this matter, and when saying it would not go unnoticed. How could Sir Paul give thanks for something he knew nothing about? And why should he feel 'grateful'? If Sir Paul were privy to such a serious criminal investigation then there must have been an appalling breach of protocol.

Badger asked himself if he'd simply grasped the wrong end of the stick. Perhaps the AC *assumed* that thanks would be forthcoming. But Badger was still not satisfied. Had these two men gained prior knowledge of how the case was developing? Did they know more about the case than he did? Then there was the question why the arrest was not carried out by DI Tykett, who had initiated the investigation. For that matter, why not just let the Leicester City Police deal with it? It seemed a darned odd decision to bring in Special Branch, who had a pretty dreadful record for being heavy handed. Were they not reserved for the more unpleasant and gang-related crimes?

He went downstairs in his dressing gown and sat in near-darkness, a whisky in his hand, and asked himself questions that previously he'd refused to contemplate. Why had he been so suddenly invited into Sir Paul's inner circle? It was flattering, but if he were completely honest, there was something 'forced' about it. He had been pretty much ignored for most of the evening. But then they'd suddenly sought him out and dangled the carrot of a greatly expanded railway police service in front of him, whilst offering exceptionally fine brandy, perhaps to dull his senses. There was something unnatural about the pattern of events. Badger began to wonder if he were being 'bought'.

The change from being ignored to being sought out had occurred immediately after Sir Paul had received the telephone call. He'd suppressed the memory until this afternoon, when Vignoles's comments had reawakened it. Yes, Vignoles could be a prize pain in the backside at times, but it couldn't be denied the man knew his stuff. And he'd hinted that there was something fishy about the baronet, and even suspected him of being linked to a crime.

Badger drained the glass and had to concede that Vignoles might be on to something. He poured another stiff measure. A cold shiver of revulsion ran through his body as he recalled the scene he had glimpsed through the window at Sir Paul's. The baronet barked a command, his subordinate stood ramrod straight as if to attention: chest out, chin up, then, for just a brief moment, giving a salute. But not the flattened hand held at right angles to the temple, as all right-minded allied fighting forces would give. This was no throwback to his service days of a few years ago with the British army. No, it was a short lift of the right arm, hand curled back against the shoulder ready to be extended forward and upwards as his arm straightened into... The Nazi salute. Sir Paul had instantaneously reached out and stayed the man's hand before he could complete the gesture, then glanced nervously out of the window as he hastily pulled down the blind. No matter how hard he tried, Badger could find no other explanation for the gesture. He had in a quiet moment in the bathroom even rehearsed it in the mirror. Replicating the hand position, so familiar on the newsreels, often held by Hitler as he rode past the crowds standing in an open car. He tried to make it a gesture of acceptance, or acquiescence, but it just did not work. The men had been having an altercation, of that Badger was in no doubt, so the gesture could not be explained away as a lampoon of the despised dictator.

This chilling image, combined with Vignoles's remarks, prompted Badger to speak on the telephone with Digby Wyatt of the *Daily Telegraph*, a journalist known for being particularly well-informed on matters pertaining to the aristocracy, the landed gentry and the glittering circle of acolytes that fluttered around them at balls, gala dinners, shooting parties and other such social occasions. Badger pulled a face registering disgust as he recalled Wyatt's mincing, effeminate mannerisms. However, Wyatt had an irrepressible love of scandal and gossip, matched only by his ability to show discretion and tact when deploying such information. Badger intimated that he wanted some background on the baronet.

'Oh, my dear man, you want to dig the dirt on Sir Paul Frobisher eh? Haha! Well, shall we just say that his terribly dashing good looks and willingness to open a very large cheque book prevent many from asking questions.' He trilled a laugh. 'And of course, don't forget that his is a very *minor* title.'

'What precisely do you mean?'

'You policemen are all the same! So bluff and direct — it quite leaves me breathless,' Wyatt purred. 'You want everything so neat and tidy. Life is just not like that, my dear chief superintendent.'

'I deal with facts, so offer me some.'

'Don't be so hasty. What I can say? That he's been living it up since the end of the war and managing to attract quite a few friends of influence; though I stress, they are strictly from the more *business* end of society.' He spoke the words as if they were somehow tainted and distasteful. 'He is virtually ignored by the truly blue-blooded, who consider him rather gauche and *nouveau riche* for polite society. It hardly needs saying he is excluded from court. However, he claims to have had a rather good war, if somewhat clandestine, and thereby rendered unmentionable. Jolly useful having a secretive war job. One can hint at all manner of dashing exploits without having to prove a thing!'

'Hmm... trouble is, I need to know if he's playing us a straight bat.'

'What do you mean?' Wyatt spoke softly and conspiratorially.

'He's up for election to the board of the Met.'

'Well, his title is perhaps a touch questionable, but no more, and of course he remains a commoner. I did once hear tell that his father died on the Somme, unmarried and without issue. That does rather raise the question of whether he is the result of an illegitimate union. A bastard in the ranks...'

'Where did he get his fortune?'

'No idea, old chap. There was word that his mother was a German girl and perhaps from wealthy stock. He has remained somewhat shy on the matter and nobody has ever met her.'

'But his business affairs? Have you anything you can tell me?'

'Not my forte! Strictly social. All I know is that Sir Paul is very much at the business end of things. Darn it, I wish I had his acumen for amassing wealth.' Wyatt paused a moment. 'I heard he has business affairs overseas, South America and Spain, but I cannot be firm on this point.'

The call left Badger unconvinced of any wrong-doing, but raised intriguing questions. There were reports from Interpol and MI6 that former Nazis were holing up in countries sympathetic to their cause, and the baronet was trading in similar territories. Could this just be coincidence? And if he really was half German...

He picked up the telephone and asked the operator to connect him. The number rang for a long time. *Come on, come on, get up man!*

Eventually it stopped and a bleary voice answered, 'Hello... who is this?'

'Pedder? It's Badger. Get dressed and get over here as fast as you can. Make sure the Rover's got a full tank of petrol and don't spare the coupons. We're going to Leicester!'

Chapter Thirty

Your Red Wagon
Count Basie Orchestra

It was only Signalwoman Green's second day at work in the lonely outpost of Akeman Street, and already she was of the opinion that perhaps it was not going to be quite as dull as she first feared.

For a start, there was the almost-continual procession of trains that passed through her section. Her favourites were the fast or semi-fast expresses that churned and chugged in a thrilling roar towards the signalbox, tearing along the straight approach lines, trailing flags of pale steam in the chill autumn air, chiming their whistles with beautifully haunting notes that carried far across the open countryside, startling flights of lapwing from the fields or provoking a great grey heron to lift itself and flap heavily away, neck folded and long legs trailing. Then there were the lengthy coal trains that clanked and rumbled south, taking what seemed an age before the little guard's van with its smoking stovepipe drew level and she would give the lonely guard at the end of these gargantuan trains a cheery wave. The coal empties, in turn, rattled and banged in a raucous din and clamour on their way back north, then in between were the bustling suburban commuter trains. The most diverting, however, were the lazy pick-up goods, the crews of which tried to find an excuse to loiter for a few minutes longer than necessary on the goods avoiding loop as they exchanged pleasantries and grinned and winked as she leant out of an opened window. No, she was far from bored.

Added to which, despite Edward Earnshaw's conviction that 'nothing ever stopped there', she had been more than a little surprised to discover, as she propped her Rudge-Whitworth bicycle against the side of the box that morning, a row of container wagons on their neat, four-wheeled trucks parked on the rather rusty and weed-strewn siding. They were bright bauxite orange and appeared to glow when a shaft of the rising sun cut through the pale wreaths of low-lying mist, burnishing everything it touched with copper and gold, illuminating the drops of dew caught in spiders' webs between the wooden rails of the steps up to the cabin and casting elongated shadows of the wagons across the gleaming running tracks of the main line.

The signalman she was relieving from night duty informed her the wagons were a delivery for farmer Tim Swithibank at Ham Farm — a rare, but eagerly anticipated occurrence. Apparently, his harrow was unserviceable and urgently required some new parts. Farmer Swithibank had already been telephoned by the signalman and advised that his delivery was waiting, so she was expecting him any time soon. Laura Green looked forward to meeting one of her neighbours and starting the process of getting to know the various characters from the tiny hamlets and isolated farms, who worked in the fields and woods that stretched as far as she could see in all directions.

Her first impression of Swithibank, however, was of a man bright purple in the face and in an absolutely foul mood, literally hopping from one foot to another and pounding a massive fist in frustration upon the solid wooden body of one of the containers. He swore profusely until, catching sight of Laura, he instantly took control of his tongue. It was not the done thing to swear in front of a lady; however, this didn't inhibit him from standing in the doorway of her signalbox and expounding at length upon how incompetent the railways were 'these days' for sending him 'the wrong bloomin' delivery'.

It was a colourful start, but she dutifully recorded the problem in the logbook and called Rugby Control. She then phoned Woodford No.1 box to say the same and warn them there had been a mix up in the yard. Signalman Howerth (whom she knew) said he would pass the message on to Woodford engine shed and they would no doubt arrange for the wagons to be collected and taken to their correct destination.

And so it was that word passed along the railway, thrumming along the looping wires beside the tracks, passed by telephone, telegraph and handwritten note between different railway clerks and signalmen and soon word landed on Anna Vignoles's desk in the goods despatching office at Leicester Central. Anna, primed by her husband, was on the lookout for just such a consignment. She made a cross-check with Woodford Halse and soon had all the details of the pick up goods that had delivered the wagons early that morning, and even better, she made a reverse connection with three wagons already reported by Marylebone goods as being in the wrong place. It fitted together. The deliveries had been transposed and she could correct this quite easily.

She quickly typed out instructions for the recovery and redelivery of the two sets of misplaced wagons; however, Vignoles wanted the container wagons at Akeman Street brought to Leicester and placed within the goods shed under police guard. Having dispatched the telegrammed instructions, one urging the immediate recovery of the containers sent to Mr Saunders at Woodford loco, she typed out a brief report that summarised what she had done and had this hand-delivered to her husband's office on the opposite platform with a sense of satisfaction at a job well done, even if she was not entirely sure of the significance of her actions.

It was midmorning when Laura Green, during a momentary lull in allowing a succession of trains to pass her little outpost, found her attention drawn to the sound of diesel engines chugging as they idled somewhere close. Stepping onto the little wooden verandah of the signalbox, she looked behind and was surprised to see three British Road Services flatbed lorries neatly parked beside the A41, with a road-mounted crane slowly approaching the siding holding the container wagons, quite obviously with the intention of lifting these onto the lorries. A small group of donkey-jacketed men in flat caps were in attendance. They looked purposeful and focused on the task, and yet she was a little taken aback. This was not what she had expected as resolution to the mistaken delivery, nor had she been given word to expect their arrival. However, the ringing bells of her block instruments were calling her back inside and the men looked like they knew what they were doing, so, with a shrug, she returned to the vital task of handling the trains.

She was kept busy for a few minutes, but there was something about the look of these men and the whole situation that did not feel right, so when the telephone rang she jumped like a startled cat, her surprise not eased by the voice of Detective Inspector Vignoles on the other end.

He said nothing that set her mind at rest.

'A diversion? But how? What should I do?'

'Think of something — anything! You need to delay them from leaving until support arrives. About forty minutes might do it.'

Chapter Thirty-one

CHANGE PARTNERS
Fred Astaire

If Laura Green thought her day had started unexpectedly and was concerned about the activities outside Akeman Street signalbox, this was nothing compared with how Vignoles and the British Railways detective department were feeling that same morning. This was going to take the biscuit for surprises. It was one discovery after another in an almost overwhelming stream of developments that stretched their limited resources to breaking point. However, it was clear that matters were coming to a head. The case appeared to have broken wide open and it was up to them to interpret the many pieces on the table and make sense of it all. But they had to work quickly.

As he and Anna stepped off the local train that had brought them from Belgrave and Birstall that morning, Vignoles had been feeling quite chipper about the investigation and so was dismayed by the unannounced arrival of Badger — demanding an urgent and private conversation — and surprised by the almost simultaneous arrival of a bedraggled, bothered and bewildered figure of Simon Howerth, grasping a water-stained briefcase, accompanied by an older man who resembled a ship's captain, and a dog. The latter was wagging its tail with boundless enthusiasm, but the other two looked bushed after having travelled all night up the Grand Union canal.

Vignoles asked Sergeant Trinder to deal with the Howerth lad, whilst he holed up with Badger. However, Trinder was not gone long before he requested to communicate an important discovery made by Simon. All three policemen immediately appreciated the significance of the lad's finding, and Badger surprised his colleagues by suggesting that this might relate to why he also had raced north that morning with such unprecedented urgency. After admitting that he was having second thoughts about the Pym case, everything had changed. Badger was now reacting quickly and in a manner to which neither Vignoles nor Trinder were accustomed. Whilst Trinder took more detailed statements from Simon and his uncle before packing them both off to the *Primrose*, moored near the North Bridge, Vignoles made a telephone call to Scotland Yard to instruct DI Tykett to get some bobbies to the Marylebone area to search for the old man who'd rescued Pym's briefcase and to bring him in for immediate questioning.

However, this conversation with Tykett had led to another revelation. The laconic and weary DI advised Vignoles that Special Branch had already travelled to Leicester during the night and arrested Mrs Pym and Terence Wilde in the early hours, had interrogated them in double-quick time at the Leicester City Police headquarters and obtained full confessions from both — confessions to *successfully* plotting and ordering the murder of Jack Pym. Terence Wilde even offered the name and address of the thug paid to do the deed and it was expected that the man in question would be pulled in before the day was out. Special Branch had succeeded in obtaining their full and complete cooperation — no doubt in expectation of a reduced sentence in court, as Badger ruefully observed.

If all that were not enough drama, whilst PC Blencowe was sent across the city to try and obtain a carbon copy of these confessions, Anna's note had been delivered to Vignoles, who immediately telephoned Miss Green in the Akeman Street signalbox and urged her to devise some manner of delaying tactic.

'Botheration! The gang has been sent to collect the containers. I wouldn't mind betting some of the characters we are interested in are there right now. We could catch them red handed!'

'Then what the devil are you waiting for?' Badger urged. He was silently kicking himself for his hasty decision to instruct Scotland Yard to make the arrest of Pym and Wilde. It had been a mistake, and he was now going to make amends.

There was indeed no time to lose, and Vignoles made the snap decision to send the two WPCs straight down to Akeman Street with six burly male constables from the city force and instructions to 'arrest the bloody lot of them.' Sergeant Trinder wanted to join the party, but Vignoles needed him in Leicester to help make sense of these developments.

The chief superintendent enthusiastically agreed to the plans, and it was he who spoke to Mr Saunders, the shedmaster at Woodford (who was now thoroughly perplexed by this succession of calls about three uninteresting 'conflat' wagons berthed in an obscure outpost of the railway), demanding the urgent despatch of an engine and brakevan to whisk his officers to Akeman Street. 'We'll get clearance on the line and treat this as a crack express! Straight there, full speed ahead, and that's an order!'

Badger also telegrammed Aylesbury station, ordering the two railway police based there make their way to Akeman Street to offer extra help. They could be on site far more speedily than the main force. He then telephoned the Buckinghamshire Constabulary and managed to convince the station superintendent to send two officers in a car to intercept the lorries, again with the clear imperative of preventing them from leaving.

The net was cast.

This was policing by instinct, with Vignoles and Badger as good as flying in the dark, using only their years of expertise to guide them as they made decisions based more upon hunch than certainty, and working for the first time as a partnership. It had been a breathless and hectic forty minutes, but exhilarating. Strangely, Badger suddenly appeared younger, more dynamic and invigorated as he barked orders to subordinates and down the telephone lines in a manner that demanded a decisive reaction and yet inspired respect rather than the habitual weary acquiescence. His usual reticence and caution were nowhere to be seen, and Vignoles for one was grateful, if more than a little surprised.

Vignoles, Badger, Trinder and Blencowe (the latter breathless from cycling across Leicester like the wind to collect carbon copies of the confessions obtained by Special Branch) were now assembled around the desk in an informal muddle in Vignoles's office, a tray with a cup of coffee, a huge aluminium teapot, various ill-assorted cups and saucers and a box of slightly damaged Macfarlane Lang's Family Assorted biscuits as the temporary focus of their attention. This 'council of war', as Blencowe dubbed it, had been hastily convened following their flurry of activity. Whilst they anxiously awaited news from DI Tykett and prayed that the gang had been stopped from escaping with the containers before reinforcements arrived, it was time to assess how Simon Earnshaw's revelations changed their understanding of the situation.

'Get yourselves a brew, stock up on biscuits, then settle down and pay attention. We have a lot of ground to cover and little time to do it. We need a frank discussion, but nothing will be repeated outside these four walls unless it comes from Vignoles or myself.' Badger looked both Sergeant Trinder and PC Blencowe in the eye to emphasise the point.

Despite his admonishing words, Badger was not his usual self, and although his gaze was as steely and unnerving as ever, there was a feverish excitement bubbling beneath the frosty surface. He was as clean-shaven and immaculately groomed as always, belying his early start, whilst the creases were still razor sharp in his trousers. The soft kid gloves and ostentatious cap lay on the desk, his swagger stick resting against the wall, but he caused more than a little surprise by unbuttoning his uniform jacket and loosening his tie and top collar button. The hot water pipes and cast iron radiator were working especially well, and Vignoles's office was becoming hot, but this was still an unprecedented move. Badger allowed the others to similarly relax, and Trinder also removed his jacket. Cigarettes and Vignoles's pipe were fired up. They looked like men settling down to serious, hard work.

'Events are moving quickly, however, we need to draw breath and analyse everything we know and the new information received today. You may wonder at my unexpected appearance this morning,' Badger looked at Vignoles, who raised an eyebrow as he drew on his pipe, expertly communicating that he was indeed surprised, but not ungrateful. 'Well, I have formed my own suspicions about some of the characters under investigation, and quite frankly, I am not prepared to let someone make a laughing stock of me. Before the war, when I was plain old Inspector John Badger, I could spot a villain and bring him to book like the rest of you!'

Everyone laughed politely, but they leaned a little closer, placing tea cups on saucers and concentrating on Badger's words. 'I will not pretend to have the same grasp of the all the complexities, though the DI here has given me a pretty succinct briefing. As time is of the essence, we shall pursue his line on this.' He cast a steely glance at Vignoles. 'Let's just pray we don't make a pig's ear of it all! Now, the easy part first. I am in agreement with the DI that the wife and her lover can be discarded. They plotted to kill this Pym chap and claim the insurance, but despite these...' Badger pointed to the carbon copies of the statements from Adeline Pym and Terence Wilde onto the desk, '...I am sure the confessions are a fix up, a ploy to keep someone's feathers from being ruffled, someone in a *high place*.' Badger growled this last part, his anger barely concealed.

'Good heavens, sir, you really think so? Then why did they confess to murder?' asked Trinder.

'To cut a deal,' interjected Vignoles. 'They are amateurs and ill equipped to deal with the intimidatory tactics of Special Branch. Few of us could.' Badger nodded, unhappily. 'If the SB want a confession, they'll get one.' Vignoles paused a beat to allow this statement to sink in. 'Full cooperation was a way to ameliorate the stiff jail sentences coming their way, no doubt hastened by a few slaps around the face. On top of that, these two lovebirds paid their man to kill Pym but harboured doubts as to whether their instructions were carried out. This put them in a weak position under interrogation and we can read here how they were reminded that a merciless judge might consider hanging them. They were willing enough to take any deal offered.'

'The hired killer will receive the same treatment in due course. Doubtless he was advised to confess to the murder, and to a few other crimes at the same time, I wouldn't mind betting, thereby helping improve the crime statistics. His lawyer will get him life rather than the rope, in return for his cooperation.' Badger gave a sour grimace. 'Case closed. Neat. Not pretty, not fair, but it's the way of the world.'

'The question is, why are Scotland Yard so desperate to see this closed?' Vignoles looked grim.

'Why, indeed?' Badger bit his lower lip. 'Sir Paul Frobisher, the so-called baronet,' he almost spat the words out, 'has already come under your spotlight. I admit I was not happy about the direction in which DI Vignoles was steering the investigation in this regard. I allowed his title and social standing to colour my judgement, but the DI got my mind working and something about the fellow just does not sit right. I fear this man is not who or what he claims to be and, if my suspicions are correct, then he is nothing less than an enemy of the state. A traitor to the king!' He stopped and sniffed, trying to control his anger. 'I shall say no more until we get some concrete proof, because this bounder has the ear of some pretty important chaps in Scotland Yard. Not that I'm suggesting complicity by anyone within the Yard, merely suggesting that this—this Frobisher, has his own reasons for wanting to see the case closed and has used all his charm and influence to see it done. He's no gentleman. This "Sir Paul" business sticks in my craw.'

Badger explained about his conversation with Digby Wyatt. 'Frankly, if Frobisher is the illegitimate son of a long-dead baronet who may have purchased the title in return for favours, so be it. No, what interests me is his background, his real motivation, the strength of his allegiance to king and Empire, and pertinently, the source of his wealth. I think his money and how he acquires it will explain much about this case.'

'Where does his money come from indeed?' Vignoles nodded appreciatively. His boss had made a perceptive observation. 'Owning a large house and funding the extravagant life style he maintains, not to mention setting up Hendon Pharmaceuticals, requires very significant capital. The discovery of a plate in Pym's briefcase that could be used to print counterfeit money raises intriguing questions. Blencowe, what have you discovered about his finances?'

'In a nutshell: the company was set up in January 1946 with capital provided by Sir Paul—er, by Frobisher, to the tune of £580,000. It's been very successful, initially manufacturing cough medicines, aspirin and various vaccines under license for the export trade; later developing a number of it own products, including the powerful pills apparently forced inside Mr Pym. It appears legitimate and very profitable, and invests heavily overseas. None of which helps explain how Frobisher got the capital to start the company, unless he printed it, of course.'

Everyone exchanged knowing looks.

'The only suggestion that all is not strictly above board is the fact that their unusual pills helped kill Pym,' continued Blencowe, 'and that Henry Bish is also the assistant director of HP. I found pictures of Frobisher and Bish in a company shareholder's statement from last year.' He pulled out a smart booklet from the folder of notes and opened it to reveal two black-and-white photographs.

'Who the devil's this?' Badger sat bolt upright and jabbed a forefinger at one of the photographs.

'That's Henry Bish. Do you know him?' asked Vignoles.

'Damned right I do! Correction. I don't *know* him, but I *saw* him at Frobisher's place, in the backroom office. He was the man I assumed was the estate manager.' Badger stared at the photograph. 'But if he is the assistant director of a successful company, why wasn't he dressed up like a king penguin like the rest of us?' Badger gave a quick resume of what he had observed. 'But there was something else, something shocking.' He described the chilling salute.

'A Nazi?' Trinder's eyes were wide.

'Hardly credible. You are quite sure?' Vignoles was floored.

'Never been more certain!'

'This gives everything a darker slant than I could ever have imagined.' Vignoles looked grim.

'It would explain the great efforts being made to conceal the truth.' Badger added.

Vignoles puffed out his cheeks. 'This has rather winded me... Ok, let's think now. This would be the same evening I was knocked out... the night Jordan's abandoned ship.' Vignoles was thinking intensely, holding his pipe and his other hand gesticulating, 'And Bish is the link between these two events. Now, he would have told Frobisher earlier in the day that I had been asking questions — I gave him my card. They may have determined it was unsafe to maintain the operation in Loughborough following my earlier visit and ordered the evacuation and destruction of all paper records.'

'Is it possible you observed Bish receiving word that Vignoles was on the premises again that evening, sir?' Trinder asked Badger.

'Hell's bells, you're both right.' Badger looked up with excitement in his eyes. 'Bish took a telephone call whilst I was watching and he looked very worried, maybe even angry. They had a quick consultation, during which I suspect your name came up. Shortly after, that weasel Frobisher collared the AC. Before I knew what was happening, I was drinking cognac and being buttered up like a goose at Christmas. They said all manner of flattering things, but what made me uneasy was their interest in seeing you off the case.'

'We must arrest Henry Bish. He has to be our way into all this.' Vignoles looked determined. 'If we can get Bish to crack we just might pin something on Frobisher. I firmly believe that the baronet was behind the Water Street counterfeiting gang we smashed in 1946. We never got the man, or men, at the top of that operation. We caused a temporary halt, but they moved on to other schemes and swindles. These are master criminals working at the top end of the scale.'

'We need to catch the Mr Big!' added Trinder.

'Top Link, to be exact.' Vignoles explained about his visit to Wormwood Scrubs. 'Whilst I'm convinced about the veracity of Price's testimony, we have nothing to offer the courts. Frobisher is going to prove slippery and elusive. I doubt we will find many who know anything strong enough to use against him, or who are willing to testify if they did.

Badger slammed his hand down on the table, making everyone jump. 'Then we had better start putting the fear of God into this blighter! Make him sweat and force his hand! Let's see what he does when cornered, when he realises we are on to him. He must slip up at some point.'

'Won't he just call upon his powerful friends?' asked Vignoles, startled by this dynamic suggestion.

'If we get Bish into custody and squealing — we'll get the boys to give him a good working over — by the time we speak to Frobisher he'll have to be more circumspect than just going running to his friends. I find it impossible to countenance that senior members of the Met and possibly even the shadow cabinet are knowing players in his nefarious plans — they trust him and they like him, but only because they have no reason to doubt his word. Frobisher can only push things so far without risking their turning on him.'

'My worry is, the moment we arrest Bish, Frobisher will have the AC bawling at us to release him before he has time to squeal.'

'Then I think it only right to communicate our suspicions to him. He'll drop that charlatan like a hot brick when he hears what I have to tell him!'

The telephone jangled beside Vignoles's right arm.

'Vignoles? Tykett here.' A smoky voice growled down the line. 'I've some good and some bad news for you. We picked up that old geezer like you asked; found him almost unconscious in a hovel of a shed down by the power station, just like the kid said. He looks a right freak, face all burnt and hands mangled. Took him straight to hospital. Christ, he stank the car out something rotten. We managed to get bit out of him, but not much, because the doctor blew a fit and tried to stop us speaking to him. Luckily, I can be a persistent bugger when I have to be.'

Vignoles gestured to his colleagues that the call was important, then prompted Tykett to continue.

'He rambled on and I couldn't make head nor tail of a lot of it. Trouble is, the doc reckon he's on the way out. Just a few hours left. Lungs wrecked by smoke and on top of that he's got pneumonia. Sidlow's keepin' an eye on him, case he rallies round, but I'm not hopeful. He says Pym had some documents, important stuff, but nothing to do with money. What's this about money? I didn't know there was any. Oh, I see... a printing plate? Well that's not it. Nah, it's the other stuff that's vital... Pym must have hidden it somewhere safe... No, I don't know what... something to do with a geezer called Sir Frobisher and some bloke called Bash. Eh? You know them? It was this Bash bloke who torched him in his shop. Yeah... attempted murder. Used the same two thugs who he saw dump Pym in the river... Oh yes, he's a witness; but, like I said, also soon to be a dead one. He watched them slide Pym down that coal chute. Yep, your sergeant was spot on.'

'How did he escape? He knew they might come for him, and when they did he was looking out from the top floor of his premises and crawled through the roof space into next door. The fire and smoke knocked him up very bad, but he survived. I suppose they thought the old guy was burnt to a cinder along with his shop.'

'Yeah, we remember the fire. A printing shop that went up like nobody's business. Just an empty shell was left. We knew about this geezer. He was known as "Papers", because if someone needed an ID card, passport, ration cards or whatever, they went to him. Sidney Greenfall is his real name. One of the very best forgers in London. He was so good that we could never pin anything on him. Besides, it pays to know who's doing this kind of work so we'd left him alone and preferred to try and nobble his clients. After the fire, he just disappeared, so we presumed he was ash.'

'If I understood what Greenfall told me — and he was rambling — Pym was working on an insurance claim lodged by the shop next door to Greenfall's. There was a lot of smoke and water damage as a result of the dodgy print shop gettin' torched, and I suppose Pym must have stumbled across Greenfall skulkin' about the place whilst he was down there and felt sorry for him. Of course, Greenfall couldn't make a claim himself, nor even check into hospital, because he knew his only option was to act as though he really was dead. However, he wanted revenge and saw Pym as a means to get it. We know Pym was not exactly averse to a bit of extra income, so they struck a deal of some sort. That's the best I could do. I'll write it all up and get it in the post.'

After Tykett hung up the phone, Vignoles shared the contents of the conversation with his officers.

'So this forger, Sidney "Papers" Greenfall, saw two men dump Pym in the canal and another man take the briefcase, only to cast it in the water a short while later?' asked Trinder.

'It tallies with what the Howerth boy told us. Greenfall's statement might stand as evidence, but my hunch is that one of the killers is already past caring about hanging. The sudden death of Rodney Mattox might be a case of the gang leaders trying to cut their losses. They know we've rumbled the murder of Pym and they're punishing the workers for a bad job. It would not surprise me if the other men involved found their life span shortened any day soon.'

Badger was drumming his fingers on the desktop. 'You'd better get searching for whatever it was Greenfall gave Pym. Whatever it is, it sounds like it could bring these two felons to book.'

'But where shall we start?' asked Trinder.

'Pym's house. We'll need a search warrant.' Vignoles looked at Badger. 'That might prove tricky, thanks to Special Branch barging in on the scene like a bull in a china shop.'

'Yes, and it will take too long.' Badger scowled. 'These spurious confessions will make the magistrate question why we need a warrant, especially as it's no longer our case.' He paced the room, scratching his chin. 'Hang it! DI Vignoles, we can't delay a moment longer. You're not averse to a bit of cloak and dagger stuff; after all, you got into that Jordan's place with no problem.' Badger gave Vignoles a sharp look that made it clear he had never been under any illusions about what had happened that night, but there was a glint in his eye, 'Get yourselves over there. No questions asked. Just don't get caught by Special Branch! If you do find something we'll find a way to play it afterwards. Pedder will drive you over.' Badger paused a moment. 'You realise that, if we get this wrong, we're all for the high jump. Dropped in the hottest of water.'

'I'm game, sir!' Trinder added without hesitation. 'One for all, and all for one!'

'I'll get those pick-locks…' Vignoles had his pipe jutting from his mouth at a determined angle, hat already on his head, his opinion on the matter quite clear.

'I'll hold the fort here and see if they've made any arrests at Akeman Street.'

Chapter Thirty-two

IT LOOKS LIKE RAIN ON CHERRY BLOSSOM LANE
Guy Lombardo

Vignoles and Trinder stood at the front gate of number 56 and looked at the silent house. Despite the red roof tiles it looked grey and sad, the garden even more so in the dank, misty air that clung around the dripping trees and tall evergreen shrubs against a gunmetal sky. The presence of leaves unswept from the lawn told their own tale. Nothing appeared to have changed, apart from the garage doors being closed, but this was no longer a family home. The house was empty and was likely to remain so for the foreseeable future. Oliver Pym would never again play with his O gauge train set on the bedroom carpet, and his mother would need a spectacularly brilliant defence counsel if she were ever to host another evening of bridge with her neighbours, even if they wanted to socialise with a woman guilty of plotting the murder of her husband.

'Round the back! It will be less obvious that we don't have a key,' Vignoles told Trinder, then adjusted his hat and turned up the collar on his unfamiliar new buff raincoat that Anna had purchased pending attempts to clean his bloodstained favourite. He walked purposefully down the curving path of crazy paving as a pied wagtail trotted ahead in rapid movements of its tiny legs, hopping from stone to stone. Trinder glanced across to the adjacent house and saw a corner of a net curtain fall back into place.

'They'll probably call the civvies. That could be a bit embarrassing.'

'They don't know we lack a warrant or a key. Once inside we'll put all the lights on and open the curtains wide, look confident and they won't challenge our right to be here. With Badger's car parked outside it will look like an official visit. We just have to pray that Special Branch don't come past.'

Vignoles surprised himself by working the pick-locks perfectly and having the back door open in less than thirty seconds. They exchanged grins like naughty school kids and stepped inside. Although they knew the house to be empty, they still remained quiet at first, moving with caution across the kitchen and peering along the hallway, listening for any sound of movement. All they heard were ticking clocks. The house was indeed empty, but they knew better than to go barging in. Special Branch might have left someone behind to keep an eye on the place, and neither of them fancied surprising one of these notorious law enforcers.

They worked diligently, opening every drawer, cupboard, storage tin and box, sifting through papers, riffling through the pages of every book and magazine, probing between piles of sheets and blankets in the airing cupboard, under the settee, behind the pictures on the walls, even beneath the rugs. Trinder searched the motor car in the garage, enjoying the smell of new leather and trim as he did so, but found nothing. He even took the back off an impressive and new Sobell model 717 radio and admired the seven valves inside that he recalled had been advertised as featuring 'a super superheterodyne receiver giving eight watts undistorted power', but whilst he could admire the engineering, there was nothing hidden inside.

After three long, frustrating hours they came to a halt, both tired, hungry and thirsty and feeling pangs of disappointment dull the anticipation they had felt when they believed they were about to make the final breakthrough.

Vignoles sat in Pym's desk chair in the little upstairs office, ran his hands through his hair and over his face in a vain attempt to wipe away the tiredness. The back of his head throbbed angrily, though he had long since abandoned the bandage. Trinder, meanwhile, sat in the old armchair and stared at the carpet.

'Blast it, sir. We've drawn a blank.'

'I fear so. I was perhaps too optimistic. Maybe he tucked the papers into an obscure file at work.'

'We'd have to search every sheet of paper in an insurance office. Hard to get a warrant, and even if we could, I'm not sure I could stomach it.' Trinder gave a wry smile, knowing that, if his boss decided in favour of such a search, he'd have to knuckle down to the task regardless.

Vignoles gave a weary smile in sympathy. 'I suppose we could try and enlist the helpful Miss Buckland.' He fell silent for a few moments. 'No, it would have been too risky for Pym to have hidden something at work. The papers must be here.'

'It would help if we knew what we are looking for. Perhaps we've found them but just don't realise. Why did the old geezer have to take so bad at the critical moment?'

'Greenfall's a very unwell man in terrible physical shape living rough in the appalling smog London has been blanketed in. I'm amazed he's lasted this long. If only he'd gone to one of the new National Health Service hospitals, he could have received free treatment.'

'But he would have to give his name, maybe he feared his enemies might have got to hear,' offered Trinder.

'True. He was a crook, and normally one does not feel much sympathy for his sort, but he must have suffered appallingly. It could be just a matter of hours before the end, poor blighter. Just another hour of lucidity and he might have told us what we need.' Vignoles sat back, stretched his legs out and stared at the bureau, the many papers that had been inside now piled in heaps, the drawers pulled open after a second thorough exploration. 'He was a forger, so I guess we should be looking for passports, ration cards, work permits, that kind of thing. All we've come up with is a bundle of illicit love letters from Wilde to Mrs Pym. They may be mildly diverting, but I cannot believe that is what Greenfall meant.'

'No. They don't say much.' Trinder was reading one of the letters as Vignoles was talking, but it was sugary, empty-headed piffle. Hiding them beneath a loose floorboard was purely Mrs Pym's way of keeping her affair secret. None of the letters he browsed mentioned killing her husband.

Vignoles made one more effort to try and think of a suitable hiding place. His eyes roved about the room that he believed was Pym's private den. They had a woman in to do the cleaning, so Mrs P. didn't even enter to dust the shelves. This simply *had* to be the location.

Trinder's thoughts fell upon Oliver. 'I wonder what's going to happen to the lad. He's as good as orphaned now.' He tossed the most recent letter onto the floor in disgust.

Vignoles nodded sadly. He thought about Oliver's beloved model railway, the prized engines standing silent on their tracks, then suddenly decided to have it sent on to wherever Oliver was living. He'd need a pretty big and stout box, though. Picking up the broken model railway van from the bureau he noticed what was wrong: one of the axle boxes had bent out of shape causing the wheels to drop out. The poor boy no longer had a dad to mend anything for him. Vignoles's compassion prompted him to repair the van before sending the whole railway set to Oliver. As he used his hands to bend the tin plate, he noticed that the little lugs securing the roof in place on the body were slightly proud of the surface and one had lost a flake of paint, revealing shiny metal beneath. That was odd. The wagon looked almost new. It was as though someone had removed the roof but failed to refit it as perfectly as had the factory.

'What an inspired choice,' thought Vignoles. Feeling both impressed and triumphant, he wielded a screwdriver and winked at Trinder. 'Here we go...'

Trinder stood up and watched attentively as Vignoles prised the little folded metal tags open so the white enamelled roof could be eased off. Looking down into the box van they saw a neat bundle carefully folded and secured by an elastic band. Vignoles eased them out and placed the wagon and the roof to one side as he slipped off the band.

'What have we here?'

He carefully unfolded a page from a passport. It bore the photograph of a woman neither of them recognised. She was in her late forties and named as Mrs Mercedes Porta, with an address in Buenos Aires and the inked stamps of the issuing authority in that city. They exchanged puzzled looks. What on earth could be the significance of this?

Vignoles smiled to himself as the next items were laid out. Four passport photographs held together by a paper clip, the first was of a good-looking man with a suntan and a dark moustache sitting in front of a plain-curtained backdrop. He looked South American, but when Vignoles laid a finger across the lower half of the man's face to hide the moustache, Trinder exclaimed 'Frobisher!'

Next came an almost identical photograph, showing the curtain with exactly the same folds in the fabric and no one sitting in front, as though snapped immediately after the subject had stood up and left. The third photograph showed a man with a neatly-trimmed beard and hair brushed and Brylcreemed into a shiny side parting sitting with the same curtain backdrop. Vignoles and Trinder squinted at this for a few moments and tried covering first the chin, then the top of his head and puzzling over it, until Trinder made the connection.

'Henry Bish! It's a good disguise, though. The beard has to be false. He looks convincingly "foreign" though.'

The final image was of a bald man with thick-framed glasses. The deceptions became easier to spot now that they were attuned to the task.

'The union rat! Gotcha!' Trinder balled a fist and made a short jabbing gesture. 'I just knew there was something about him.'

Vignoles agreed. 'I understand what we have here. Our forger was a clever man. He printed a spare copy of these pictures, which obviously are to be used on forged passports with new identities. Now, they may have been taken at different times in his shop, I should imagine for the sake of security as they would not all troop in as a group.'

'The shop that was burnt down?'

'Greenfall's, yes. Where he was clever was that he also took a photograph of the curtain used as a backdrop, careful to retain the same lighting each time and not to allow the curtain to be touched. Notice how the folds are absolutely identical in all four pictures?'

'Almost like a finger print?' observed Trinder.

'Correct! These men will have taken every precaution to cover their tracks in having these taken, but who thinks about the folds on a dull curtain backdrop? If they had swished it to one side or pulled it down they just might have helped protect themselves, but I doubt anyone would think to do that.'

'A husband and wife obtaining passports at the very same time might have consecutive images taken by the same photographer with the same background, but three men of different ages—'

'—and probably with different nationalities — impossible. No matter how good the forgeries are, and I suspect they are virtually undetectable, this blank image is the key that reveals them to be fakes. My guess is that our English baronet is able to become an Argentinean — thanks to a false moustache and a tube of Cow Gum to hold it in place — and poor, innocent Mercedes Porta, who has long since had a replacement passport issued, but who unwittingly provided the page that was copied for the forgery.'

Trinder opened a small envelope and extracted a roll of negatives, holding the strip up to the light from the window. 'Here they are. The negatives of the prints and photographs of their completed passports.'

'Bingo!' Vignoles peered at the tiny frames, but could make out little without a magnifying glass, though it was obvious what they were. 'I suspect Frobisher's new passport will bear exactly the same number, and the inked stamps placed by the embassy across his picture will be unfeasibly identical to those we see here on Mrs Porta's original — again, it acts like an embedded fingerprint. Look at how carefully this has been removed. I think our clever forger friend unbound the original passport and extracted this page with consummate care, he then made an exact copy for Frobisher and rebound the booklet, thus providing an authentically worn and aged document, complete with visas.'

'What's this?' Trinder had been smiling, sharing the enjoyment of Vignoles unravelling the documents and the potency of their meaning as he picked up the final item: a small fold of card slipped inside an envelope. He removed this as Vignoles was speaking, but now he was looking in puzzlement at what he held in his hands. 'I can't read German, but this looks ominously like it might be an "SS" membership card. Good God! That face — it's *Frobisher*!' Vignoles exhaled long and slow, puffing out his cheeks as he did so, trying to take in this devastating piece of information. 'Badger was right: a traitor in our midst.'

Both men stared in mute horror at the little card, attempting to assimilate the information it contained.

'My God, has this man been a Quisling, right here, all through the war?'

'This is a dangerous revelation. We will need to think how we handle this — it's almost like carrying a UXB in our hands.'

Trinder had a look of intense concentration on his face. 'So Pym must have realised that Top Link was Frobisher — remember that little note under his desk blotter? Perhaps at first this was nothing more than information useful to keep under his hat whilst he continued to help them work their frauds and take backhanders in return. However, fate then determined that Pym met Greenfall following that fire — he was looking into the insurance claim for the neighbouring property. He must have helped Greenfall. Perhaps he felt sorry for him. By so doing, Pym was taken into his confidence.'

'It's starting to make sense,' agreed Vignoles. 'Yes, Greenfall must have offered these documents to Pym as weapons to obtain some form of revenge, not knowing that Pym was actually working for these very men. Pym was caught in between. He had inadvertently discovered that he was not just helping make money on the black market, but was actually aiding a traitor to his own king and country. Pym was probably as good as dead from the moment he was given these.'

'Too hot to handle?'

'I'd say so. I'm sure Pym did not know how to handle the enormity of this revelation. He opted instead to try and gain money or power — we may never know exactly what — by threatening to report Bish to the police for having the printing plate, whilst concealing the fact he had these documents. I think this could have been the poisonous conversation overheard by Oliver.'

'You're not kidding. Bish must have realised that if Pym had that printing plate, then he probably had the documents as well. Pym showed his hand inexpertly, revealing that he had made contact with Greenfall at some point. I think they interrogated him, got the printing plate and then decided that, by killing him, Bish could stop their cover being blown.'

Vignoles nodded agreement. 'Bish and Millett are part of this evil conspiracy, as we can see — possibly former members of the SS as well. I wonder who they really are,' Vignoles looked grim, 'and who the devil is this Frobisher? What we do know is they have false identities ready to use to effect an escape. The good news is that Bish, and perhaps Millett, could be under arrest right now if our girls got to Akeman Street in time.'

Trinder nodded in agreement. 'Gosh, I do hope they're all right. These men are dangerous.' They both fell silent for a moment as they considered what this implied.

'We hold a rather nice ace up our sleeve, however. We now know Frobisher's false identity, but he does not know that we do. If I can force him to bolt, we can be ready and waiting.'

Chapter Thirty-three

My Shining Hour
The Casa Loma Orchestra

Edward Earnshaw could hardly believe his luck. He was unclear exactly what was happening, but it was something big. A hastily-prepared locomotive coupled to two guards' vans filled with policemen (and two policewomen) and permission to 'go as fast as you can' up the line, with all signals cleared and no stops was something unique, and it was going to make for an exhilarating run.

He'd been rostered for the job only because there was no one else available, (a situation not helped by the non-appearance of his unreliable friend Simon Howerth, as Shedmaster Saunders made a point of repeating). Eddie was to be paired with driver Boswell and their steed for the day was a splendid V2 class locomotive numbered 60820, one of a type of engine that Eddie only dreamed of being able to fire and which were undoubtedly the most glamorous, the sleekest and the fastest of the engines stabled at Woodford Halse.

The decision that led to his being allowed to fire this special was made following a flurry of messages and telephone calls for Mr Saunders and an urgent re-jigging of the few men and locomotives remaining on shed — the majority already far away, pulling other trains, leaving the cavernous, smoky shed virtually empty of both men and machines. The shedmaster dashed to and fro in urgent consultation with his foreman and the head fitter and stared at the grand roster board at the back of the shed that bore the chalked names of the crews beside the numbers of the locomotive assigned to them. After much discussion and scratching of heads and some wiping out of names with a damp cloth and the chalking of adjustments, Eddie had been called to an urgent briefing.

'It's a very light train and a beauty of an engine, so you should be up to the task — but do not let us down!' Saunders looked stern. 'You've got a crack man on the regulator and it's a straight run. On the return you'll have just three more on the back, plus the two vans, so again a light and easy train — but speed is of the essence, on the strict orders of the detective department — I can say no more. Now lad, the engine is fresh from having a few boiler stays fixed and the sticking injector does now work, apparently. She was going to be rostered on the York express, but you've now got her, so make the most of it. Heaven knows what the York roster will think of having a clapped out Great Western Hall on the front, but that's my problem. The fire raiser has her almost up to pressure, so you be ready to roll the moment I give word.'

'Yes, Mr Saunders. But where are we going?'

'Did I not say? To Akeman Street to lend assistance to the signalman — er, signal*woman*, I should say.'

'Oh! Miss Green. Gosh, I know her.' Edward grinned, although he felt a stab of apprehension. The combination of police and extreme urgency now had him worried about her safety; however, the overwhelming sensation was one of excitement at the thought of racing south to see the lovely Laura.

'Then I'm sure you'll find steam enough to get there double-quick, eh lad!' said Saunders, slapping him on the back.

❖   ❖   ❖   ❖

Signalwoman Green was trying to think how she could delay these rough looking men from driving away in their lorries. How on earth could she hope to stop them on her own — and why did she have to? The implication was that these men were stealing the containers, and therefore might turn aggressive. DI Vignoles had just ordered her to delay them by any means possible and assured her help was on the way.

There was only one thing for it. She would have to adopt the 'innocent' approach, that way they could have no reason to turn nasty. She just needed something to delay them in their work...

Signalling folk love their tea and Akeman Street box came equipped with a huge black kettle that spent its life on the iron stove top, and an impressive brown-and-cream teapot wearing a crocheted cosy bearing a Union Flag design in striking colours. There was also a surprisingly large array of enamel mugs that suggested the local platelayers were in the habit of calling in for a brew when they walked the line. Laura also had a precious, unopened packet of biscuits and a complete, home-baked plum cake, both presents from her mother. It was time to deploy these domestic weapons in her campaign to buy time. Laura knew that few workmen, honest or not, could resist a mug of hot tea, a lovely cake and a plate of biscuits.

She was correct.

The gang leader was unhappy when she arrived at the bottom of the steps, calling 'tea up!' and bearing a tray laden with teapot and mugs, but his look of barely-concealed anger washed over the heads of the others, who instantly dropped everything, cutting the motor on the self-propelled crane that was now dangling the first container in the air, making it clear that a tea break offered by a young, attractive signalwoman was not to be ignored. The unhappy man consulted briefly with another

~ 260 ~

rough-looking sort with a little moustache, before deciding it was easier to give in and let the men take a break than to make a scene.

This tea diversion was not going to buy her more than ten minutes, however, and Laura reckoned they would have all three containers lifted off and away in under half an hour. Returning to her box she pulled the long, steel signal levers into place and chewed over her options. She had an idea. It involved telling a lie and the consequences might be messy, but the inspector had been insistent she must not fail in her task.

Glancing out of the window to check that no one was coming up the signalbox stairs, Laura quickly dialled Ham Farm. It was fortunate that her telephone, unlike most, was provided with an outside line during the war when the lonely signallers would have been at the mercy of enemy aircraft or the constant threat of German parachutists and might have need to call outside for assistance. The phone rang and rang, but eventually the brusque voice of the short-tempered farmer answered. She took a deep breath and launched into the lie.

To her relief, she had to say very little to get the man into an absolute fury. He did not question for a moment the improbability of the railway swapping the wrong deliveries around in such a short time, but instantly reacted to her concern that a bunch of suspicious men were trying to drive off with his precious harrow parts in their lorries. He swore down the telephone and promised to 'bring the lads with him and give 'em a piece of my mind!' then slammed the receiver down.

Laura prayed that the police would arrive on the scene first, as this was surely going to become very heated and she would be entirely responsible. She sat down on the hard wooden chair and willed the instruments to inform her that help was on the way.

＊　　＊　　＊　　＊

It was called the 'Battle of Akeman Street' by the local newspaper the following day. A description that made it appear more noble and more exciting than the fisticuffs and bar room slugging, the rolling in mud, the jabbing of pitchforks and uncontrolled brawling that ensued, but it did have a certain ring to it and many a reader enjoyed the stirring images of Roman centurions doing battle with native, blue-woad-daubed Britons that the paper's fantastical description evoked in their minds.

The reporter really got into his stride when he wrote of how *the two trains steamed towards this lonely, beleaguered signalbox from opposing directions, with long battle colours of smoke trailing, whistles blowing across the distant fields like horns calling men to battle, both playing out the role of Roman chariots or Boadicea's battle carts — depending upon the good reader's preference — to heart-racing perfection.*

In reality, it was the Buckinghamshire Constabulary who arrived first, in a wheezing old Austin with a blowing exhaust. This *avant garde* consisted of two constables, one of extreme youthfulness and the other tending towards retirement age and, perhaps unsurprisingly, they adopted a cautious approach to the situation, cruising past the parked lorries before pulling over and casually enquiring if all was in order.

They made a point of appearing to be reassured that all was indeed 'perfectly in order, thank you' by the smooth talking Henry Bish, but not before they had slowly walked around the three red-and-black vehicles and the crane, kicking the tyres and noting the registration plates, whilst the drivers stood silent and watched, sipping more of Laura's tea. The constables succeeded in wasting a few more valuable minutes by checking the papers for each vehicle, which they found in order, asking to see driving licences, which also appeared satisfactory, before enquiring why three teams of lorries and crew had driven all the way from London. Bish and Millett made great efforts to be patient and were careful to offer something close to the truth as an explanation — the urgent recovery of containers inadvertently delivered to the wrong location.

'No, constable, we don't know the nature of what is being conveyed, nor do we have the keys — we're tasked only with effecting the speedy recovery of said containers for the company in question. Road haulage is our job, constable; we do our bit and let others do theirs.' Millett fell back into his role as union rep. with ease.

The constables were aware that all was not as it should be, but they were unable to tackle six men and a crane operator, so professed to be satisfied and motored away in their beetle-black car, only to stop at the next junction, set up a road block and stand guard, aware that the lorries could not turn and would be obliged to travel in their direction when they came to leave. They passed the time debating what would happen if the thieves decided to take a run at the combination of a small Austin and the plank of wood balanced on two wooden vegetable crates that blocked the road. They concluded that it would not play out well for the car.

However, no sooner had Bish ordered the men back to work unloading the second of the containers, than Millett's attention was drawn to a tractor driven by a florid-faced man with a grim look on his face, towing a trailer laden with four burly farmhands wielding pitchforks.

He whistled and drew Bish's attention. 'Looks like trouble is on the way.'

Bish squinted as he looked along the road. 'That's all we need: dumb yokels come to teach the townies what's what.'

'What should we do?'

'Maintain discipline and stay calm. We're equal in number, so if it comes to a fight we could manage, but we'll avoid that or else the signal girl will call those policemen back.'

Millett glanced up at the signalbox and caught a glimpse of a pale face watching. He curled a lip. 'I think she might be responsible...'

'Never mind her.' Bish put a hand on Millett's arm and turned to face the Massey-Harris tractor with its bulbous, olive green nose and wide-set headlamps that gave it the look of a frog, now vibrating with the engine as the farmer swung down from the curved metal seat.

'Oi! What are you up too? Bit of thieving is it, lads?' He stood close to Bish and snarled. 'We don't take kindly round here to people nicking things!'

'You've got this all wrong...'

Signalwoman Green could not say with certainty who threw the first punch, but she clearly recalled the farmer and his men squaring up to the gang leader and his assistant. There was a lot of shouting, arm pointing and waving, a cap was tipped off to reveal a bald crown ringed by salt-and-pepper hair, fingers were jabbed at chests, then an animal roar as a full-blown punch-up ensued. Laura's attention was diverted away at this critical moment by the arrival outside the signalbox of the local stopping passenger train that she had been forewarned conveyed two railway policemen.

The train sighed to a halt in a cloud of steam and she watched as the uniformed men dropped to the tracks and hurried into the mêlée, hands holding their caps in place and truncheons drawn. The passengers and engine crew strained to watch, although their view was partially masked by the containers on the siding; windows were dropped down and heads peered out, accompanied by shouts and whistles, all adding to the mounting sense of drama and confusion.

It was hard to tell who was slugging whom, as the men steadily became muddier and more dishevelled and the two policemen only made matters worse by throwing punches at anyone and everyone, receiving for their trouble a fist or two in return. A plank of wood was deployed, a spanner swirled and jabbed and blood started to flow, along with the rivulets of muddy water staining faces and hands.

The chubby N2 class locomotive and its train were due to leave. Having never been timetabled to stop at Akeman Street the guard was anxiously flapping his flag in annoyance. The driver appeared eager to offer help but Laura warned him that passengers might climb down to join in the fight. Reluctantly, he chuffed his engine off into the distance. However, to Laura's immense relief, she soon got word of the imminent arrival of reinforcements, stood at the top of the box steps and watched for the distant plume of white smoke that would herald their arrival.

There was little doubt that Driver Boswell and Fireman Earnshaw made a grand entrance. Their engine was sparkling clean. The green livery with 'British Railways' in large, cream Gill Sans lettering glinted like a box of apples in the pale wintry sun, the chill air forming a volcanic eruption of brilliant white steam that hung in a trail of cumulus nimbus a good mile above the flatlands, the engine roaring out of this expanding vapour cloud in a smooth and rhythmic beat, chattering and echoing, the haunting whistle held too long by an excited fireman leaning out of the cab, with one hand holding his cap in place, startling great flocks of crows into the air and scattering them like dust in the wind. Even the fighting men momentarily stopped and stared.

Driver Boswell knew that with such a light train, and permission to push the upper edge of the speed limit, he could afford to brake late and was reluctant to shut off steam until the last moment. They were approaching the box at an exhilarating pace that had the guard frantically screwing down the brakes onto the van wheels in alarm, whilst policemen and women leant out of the verandahs at each end of the van, ready to jump down the moment the panting beast came to a standstill. Shrill police whistles peeped and booted feet crunched on ballast. The charge of the 'serge brigade' was over almost before it had started; they soon overpowered those few still willing to resist arrest, the others eager to desist and start to nurse bruised arms, shoulders and blackening eyes while wondering why they had even been fighting. Handcuffs were snapped on wrists, orders barked and two railway WPCs had the satisfaction of watching their civvy colleagues bring some semblance of order to the mud-caked chaos they had encountered just minutes before.

Signalwoman Green leant out of one of her windows, the cab of the V2 just a few feet away, and grinned at the coal-blackened faces of the crew, the driver leaning on the metal cab door and fireman deep in the shadows behind.

'You all right, love? They didn't lay a finger on you, I hope?' asked Driver Boswell.

'I'm quite OK. But thank goodness you arrived when you did! It was getting very ugly.' She laughed nervously but was visibly relieved.

There was another wave of angry, raised voices and barked commands.

'So what's up, duck? Looks like a right set-to!'

'I think they're thieves. It must be something valuable too, looking at this operation. I don't know more than that. I just had strict orders from the detective department to delay them until you arrived.'

Driver Boswell grinned, his teeth flashing bright white. 'Well, it's a rum do. Say, have you got any tea, miss? I'm parched.' Without waiting for an answer he swung out of the cab and dropped down, his enamelled tea can in one hand. As he walked around to the cabin steps the fireman took his place leaning on the cab side.

'Hullo Laura! Bet you didn't expect to see me here.'

'Eddie! Oh my goodness! With your face all black and cap pulled down, I didn't recognise you.' Laura smiled and felt glad. His was a friendly face amidst all this anger and violence and she suddenly realised how nerve-wracking the last few hours had been. As the big engine sighed, ticked and hissed, she felt all her bottled up apprehension drain away.

'We steamed here so fast, Laura. Really, it was like the *Master Cutler* all the way, but of course we had almost nothing to pull. We were at top speed from Woodford — and even a bit more at times!' Eddie grinned. 'It was the thrill of a lifetime flashing through the stations with the whistle screaming!'

'Golly. This must be something awfully serious, you lot rushing down in this manner.' She glanced across at the hook of the self-propelled crane and the mass of muddy people standing below. It looked unpleasantly like a gibbet. 'This engine is usually for express trains, Eddie, and you not even a passed fireman! How on earth did you manage that?'

'Ahh, I just couldn't keep away from you,' Edward joked.

They exchanged knowing looks then fell silent. She looked at him a moment, unable to read his expression, though his eyes sparkled with that intensity miners and footplate men have with their blackened faces. Eddie broke the awkwardness.

'I didn't expect to fire one of these engines for many years.'

'I suppose you need to rest after all that hard work.'

'Not a bit of it!' He offered a smile, 'though I have shovelled coal like there's no tomorrow to get us here — and Driver Boswell drove like a demon!'

'Aye well, I wouldn't go that far, lad, but it was a grand run,' Boswell chipped in, now standing inside the box making the floor ash grey, a thin, hand-rolled cigarette in his mouth. 'If you two could just stop yer courting for a moment, I want to mash a fresh brew. Where's the tea pot, miss?'

Courting? Laura flushed red at his word and swiftly changed the focus of attention onto the teapot. 'Those men have it somewhere — and take those filthy boots off before you come in again!'

She and Edward looked across at the police marshalling handcuffed men into ragged rows, the two WPCs with open notebooks taking names and details. Eddie took a moment to put the steam injector on, and as it gurgled and the copper overflow dribbled hot water onto the track below, he and Laura shared a quiet moment amidst the fuss and anger still almost palpable in the air. He was close enough to reach out and touch her. All he had to do was stretch out his arm... He glanced across but hurriedly looked away as Laura caught his gaze.

After a moment she spoke.

'Thank you for coming to my rescue.'

'Thank Shedmaster Saunders, he gave me the job.'

'Yes, but you did it.'

'I think you were doing a pretty splendid job here without us.'

'I'm not sure; I might have made complications. I'll tell you the whole story one day.'

'I'd like that very much. Gosh, Laura, this makes you every bit the detective, like Simon and me! A worthy addition to the service, Simon will agree!' Eddie was about to laugh, but hesitated, suddenly looking serious. 'If we ever find where he's got to, that is. I'm hoping the police might be able to tell me something.'

They exchanged worried looks, and the locomotive hissed as though it was breathing, masking a quickening of breath across the divide.

'It think it was super we shared this adventure.'

'Even though I took you down that dingy lane and Simon shoved you?'

Laura laughed, 'yes, even after *that*!'

She heard the sound of instrument bells and made as if to move, but just before doing so she leant even closer and quickly whispered 'You were like a knight on a great charger riding to my rescue!' She walked away, picked up a cloth and used it to cover a heavy iron signal lever before pulling it towards her with one smart movement that caused a series of deep, solid clunking sounds from the locking room below.

Chapter Thirty-four

ULTRAFOX
Django Reinhardt & Stephane Grappelli

It was the following day and with Henry Bish and Victor Millett in custody and the three containers impounded, it was time to put the final stage of the plan in action.

'With his deputies under arrest, Frobisher must be feeling the heat,' declared Vignoles to his assembled colleagues. Both he and Badger were of the belief the traitor would now attempt to flee the country. They hoped that their knowledge of the name under which he was likely to travel would to be his downfall. Better still, thanks to some sterling work on the telephones and telegraph machine by PC Blencowe and Sergeant Trinder, they had traced a ticket reservation, and knew through which port Sir Paul Frobisher hoped to escape, and at what time.

'DI Vignoles, I still cannot believe this is true. Can this scoundrel really be a Nazi collaborator?' Badger was sitting behind his desk at 222 Marylebone Road.

'The revelation is hard to stomach, but those documents appear to tell the tale. We've read in the papers how some of the Nazis evaded capture and are supposed to be hiding in Spain, Egypt or Argentina, and we have the proof here that he commissioned a fake identity as an Argentinean businessman.'

'What about this SS membership business? Could it not just be a fake? The forger was considered good at his work, so perhaps it's just a vicious hoax.'

'That's not impossible, sir, but we can leave it to the security services to unpick the layers of deception involved and discover the truth about his past and political allegiance. We know Frobisher was with the Special Operations Executive, so deception and duplicity are his forte.'

'Looks like he was working for the wrong side!' fumed Badger.

'It's certainly a mystery how Greenfall came into possession of that card,' Trinder added, 'but of one thing we can be certain, he and his men were scared by the possibility of these documents falling into the wrongs hands — so they murdered Pym and tried to kill Greenfall and burn everything in his shop. They even killed their own foot soldiers — once those body parts found on the Bakerloo Line are identified, I'm sure it will be Dennis Parkey, and we already know what they did to Ron Mattox. We now hold the information that can nail them all!' Trinder nodded with grim satisfaction.

'It's time for action, sir,' added Vignoles. 'Much as I want to agree with my sergeant, I suspect Frobisher is going to be the slipperiest of fellows to pin a charge on, so our best bet is to flush him out and nab him. We can at the very least arrest Frobisher for travelling under a false passport — not the greatest of offences, but it will do for now. The hard work will come later to build a full case against him and his cronies.'

'Agreed, Charles. Get the crafty fox whilst on the run, eh? Hunt him down and corner the coward! He'll start blabbing soon enough when he knows he's done for, you mark my words. These collaborators are weak, lily-livered sorts. No moral fibre or backbone, it stands to reason.' Badger sniffed with displeasure.

'If he is more than just an honorary member of the SS, I fear it will take a lot for him to crack.'

'Perhaps. Look here, are you quite sure about his escape route?' Badger was back to his usual smartly-buttoned-down self, standing behind his desk pulling on his expensive kid leather gloves, swagger stick lying across his desk ready to be deployed under his left armpit. 'You've time to get yourselves in place, but if he gets just a sniff you're waiting to pounce, he'll change his plans and then the balloon will really go up. We could be left with egg on our faces.'

'That's why Bish and Millett were brought back to Leicester and only questioned about their work with Jordan's Import and Export, for now. We could not prevent the newspapers from reporting the incident at Akeman Street, but we have managed to keep it strictly within those limits. If we maintain it was nothing more than an audacious robbery attempt as part of a black marketeering ring, no one should suspect anything about the darker side of the story. Frobisher will be worried his frauds and other such schemes are in jeopardy, but unaware that we've unmasked him as a German sympathiser.'

'I want to confront him now! Make the coward sweat with fear!' Badger glared out of his office window in the direction of Frobisher's house.

'I understand your sentiments, sir, but an unexpected appearance could have him wondering what's up. We cannot be sure he has not an alternative disguise and escape plan to call upon,' replied Vignoles.

Badger eyed his DI for a moment, 'I suppose you're right.' He sighed deeply. 'I just want to look him in the eye one last time, see the evil behind those Farley Granger good looks and make him squirm like the worm that he is.' He lowered his voice. 'Truth is, Vignoles, I might be tempted to put a bullet in his head.' Badger did not look like he was joking.

'Apart from the two photographs, I've never even seen the baronet.' Vignoles replied. 'In fact, I've hardly spoken to the ones we've arrested, either. I'd like to see him, but we can't take the risk and time is passing.'

'It's quite extraordinary, sir, Not one of us has properly questioned any of the perpetrators. This whole case has been run at arm's length. Most peculiar, don't you think?' asked Trinder.

'Yes, but good detective work — and teamwork — will bring them all to book.' Badger now had his cap on his head. He swiped up his stick from the desk, using it to emphasise his point. 'This could be the modern face of policing. Using deduction and paperwork to bag the felons. Hell's bells, I appear to have become an innovator! Most unsettling.' Badger pondered this thought for a moment. 'Look, are you quite sure I cannot join you? If I hung well back and kept my head down? I think too much deskwork — the inescapable trappings of this blasted new-fangled style of policing — has rather dulled me. Reading the report of the Akeman incident had me longing to be there and get stuck right into it!' He made a few showy cuts and thrusts with his stick as if he were in a Robin Hood film, much to the surprise and amusement of his officers. 'I'd love the chance to snap the cuffs on him — for old time's sake.'

'Sorry, sir, but he knows your face. If he caught even a glimpse of you, he would suspect a trap.' Vignoles smiled apologetically at his chief. The truth was, having the Badger breathing down his neck was the last thing Vignoles needed.

'Yes, I take the point. Well, just get him, Vignoles! I want the detective department to take full credit for this extraordinary arrest. We can punch well above our weight on this and I can give Sir Ronald Vallance something to really sit up and think about!'

∗   ∗   ∗   ∗

The plan was that Vignoles, Trinder, Blencowe, Lansdowne and Benson would travel from Waterloo to Southampton docks to arrive two hours in advance of Frobisher's known departure time, giving them time to scout the layout of the dock terminal to see how best to make the arrest. Nothing could be left to chance.

It was a fine and blustery day in the capital. Although the sky was still laden with the smoke from a million chimney pots, the smog had been lifted and shredded by a gathering wind during the night. The city could breathe easily at last, taking deep lungfuls of cleaner air as the sun beamed from the blue above, and Londoners felt grateful to have some colour and clarity in their daily lives.

With better weather and a little time on their side, Vignoles allowed himself a few moments of respite after his exertions, both mental and physical, of the past week. The bash on his head was still sore and he felt deserving of ten minutes train spotting whilst they awaited the coaches forming their train to be pushed into place by the Waterloo station pilot. As he stood near the platform end, the others bought wafer-thin, paper-rationed newspapers or magazines at the WH Smith stall and Blencowe splashed out on a Mars bar, using his last coupon to secure it, before generously cutting the short bar into five equal pieces with his penknife and sharing it around.

The Southern Region was foreign territory for Vignoles and he wanted to make the most of looking at the sometimes odd, and often striking engines the region deployed, drinking in the sight of two magnificent streamliners at the head of their trains in this continually busy, noisy, smoky station that made up with relentless clattering activity what it lacked in beauty and grace.

One of the streamliners sported the tatty remnants of a grubby Southern Railway livery dating long before 1948, and now was not only filthy, but ruined by deep orange and black scorched patches where the paint had burnt off in livid, ugly blisters, scars that reminded Vignoles of the description of the painful burns on the face of Sidney Greenfall. *Westward Ho!* had suffered a spectacular fire in the oil bath between the wheels that encased the revolutionary, if not always reliable, chain drive of these innovative engines. Vignoles pondered the finer points of modern locomotive design for a moment as he smoked a pipe filled with fresh Goldflake Honeydew tobacco that he'd eagerly snapped up from a kiosk in the station concourse.

Their boat train was to be hauled by a sister locomotive to this poor, scarred beast, but theirs was wearing an immaculate coat of malachite green branded by the fledgling nationalised railways in large, 'sunshine' lettering that lent it an optimistic note in the clear morning light. The engine's slab sides of air-smoothed steel were polished and buffed to perfection, reflecting slightly distorted images of his officers standing in a companionable group a way back along the platform. The enormous nameplate and badge framed by three thin yellow stripes that ran its length set off the ensemble perfectly. Vignoles felt there was something appropriate, perhaps symbolic, that an engine named *Fighter Command,* one of the Battle of Britain class, was taking them on the hunt for a Nazi.

The trip to Southampton was uneventful, with the powerful engine roaring along at a terrific speed, the harsh exhaust beats pounding like explosions from the houses in their tree-lined avenues, from the Art

Deco shops and new concrete and glass training colleges and motor car dealerships forming the relentless miles of south London suburbs. The sun cast a shadow of the locomotive exhaust like a towering mushroom cloud far across the pretty, village-strewn countryside with willow-banked rivers and cow-dotted fields with that opened out once they escaped into the green belt encircling the capital.

The detective department collectively dozed, with papers on their laps. Even Vignoles found his eyes heavy with sleep as he tried to glimpse the small engines from the Victorian age that the region still favoured as they roared through pretty stations, scattering the autumn leaves and leaving a puff ball of smoke above the tracks to be gently teased apart by the skeletons of trees, electric lamps and concrete footbridges.

Southampton docks were vast, and after the frequent attentions of the Luftwaffe, much of the sprawling complex still lay in ruins or showed signs of having been hastily patched up. However, the new Art Deco-styled Ocean Terminal was nearing completion and now gleamed in a fresh coat of white distemper offset by pale blue rectilinear windows; it was a long expanse of concrete and glass that looked very racy and modern, with its artfully curved glass entrance topped by an ornamental tower shaped like a Cunarder's funnel. They caught tantalising glimpses from their carriage window of an ocean liner that lay behind this entrancing new building. The *RMS Mauretania* could be glimpsed across the roof and through the long stretches of terminal windows, her hull studded with portholes, windows and doors, the raked funnels glossy black and startling red, shining in the sun like the wing covers of a freshly hatched ladybird. People swarmed across the approach ways and around the clutch of temporary huts that served until the Ocean Terminal was opened, the scene one of tremendous hustle and fuss as the ocean cruiser, now spruced up after years in battleship grey, disgorged her first class passengers towards a line of beautiful umber and cream Pullman cars, each carriage named and replete with ornate table lamps and silver cutlery, the starched white table cloths and crystal wine glasses catching the brilliant clear light. The 'Bournemouth Belle' was filling; preparing to whisk its wealthy clientele to London, whilst liveried staff served champagne cocktails and offered cigars and cigarettes.

Vignoles was wide awake now, as were his officers, captivated by this vision of the unattainable (leastways, on a policeman's pay), marvelling at the colours and the quality of the fine clothes worn by these well-heeled travellers, at the cut of the stylish American suits and overcoats, the glitter of jewels at pale throats and on the fingers of soft hands, noting the haughty expressions and indulgent smiles of those taking their extravagantly expensive Pullman seats.

Their train did not stop, however, for their destination lay beyond the berths of the mighty Cunard liners, and it was now moving at walking pace and with almost thoughtful exhalations from the chimney. With the crew leaning from the cab, their train threaded its way along the dock, wheels squealing in protest as it snaked towards the Harland and Wolff jetty. The rails were so close to the harbour edge that at times it felt as though they would be plunged into the greenish waters below. Eventually the train eased alongside a curving platform protected by a canopy of glass and wood that caught the refracted light from the harbour and made endless dancing circles and spinning shapes that rapidly expanded and contracted upon all it touched.

This light-dappled platform opened into a covered waiting hall with booking office, a little café and the smart Wayfarer restaurant running along one end, flanked on the other side by a line of tall metal railings offering a view of a ship in a dry dock surrounded by a cluster of offices, sheds, cranes, piles of machinery and all the clutter of a busy shipyard. What immediately grabbed their attention as they stepped onto the platform, however, was the sensation of being at the end of a narrow peninsula with water and the smell of the sea all about. A stiff breeze carried ozone in the air along with the scent of rotting seaweed and coal smoke from *Fighter Command*, but above all this was the unmistakably heady odour of aero engine fuel. Below the hiss of the steam engine at the buffers and the clamour of passengers talking and walking, and far deeper than the metallic boom of hammers in the dry dock, there was a low bass roar, like a giant animal purring or growling. It was the sound of four aircraft engines, and then, as they momentarily revved up, the sound resonated physically in their chests.

'My word! What a wonderful sound!' Trinder grinned like a boy.

Lansdowne had her hands over her ears. 'It's ear-splitting!'

'Come along, we should watch her leave!' Vignoles urged them forward and through the metal gate that barred the exit from the platform, their warrant cards serving to allow access, having telephoned an advance warning of their impending visit.

'I've always wanted to see one of these.' Benson exchanged excited looks with Trinder as they dashed towards the far end of the hall and gained a clear view of the harbour beyond where, moored beside a smaller jetty that extended from the Harland and Wolff terminal building, they could see the wide span of wings hunched down behind the pert, uplifted nose and cockpit windows of the white fuselage, the broad wings bearing the furiously spinning propellers of four Pratt and Whitney engines now roaring and spitting with anticipation.

They walked quickly along the jetty, but were held back from the final approach by another gate, now closed and guarded by more officials, and Vignoles did not demand they were let through, for he knew the magnificent flying boat, operating under the flag of the British Overseas Airways Corporation, was just about to depart. They formed a line and watched as the engines ratcheted up a notch and the extraordinary flying machine eased away from its mooring with a great mist of water kicked up by the propellers and fuming exhaust, bisected by a rainbow of shimmering colour as the sun pierced the light cloud of spray. The lumbering bulk of the Short S.25 Sandringham moved like a strange steel swan into the harbour bay.

'I love it...' Benson looked dreamy.

The Sandringham turned its chunky, salt-stained tail towards them and sat back in the water with a raging assault of noise and stinking blue exhaust as it powered up, creating a deep wash of white that churned a ragged furrow through the water, until, with almost gentle grace, the pot-bellied beast lifted clear, its shadow dipping and rising across the playful, white-horse crested waves. With orange fire crackling from the exhaust pipes, it pulled upwards in a long and slow ascent, sending seagulls wheeling below.

'Unmissable!' Trinder was shading his eyes.

'What a delight!' Lansdowne was grinning.

'Impressive indeed. Our job now is to ensure that a certain person *does* miss the next flight — which, if I am not mistaken, will be in that machine there.' Vignoles allowed one last glance at the diminishing shape of the white metal bird, then pointed out another Sandringham, moored a little distance away to a buoy and rocking and bobbing on the disturbed waters. It was emblazoned with the words 'Aquila Airways', a private airline company that had evaded nationalisation and which also flew these grand symbols of the now rapidly-fading empire.

'We need to assess every step of the route he will take to board the flying boat; from disembarking the train, through passport control, right up to the gangplank and into the cabin. We need to decide where to move in and arrest him, where to escort him with the minimum of fuss after we do so, and where to place ourselves to cut off any possible escape routes if he tries to run. We have exactly two hours, so let's jump to it!'

✻   ✻   ✻   ✻

All was set. Each was in place, wristwatches synchronised, handcuffs in handy coat pockets and suitable props deployed to aid their blending into the scene. Trinder had purchased the latest *Melody Maker*, his eyes glancing across the top of the pages rather than onto articles about his favourite dance bands as he sat beside the woman whom most would assume to be his wife, but was actually WPC Benson, in turn, busy studying the latest photographs of the two princesses in the copy of *Picture Post* that lay open on her lap.

Blencowe was much further away, wrapped in a green army overcoat and poorly-fitting suit, a kit bag under his feet. He was playing a soldier who was sleeping after a tiresome journey following demobbing. A Wild West paperback rested on his nose, allowing a perfectly adequate field of vision in the narrow slit between this and his cap. Vignoles and Lansdowne were taking refuge in the fact that a couple rarely attracts attention. They sat patiently on a bench, she with a tatty, pre-war guide book to Lisbon (Vignoles had spotted this on a table outside a second-hand bookshop near Leicester Central just the day before) from which she was apparently indicating to her husband the unmissable highlights of the ancient port.

The inbound boat train eased to a halt exactly on time, hauled by an engine with the splendid name of *Sir Mador de la Porte*. Carriage doors opened and a modest number of passengers disembarked. The Aquila Airways flying boat to Lisbon appeared not to be as popular as the flight to Durban they had seen depart, and this worked to their advantage. Fewer passengers meant it would be easier to spot their man.

Vignoles smiled as he gently nudged Lansdowne, careful not to stare at the man now walking confidently along the platform, separated from them by the high metal railings. He had a way to walk, having disembarked from one of the far carriages, his expensive leather holdall swinging at his side, an umbrella slipped across the top between the handles and bundled together with a folded newspaper. Señor Santos Rodriguez was convincingly Argentinean, his skin just a little more tanned than the average pale and pasty Englishman (Badger said Frobisher had the sort of tan associated with actors living it up in California or Miami), his hair now dark brown and slicked into place with oil, neatly trimmed and perfectly matching his luxuriant moustache, which certainly did not look fake. A pair of silver-framed glasses with a slight green tint to the lens and a hat in a style different from those fashionable in Britain, completed the transformation.

Vignoles felt a strange twinge of doubt. Frobisher was almost too good. He looked exactly as he did in the passport photo, capturing the look to perfection and was unrecognisable as Sir Paul Frobisher, the English baronet. If Vignoles had not known differently and not imprinted the image in his mind, Señor Rodriguez would almost certainly have eluded them. Vignoles stood up, Lansdowne did the same, holding the guidebook prominently so they might look like tourists waiting for the same flight, and they walked arm-in-arm towards the gate through which their quarry would soon pass. Vignoles stood up, Lansdowne did the same, holding the guidebook prominently so they might look like tourists waiting for the same flight, and they walked arm-in-arm towards the gate their quarry would soon pass through. A queue had formed as the train passengers waited to have their tickets and passports examined. Once through the gate they would have access to the waiting flying boat that was noisily taxiing into position, or they could cross the hall to the ticket counter to buy or collect their flight tickets. Vignoles had already established that Frobisher had booked a single flight to Lisbon, but knew that he needed to collect and pay for this. For that reason Trinder and Benson were seated just inside the ticket office vestibule.

✢   ✢   ✢   ✢

Frobisher was using all his powers of concentration to remain calm. He had to act as normal as possible, and the best way to do this was to 'become' his new character. He must now think only in Spanish and try to act the way he imagined an Argentinean might on his way to Lisbon for a business meeting. He ran the bogus details of this 'business' over and over in his mind, practising the lie so that it might trip more easily from his tongue, cementing his constructed story of how and why he was to later board a ship that would take him on to Buenos Aires. He was conscious that he must not make any odd, nervous movements and try to resist studying his fellow passengers too earnestly, although his limbs almost itched with the desire to do turn about and search each face for a waiting threat.

Slow breaths. He had to take slow breaths. His palms were sweaty and he could feel his hatband dampen despite the brisk, cold wind from the sea. If he started to sweat it could loosen the glue that held his moustache in place. He dabbed the false band of hair gently with a gloved hand, pretending to mask a slight cough. *What is the hold up? Is it that silly blonde struggling to find her ticket? It will be in her handbag... Oh, don't say she's left it behind! Come on... come on! Get on with it...*

He stared enviously as each passport was approved and stamped and the queue shuffled forward. *Don't let there be a problem. Not now I am so close.*

His gaze swept the concourse and located the ticket desk and a young woman in a neat blue suit and pale blouse seated behind the counter. He just had to get past this gate then walk across to the counter — no need to rush as there was plenty of time and only three others in the queue. He would smile, greet her, and pay for the ticket. Simple.

'Good afternoon sir, can I see your railway ticket please?'

He proffered the card rectangle and watched intently as it was punched by the inspector, accepting it back with a slight smile, then faced the other uniformed man, a tall, unsmiling fellow with a cap slightly too big for his head and a food stain on a cuff.

'Passport?' The officer held out his hand and Frobisher handed over the Argentine document and watched, his breath shallow as he fought to contain the tension in his chest whilst the man flicked through the pages, pausing to study the visas pasted on some of them. The man's eyes moved expertly from page to face as he compared the photograph with the man standing before him.

'Where are you travelling to today, sir?'

'Lisboa.'

'Lisbon, uh huh. Do you have your aeroplane ticket with you, sir?'

'Er, no. I, er, must collect it. I already have telephoned and made my reservation. Is it close, where I collect this, please?' His accent was deliberately subtle but effective; this was the voice of a regular traveller, both familiar and comfortable with English, and yet the slight hesitation was convincing, and gave him time to measure his response.

'It's just across the way, sir. I see you have very little luggage with you today. Not staying long?'

'Yes, er, that is, I am travelling light as I stay only for one night, and my trunks are being forwarded ahead to my ship. I sail home to Argentina from Lisboa.'

'Business, is it?'

'Correct.'

'Very well, have a good flight, and we hope to see you back in England one day.'

'Thank you.' Frobisher lifted his hat and felt a flood of relief as another hurdle was passed. He forced himself to take a few steps beyond the barrier and casually slip his passport inside a pocket, using the time to run his expert eye over his fellow travellers. What about that dozing soldier? Did he detect a tiny glint of an open eye beneath the cap?

He held his breath for a moment to try and calm his rapidly beating heart. He wondered what was happening to Bish and Millett. What had gone so wrong? They would never crack under interrogation, would they? Not for a few days, at least. If they could buy him just that much time, he would be sailing across the Atlantic and far away from British jurisdiction. Once he was in Argentina, the organisation would step in and get him back on his feet and settled into a new life there. He'd funded them to the tune of many thousands of pounds, keeping the rescue fund healthy for just such an operation, so he could be sure of a warm reception.

He opened his eyes with a jolt.

'Excuse me, Señor Rodriguez?' The man addressing him wore a trenchcoat with a paper poppy pinned in the lapel, a fedora hat angled over his brow and rectangular glasses with a sun visor clipped over the lenses that did not completely conceal a spectacular black eye. A pipe jauntily protruded from the corner of his mouth, making him look more than a little raffish.

'Eh? I am sorry, what do you want?'

The man smiled, the pipe skilfully balanced in his mouth as he spoke, his hand extended as if he wished to shake hands. 'Look, sorry to spring on you like this, and of course you won't know us from Adam,' his voice was light and affable, 'but we have a mutual acquaintance in common and they told us we should look you up. Betty and I are off to Lisbon too, ripping good luck, eh? Thought you'd like some company...'

'I know nothing about this. Sorry, I must get my ticket. Excuse me.' Frobisher felt a dizzying sensation inside, touched his hat and put his head down, making to walk away.

'You see, we both know the Pyms. Jack Pym? Played bridge with him and his charming wife Adeline — that was, until his awful accident.' The man stepped closer. 'He worked for you, I understand?' The man maintained his smile but his dark-lensed glasses stared blankly as he tried to usher them to one side and his voice was no longer so cheerful. Frobisher noticed that the man's young wife was now standing to one side, not quite in his line of sight. He swallowed, trying not to show his growing apprehension and feeling a tickle of fear in the nape of his neck. He slid his free hand into his coat pocket.

'Join us for a cup of tea? The café here is very quiet,' the man placed an arm on Frobisher's. 'More discreet.' His voice was low but clear. 'You see, we just need to have another look at that passport, Sir Paul.'

'I have no idea what you are talking about! What this is crazy nonsense?'

'You know perfectly well.' The man's voice was quiet and level. 'Now if you will just step this way...'

'Get off me!'

'Paul Frobisher, I am arresting you...'

Frobisher spun around and saw a couple striding out of the ticket office. He guessed they were moving in for the sting. Without a moment's hesitation he swung his heavy bag squarely into the face of the young woman, making her stagger backwards and momentarily lose balance, one hand clutching her ear where the point of the umbrella had struck. His other hand was out of his coat pocket, the switchblade flashing as it caught the pools of swimming light refracted from the sea.

He swept the knife in a swift arc that made the policeman leap backwards as it flew past his nose with fractions of an inch to spare. He had but a moment to react, sprinting across the smooth tiles of the floor, feeling his expensive, leather-soled shoes slip and slide as they struggled to find grip, but he was fit, and a good runner and, although he could hear the sound of feet following, he had the lead.

Head down he dashed as fast as he could towards a door marked 'No Exit', body charging this open as he rushed from the echoing concourse into the bright freshness of the open air, aware of the mighty prow of a ship above his head, the cluttered dockside all about and the clanging of an alarm bell he had set off. His shoes now gripped the concrete as he gathered speed, but where could he go?

Towards land was his only option, but as he drove his legs harder and tried to gain some distance, he was aware of a small shunting engine pulling a couple of wagons rapidly approaching from his left around a sharp corner, wheels squealing and complaining on the tightly curved dock railway. Its little pistons were working as frantically as his legs were pumping, and their speed was evenly matched. Unless he slowed, the short train would cross at right angles and cut off his escape. The engine peeped its whistle angrily and he knew it could not stop, for its momentum would carry it forward many yards even if the driver screwed the brakes down hard. If he carried on running forwards he would be cut to pieces.

He would at least die with some measure of honour by taking his secrets with him, protecting those far greater and more powerful than he; protecting the surviving hierarchy of the SS — the men who one day might still see a fourth *Reich* rise to rule the world, and this time, for the promised thousand years.

What if he turned around? He would have to submit to the humiliation of arrest, to an endless trial that would probably last many agonising, stifling months, maybe years. The days and nights of stomach-wrenching terror anticipating the death that surely would be the only outcome. Enduring the hatred of people stupidly unable to understand the contamination of the Jews that he could see was eating away at the integrity of the only true master race. He ran forwards, heart beating hard, breath forced from his lungs in sharp blasts as from a snorting bull in the ring... all that lay ahead now was loathing and hatred until the final release with a noose around his neck. He had sworn allegiance until death... there was no other way.

∗   ∗   ∗   ∗

Vignoles ran as fast as he could, conscious that Blencowe was breaking away on the flank to cut off Frobisher's escape, and that others were joining him in hot pursuit. Their man could not go far. There were gates and fences and all manner of controls to pass through. He was penned in and there could be no way out, and Vignoles cursed Frobisher for running like a chased cat. You can climb up a tree, but then what? We've got you to bang to rights and can wait all day until you come down and accept your fate.

He felt a jolt of horror. *Oh no! He isn't going to—*

Vignoles could see the collision unfold in slow motion, the running man with his coat tails flapping, his hat lofted from his head by a gust of salty air and the stubby tank engine steaming fussily forwards with its small wheels spinning and short pistons busy with their rapid to-ing and fro-ing motion, the face of the startled fireman leaning on the whistle cord as the driver furiously worked the brakes.

Frobisher glanced back and their eyes met briefly, for the first and the last time.

'Stop! Stop!' In that moment Vignoles was unsure why he should wish so fervently that a man who would almost certainly be hanged would bother to save his life.

Time seemed to stretch to an eternity. Later everyone agreed they could remember every detail as vividly as if in a film running in slow motion, a ghastly, horrific film, as Sir Paul Frobisher, baronet, collided with the buffers, buckling and crumpling like a rag doll, his legs twisting into impossible angles, his head slamming with a grotesque crack against the upturned coupling hook on the centre of the buffer beam, his body dragged immediately beneath the low-slung engine. The next few grisly moments, as his limbs were sliced and crushed, were thankfully masked by a wreathe of steam, stained for one moment, the palest of candyfloss pink.

Chapter Thirty-five

TAILSPIN
The Dorsey Brothers

Remembrance Sunday. It was early evening and Charles and Anna Vignoles were hiking out of Belgrave and Birstall station onto Mowmacre Hill. Earlier that day they had attended the remembrance service in Leicester then lunched in the J. Lyons tearooms. However, as the day remained clear and the low winter sunlight took the edge off the rawness of the afternoon, they decided to return homewards and take their favourite walk so as to make the best of the dying embers of the weekend. They were risking spoiling their shoes, but both agreed that sometimes moments were to be seized that demanded one pushed aside such concerns.

They climbed a stile and skirted one of the brown fields of earth that looked like damp corduroy laid over the slope of the land, and which formed part of the transition from the smooth greens of the golf course to rolling farmland. They walked on the pale, wintry grass at the side of the field to keep the worst of the mud from their shoes, smelling the tilled loam and recently burnt stubble. Autumn hawkbit flamed like little yellow candles studding the field edge and the hawthorn hedgerows were heavy with berries. Two late feeding waxwings bobbed and fluttered between the festoons of Old Man's Beard caught amongst the spiky branches, the beads of brilliant colour on their wings like little jewels. The elms, oaks and whitethorns stood immobile in the windless air, dark and grey where not coloured silver by the disc of the rising moon or tinged pink by the last glow of the dying sun, now dipped below the horizon. A cow lowed in a distant field. They stopped and turned to look down onto their little community beside the railway and the twinkling lights just starting to come alive in the far off city. A distant whistle hung on the still air. Smoke stood straight up from countless chimney pots like stiffened threads of grey wool.

Vignoles had been talking about the case as they walked. He'd not said much to Anna since the bloody conclusion in Southampton docks, but was now explaining his dissatisfaction, of how it was hard to consider it a successful conclusion, with so many dead and a case now set to become shrouded behind ever thicker layers of secrecy as the security services took hold of it and buried the uncomfortable truth behind yet more careful sleights of hand.

'I'm not sure we will ever discover the complete truth about Frobisher. He took most of his secrets to the grave and those he left behind will be hidden away by MI5 or MI6.'

Anna squeezed his arm but remained silent.

'I had an office full of "men from the ministry" on Friday. All odd, sallow types with bowler hats and barely a civil word between them, and they were taking every last scrap of evidence away and forcing us all to sign the Official Secrets Act.'

'But he was who he said he was?' asked Anna.

'Oddly, yes. He was indeed born Paul Frobisher — the illegitimate son of the rakish Henry Frobisher, baronet, and a young woman who gave him away to an orphanage. She has completely disappeared, but the rumour persists she was German, though that may be just a wish to seek an easy explanation for his love for all things Nazi. Who knows?' Vignoles shrugged. 'Certainly Sir Paul travelled extensively before the war in Germany and Austria, developing various business interests. He always was an entrepreneur, and a good one by the sound of it.'

'Would his travels not have alerted the authorities? What I mean is, surely that would have made him a security risk?'

'Far from it. A great many British businessmen had such dealings right up until the last moment war was declared, some even managed to continue for a time after. His fluency in German, and indeed his natural flair for languages and extensive knowledge of mainland Europe, made him a natural for the SOE, who eagerly came recruiting — though I am not supposed to have told you that.' Vignoles exchanged a guilty look with Anna, who smiled. 'They were desperate for people like Frobisher and he must have played the role perfectly. I assume he infiltrated the SS — on our orders — but actually used his cover to help smuggle some of these unsavoury types to safety.'

They stood in silence, the coldness of the air feeling as though it were cleansing them inside.

'The other two are Germans. Their stories will be unravelled in time and no doubt a big play will be made about them in the courts, as they can more easily be painted as the villains, especially as they killed some members of the gang.' Vignoles dropped his voice to barely more than a whisper. 'The rumour is, they worked a pretty audacious campaign in 1944, under an especially duplicitous commander called Skorzeny. They broke the Geneva Convention by operating in uniforms taken from the dead bodies of British and American soldiers, speaking English fluently and causing absolute havoc behind the lines. I suspect Frobisher was part of this set up.' Vignoles sighed. 'Damned awkward to have a security lapse as big as that.'

Anna drew closer, her arm around his waist, head nestling on his shoulder. Vignoles pressed his face into her hair.

'You suspect there will be a cover up?'

Vignoles took a while to answer. 'It would be far easier to draw a veil over Frobisher's darker side and announce an "unfortunate accident that killed a decorated member of the SOE". The establishment would prefer things not stirred up too much. Faces must be saved. Badger's new best friend, the assistant commissioner, can pretend to mourn an acquaintance and be spared a damaging revelation.'

'They'll brush it under the carpet?'

'Possibly.'

'You mentioned earlier in the week about an especially incriminating document found in Pym's house. How did Frobisher come to lose such a thing?'

'As ever, darling, you are perceptive.' Vignoles checked the fields around were still empty. 'The nature of all these items, and indeed their very existence, is top secret now. But my personal hunch is that he, or one of his cronies — and my money is on Bish — took some items to the hapless forger, Greenfall. They would need all manner of documents, both for their life in Britain and for their escape plans, and this little item was accidentally included, perhaps caught between some pages or in a fold of an envelope. The item in question is quite small. However, there is a vital dimension to the story...' Vignoles scanned the darkened fields but could detect no sign of human activity. He still kept his voice low. 'DI Tykett knows a lot about this particular forger, who was a man with few moral standards. Greenfall cared not a hoot what someone was planning to do with whatever documents he made for them — except when it came to one particular thing....'

Anna looked at Vignoles, her dark eyes bright.

'You see, his grandmother was a Jewess. A Russian escapee from the pogroms of the last century. The family always played this down and they were to all intent and purposes as English as anyone. Tykett doubts Greenfall believed in much except making money by any means, fair or foul. But even he must have bridled at helping the SS.'

'Everyone has his limit. And those terrible things we saw in the newsreels... beyond imagination. Yes, you're right. A part-Jewish crook would easily find his stomach turned.'

They embraced, preferring to turn away from such horrific images. After a minute or so, Anna reopened her eyes and exclaimed.

'Oh Charles, look!'

Out of the eastern sky a large, white 'v' appeared, moving across the clear sky that moved from black to indigo near the western horizon, where a faint glimmer of the lost sun still gamely clung on. Geese flying in formation, their honking calls, though distant, clearly audible. The birds were flying at so great a height that the moon and a trace of daylight illuminated them so they resembled a piece of white silk ribbon fluttering in the wind.

'How beautiful!' Anna craned her neck to watch them flap above their heads, their long necks stretched out as if straining to reach their destination that bit quicker.

Vignoles was grinning. Standing there with Anna, looking at the wild birds flying free, he felt able to cast off the sordid taint of unpleasant thoughts and reflect on more positive things. As the tumbling 'v' of pale ribbon dropped behind a line of trees, they started to walk back towards Station Road and the long, gentle descent past the straggle of old cottages and the allotment gardens, and then home.

'I've made a decision about something.'

'Oh, yes?' Anna linked her arm through his.

'It's about that Simon Howerth lad. He's got himself into a right pickle and is currently under suspension, with a disciplinary hearing next week. He's going to be dismissed, of that I am quite sure, and there could even be a case for pressing charges.'

'That sounds awfully harsh. Golly, it will ruin his whole life.'

'I know. Sadly, the law can only see as far as the facts. And he committed some unlawful acts. There are those who feel he should be punished. I, however, am not convinced that a harsh judgement will offer the best solution for society and for his long term development. I think he has a spark about him, a natural inquisitiveness and a sharp mind, he's pretty brave as well, and we must accept that, without him, we would never have got where we did. Top Link could possibly be free; a Nazi and a traitor who had operated in the heart of British society, living it up in the South American sun.'

'What can you do?'

'I may not be able to swing it, but I'll give it my best shot. I want to take him into the detective department. Get him under my wing. Direct him, guide him, because otherwise he'll serve time, become bitter and mean-spirited and come under the influence of crooks and thieves and learn the tricks of the trade. Upon release he will probably become an able criminal. Hardly a success story.'

'Charles, your idea is splendid. It's time society tried to cure and not just punish mistakes made by youngsters.'

'Indeed. Of course, he'll start at the bottom. No more than an office tea boy at first and on pretty thin wages. He'll have to earn his right to even be there and learn to stick to the rules like glue. We might have to dock his pay until the value of the money he gained illegally is paid into the police retirement fund, but he will have a future.'

Anna smiled and hugged her husband closer. They walked in companionable silence for a while as the lane grew steadily darker and their breath formed clouds. Tall clusters of yarrow stood tall on either side, the white flowerheads tinged with pink and intermingled with cheery Michaelmas daisies, escapees from a nearby cottage garden, their misty blue rays capturing something of the moon's pale light.

'Charles, talking of the future, has John said anything to you?'

'Trinder? He says quite a lot of things, Anna, often about Ella Fitzgerald. In what particular respect?'

'Something... out of the ordinary. But a good thing.'

'I say, you're talking in riddles. What *do* you mean?' Vignoles frowned in concentration. 'Oh yes, I remember! He finally settled on the new Louis Armstrong 78. He was quite excited about it, I recall.'

'You men are quite hopeless!'

'Why? What on earth have we done now?'

'He's really said nothing at all? Have you not even noticed?'

'Noticed what?' Vignoles stopped and looked at Anna, 'tell me!'

Anna's reply was to pull a pocket diary from her handbag and extract the thin pencil from its place in the spine, and although she could barely see the pages, she made a cross beside November 13th. 'There! You will wait for John to speak up, and I shall see just how long it takes from today for him to do so.' She gave a wicked grin.

Vignoles was laughing, as was Anna.

'Tell me what? How will I know when he's told me, if you don't say what it is?'

She laughed. 'Charles, it's Violet. She's going to have a baby!'

'Good heavens! What I mean is, that's super news, of course. He never said a word. Gosh, but we must hurry home and telephone them at once. We must celebrate... I know, we have that bottle of claret tucked away!'

'Let's hurry home indeed, but you can leave them in peace tonight. Poor Violet has hardly seen her husband for days and we can all celebrate sometime later. I think they might appreciate some time alone together. And besides, I don't think I've seen enough of *my* husband either! So what say we bank up the fire in the bedroom, light the candles and take that bottle of claret upstairs?'

THE END

The fifth book in the Inspector Vignoles series will be steaming into the shops in the spring of 2012. Here's a taste of things to come...

THE LAST TRAIN (TO BRACKLEY CENTRAL)
(1950)

Chapter One

The Cobra's Eye

Egypt. October 1942. Private Raymond Coulson of the 7th Armoured Division opened his bedroll and dropped his pack beside it. He then drank heartily from a water bottle to wash the dust from his throat.

Riding a Humber armoured car across a scorching desert was hot and sweaty work. His clothes were damp, his neck and forearms burned pink from the sun and his eyes dry from staring into the heat haze, peeled raw trying to detect the Afrika Korps they knew were waiting for them.

The crew had lashed up a canopy of pale canvas to one side of their vehicle and the others had chosen to bed down beneath this in what would be a crowded huddle, but Coulson needed space. Squeezed into the pint-sized vehicle all day, smelling their sweat and fear, their arms and legs continually pressed close together and with no room to stretch or move, he needed to be away from them. He wanted to lie on his back and stare at the stars during the clear desert night, feeling his body cool after roasting in the oven of the Humber, gratefully drinking in the fresh chilled air and seeking to eradicate the constant stink of exhaust fumes and motor oil.

Loosening his blouson jacket to allowing the air to circulate, he flopped down onto the bedroll to remove his boots. Stuffing his noxious socks into the boot openings to prevent scorpions climbing inside, he wriggled his toes and already felt more comfortable. He pulled a packet of Camel cigarettes from a breast pocket, extracted one and rested it on his cracked lips. Catching the eye of 'Bounder' Baker leaning against a stack of water cans, he raised the packet in a gesture of silent invitation. Bounder grinned and Coulson expertly flipped the cigarette across the divide in a spinning Catherine wheel flight.

He lit his cigarette and lay down for a few minutes of luxury with his legs stretched out fully for the first time that day. He adjusted his back for a moment, trying to get comfortable, but then sat up, patting the bedroll and feeling for the lump jabbing into his spine. Stones were the impediment to a good night's sleep when off the deeper and softer dunes. The land near El Alamein was relatively flat and the sand partially masked the rocky terrain below, better for their vehicles to traverse but a right pain in the backside when bedding down. He noted the many stones on either side of his bedroll and decided against trying another spot and so he knelt down and peeled the top corner back to reach underneath and explore with his fingers.

He was surprised at the neat and regular shape he encountered and the sharply defined corner that was proud of the sand. How odd? It was not a stone. Coulson saw a little ornamental box lying at an angle with one corner poking out of the sand and immediately felt a tingle of curiosity. He swiftly palmed the box in one of his big hands and checked that no one had noticed his discovery. He lay down, this time on his side with his back to his crewmates. Placing the little box close to his body, he opened the lid.

He dragged heavily on his cigarette to mask the involuntary inhalation of breath he was forced to make. The diamond sprang alive as the evening sun filled it with light for the first time since the day had been lost, many years before. Coulson stared in wonderment at the yellow fire inside the perfectly cut diamond, marvelling at how it appeared alive as he slowly turned the golden ring in his fingers, making it glint and sparkle. He knew nothing of gemstones, but he knew quality and beauty when he saw it. This was special. It was bewitching, entrancing.

This was a ring any woman would love, and now he, humble private Ray Coulson, the garage mechanic from a little town in Northamptonshire, was the man to give this beautiful creation to his darling Betty Boo. It would be the perfect engagement ring, and he felt a rush of excitement course through his veins as he imagined Betty's face when she saw it. If he could just get through this next campaign and return home on leave. He closed his eyes and offered a brief, silent prayer.

He kissed the cold stone thanking the Lord for this extraordinary piece of good fortune then closed his fist, hiding it from view. Hauling his pack towards him with his free hand and puffing on the fag secured between his cracked lips, he quickly stuffed the empty box into the bottom and rummaged about until he located the emergency sewing kit.

As the red ball of the sun slipped towards the horizon, sending long shadows across the undulating desert towards them and burnishing a wrecked locomotive in the distant station, he carefully sewed the precious ring into the bottom edge of one of the pockets of his shorts under the pretence of mending a hole. It would now be safe from loss or detection, yet remain with him at all times. If the Humber took a hit and they had to bale out, his pack might be lost, and they often shed their jackets and undershirts in the terrible heat of the day, but he would always be in his voluminous army shorts.

To be continued...

THE INSPECTOR VIGNOLES MYSTERIES

'Highly recommended to lovers of steam strains who don't mind being frozen to the marrow by murder.' *Oxford Times*

'Amongst the best books I have read in recent years.' *Steve Masters*

'Thoroughly recommended for providing an exciting and captivating read... Each move is meticulously told and there is a pace to the story that keeps one wanting to turn the pages.' *Mainline magazine*

'*The Torn Curtain* is a gripping rollercoaster of a novel that demands the reader keep the pages turning. The best of the "railway detective" novels on the market.' *Steam Railway*

'I love it! A real page-turner.' *Daily Mirror*

'An absolutely riveting story that has all the elements of a cracking yarn... A most satisfyingly spectacular, albeit gruesome conclusion.' *British Railway Modelling*

'An intriguing mystery, warm-hearted and evocative.' *Dave Baker*

'Atmospheric and gripping... the characters are painted very vividly.' *Sian Harrington*

'Skillfully constructed and features a host of well-observed characters. Bags of wonderful nostalgia and a gripping denoument.' *Tony Boullemier*

'Not just splendidly paced crime thrillers, not just delicious treats for all steam train enthusiasts but really vibrant social portraits... I intend putting them in my Best Read of the Year slot in the run-up to Christmas.' *Ewan Wilson, Waterstone's*

'Stephen has originated the new literary genre of Post-war Austerity Gothic.' *Liverpool Daily Post*

For more information, please see overleaf

The Inspector Vignoles Mysteries comprise

SMOKE GETS IN YOUR EYES

Published 2007   ISBN 978-1-904109-1-74

THE MURDER OF CROWS

Published 2008   ISBN 978-1-904109-1-98

THE TORN CURTAIN

Published 2009   ISBN 978-1-904109-20-4

THE MARYLEBONE MURDERS

Published 2011   ISBN 978-1-904109-21-1

THE LAST TRAIN (TO BRACKLEY CENTRAL)

Planned for spring 2012   ISBN 978-1-904109-22-8

Each book is priced at £8.99

All titles in the series can be ordered from any bookshop or online store such as Amazon. Books ordered directly from the author can be signed and/or dedicated to your requirements upon request.

Postage and packing: £2.75 for the first book and £1 for each additional book. Please send cheques, made payable to Stephen Done, to:

5 Richmond Street,
New Brighton, Wirral
CH45 2LE

To pay by credit card, visit our website hastingspress.co.uk

If you have any queries about ordering, please telephone 01424 442142 or email hastings.press@gmail.com